William Makepeace Thackeray, Richard Herne Shepherd

Sultan Stork, and other Stories and Sketches

William Makepeace Thackeray, Richard Herne Shepherd

Sultan Stork, and other Stories and Sketches

ISBN/EAN: 9783743338548

Manufactured in Europe, USA, Canada, Australia, Japa

Cover: Foto ©Andreas Hilbeck / pixelio.de

Manufactured and distributed by brebook publishing software
(www.brebook.com)

William Makepeace Thackeray, Richard Herne Shepherd

Sultan Stork, and other Stories and Sketches

SULTAN STORK

AND OTHER STORIES AND SKETCHES

BY

WILLIAM MAKEPEACE THACKERAY

(1829-1844)

NOW FIRST COLLECTED

TO WHICH IS ADDED

The Bibliography of Thackeray

REVISED AND CONSIDERABLY ENLARGED

LONDON
GEORGE REDWAY
YORK-STREET, COVENT GARDEN
1887

INTRODUCTION

BY THE EDITOR.

HAT so exquisite and finished a product of
Thackeray's mature genius and humour as
Sultan Stork should have escaped the author's
attention when republishing his *Miscellanies*
thirty years ago is perhaps more easily intelligible than
its omission from the two supplementary volumes,
containing pieces hitherto uncollected, issued in the
winter of last year by the publishers of his collected
Works, and which must be taken to represent and
include their final gleanings in that field. In neither
case is the omission of the radiant and sunny little
jeu d'esprit which gives its leading title to the present
volume easily explicable, except on the assumption of
forgetfulness of its existence on the one hand on the
part of the writer, or of ignorance of its existence
on the other on the part of his posthumous publishers
—a supposition rendered all the more likely in the
latter case by the fact that "Sultan Stork" does not
happen to be recorded in the original edition of the
"Bibliography of Thackeray."

    At any rate it seemed to us, with every desire to
leave the territory, if possible, in possession of its

645978

aboriginal occupants, that the two volumes heralded
with such a flourish of trumpets were very far from
being either satisfactory or exhaustive, that they
included much that might have been wisely left to
oblivion, or to the industrious curiosity of research,
and excluded much that was in every way worthy to
rank with the best of Thackeray's *opera minora*. The
time therefore appeared to have arrived for carrying
out and fulfilling, in a somewhat modified form, a
project announced and a promise made in the summer
of 1882.

For the three boyish contributions to the Cambridge
"Snob," written by Thackeray as an undergraduate
in his later teens, no special significance is claimed;
but they are at least as characteristic and amusing as
the mock prize-poem of *Timbuctoo*, given by Messrs.
Smith and Elder in the first of their supplementary
volumes; and the personality and style of Mrs. Ramsbottom, originated by Theodore Hook and then still
fresh in the memories of the readers of *John Bull*, are
not unsuccessfully imitated. The earliest piece of any
importance, and the longest piece included in this
volume, is the tale of *Elizabeth Brownrigge*, published
in *Fraser's Magazine* in the summer of 1832, when
Thackeray was in his twenty-second year. That
he was a recognised contributor to *Fraser's Magazine*
in the early thirties is established by the fact that
his figure appears in Maclise's group of the *Fraserians*
published in the magazine in 1835.

This tale was first attributed to Thackeray by Dr. John
Brown, of Edinburgh, in an article published in the
North British Review, in February 1864, a month or
two after Thackeray's death. It was not recorded,

however, in the original issue of the *Bibliography of Thackeray* — an omission to which Mr. Swinburne (whose knowledge of the remotest recesses of modern as well as of ancient literature is almost phenomenal, and whose critical faculty is hardly less remarkable than his poetic genius,) obligingly drew the compiler's attention. Mr. Swinburne has courteously accorded the editor permission to publish this communication, which ran as follows:—

The Pines, Putney Hill,

Dec. 24, 1880.

DEAR SIR,

Pray accept my sincere thanks for your very handsome present, which I have begun to examine—with what interest you will see when I tell you that I suspect—though it is mere suspicion—that you have not exhausted the list of Thackeray's contributions to *Fraser*. When an undergraduate, I looked up some of these in the Union Library, and detected in a review (for instance) either of the pictures of the year (about '38) or of its illustrated books, a well-known passage in *Vanity Fair*—where it appeared some ten years later. And just before 'Catherine' appeared another burlesque or grotesque horror—'Elizabeth Brownrigge,' a story in two parts, which ought to be Thackeray's, for, if it is not, he stole the idea, and to some extent the style, of his parodies on novels of criminal life, from this first sketch of the kind.

Yours very truly

A. C. SWINBURNE.

We could not help regarding this independent confirmatory evidence as highly important, if not absolutely decisive; and the lingering incredulity which, though Dr. John Brown's account of the tale had been familiar to us for many years, forbade us to chronicle it as an item in the original issue of the "Bibliography of Thackeray," was gradually dissipated. Lest, however, Mr. Swinburne should be unjustly saddled with any share of moral responsibility in the matter, or be erroneously regarded as the motor, fautor or sponsor of this section of our enterprise, it is due to him to add that in granting free leave for the publication of his own letter, he expressed himself "half sorry that this burlesque should be revived."*

In his paper on Thackeray in the *North British Review* for February 1864, the late Dr. John Brown of Edinburgh writes as follows:—

"In 1832, when Mr. Thackeray was little more than twenty-one, *Elizabeth Brownrigge: a tale*, was narrated in the August and September numbers of *Fraser*. This tale is dedicated to the author of *Eugene Aram*, and the writer describes himself as a young man who has for a length of time applied himself to literature, but entirely failed in deriving any emoluments from his exertions. Depressed by failure he sends for the popular novel of *Eugene Aram* to gain instruction therefrom. He soon discovers his mistake :—

"From the frequent perusal of older works of imagination I had learnt so to weave the incidents of my story as to interest the feelings of the reader in favour of virtue, and to increase his detestation of vice. I have been taught by *Eugene Aram* to mix vice and virtue up together in such an inextricable confusion as to render it impossible that any preference should be given to either, or that the one, indeed, should be at all distinguishable from the other. . . . In taking my subject from that walk of life to which you had directed my attention, many motives conspired to fix my choice on the heroine of the ensuing tale ; she is a classic personage,—her name has

---

* *The Pines:* July 3, 1886.

DEAR MR. SHEPHERD,

Dr. John Brown's opinion is worth so much more than mine that it seems to me quite superfluous for you to quote my letter ; but certainly, if you think otherwise, I can have no objection to your doing so. Thanks for the proofs. The parody is amusing, as my memory assured me ; but I wish Thackeray (if it be he) had not taken a subject so horribly disgusting to crack jokes upon. On the other hand 'Eugene Aram' is so provocative of ridicule that nothing (from that point of view) can be too strong or violent to be just or reasonable. Still, on reading it again, I am half sorry that this burlesque should be revived—though no doubt it is not wanting in cleverness of a rather coarse kind.

Yours very truly
A. C. SWINBURNE.

been already 'linked to immortal verse' by the muse of Canning. Besides, it is extraordinary that, as you had commenced a tragedy under the title of *Eugene Aram*, I had already sketched a burletta with the title of *Elizabeth Brownrigge*. I had, indeed, in my dramatic piece, been guilty of an egregious and unpardonable error : I had attempted to excite the sympathies of the audience in favour of the murdered apprentices, but your novel has disabused me of so vulgar a prejudice, and, in my present version of her case, all the interest of the reader and all the pathetic powers of the author will be engaged on the side of the murderess."

According to this conception the tale proceeds, with incidents and even names taken directly from the *Newgate Calendar*, but rivalling *Eugene Aram* itself in magnificence of diction, absurdity of sentiment, and pomp of Greek quotation. The trial scene and the speech for the defence are especially well hit off. *If Elizabeth Brownrigge was written by Thackeray, and the internal evidence seems to us strong,* the following is surprising criticism from a youth of twenty-one—the very Byron and Bulwer age :—

"I am inclined to regard you [the author of *Eugene Aram*] as an original discoverer in the world of literary enterprise, and to reverence you as the father of a new '*lusus naturæ* school.' There is no other title by which your manner could be so aptly designated. I am told, for instance, that in a former work, having to paint an adulterer, you described him as belonging to the class of country curates, among whom, perhaps, such a criminal is not met with once in a hundred years; while, on the contrary, being in search of a tender-hearted, generous, sentimental, high-minded hero of romance, you turned to the pages of the *Newgate Calendar*, and looked for him in the list of men who have cut throats for money, among whom a person in possession of such qualities could never have been met with at all. Wanting a shrewd, selfish, worldly, calculating valet, you describe him as an old soldier, though he bears not a single trait of the character which might have been moulded by a long course of military service, but, on the contrary, is marked by all the distinguishing features of a bankrupt attorney, or a lame duck from the Stock Exchange. Having to paint a cat, you endow her with the idiosyncrasies of a dog."

At the end, the author intimates that he is ready to treat with any liberal publisher for a series of works in the same style, to be called *Tales of the Old Bailey, or Romances of Tyburn Tree.* The proposed series is represented only by *Catherine*, a longer and more elaborate effort in the same direction. It is the narrative of the misdeeds of Mrs. Catherine Hayes, an allusion to whose criminality in after years brought down upon the author of *Pendennis* an amusing outburst of fury from Irish patriotism, forgetting in its excitement, that the name had been borne by a heroine of the Newgate Calendar as well as by the accomplished singer. The purpose of *Catherine* is the same as that of *Elizabeth Brownrigge*—to explode the *lusus naturæ* school ; but the plan adopted is slightly different. Things had got worse than they were in 1832. The public had called for coarse stimulants and had got them. *Jack Sheppard* had been acquiring great popularity in *Bentley's Miscellany;* and the true feeling and pathos of many parts of *Oliver Twist* had been marred by the unnatural sentimentalism of Nancy.

Neither of these tales, though it is very curious to look back at them now, can be considered quite successful. And the reason of this is not hard to find. It was impossible that they could be attractive as stories; while on the other hand, the humour was not broad enough to command attention for itself. They were neither sufficiently interesting, nor sufficiently amusing. They are caricatures without the element of caricature. In *Elizabeth* we have little but the story of a crime committed by a criminal actuated by motives and over-flowing with sentiments of the Eugene Aram type. *Catherine* is more ambitious. In it an attempt is made to construct a story—to delineate character. But nothing could make a story interesting which consists of little more than the seduction of a girl, the intrigues of a mistress, the discontent of a wife growing into hatred and ending in murder. At the close, indeed, the writer resorts to the true way of making such a *jeu d'esprit* attractive—burlesque. He concludes, though too late altogether to save the piece, in a blaze of theatrical blue-fire; and it was this idea of burlesque or extravagant caricature which led to the perfected successes of "George de Barnwell" and "Codlingsby." *In a literary point of view, it is well worth while to go back upon those early efforts;* and we have dwelt upon them the more willingly that their purpose and the literary doctrine they contend for would be well remembered at this very time. We have given up writing about discovered criminals, only to write more about criminals not yet found out; the *lusus naturæ* school has given place to the sensational; the literature of the *Newgate Calendar* has been supplanted by the literature of the detective officer—a style rather the worse, and decidedly the more stupid of the two.

In 1833 Thackeray became connected as editor, and also in some measure, as proprietor, with a weekly literary journal, the fortunes of which were not prosperous. The journal bore the imposing title of "The National Standard and Journal of Literature, Science, "Music, Theatricals, and the Fine Arts." Thackeray's editorial reign began about the nineteenth number, after which he seems to have done a good deal of work—reviews, letters, criticisms and verses. There is a mock sonnet by W. Wordsworth, illustrative of a drawing of Braham in stage nautical costume, standing by a theatrical sea-shore; in the background an Israelite, with the clothes'-bag and triple hat of his ancient race; and in the sky, constellation-wise, appears a Jew's harp, with a chaplet of bays round it. We have here the germ of a style in which Thackeray became famous, though the humour of attributing this nonsense to Wordsworth, and of making Braham coeval with Queen Anne, is not now very plain. There is a yet more characteristic touch in a review of a poem by poor Robert Montgomery, who had the misfortune to become the butt of more than one famous writer, winding up with a quotation of some dozen lines, the order of which, says the critic, has been reversed by the printer, but as they read quite as well one way as the other, he does not think it worth while to correct the mistake ! A comical tale called "The Devil's Wager," afterwards reprinted in the *Paris Sketch-book*, also appeared in the *National Standard*, with a capital woodcut, representing the devil as sailing through the air, dragging after him the fat Sir Roger de Rollo by means of his tail, which is wound round Sir Roger's neck. The idea of this tale is characteristic. The venerable knight already in the other world, has made a foolish bet with the devil involving very seriously his future prospects there, which he can only win by persuading some of his relatives on earth to say an *Ave* for him. He fails to obtain this slight boon from a kinsman successor for obvious reasons ; and from a beloved niece, owing to a musical lover whose serenading quite puts a stop to her devotional exercises ; and succeeds at last, only when, giving up all hope from compassion or generosity, he appeals by a pious fraud to the selfishness of a brother and a monk.

Perhaps best of all is a portrait of Louis Philippe, presenting the Citizen King under the Robert Macaire aspect, the adoption and popularity of which Thackeray so carefully explains and illustrates in his Essay on "Caricatures and Lithography in Paris." Below the portrait are some lines, not themselves very remarkable, but in which, especially in the allusion to snobs by the destined enemy of the race, we catch glimpses of the future.

The journal seems to have been an attempt to substitute vigorous and honest criticism of books and of art for the partiality and slipslop general then, and now not perhaps quite unknown. It failed, partly, from the inexperience of its managers, but still more from want of the capital necessary to establish anything of the sort in the face of similar journals of old standing. People get into a habit of taking certain periodicals unconsciously, as they take snuff. *The National Standard* came into existence on the 5th January 1833, and ceased to be on the 1st February 1834.*

All Thackeray's ascertainable contributions to the *National Standard* (with the exception of the tale already alluded to as reprinted in the *Paris Sketch-book*)—all at least possessing anything but the merest ephemeral interest—are included in the present volume. And so ends the chapter of Juvenilia.

Four years later (1837) we find Thackeray engaged as a serious critic, reviewing Thomas Carlyle's newly-published "French Revolution," in the columns of the *Times*. This interesting notice has only been identified within the last few years, through a mention of it by Carlyle himself, in a letter to his brother, printed by Mr. Froude, in the volumes entitled "Carlyle's Life in London." "The writer," says Carlyle in his trenchant pungent way, "is one Thackeray, "a half-monstrous Cornish giant, kind of painter, "Cambridge man and Paris newspaper correspondent, "who is now writing for his life in London. His article "is rather like him, and I suppose calculated to do the "book good." It should be added that, in resuscitating this article from its old *oubliette* of half-a-century back in the *Times*, the quotations and excerpts, there very incorrectly given, partly perhaps through haste and want of opportunity or leisure to correct the press, have been carefully collated with the first three-volume edition of the book reviewed, and silently set right wherever wrong. That humble little service was due alike to the memory of Thackeray and of Carlyle in

---

* *North British Review*, February, 1864.

bringing back this interesting and characteristic notice to the light of day.

"Little Spitz: a Lenten Anecdote," was contributed to George Cruikshank's *Omnibus* in October 1841, accompanied by a very humorous illustration by that artist. Although never hitherto included in any volume or collection of Thackeray's writings (at any rate in this country), it will perhaps be better known to the general reader than any of the other contents of the present volume,—Cruikshank's *Omnibus* being, especially in the later re-issue, an easily procurable book.

"Sultan Stork" (also illustrated by George Cruikshank) appeared in the first volume of *Ainsworth's Magazine*, now somewhat of a rarity; as did also an art-paper entitled "An Exhibition Gossip, by Michael Angelo Titmarsh," followed next year (1843) by a series of "Letters on the Fine Arts," contributed to a newly-started illustrated weekly paper called the *Pictorial Times.**

---

* *The Pictorial Times, a Weekly Journal of News, Literature, Fine Arts and the Drama,*—Office 135, Fleet-street, London,—was started on Saturday, March 18, 1843.

The first volume, dating from March 18 to August 19, was "illustrated with nine hundred engravings on wood, executed by Henry Vizetelly and others." Each number consisted of sixteen pages folio. In the opening number appeared the first of the series of Thackeray's "Letters on the Fine Arts," written under the pseudonym not even then entirely unknown to fame of "Michael Angelo Titmarsh," and purporting (like the Fraserian article on the French School of Painting), to be addressed to Sanders McGilp, Esq. Mr. Henry Vizetelly, who was part proprietor of this journal and connected with its artistic department, informs me that Thackeray, besides the "Letters on the Fine Arts," contributed several literary criticisms, among which he asserts the notice of Macaulay's Essays (p. 43, April 1, 1843) to be certainly Thackeray's,—an assertion well borne out by internal evidence of style. *The Pictorial Times* was still extant at the end

"Dickens in France" appeared in *Fraser's Magazine*, March 1842; and "The Partie Fine" and "Arabella" (or its moral) in *Colburn's New Monthly Magazine*, May and June 1844. These three papers will speak for themselves and appeared to us to be well worthy of preservation.

There remains only one short piece of verse that requires further explanation—the lines which close the original text of the present volume, entitled " Daddy, I'm hungry. A Scene in an Irish Coachmaker's Family." To render these intelligible at this distance of time to the ordinary reader we have to recur to the narrative of Sir Charles Gavan Duffy, who, in his book entitled *Young Ireland*, has related in detail the circumstances which led to their publication in the Dublin newspaper, *The Nation* :—

" In 1842 there were no railways in Ireland except local lines a few miles in length, and the mails were still carried by coaches . . . . Coach-building was still a prosperous pursuit in Dublin, and five hundred artisans were constantly engaged, making, painting and repairing the vehicles employed by the Post-Office. For thirty years the contract for carrying the Irish mails had been in the hands of Mr. Peter Purcell, either singly or in conjunction with other capitalists. Lord Lowther, Postmaster-General at this time, invited tenders in England and Scotland for the Irish service of 1843, and the tender of Mr. Croal, a Scotch contractor, being the lowest, was accepted. To fulfil his contract in good time Mr. Croal must bring coaches ready made to Ireland. As this result would throw a crowd of workmen out of employment, it created an angry feeling among the artisans of Dublin. But although it was contended that

---

of 1844, and reached at any rate a fourth volume ; but Thackeray apparently ceased to contribute after the first volume. He seems to have been content, however, during his connexion with the journal, to write anything to order, either on artistic or literary subjects, for the modest remuneration of three guineas a week, surely an extremely low rate of pay when we consider the pinnacle of literary fame he was to reach only five years later.

Mr. Purcell's tender was practically the lowest, and the subject was mentioned in Parliament and a memorial presented, it came to nothing, and Mr. Croal was left in possession of his contract.

"While the result was still in doubt an unexpected ally presented himself in the person of a young English artist who had recently written a bantering book upon Ireland under the *nom de guerre* of Michael Angelo Titmarsh. What he was to become in the fulness of time was scarcely anticipated in England at that period, and not at all anticipated in Ireland. He had dedicated his "Irish Sketch-Book" to "Harry Lorrequer," but had not apparently established himself in the good graces of the literary Tories; for he was understood to be the original of an English tourist in Ireland bitterly burlesqued in one of Dr. Lever's novels: and the nationalists only remembered that he had been contemptuous of Repeal, and had caricatured O'Connell with a face of the type which Cockney artists associate with a blunderbuss. Mr. Purcell (the Mr. P. whose agricultural improvements are described in the second chapter of the *Irish Sketch-Book*, and the Catholic gentleman whom the neighbouring parson did not visit,) had treated the young artist with consideration and hospitality during his visit to Ireland; and out of gratitude, perhaps, he took sides promptly in the Croal and Purcell contest. A friend brought me for anonymous publication in the *Nation*, two illustrations with accompanying verses, enclosed in a note from Mr. Thackeray. One drawing presented a stage-coach driven by a Highlander plaided and plumed, and with another Highlander for guard, but without a single passenger; while the country children jeered at the empty vehicle and its outlandish officials. The second illustration and the accompanying squib, by the same hand, which was published in *The Nation*, I have thought worth reproducing as a curiosity of literature. It will make a pleasant offset for the Battle of Limerick."*

The Bibliography of Thackeray, which concludes the present volume, will, we trust, in its amended and enlarged form, prove useful for reference to students and collectors, as well as to ordinary readers. When originally published in a separate form six years ago,

* *Young Ireland. A Fragment of Irish History*, 1840-1850. By Sir Charles Gavan Duffy. London: Cassell, Petter, Galpin and Co., 1880, pp. 231-235.

in the winter of 1880, it could be little more than tentative and experimental: much new information has since come to light; and in the labour of revision and addition no pains have been spared in pursuing research and inquiry in every available or accessible quarter. The General Index, which includes references to the Bibliography as well as to the text, will, it is hoped, be found if not entirely exhaustive, at least sufficiently copious and serviceable.

CONTENTS.

SULTAN STORK

BEING THE ONE THOUSAND AND SECOND NIGHT

SULTAN STORK.

BEING

THE ONE THOUSAND AND SECOND NIGHT.

TRANSLATED FROM THE PERSIAN,

BY MAJOR G. O'G. GAHAGAN, H.E.I.C.S.

PART THE FIRST.

THE MAGIC POWDER.

FTER those long wars," began Scheherazade, as soon as her husband had given the accustomed signal, "after those long wars in Persia, which ended in the destruction of the ancient and monstrous Ghebir, or fire-worship, in that country, and the triumph of our holy religion: for though, my lord, the Persians are Soonies by creed, and not followers of Omar, as every true believer in the prophet ought to be, nevertheless——"

"A truce to your nevertheless, madam," interrupted the Sultan, "I want to hear a story, and not a controversy."

"Well, sir, after the expulsion of the Ahrimanians, King Abdulraman governed Persia worthily until he died after a surfeit of peaches, and left his throne to his son Mushook, or the Beautiful,—a title by the way," remarked Scheherazade, blushing, and casting down her lovely eyes, "which ought at present to belong to your majesty."

Although the Sultan only muttered, "Stuff and nonsense, get along with you," it was evident, by the blush in the royal countenance, and the smile which lightened up the black waves of the imperial beard, as a sunbeam does the sea, that his

B

majesty was pleased, and that the storm was about to disappear. Scheherazade continued:—

"Mushook, ascending the throne, passed honourably the first year of his reign in perfecting the work so happily begun by his royal father. He caused a general slaughter of all the Ghebirs in his land to take place, not only of the royal family, but of the common sort; nor of the latter did there remain any un-killed (if I may coin such a word) or unconverted; and, as to the former, they were extirpated root and branch, with the exception of one most dogged enchanter and Ahrimanian, Ghuzroo by name, who, with his son Ameen-Adhawb, managed to escape out of Persia, and fled to India, where still existed some remnants of their miserably superstitious race. But Bombay is a long way from Persia, and at the former place it was that Ghuzroo and his son took refuge, giving themselves up to their diabolical enchantments and worship, and calling them-selves king and prince of Persia. For them, however, their plans and their pretensions, King Mushook little cared, often singing, in allusion to them, those well-known verses of Hafiz:—

> "'Buldoo says that he is the rightful owner of the rice-field,
> And declares that the lamb is his undisputed property.
> Brag, O Buldoo, about your rights and your possessions;
> But the lamb and rice are his who dines on the pilau.'"

The Sultan could hardly contain himself for laughing at this admirable epigram, and, without farther interruption, Schehera-zade continued her story.

"King Mushook was then firmly established on his throne, and had for his vizier that famous and worthy statesman Munsoor; one of the ugliest and oldest, but also one of the wisest of men, and attached beyond everything to the Mushook dynasty, though his teeth had been knocked out by the royal slipper."

"And, no doubt, Mushook served him right," observed the Sultan.

"Though his teeth had been knocked out, yet wisdom and persuasion ever hung on his lips; though one of his eyes, in a fit of royal indignation, had been closed for ever, yet no two eyes in all the empire were as keen as his remaining ball; he was, in a word, the very best and honestest of viziers, as fat and merry, too, as he was wise and faithful.

"One day as Shah Mushook was seated after dinner in his beautiful garden-pavilion at Tehran, sick of political affairs, which is no wonder,—sick even of the beautiful houris who had been dancing before him to the sound of lutes and mandolins—tired of the jokes and antics of his buffoons and story-tellers,—let me say at once dyspeptic, and in a shocking ill-humour; old Munsoor (who had already had the royal pipe and slippers flung half-a-dozen times at his head), willing by any means to dissipate his master's ill-will, lighted in the outer courts of the palace, as he was hieing disconsolately home, upon an old pedlar-woman, who was displaying her wares to a crowd of wondering persons and palace servants, and making them die with laughing at her jokes.

"The vizier drew near, heard her jokes,* and examined her wares, which were extraordinarily beautiful, and determined to conduct her into the august presence of the king.

"Mushook was so pleased with her stock in trade, that, like a royal and generous prince, he determined to purchase her whole pack, box, trinkets, and all; giving her own price for them. So she yielded up her box, only taking out of one of the drawers a little bottle, surrounded by a paper, not much bigger than an ordinary bottle of Macassar oil."

"Macassar oil! Here's an anachronism!" thought the Sultan. But he suffered his wife to proceed with her tale.

"The old woman was putting this bottle away into her pocket, when the sultan's eye lighted upon it, and he asked her in a fury, why she was making off with his property?

"She said she had sold him the whole pack, with the exception of that bottle; and that it could be of no good to him, as it was only a common old crystal bottle, a family piece, of no sort of use to any but the owner.

"'What is there in the bottle?' exclaimed the keen and astute vizier.

---

* These, as they have no sort of point except for the Persian scholar, are here entirely omitted.—G. O'G. G.

"At this the old woman blushed as far as her weazened old face could blush, hemmed, ha'd, stuttered, and shewed evident signs of confusion. She said it was only a common bottle— that there was nothing in it—that is, only a powder—a little rhubarb.

"'It's poison!' roared Mushook; 'I'm sure it's poison!' And he forthwith seized the old hag by the throat, and would have strangled her, if the vizier had not wisely interposed, remarking, that if the woman were strangled there could be no means of knowing what the bottle contained.

"'To shew you, sire, that it is not poison,' cried the old creature to the king, who by this time had wrenched the bottle out of her pocket, and held it in his hand; 'I will take a little of the powder it contains.' Whereupon his majesty called for a teaspoon, determined to administer the powder to her himself. The chief of the eunuchs brought the teaspoon, the king emptied a little of the powder into it, and bidding the old wretch open her great, black, gaping, ruinous mouth, put a little of the powder on her tongue; when, to his astonishment, and as true as I sit here, her old hooked beak of a nose (which, by way of precaution, he was holding in his fingers) slipped from between them; the old, black tongue, on which he placed the teaspoon, disappeared from under it; and not only the nose and the tongue, but the whole old woman vanished away entirely, and his majesty stood there with his two hands extended—the one looking as if it pulled an imaginary nose, the other holding an empty teaspoon; and he himself staring wildly at vacancy!"

"Scheherazade," said the Sultan, gravely, "you are drawing the long bow a little too strongly. In the thousand and one nights that we have passed together, I have given credit to every syllable you uttered. But this tale about the old woman, my love, is, upon my honour, too monstrous."

"Not a whit, sir; and I assure your majesty that it is as true as the Koran itself. It is a fact perfectly well authenticated, and written afterwards, by King Mushook's orders, in the Persian annals. The old woman vanished altogether; the king was left standing there with the bottle and spoon; the vizier was dumb with wonder; and the only thing seen to quit the room was a little canary-bird, that suddenly started up before the king's face, and chirping out 'kikiriki,' flew out of the open window, skimmed over the ponds and plane-trees in the garden, and was last seen wheeling round and round the minaret of the great mosque of Tehran."

" Mashallah !" exclaimed the Sultan. " Heaven is great : but I never should have credited the tale, had not you, my love, vouched for it. Go on, madam, and tell us what became of the bottle and Sultan Mushook."

"Sir, when the king had recovered from his astonishment, he fell, as his custom was, into a fury, and could only be calmed by the arguments and persuasions of the grand vizier.

"'It is evident, sire,' observed that dignitary, 'that the powder which you have just administered possesses some magic property, either to make the persons taking it invisible, or else to cause them to change into the form of some bird or other animal ; and very possibly the canary-bird which so suddenly appeared and disappeared just now, was the very old woman with whom your majesty was talking. We can easily see whether the powder creates invisibility, by trying its effects upon some one—the chief of the eunuchs for example.' And accordingly Hudge Gudge, the chief of the eunuchs, against whom the vizier had an old grudge, was compelled, with many wry faces, to taste the mixture.

"'Thou art so ugly, Hudge Gudge,' exclaimed the vizier with a grin, ' that to render thee invisible, will only be conferring a benefit upon thee.' But, strange to say, though the eunuch was made to swallow a large dose, the powder had no sort of effect upon him, and he stood before his majesty and the prime minister as ugly and as visible as ever.

"They now thought of looking at the paper in which the bottle was wrapped, and the king, not knowing how to read himself, bade the grand vizier explain to him the meaning of the writing which appeared upon the paper.

" But the vizier confessed, after examining the document, that he could not understand it ; and though it was presented at the divan that day, to all the councillors, mollahs, and men learned in the law, not one of them could understand a syllable of the strange characters written on the paper. The council broke up in consternation; for his majesty swore, that if the paper was not translated before the next day at noon, he would bastinado every one of the privy council, beginning with his excellency the grand vizier.

"'Who has such a sharp wit as necessity?' touchingly exclaims the poet Sadee, and so, in corroboration of the words of that divine songster, the next day at noon, sure enough, a man was found—a most ancient, learned, and holy dervish, who knew all the languages under the sun, and, by consequence, that in which the paper was written.

"It was in the most secret Sanscrit tongue; and when the dervish read it, he requested that he might communicate its contents privately to his majesty, or at least only in the presence of his first minister.

"Retiring then to the private apartments with the vizier, his majesty bade the dervish interpret the meaning of the writing round the bottle.

"'The meaning, sire, is this,' said the learned dervish. 'Whoever, after bowing his head three times to the east——'

"'The old woman waggled hers,' cried the king: 'I remarked it, but thought it was only palsy.'

"'Whoever, after bowing his head three times to the east, swallows a grain of this powder, may change himself into whatever animal he please: be it beast, or insect, or bird. Likewise, when he is so changed, he will know the language of beasts, insects, and birds, and be able to answer each after his kind. And when the person so transformed desires to be restored to his own shape, he has only to utter the name of the god "Budgaroo," who himself appeared upon earth in the shape of beasts, birds, ay, and fishes,* and he will instantly resume his proper figure. But let the person using this precious powder especially beware, that during the course of his metamorphosis he do not give way to laughter; for should he indulge in any such unholy mirth, his memory will infallibly forsake him, and

* In Professor Schwann's Sankritische Alterthumskunde, is a learned account of the transmutations of this Indian divinity.—G. O'G. G.

not being able to recall the talismanic word, he will remain in the shape into which he has changed himself.'

" When this strange document had been communicated to his majesty, he caused the dervish's mouth to be filled with sugar-candy, gave him a purse of gold, and bade him depart with every honour.

"'You had better at least have waited,' said the shrewd vizier, 'to see if the interpretation be correct, for who can tell whether this dervish is deceiving us or no?'

" King Mushook rejoined that that point should be put at rest at once, and, grimly smiling, ordered the vizier to take a pinch of powder, and change himself into whatever animal he pleased.

" Munsoor had nothing for it, but to wish himself a dog ; he turned to the east, nodded his head thrice, swallowed the powder, and lo ! there he was—a poodle—an old fat, lame, one-eyed poodle; whose appearance made his master laugh inordinately, though Munsoor himself, remembering the prohibition and penalty, was far too wise to indulge in any such cachinnation.

" Having satisfied his royal master by his antics, the old vizier uttered the requisite word, and was speedily restored to his former shape.

" And now I might tell how the King of Persia and his faithful attendant indulged themselves in all sorts of transformations by the use of the powder ; how they frequented the society of all manner of beasts, and gathered a deal of wisdom from their conversation ; how perching on this housetop in the likeness of sparrows, they peered into all the family secrets of the proprietors ; how buzzing into that harem window in the likeness of blue-bottle flies, they surveyed at their leisure the beauties within, and enjoyed the confusion of the emirs and noblemen, when they described to them at divan every particular regarding the shape, and features, and dress, of the ladies they kept so secretly in the anderoon. One of these freaks had like to have cost the king dear ; for sitting on Hassan Ebn Suneebee's wall, looking at Bulkous, his wife, and lost in admiration of that moon of beauty, a spider issued out from a crevice, and had as nearly as possible gobbled up the King of Persia.

This event was a lesson to him, therefore; and he was so frightened by it, that he did not care for the future to be too curious about other people's affairs, or at least to take upon himself the form of such a fragile thing as a blue-bottle fly.

"One morning—indeed I believe on my conscience that his majesty and the vizier had been gadding all night, or they never could have been abroad so early—they were passing those large swampy grounds, which everybody knows are in the neighbourhood of Tehran, and where the Persian lords are in the habit of hunting herons with the hawk. The two gentlemen were disguised, I don't know how; but seeing a stork by the side of the pool, stretching its long neck, and tossing about its legs very queerly, King Mushook felt suddenly a longing to know what these motions of the animal meant, and taking upon themselves likewise the likeness of storks (the vizier's dumpy nose stretched out into a very strange bill, I promise you), they both advanced to the bird at the pool, and greeted it in the true storkish language.

"'Good morning, Mr. Long Bill,' said the stork (a female), curtseying politely, 'you are abroad early to day; and the sharp air, no doubt, makes you hungry: here is half an eel which I beg you to try, or a frog, which you will find very fat and tender.' But the royal stork was not inclined to eat frogs, being no Frank.'"

"Have a care, Scheherazade," here interposed the Sultan. "Do you mean to tell me that there are any people, even among the unbelievers, who are such filthy wretches as to eat frogs?—Bah! I can't believe it!"

Scheherazade did not vouch for the fact, but continued. "The king declined the proffered breakfast, and presently falling into conversation with the young female stork, bantered her gaily about her presence in such a place of a morning, and without her mamma, praised her figure and the slimness of her legs (which made the young stork blush till she was almost as red as a flamingo), and paid her a thousand compliments that made her think the stranger one of the most delightful creatures she had ever met.

"'Sir,' said she, 'we live in some reeds hard by; and as my

mamma, one of the best mothers in the world, who fed us children with her own blood when we had nothing else for dinner, is no more, my papa, who is always lazy, has bidden us to look out for ourselves. You were pleased just now to compliment my l—— my *limbs*,' says the stork, turning her eyes to the ground; ' and the fact is, that I wish to profit, sir, by those graces with which nature endowed me, and am learning to dance. I came out here to practise a little step that I am to perform before some friends this morning, and here, sir, you have my history.'

" ' I do pray and beseech you to let us see the rehearsal of the step,' said the king, quite amused; on which the young stork, stretching out her scraggy neck, and giving him an ogle with her fish-like eyes, fell to dancing and capering in such a ridiculous way, that the king and vizier could restrain their gravity no longer, but burst out into an immoderate fit of laughter. I do not know that Munsoor would have laughed of his own accord, for he was a man of no sort of humour; but he made it a point whenever his master laughed always to roar too; and in this instance his servility cost him dear.

" The young female stork, as they were laughing, flew away in a huff, and thought them no doubt the most ill-mannered brutes in the world. When they were restored to decent gravity, the king voted that they should resume their shapes again, and hie home to breakfast. So he turned himself round to the east, bobbed his head three times according to the receipt, and—

" ' Vizier,' said he, ' what the deuce is the word ?—Hudge, kudge, fudge—what is it ? '

" The vizier had forgotten too; and then the condition annexed to the charm came over these wretched men, and they felt they were storks for ever. In vain they racked their poor brains to discover the word—they were no wiser at the close of the day than at the beginning, and at nightfall were fain to take wing from the lonely morass where they had passed so many miserable hours, and seek for shelter somewhere."

PART THE SECOND.

THE ENCHANTED PRINCESS.

"After flying about, for some time, the poor storks perched upon the palace, where it was evident that all was in consternation. ' Ah!' said the king, with a sigh, ' why, O cursed vizier, didst thou ever bring that beggar-woman into my presence? here it is, an hour after sunset, and at this hour I should have been seated at a comfortable supper, but for thy odious officiousness, and my own fatal curiosity.'

" What his majesty said was true ; and, having eaten nothing all day (for they could not make up their stomachs to subsist upon raw frogs and fish), he saw, to his inexpressible mortification, his own supper brought into the royal closet at the usual hour, taken away from thence, and the greater part of it eaten up by the servants as they carried it back to the kitchen.

" For three days longer, as they lingered about Tehran, that city was in evident dismay and sorrow. On the first day a council was held, and a great deal of discussion took place between the mollahs and emirs ; on the second day another council was held, and all the mollahs and emirs swore eternal fidelity to King Mushook ; on the third day a third council was held, and they voted to a man that all faithful Persians had long desired the return of their rightful sovereign and worship, and proclaimed Ghuzroo Sultan of Persia. Ghuzroo and his son, Ameen Adawb, entered the divan. What a thrill passed through the bosom of Mushook (who was perched on a window of the hall) when he saw Ghuzroo walk up and take possession of his august throne, and beheld in the countenance of that unbeliever the traits of the very old woman who had sold him the box!

" It would be tedious to describe to your majesty the numberless voyages and the long dreary flights which the unhappy sultan and vizier now took. There is hardly a mosque in all Persia or Arabia on which they did not light ; and as for frogs and fishes, they speedily learned to be so little particular as to swallow them raw with considerable satisfaction, and, I do believe, tried every pond and river in Asia.

" At last they came to India; and being then somewhere in
the neighbourhood of Agra, they went to take their evening
meal at a lake in a wood : the moon was shining on it, and there
was upon one of the trees an owl hooting and screaming in the
most melancholy manner.

" The two wanderers were discussing their victuals, and it
did not at first come into their heads to listen to the owl's
bewailings; but as they were satisfied, they began presently to
hearken to the complaints of the bird of night that sate on a
mango-tree, its great round, white face shining in the moon.
The owl sung a little elegy, which may be rendered in the
following manner : —

> ' *Too—too—too—oo* long have I been in imprisonment ;
> *Who—o—o—o* is coming to deliver me ?
> In the darkness of the night I look out, and see not my deliverer ;
> I make the grove resound with my strains, but no one hears me.
>
> I look out at the moon :—my face was once as fair as hers :
> She is the queen of night, and I was a princess as celebrated.
> I sit under the cypress-trees, and was once as thin as they are :
> Could their dark leaves compare to my raven tresses ?
>
> ' I was a princess once, and my talents were everywhere sung of ;
> I was indebted for my popularity not only to beauty but *to whit* ;
> Ah, where is the destined prince that is to come to liberate, and *to who—o ?*

" Cut the verses short, Scheherazade," said the Sultan.   And
that obedient princess instantly resumed her story in prose.

" ' What,' said King Mushook, stepping up to the owl, ' are
you the victim of enchantment ? '

" Alas ! kind stranger, of whatever feather you be—for the
moon is so bright that I cannot see you in the least,—I was
a princess, as I have just announced in my poem ; and famous,
I may say, for my beauty all over India.   Rotu Muckun is my
name, and my father is King of Hindostan.   A monster from
Bombay, an idolater and practiser of enchantments, came to my
court and asked my hand for his son ; but because I spurned
the wretch, he, under the disguise of an old woman——'

" ' With a box of trinkets,' broke out the vizier.

" ' Of no such thing,' said the owl, or rather the disguised
Princess Rotu Muckun; ' with a basket of peaches, of which I was

known to be fond, entered the palace garden one evening as I was seated there with my maidens, and offered me a peach, of which I partook, and was that instant turned into an owl. My attendants fled, screaming at the metamorphosis; and as the old woman went away, she clenched her fist at me and laughed, and said "Now, princess, you will remember the vengeance of Ghuzroo." '

" ' This *is* indeed marvellous!' exclaimed the King of Persia. ' Know, madam, that the humble individual who now addresses you was a year since no other than Persia's king.'

" ' Heavens!' said the princess, trembling, and rustling all her feathers; ' can you be the famous and beautiful Mushook, who disappeared from Tehran with his grand vizier?'

" ' No other, madam,' said the king, laying his claw on his breast; ' and the most devoted of your servants.'

" ' Heigho!' said she; ' I would that you had resumed your former shape, and that what you said were true; but you men, I have always heard, are sad, sad deceivers!'

" Being pressed farther to explain the meaning of her wish, the princess said that she never could resume her former appearance until she could find some one who would marry her under her present form; and what was more, she said, an old Brahmin had made a prophecy concerning her, that she should be saved from destruction by a stork.

" ' This speech,' said the vizier, drawing his majesty aside, ' is the sheerest and most immodest piece of fiction on the part of Madam Owl that ever I heard. What is the upshot of it? The hideous old wretch, pining for a husband, and not being able on account of her age and ugliness, doubtless, to procure one among birds of her own degree, sees us two slim, elegant, fashionable fellows pass, and trumps up instantly a story about her being a princess, and the deuce knows what. Even suppose she be a princess, let your majesty remember what the poet Ferooz observes—

" Women are not all beautiful—for one moon-eyed,
       Nine hundred and ninety-nine are as ugly as Shaitan."

Let us have a care, then, how we listen to her stories.'

" ' Vizier,' answered his majesty, ' I have remarked that you are always talking about ugliness; and, by my beard! you are the ugliest man in my dominions. Be she handsome or hideous, I am sure that there is something in the story of the princess mysteriously connected with our fate. Do you not remember that extraordinary dream which I had in my youth, and which declared that I too should be saved from danger by an owl? Had you not also such a dream on the self-same night? Let us not, therefore, disregard the warnings of Fate:—the risk shall be run, the princess shall be married, or my name's not Mushook.'

"'Well, sir,' said the vizier, with a shrug, 'if you insist upon marrying her, I cannot, of course, give any objection to the royal will: and your majesty must remember that I wash my hands of the business altogether.'

"'*I* marry her!' screamed the king, in a rage; 'Vizier, are you a fool? Do you suppose me such a fool as to buy a pig in a poke, as they say at Bagdad?'

"'I was sure your majesty would not be so imprudent,' said the vizier, in a soothing tone.

"'Of course, I wouldn't; no, vizier, my old and tried servant, *you* shall marry the Princess Rotu Muckun, and incur the risk of this adventure.'

"The poor vizier knew he had only to obey, were his master to bid him to bite off his own nose; so he promised compliance in this instance with as good a grace as he could muster. But the gentlemen, in the course of this little dispute, had not taken into consideration that the owl had wings as well as they, and had followed them into the dark brake where the colloquy took place, and could see them perfectly, and hear every word that passed.

"'Tut-tut-tut-too!' shrieked out the owl, in a shrill voice, 'my lord of Persia, and you, grand vizier, do you suppose that I, the Princess of Hindostan, am to be cast about from one person to another like a shuttlecock? Do you suppose that I, the loveliest woman in the universe, am tamely to listen to doubts regarding my beauty, and finally to yield up my charms to an ugly, old, decrepit monster, like your grand vizier?'

"'Madam—' interposed the King of Persia.

" ' Tut-tut-too ! don't madam me, sir,' said the princess, in a fluster,—' mademoiselle, if you please; and mademoiselle to remain, rather than be insulted so. Talk about buying a pig in a poke, indeed ! here is a pretty gentlemanlike phrase for a monarch who has been used to good society !—pig in a poke, indeed ! I'll tell you what, my lord, I have a great mind to make you carry your pigs to another market. And as for my poor person, I will see,' cried the owl, sobbing, ' if some noble-hearted person be not more favourable to-tu-to to-*it*-to-oo-oo-oo-oo !' Here she set up such an hysterical howling, that his majesty the King of Persia thought she would have dropped off her perch.

" He was a good-natured sovereign, and could not bear to see the tears of a woman."

" What a fool !" said the Sultan. But Scheherazade took no notice.

" And having his heart melted by her sorrows, said to her, ' Cheer up, madam, it shall never be said that Mushook deserted a lady in distress. I swear to you by the ninth book of the Koran, that you shall have my hand as soon as I get it back myself; in the meanwhile accept my claw, and with it the heart of the King of Persia.'

" ' Oh, sir !' said the owl, ' this is too great joy—too much honour—I cannot,' said she, in a faint voice, ' bear it ! — O Heavens !—Maidens, unlace me !—Some water—some water—a jug-jug-jug——'

" Here what the king had formerly feared actually took place, and the owl, in an excess of emotion, actually tumbled off the branch in a fainting fit, and fell into the thicket below.

" The vizier and his majesty ran like mad to the lake for water ; but ah ! what a scene met their view on coming back !

" Forth there came to meet them the loveliest damsel that ever greeted the eyes of monarch or vizier. Fancy, sir, a pair of eyes ——"

" Cut the description short, Scheherazade," interrupted the Sultan ; " your eyes, my dear, are quite pretty enough for me."

" In short, sir, she was the most lovely woman in the world of her time ; and the poor old vizier, as he beheld her, was mad to think what a prize he had lost. The King of Persia flung himself at her feet, and vowed himself to be the happiest of men."

" Happiest of men ! " roared out the Sultan. " Why, woman, he is a stork : how did he get back to his shape. I want to know ? "

" Why, sir, it must be confessed that when the Princess of Hindostan, now restored to her pristine beauty, saw that no sort of change had taken place in her affianced husband, she felt a little ashamed of the connexion, and more than once in their journey from Agra to the court of her father at Delhi, she thought of giving her companion the slip : ' For how,' said she, ' am I to marry a stork ? ' However, the king would never leave her for a moment out of his sight, or, when his majesty slept, the vizier kept his eye upon her : and so at last they walked and walked until they came near to Delhi on the banks of the Jumna.

" A magnificent barge was floating down the river, pulled by a hundred men with gilded oars, and dressed in liveries of cloth of gold. The prow of the barge was shaped like a peacock, and formed of precious stones and enamel ; and at the stern of the vessel was an awning of crimson silk, supported by pillars of silver, under which, in a yellow satin robe, covered with diamonds of intolerable brightness, there sat an old gentleman smoking, and dissolved seemingly in grief.

" ' Heavens ! ' cried the princess, ' 'tis my father ! ' and straightway she began flapping her pocket-handkerchief, and crying at the top of her voice, ' Father, father, 'tis your Rotu Muckun calls ! '

" When the old gentleman, who was smoking in yellow satin, heard that voice, he started up wildly, let drop his hookah, shouted hoarsely to the rowers to pull to the shore, and the next minute tumbled backwards in a fainting fit.—The next minute but one he was in the arms of his beloved girl, the proudest and happiest of fathers.

" The princess at the moment of meeting, and in the hurry of running into the boat, had, it must be confessed, quite for-gotten her two storks ; and as these made an effort to follow her, one of the rowers with his gilded oar gave the grand vizier a crack over the leg, which caused that poor functionary to limp for many years after. But our wanderers were not to be put off so. Taking wing, they flew right under the awning of the boat, and perched down on the sofa close by the King of Hindostan and his daughter.

" ' What, in Heaven's name,' said Hindostan, ' are these filthy birds, that smell so horribly of fish ? Faugh ! turn them out."

" ' Filthy yourself, sir, my brother,' answered the King of Persia, ' the smell of fish is not much worse than that of tobacco, I warrant. Heigho ! I have not had a pipe for many a long day !'

" Here Rotu Muckun, seeing her father's wonder that a stork should talk his language, and his anger at the bird's impudence, interposed, and related to his majesty all the circumstances attending the happy change that had taken place.

" While she was speaking (and her story was a pretty long one), the King of Persia flung himself back in an easy attitude on one of the sofas, crossing his long legs, and folding his wings over his chest. He was, to tell the truth, rather piqued at the reception which his brother of Hindostan had given him. Old Munsoor stood moodily at a little distance, holding up his game leg.

" His master, however, was determined to shew that he was perfectly at his ease. ' Hindostan, my old buck,' said he, ' what a deuced comfortable sofa this is ; and, egad, what a neat turn-out of a barge.'

" The old gentleman, who was a stickler for ceremony, said drily, ' I am glad your majesty finds the sofa comfortable, and the barge to your liking. Here we don't call it a barge, but a BUDGEROW.'

" As he spoke this word, the King of Persia bounced off his seat as if he had been shot, and upset the hookah over the King of Hindostan's legs ; the moody old grand vizier clapped his wings and screamed for joy ; the princess shrieked for astonishment ; and the whole boat's crew were in wonder, as they saw the two birds turn towards the east, bob their long bills three times, and call out ' Budgerow !'

" At that word the birds disappeared, and in their place,

before the astonished sovereign of Hindostan there stood two
gentlemen in the Persian habit. One of them was fat, old, and
one-eyed, of a yellow complexion, and limping on a leg—'twas
Munsoor, the vizier. The other—ah, what a thrill passed
through Rotu Muckun's heart as she beheld him :—had a dark
countenance, a dark flashing eye, a royal black beard, a high
forehead, on which a little Persian cap was jauntily placed. A
pelisse of cashmere and sables covered his broad chest, and
showed off his excessively slim waist to advantage ; his little
feet were encased in yellow slippers : when he spoke, his
cornelian lips displayed thirty-two pearly teeth ; in his girdle
was his sword, and on the hilt of it that famous diamond, worth
one hundred and forty-three millions of tomauns.

" When the King of Hindostan saw that diamond, he at once
knew that Mushook could be no impostor, and taking him
heartily by the hand, the good-natured monarch ordered
servants to pick up the pieces of the chillum, and to bring fresh
ones for the King of Persia and himself.

" ' You say it is a long time since you smoked a pipe,' said
Hindostan, waggishly ; ' there is a lady here that I dare swear
will fill one for you.' With this and other sallies the royal
party passed on to Delhi, where Munsoor was accommodated
with diaculum and surgical aid, and where the marriage was
celebrated between the King of Persia and the Princess of
Hindostan."

" And did the King of Persia ever get his kingdom back
again ? " asked the Sultan.

" Of course he did, sir," replied Scheherazade, " for where did
you ever hear of a king who had been kept out of his just
rights by a wicked enchanter, that did not regain his possessions
at the end of a story ? No, sir, at the last page of a tale,
wicked enchanters are always punished, and suffering virtue
always rewarded ; and though I have my doubts whether in
real life ——"

" Be hanged to your prate, madam, and let me know at once
how King Mushook got back his kingdom, and what he did to
Ghuzroo and his son Ameen Adawb ? "

" Why, sir, marching with five hundred thousand men, whom

c

his father-in-law placed under his command, King Mushook went, via Caubul and Affghanistan, into Persia; he defeated the usurping Ghuzroo upon the plains of Tehran, and caused that idolatrous monarch to be bastinadoed to death. As for his son, Ameen Adawb, as that young prince had not taken any part in his father's rebellion, Mushook, who was a merciful sovereign, only ordered him to take a certain quantity of the powder, and to wish himself to be a stork. Then he put him into a cage, and hung him outside the palace wall. This done, Mushook and his princess swayed magnificently the sceptre of Persia, lived happily, were blest by their subjects, had an infinite number of children, and ate pilau and rice every day.

"Now, sir, it happened, after several years' captivity in the cage, that the Prince Ameen Adawb ——" * * *

Here Scheherazade paused; for, looking at her royal husband, she saw that his majesty was fast asleep, and deferred the history of Prince Ameen Adawb until another occasion.

LITTLE SPITZ.

A LENTEN ANECDOTE, FROM THE GERMAN OF PROFESSOR
SPASS.

By MICHAEL ANGELO TITMARSH.

 THINK," said Rebecca, flinging down her beautiful
eyes to the ground, and heaving a great sigh—" I think,
Signor Lorenzo, I could eat a bit of—sausage."

" Of *what?* " said Lorenzo, bouncing up and forgetting all sense of politeness in the strange demand. " My dearest
madam, *you* eat a sausage ? "

" Ha, ha, I'm blesht," shouted Abednego, the banker, Rebecca's
papa, " I'm blesht, if Signor Lorenz does not think you want to
eat the unclean animal, Rebecca, my soul's darling. These
shtudents are dull fellows, look you, and only know what's in
their books. Why, there are in dis vicked vorld no less than
four hundred kindsh of shausages, Signor Lorenz, of which
Herr Bürcke, the court-butcher, will show you the resheipts.—
Confess now, you thought my darling wanted to eat pig—
faugh ! "

Rebecca's countenance, at the very idea, assumed an expression
of the most intolerable disgust, and she gazed reproachfully at
Lorenzo. That young man blushed, and looked particularly
foolish, as he said : " Pardon me, dearest madam, for entertaining a thought so unworthy. *I did,* I confess, think of pork-
sausages, when you spoke, and although pretty learned on most
subjects, am indeed quite ignorant upon the matter of which
Herr Abednego has just been speaking."

"I told you so," says Abednego. "Why, my goot sir, dere is mutton-sausages, and veal-sausages, and beef-sausages, and—"

"Silence, papa," said Rebecca, sharply : "for what has Signor Lorenz to do with such things ? I'm very sorry that I—that I offended him by asking for any dish of the kind, and pray let him serve us with what he has."

Rebecca sunk down in a chair, looking very faint; but Lorenzo started up, and swore that he would have himself cut up into little pieces, stuffed into a bladder, and made sausage-meat of, rather than that the lovely Israelite should go without the meat that she loved. And, indeed, such was the infatuated passion which this young man entertained for the Jewess, that I have not the least doubt but that he would have been ready to do as he said. "I will send down immediately into the town," continued he, "and in ten minutes, my messenger will be back again."

"He must run very fast," said the lady, appeased, "but I thought you said, Signor Lorenz, that you kept but one servant, and that your old housekeeper was too ill to move ?"

"Madam, make your mind quite easy.—I have the best little messenger in the world."

"Is it a fairy," said the Jewess, "or a household demon ? They say that you great students have many such at your orders, and I should like to see one of all things."

"You shall see him, dearest lady," replied the student, who took from a shelf a basket and a napkin, put a piece of money into the basket (I believe the poor devil had not many of them), and wrote a few words on a paper which he set by the side of the coin. "Mr. Bürcke," wrote he, "Herr Hofmetzler (that is, Mr. Court-butcher), have the goodness to send, per bearer, a rixdollar's worth of the best sausages—*not* pork." And then Lorenz opened his window, looked into his little garden, whistled, and shouted out, "Hallo ! *Spitz !* "

"Now," said he, "you shall see my familiar;" and a great scratching and whining was presently heard at the door, which made Rebecca wonder, and poor old fat Abednego turn as yellow as a parsnip. I warrant the old wretch thought that a demon with horns and a tail was coming into the room.

The familiar spirit which now made its appearance had a tail certainly, and a very long one for such a little animal; but there was nothing terrible about him. The fact is, it was Lorenz's little turnspit-dog, that used to do many such commissions for the student, who lived half a mile out of the city of Krähwinkel, where the little dog was perfectly well known. He was a very sagacious, faithful, ugly little dog as ever was seen. He had a long black back and tail, and very little yellow legs; but he ran excessively fast on those little legs, and regularly fetched his master's meat and rolls from the city, and brought them to that lovely cottage which the student, for quiet's sake, occupied at a short distance from town.

"When I give him white money," said Lorenz, caressing the little faithful beast, that wagged his tail between the calves of his master's legs, and looked up fondly in his face, "when I give him white money, he goes to the butcher's; when I give him copper, he runs to the baker's,—and was never yet known to fail. Go, my little Spitz, as fast as legs will carry thee. Go, my dog, and bring with thee the best of sausages for the breakfast of the peerless Rebecca Abednego." With this gallant speech, which pleased the lady greatly, and caused her to try to blush as much as possible, the little dog took the basket in his mouth, and trotted down stairs, and went off on his errand. While he is on the way to Krähwinkel and back, I may as well mention briefly who his master was, how he came to be possessed of this little animal, and how the fair Jewess had found her way to a Christian student's house.

Lorenz's parents lived at Polkwitz, which everybody knows is a hundred leagues from Krähwinkel. They were the most pious, orderly, excellent people ever known, and their son bade fair to equal them in all respects. He had come to Krähwinkel to study at the famous university there; but he never frequented the place except for the lectures; never made one at the noisy students' drinking bouts; and was called, for his piety and solitary life, the hermit.

The first year of his residence he was to be seen not only at lectures, but at church regularly. He never ate meat on a Friday; he fasted all through Lent; he confessed twice in a month; and was a model for all young students, not merely at Krähwinkel, Bonn, Jena, Halle, and other German universities; but those of Salamanca and the rest in Spain, of Bologna and other places of learning in Italy, nay, of Oxford and Cambridge in the island of England, would do well to take example by him, and lead the godly life which he led.

But I am sorry to say that learning oftentimes begets pride, and Lorenzo Tisch, seeing how superior he was to all his companions, ay, and to most of the professors of the university, and plunging deeper and deeper daily into books, began to neglect his religious duties at first a little, then a great deal, then to take no note of them at all; for though, when the circumstances of this true history occurred, it was the season of Lent, Lorenzo Tisch had not the slightest recollection of the fact, not having been at church, or looked into an almanack or a prayer-book, for many months before.

Lorenzo was allowed a handsome income of a hundred rix-dollars per year by his parents, and used to draw this at the house of Mr. Abednego, the banker. One day, when he went to cash a draft for five dollars, the lovely Miss Rebecca Abednego chanced to be in the room. Ah, Lorenzo, Lorenzo! better for you to have remained at home studying the Pons Asinorum; better still for you to have been at church, listening to the soul-stirring discourses of Father Windbentel; better for you to have been less learned and more pious: then you would not have been so likely to go astray, or allow your fancy to be inflamed by the charms of wicked Jewesses, that all Christian men should shun like poison.

Here it was Lent season—a holiday in Lent, and Lorenzo Von Tisch knew nothing about the matter, and Rebecca Abednego, and her father, were absolutely come to breakfast with him!

But though Lorenzo had forgotten Lent, the citizens of Krähwinkel had not, and especially one Herr Bürcke, the court butcher, to whom Tisch had just despatched Spitz for a dollar's worth of sausage-meat.

The visits of Tisch to the Jew's house had indeed caused not a little scandal. The student's odd, lonely ways, his neglect of church, his queer little dog that ran of errands for him, had all been talked of by the town's-people, who had come at last to believe that Lorenzo was no less than a magician, and his dog, as he himself said in joke, his familiar spirit. Poor Spitz!—no familiar spirit wert thou; only a little, faithful, ugly dog—a little dog that Tisch's aunt Konisgunda gave to him, who was equally fond of it and him.

Those who know Krähwinkel (and who, I should like to know, is not acquainted with that famous city?) are aware that Mr. Bürcke, the court butcher, has his handsome shop in the Schnapps-Gasse, only a very few doors from Abednego's banking-house. Mrs. Bürcke is, or used to be, a lady that was very fond of knowing the doings of her neighbours, and passed many hours staring out of her windows, of which the front row gave her a command of the whole of that beautiful street, the Schnapps-Gasse, while from the back the eye ranged over the gardens and summer-houses without the gates of the town, and the great road that goes to Bolkum. Herr Lorenzo's cottage was on this road; and it was by the Bolkum-gate that little Spitz the dog entered with his basket, when he went on his master's errands.

Now, on this day in Lent, it happened that Frau Bürcke was looking out of her windows instead of listening at church to Father Windbeutel, and she saw at eleven o'clock Mr. Israel Löwe, Herr Abednego's valet, porter, coachman, gardener, and cashier, bring round a certain chaise that the banker had taken for a bad debt, into which he stepped in his best snuff-coloured coat, and silk stockings, handing in Miss Rachael,* in a neat dress of yellow silk, a blue hat and pink feathers, and a pair of red morocco slippers that set off her beautiful ankle to advantage.

"Odious people!" said Mrs. Bürcke, looking at the pair whom Mr. Löwe was driving, "odious, vulgar horse!" (Herr Bürcke kept only that one on which his lad rode;) "Roman-nosed beast! I shouldn't wonder but that the horse is a Jew too!"—and she saw the party turn down to the left into Bolkum-Strasse, towards the gate which I have spoken of before.

---

* Presumably a slip of the pen for " Rebecca," as the name appears throughout elsewhere ; but we have not ventured to alter it. It may have been " Rachael Rebecca," or " Rebecca Rachael."—ED.

When Madame Bürcke saw this, she instantly flew from her front window to her back window, and there had a full view of the Bolkum road, and the Abednego chaise jingling up the same. Mr. Löwe, when they came to the hill, got off the box and walked, Mr. Abednego sat inside and smoked his pipe.

"*Ey du lieber Himmel!*" screamed out Mrs. Bürcke, "they have stopped at the necromancer's door!"

It was so that she called the worthy Tisch : and she was perfectly right in saying that the Israelitish cavalcade had stopped at the gate of his cottage ; where also appeared Lorenzo, bowing, in his best coat, and offering his arm to lead Miss Rebecca in. Mrs. Bürcke could not see how he trembled as he performed this work of politeness, or what glances Miss Rebecca shot forth from her great wicked black eyes. Having set down his load, Mr. Israel again mounted his box, and incontinently drove away.

"Here comes that horrid little dog with the basket," continued Mrs. Bürcke, after a few minutes' more looking out of the window :—and now is not everything explained relative to Herr Lorenzo Tisch, Miss Rebecca Abednego, and the little dog?

Mrs. Bürcke hated Spitz : the fact is, he once bit a hole in one of her great, round, mottled arms, which had thrust itself into the basket that Spitz carried for his master's provisions ; for Mrs. B. was very anxious to know what there was under the napkin. In consequence, therefore, of this misunderstanding between her and the dog, whenever she saw the animal, it was Mrs. B.'s wicked custom to salute him with many foul words and curses, and to compass how to do him harm ; for the Frau Hofmetzlerinn, as she was called in Krähwinkel, was a lady of great energy and perseverance, and nobody could ever accuse her of forgetting an injury.

The little dog, as she sat meditating evil against him, came trotting down the road, entered as usual by the Bolkum-gate, turned to the right, and by the time Madame Bürcke had descended to the shop, there he was at the door, sure enough, and entered it wagging his tail. It was holiday Lent, and the butcher-boys were absent ; Mr. Bürcke himself was abroad ; there was not a single joint of meat in the shop, nor ought there to be at such a season, when all good men eat fish. But how was poor Spitz to know what the season was, or tell what his master himself had forgotten?

He looked a little shy when he saw only Madame Bürcke in the shop, doubtless remembering his former disagreement with her; but a sense of duty at last prevailed with him, and he jumped up on his usual place on the counter, laid his basket down, whined, and began flapping the place on which he sat with his tail.

Mrs. Bürcke advanced, and held out her great mottled arm rather fearfully; he growled, and made her start a little, but did her no harm. She took the paper out of the basket, and read what we have before imparted to the public, viz. :—"*Mr. Court Butcher, have the goodness to send per bearer a rixdollar's worth of best sausage meat,* NOT *pork.—Lorenz Tisch.*" As she read, the dog wagged his tail more violently than ever.

A horrible thought entered the bosom of Mrs. Bürcke, as she looked at the dog, and from the dog glanced at her husband's *cleaver*, that hung idling on the wall.

"Sausages in Lent!" said Mrs. Bürcke: sausages to be fetched by a dog for that heathen necromancer and that accursed Jew! He *shall* have sausages with a vengeance. Mrs. Bürcke took down the cleaver, and

*   *   *   *   *   *   *   *

About twenty minutes afterwards Herr Lorenzo Tisch opened his garden gate, whither he had been summoned by the whining and scratching of his little faithful messenger. Spitz staggered in, laid the basket at his master's feet, licked his hand, and fell down.

"Blesh us, dere'sh something red all along the road!" cried Mr. Abednego.

"Pshaw! papa, never mind that, let's look at the sausages," said his daughter Rebecca—a sad gormandizer for so young a woman.

Tisch opened the basket, staggered back, and turned quite sick.—In the basket which Spitz had carried so faithfully lay the poor little dog's OWN TAIL!

What took place during the rest of the entertainment, I have never been able or anxious to learn ; but this I know, that there is a single gentleman now living with Madame Konisgunda Von Speck, in the beautiful town of Polkwitz, a gentleman, who, if he has one prejudice in the world, has that of hating the Jewish nation—a gentleman who goes to church regularly, and, above all, never eats meat in Lent.

He is followed about by a little dog—a little ugly dog— of which he and Madame Von Speck are outrageously fond ; although, between ourselves, the animal's back is provided with no more tail than a cannon-ball.

DICKENS IN FRANCE.

EEING placarded on the walls a huge announcement that " Nicholas Nickleby, ou les Voleurs de Londres," was to be performed at the Ambigu-Comique Théâtre on the Boulevard, and having read in the *Journal des Débats* a most stern and ferocious criticism upon the piece in question, and upon poor Monsieur Dickens, its supposed author, it seemed to me by no means unprofitable to lay out fifty sous in the purchase of a stall at the theatre, and to judge with my own eyes of the merits and demerits of the play.

Who does not remember (except those who never saw the drama, and therefore of course cannot be expected to have any notion of it)—who does not, I say, remember the pathetic acting of Mrs. Keeley in the part of Smike, as performed at the Adelphi; the obstinate good-humour of Mr. Wilkinson, who, having to represent the brutal Squeers, was, according to his nature, so chuckling, oily, and kind-hearted, that little boys must have thought it a good joke to be flogged by him; finally, the acting of the admirable Yates in the kindred part of Mantalini? Can France, I thought, produce a fop equal to Yates? Is there any vulgarity and assurance on the Boulevard that can be compared to that of which, in the character of Mantalini, he gives a copy so wonderfully close to nature? Never then were fifty sous more cheerfully—nay, eagerly paid, than by your obedient servant.

After China, this is the most ignorant country, thought I, in the whole civilised world (the company was dropping into the theatre, and the musicians were one by one taking their seats); these people are so immensely conceited, that they think the rest of Europe beneath them; and though they have invaded

Spain, Italy, Russia, Germany, not one in ten thousand can ask
for a piece of bread in the national language of the countries so
conquered. But see the force of genius; after a time it conquers
every thing, even the ignorance and conceit of Frenchmen! The
name of Nicholas Nickleby crosses the Channel in spite of them.
I shall see honest John Browdie and wicked Ralph once more,
honest and wicked in French. Shall we have the Kenwigses,
and their uncle, the delightful collector; and will he, in Ports-
mouth church, make that famous marriage with Juliana
Petowker? Above all, what will *Mrs.* Nickleby say?—the
famous Mrs. Nickleby, who has lain undescribed until Boz
seized upon her, and brought that great truth to light, and whom
yet every man possesses in the bosom of his own family. Are there
Mrs. Nicklebies—or to speak more correctly, are there Mistresses
Nickleby in France? We shall see all this at the rising of the
curtain; and hark! the fiddlers are striking up.

Presently the prompter gives his three heart-thrilling slaps,
and the great painted cloth moves upwards: it is always a
moment of awe and pleasure. What is coming? First you
get a glimpse of legs and feet; then suddenly the owners of the
limbs in question in steady attitudes, looking as if they had
been there one thousand years before; now behold the landscape,
the clouds; the great curtain vanishes altogether, the charm is
dissolved, and the disenchanted performers begin.

ACT I.

You see a court of a school, with great iron bars in front, and
a beauteous sylvan landscape beyond. Could you read the
writing on the large board over the gate, you would know that
the school was the "Paradis des Enfans," kept by Mr. Squeers.
Somewhere by that bright river, which meanders through the
background, is the castle of the stately Earl of Clarendon—no
relation to a late ambassador at Madrid.

His lordship is from home; but his young and lovely daughter,
Miss Annabella, is in Yorkshire, and at this very moment is
taking a lesson of French from Mr. Squeers's *sous-maître*,
Nickolass Neeklbee. Nicholas is, however, no vulgar usher;
he is but lately an orphan; and his uncle, the rich London

banker, Monsieur Ralph, taking charge of the lad's portionless sister, has procured for Nicholas this place of usher at a school in le Yorksheer.

A rich London banker procuring his nephew a place in a school at eight guineas per annum! Sure there must be some roguery in this; and the more so when you know that Monsieur Squeers, the keeper of the academy, was a few years since a vulgar rope-dancer and tumbler at a fair. But, peace! let these mysteries clear up, as, please Heaven, before five acts are over they will. Meanwhile Nicholas is happy in giving his lessons to the lovely Meess Annabel. Lessons, indeed! Lessons of what? Alack, alack! when two young, handsome, ardent, tender-hearted people pore over the same book, we know what happens, be the book what it may. French or Hebrew, there is always one kind of language in the leaves, as those can tell who have conned them.

Meanwhile, in the absence of his usher, Monsieur Squeers keeps school. But one of his scholars is in the court-yard; a lad beautifully dressed, fat, clean, and rosy. A gentleman by the name of Browdie, by profession a drover, is with the boy, employed at the moment (for he is at leisure and fond of music) in giving him a lesson on *the clarionet*.

The boy thus receiving lessons is called facetiously by his master *Prospectus*, and why? Because he is so excessively fat and healthy, and well clothed, that his mere appearance in the court-yard is supposed to entice parents and guardians to place their children in a seminary where the scholars were in such admirable condition.

And here I cannot help observing in the first place, that Squeers exhibiting in this manner a sample-boy, and pretending that the whole stock were like him (whereas they are a miserable, half-starved set), must have been an abominable old scoundrel; and, secondly (though the observation applies to the French nation merely, and may be considered more as political than general), that by way of a fat specimen, never was one more unsatisfactory than this. Such a poor shrivelled creature I never saw; it is like a French fat pig, as lanky as a greyhound! Both animals give one a thorough contempt for the nation.

John Browdie gives his lesson to Prospectus, who informs him of some of the circumstances narrated above ; and having concluded the lesson, honest John produces a piece of *pudding* for his pupil. Ah, how Prospectus devours it ! for though the only well-fed boy in the school, he is, we regret to say, a gormandiser by disposition.

While Prospectus eats, another of Mr. Squeers's scholars is looking unnoticed on ; another boy, a thousand times more miserable. See yon poor shivering child, trembling over his book in a miserable hutch at the corner of the court ! He is in rags, he is not allowed to live with the other boys ; at play they constantly buffet him, at lesson-time their blunders are visited upon his poor shoulders.

Who is this unhappy boy ? Ten years since a man by the name of Becher brought him to the Paradis des Enfans ; and paying in advance five years of his pension, left him under the charge of Monsieur Squeers. No family ever visited the child ; and when at the five years' end the *instituteur* applied at the address given him by Becher for the further payment of his pupil's expenses, Monsieur Squeers found that Becher had grossly deceived him, that no such persons existed, and that no money was consequently forthcoming, hence the misfortunes which afterwards befell the hapless orphan. None cared for him—none knew him, 'tis possible that even the name he went by was fictitious. That name was Smike, pronounced Smeek.

Poor Smeek ! he had, however, found one friend,—the kind-hearted *sous-maître* Neeklbee—who gave him half of his own daily pittance of bread and pudding, encouraged him to apply to his books, and defended him as much as possible from the assaults of the schoolboys and Monsieur Squeers.

John Browdie had just done giving his lesson of clarionet to Prospectus, when Neeklbee arrived at the school. There was a difference between John and Nicholas ; for the former, seeing the young usher's frequent visits at Clarendon Castle, foolishly thought he was enamoured of Meess Jenny, the fermier's daughter, on whom John too had fixed an eye of affection. Silly John ! Nicholas's heart was fixed (hopelessly as the young man thought) upon higher objects. However, the very instant that Nickleby entered the court-yard of the school, John took up his stick and set off for London, whither he was bound with a drove of oxen.

Nickleby had not arrived a whit too soon to protect his poor friend, Smeek; all the boys were called into the court-yard by Monsieur Squarrs, and made to say their lessons; when it came to poor Smeek's turn, the timid lad trembled, hesitated, and could not do his spelling.

Inflamed with fury, old Squarrs rushed forward, and would have assomméd his pupil, but human nature could bear this tyranny no longer. Nickleby, stepping forward, defended the poor prostrate child; and when Squeers raised his stick to strike—pouf! pif! un, deux, trois, et la !—Monsieur Nicholas flanquéd him several coups de poing, and sent him bientôt grovelling à terre.

You may be sure that there was now a pretty hallooing among the boys; all jumped, kicked, thumped, bumped, and scratched their unhappy master (and serve him right, too!), and when they had finished their fun, vlan ! flung open the gates of the Infants' Paradise and ran away home.

Neeklbee seeing what he had done, had nothing left but to run away too: he penned a hasty line to his lovely pupil, Miss Annabel, to explain that though his departure was sudden his honour was safe, and seizing his stick quitted the school.

There was but one pupil left in it, and he, poor soul, knew not whither to go. But when he saw Nicholas, his sole friend, departing, he mustered courage, and then made a step forward—and then wondered if he dared—and then, when Nicholas was at a little distance from him, ran, ran, as if his life (as indeed it did) depended upon it.

This is the picture of Neeklbee and poor Smeek.* They are both dressed in the English fashion, and you must fancy the curtain falling amidst thunders of applause. [*End of Act I.*

"Ah, ah, ah ! ouf, pouf."—"Dieu, qu'il fait chaud !"—"Orgeat, limonade, bière !"—"L'Entracte, journal de tous les spectacles !"

---

* Alluding to a sketch, the first of two sketches by the author, which accompanied this paper on its original appearance in *Fraser's Magazine.*—ED.

—"LA MARSEILLAI-AI-AISE!"—with such cries from pit and boxes the public wiles away the weary ten minutes between the acts. The three *bonnes* in the front boxes, who had been escorted by a gentleman in a red cap, and jacket, and earrings, begin sucking oranges with great comfort, while their friend amuses himself with a piece of barley-sugar. The *petite-maîtresse* in the private box smoothes her *bandeaux* of hair and her little trim, white cuffs, and looks at her *chiffons*. The friend of the tight black velvet spencer, meanwhile, pulls his yellow kid gloves tighter on his hands, and looks superciliously round the house with his double-glass. Fourteen people, all smelling of smoke, all bearded, and all four feet high, pass over your body to their separate stalls. The prompter gives his thumps, whack—whack —whack! the music begins again, the curtain draws, and, lo! we have

ACT II.

The tavern of Les Armes du Roi appears to be one of the most frequented in the city of London. It must be in the Yorkshire road, that is clear; for the first person whom we see there is John Browdie; to whom presently comes Prospectus, then Neeklbee, then poor Smeek, each running away individually from the Paradis des Enfans.

It is likewise at this tavern that the great banker Ralph does his business, and lets you into a number of his secrets. Hither, too, comes Milor Clarendon,—a handsome peer, forsooth, but a sad reprobate I fear. Sorrow has driven him to these wretched courses: ten years since he lost a son, a lovely child of six years of age; and, hardened by the loss, he has taken to gambling, to the use of the *vins de France* which take the reason prisoner, and to other excitements still more criminal. He has cast his eyes upon the lovely Kate Nickleby (he, the father of Miss Annabel!), and asks the banker to sup with him, to lend him ten thousand pounds, and to bring his niece with him. With every one of these requests the capitalist promises to comply: the money he produces forthwith; the lady he goes to fetch. Ah, milor! beware—beware, your health is bad, your property is ruined,—death and insolvency stare you in the face,

—but what cares Lor Clarendon ? He is desperate : he orders a splendid repast in a private apartment, and while they are getting it ready, he and the young lords of his acquaintance sit down and crack a bottle in the coffee-room. A gallant set of gentlemen truly, all in short coats with capes to them, in tights and Hessian boots, such as our nobility are in the custom of wearing.

" I bet you cinq cent guinées, Lor Beef," says Milor Clarendon (whom the wine has begun to excite), "that I will have the lovely Kate Nicklbee at supper with us to-night."

"Done !" says Lor Beef. But why starts yon stranger who has just come into the hotel ? Why, forsooth ? because he is Nicholas Nickleby, Kate's brother ; and a pretty noise he makes when he hears of his lordship's project !

" You have Meess Necklbee at your table, sir ? You are a liar !"

All the lords start up.

" Who is this very strange person ?" says Milor Clarendon, as cool as a cucumber.

" Dog ! give me your name !" shouts Nicholas.

" Ha ! ha ! ha !" says my lord, scornfully.

"John," says Nickleby, seizing hold of a waiter, "tell me that man's name."

John the waiter looks frightened, and hums and has, when, at the moment, who should walk in but Mr. Ralph the banker, and his niece.

Ralph. " Nicholas !—confusion !"

Kate. " My brother !"

Nicholas. " Avaunt, woman ! Tell me, sirrah, by what right you bring my sister into such company, and who is the villain to whom you have presented her ?"

Ralph. " Lord *Clarendon.*"

Nicholas. " The father of Meess Annabel ? Gracious heaven !"

What followed now need not be explained. The young lords and the banker retire abashed to their supper, while Meess Kate, and Smike, who has just arrived, fall into the arms of Nicholas.

Such, ladies and gentlemen, is the second act, rather feeble in interest, and not altogether probable in action. That five people running away from Yorkshire should all come to the same inn in London, arriving within five minutes of each other,

—that Mr. Ralph, the great banker, should make the hotel his
place of business, and openly confess in the coffee-room to his
ex-agent Becher that he had caused Becher to make away with
or murder the son of Lord Clarendon,—finally, that Lord
Clarendon himself, with an elegant town mansion, should receive
his distinguished guests in a tavern, of not the first respectability,
—all these points may, perhaps, strike the critic from their
extreme improbability.   But, bless your soul ! if *these* are im-
probabilities, what will you say to the revelations of the

THIRD ACT.

That scoundrel Squarrs before he kept the school was, as we
have seen, a tumbler and *saltimbanque*, and, as such, member
of the great fraternity of cadgers, beggars, *gueux*, thieves, that
have their club in London.   It is held in immense Gothic vaults
under ground : here the beggars concert their plans, divide their
spoil, and hold their orgies.

In returning to London Monsieur Squarrs instantly resumes
his acquaintance with his old comrades, who appoint him, by
the all-powerful interest of a *peculiar person*, head of the com-
munity of cadgers.

That person is no other than the banker Ralph, who, in
secret, directs this godless crew, visits their haunts, and receives
from them a boundless obedience.   A villain himself, he has need
of the aid of villany.   He pants for vengeance against his
nephew, he has determined that his niece shall fall a prey to
Milor Clarendon,—nay more, he has a dark suspicion that Smike
—the orphan boy—the homeless fugitive from Yorkshire—is no
other than the child who ten years ago—but, hush !

Where is his rebellious nephew and those whom he protects ?
The quick vigilance of Ralph soon discovered them ; Nicholas,
having taken the name of Edward Browne, was acting at a
theatre in the neighbourhood of the Thames.   Haste, Squarrs,
take a couple of trusty beggars with you, and hie thee to
Wapping ; seize young Smike and carry him to Cadger's Cavern,—
haste, then !   The mind shudders to consider what is to happen.

In Nicholas's room at the theatre we find his little family
assembled, and with them honest John Browdie, who has for-

gotten his part on learning that Nicholas was attached, not to the *fermière*, but to the mistress; to them comes—gracious heavens!—Meess Annabel. "Fly," says she, "fly! I have overheard a plot concocted between my father and your uncle; the sheriff is to seize you for the abduction of Smeek and the assault upon Squarrs," &c. &c. &c.

In short, it is quite impossible to describe this act, so much is there done in it. Lord Clarendon learns that he has pledged his life interest in his estates to Ralph.

His lordship *dies*, and Ralph seizes a paper, which proves beyond a doubt that young Smike is no other than Clarendon's long-lost son.

L'infâme Squarrs with his satellites carry off the boy; Browdie pitches Squarrs into the river; the sheriff carries Nickleby to prison; and VICE TRIUMPHS in the person of the odious Ralph. But vice does not always triumph; wait awhile and you will see. For in the

FOURTH ACT

John Browdie, determined to rescue his two young friends, follows Ralph like his shadow; he dogs him to a rendezvous of the beggars, and overhears all his conversation with Squarrs. The boy is in the Cadger's Cavern, hidden a thousand feet below the Thames; there is to be a grand jollification among the rogues that night—a dance and a feast. "*I*," says John Browdie, "*will be there.*" And, wonderful to say, who should pass but his old friend Prospectus, to whom he gave lessons on the clarionet.

Prospectus is a cadger now, and is to play his clarionet that night at Cadger's Hall. Browdie will join him,—he is dressed up like a blind beggar, and strange sights, heaven knows, meet his eyes in Cadger's Hall.

Here they come trooping in by scores,—the halt and the lame, black sweepers, one-legged fiddlers, the climber mots, the fly-sakers, the kedgoree coves,—in a word, the rogues of London, to their Gothic hall, a thousand miles below the level of the sea. Squarrs is their nominal head; but their real leader is the tall man yonder in the black mask, he whom nobody knows but Browdie, who has found him out at once,—'tis Ralph!

" Bring out the prisoner," says the black mask; " he has tried
to escape—he has broken his oaths to the cadgers, let him meet
his punishment."

And without a word more, what do these cadgers do ? They
take poor Smike and *bury him alive;* down he goes into the
vault, a stone is rolled over him, the cadgers go away,—so much
for Smike.

But in the meantime Master Browdie has not been idle. He
has picked the pocket of one of the cadgers of a portfolio
containing papers that prove Smike to be Lord Clarendon
beyond a doubt ; he lags behind until all the cadgers are gone,
and with the help of Nicholas (who, by the by, has found his
way somehow into the place), he pushes away the stone, and
brings the fainting boy to the world.

These things are improbable you certainly may say, but are
they impossible ? If they are possible, then they may come to
pass ; if they may come to pass, then they may be supposed to
come to pass : and why should they not come to pass ? That is
my argument : let us pass on to the

FIFTH ACT.

Aha ! Master Ralph, you think you will have it all your
own way, do you ? The lands of Clarendon are yours, provided there is no male heir, and you have done for *him.* The
peerage, to be sure (by the laws of England), is to pass to the
husband of Meess Annabella. Will she marry Ralph, or not ?
Yes : then well and good; he is an earl for the future and the
father of a new race of Clarendon. No: then, in order to spell
her still more, he has provided amongst the beggars a lad who
is to personate the young mislaid Lord Clarendon, who is to
come armed with certain papers that make his right unquestionable, and who will be a creature of Ralph's, to be used or cast
away at will.

Ralph pops the question ; the lady repels him with scorn.
" Quit the house, Meess," says he ; " it is not yours, but mine.
Give up that vain title which you have adopted since your papa's
death ; you are no countess,—your brother lives. Ho ! John,
Thomas, Samuel ! introduce his lordship, the Comte de Clarendon."

And who slips in ? Why, in a handsome new dress, in the English fashion, Smike, to be sure—the boy whom Ralph has murdered—the boy who had risen from the tomb—the boy who had miraculously discovered the papers in Cadger's Hall and (by some underhand work that went on behind the scenes, which I don't pretend to understand) had substituted himself for the substitute which that wicked banker had proposed to bring forward! A rush of early recollections floods the panting heart of the young boy. Can it be ? Yes—no ; sure these halls are familiar to him ? That conservatory, has he not played with the flowers there—played with his blessed mother at his side ? That portrait! Stop! a—a—a—a—ah! it is—it is my sister Anna—Anna—bella !

Fancy the scene as the two young creatures rush with a scream into each other's arms. Fancy John Browdie's hilarity : he jumps for joy, and throws off his beggar's cloak and beard. Nicholas clasps his hands, and casts his fine eyes heavenward. But, above all, fancy the despair of that cursed banker Ralph as he sees his victim risen from the grave, and all his hopes dashed down into it. Oh! Heaven, Thy hand is here ! How must the banker then have repented of his bargain with the late Lord Clarendon, and that he had not had his lordship's life insured ! Perdition ! to have been out-tricked by a boy and a country boor ! Is there no hope ? * * *

Hope ? Psha ! man, thy reign of vice is over,—it is the fifth act. Already the people are beginning to leave the house, and never more again canst thou expect to lift thy head.

" Monsieur Ralph," Browdie whispers, " after your pretty doings in Cadger's Hall, had you not best be thinking of leaving the country, as Nicholas Nickleby's uncle, I would fain not see you, crick ! You understand ?" (pointing to his jugular).

" I do," says Ralph, gloomily, " and will be off in two hours." And Lord Smike takes honest Browdie by one hand, gently pressing Kate's little fingers with the other, and the sheriff, and the footmen, and attendants form a tableau, and the curtain begins to fall, and the blushing Annabel whispers to happy Nicholas,—" Ah! my friend, I can give up with joy to my brother *ma couronne de comtesse*. What care I for rank or name with

you? the name that I love above all others is that of LADY
ANNABEL NICKLEBY."   [*Exeunt omnes.*

The musicians have hurried off long before this. In one
instant the stage lamps go out, and you see fellows starting
forward to cover the boxes with canvass. Up goes the chandelier
amongst the gods and goddesses painted on the ceiling. Those
in the galleries, meanwhile, bellow out "SAINT ERNEST!" he it
is who acted John Browdie. Then there is a yell of "SMEEK!
SMEEK!" Blushing and bowing, Madame Prosper comes forward; by Heavens! a pretty woman, with tender eyes and a
fresh, clear voice. Next the gods call for "CHILLY!" who acted
the villain : but by this time you are bustling and struggling
among the crowd in the lobbies, where there is the usual odour
of garlic and tobacco. Men in sabots come tumbling down
from the galleries; cries of "*Auguste, solo ! Eugenie ! prends ton
parapluie.*" "*Monsieur, vous me marchez sur les pieds,*" are heard
in the crowd, over which the brazen helmets of the Pompier's
tower are shining. A cabman in the Boulevard, who opens his
vehicle eagerly as you pass by, growls dreadful oaths when,
seated inside, you politely request him to drive to the Barrière
de l'Etoile. "*Ah, ces Anglais,*" says he, "*ça demeure dans les
déserts—dans les déserts, grand Dieu! avec les loups ; ils prennent
leur* beautyfine *thé avec leurs tartines le soir, et puis ils se couchent
dans les déserts, ma parole d'honneur ; comme des Arabes.*"

If the above explanation of the plot of the new piece of
Nicholas Nickleby has appeared intolerably long to those few
persons who have perused it, I can only say for their comfort
that I have not told one half of the real plot of the piece in
question ; nay, very likely have passed over all the most
interesting part of it. There, for instance, was the assassina-
tion of the virtuous villain Becher, the dying scene with my
lord, the manner in which Nicholas got into the Cadger's Cave,
and got out again. Have I breathed a syllable upon any of
these points? No; and never will to my dying day. The
imperfect account of *Nicholas Nickleby* given above is all that the
most impatient reader (let him have fair warning) can expect
to hear from his humble servant. Let it be sufficient to know

that the piece in itself contains a vast number of beauties
entirely passed over by the unworthy critic, and only to be
appreciated by any gentleman who will take the trouble to step
across the Channel, and thence from his hotel to the am-
biguously-comic theatre. And let him make haste, too; for
who knows what may happen? Human life is proverbially
short. Theatrical pieces bloom and fade like the flowers of
the field, and very likely long before this notice shall appear
in print (as let us heartily, from mercenary considerations, pray
that it will), the drama of *Nicholas Nickleby* may have disappeared altogether from the world's ken, like Carthage, Troy,
Swallow Street, the Marylebone bank, Babylon, and other fond
magnificences elevated by men, and now forgotten and prostrate.

As for the worthy Boz, it will be seen that *his* share in the
piece is perfectly insignificant, and that he has no more connexion with the noble geniuses who invented the drama than a
peg has with a gold-laced hat that a nobleman may have hung
on it, or a starting-post on the race-course with some magnificent
thousand-guinea fiery horses who may choose to run from it.
How poor do his writings appear after those of the Frenchman!
How feeble, mean, and destitute of imagination! *He* never
would have thought of introducing six lords, an ex-kidnapper,
a great banker, an idiot, a schoolmaster, his usher, a cattle-
driver, coming for the most part a couple of hundred miles, in
order to lay open all their secrets in the coffee-room of the
King's Arms hotel! He never could have invented the great
subterraneous cavern, *cimetière et salle de bal*, as Jules Janin
calls it! The credit of all this falls upon the French adaptors
of Monsieur Dickens's romance; and so it will be advisable to
let the public know.

But as the French play-writers are better than Dickens, being
incomparably more imaginative and poetic, so, in progression,
is the French critic, Jules Janin, above named, a million times
superior to the French playwrights, and, after Janin, Dickens
disappears altogether. He is cut up, disposed of, done for.
J. J. has hacked him into small pieces, and while that wretched
romancer is amusing himself across the Atlantic, and fancying,
perhaps, that he is a popular character, his business has been

done for ever and ever in Europe. What matters that he is read by millions in England and billions in America? that everybody who understands English has a corner in his heart for him? The great point is, *what does Jules Janin think?* and that we shall hear presently; for though I profess the greatest admiration for Mr. Dickens, yet there can be no reason why one should deny oneself the little pleasure of acquainting him that *some* ill-disposed persons in the world are inclined to abuse him. Without this privilege what is friendship good for?

Who is Janin? He is the critic of France. J. J., in fact,— the man who writes a weekly *feuilleton* in the *Journal des Débats* with such indisputable brilliancy and wit, and such a happy mixture of effrontery, and honesty, and poetry, and impudence, and falsehood, and impertinence, and good feeling, that one can't fail to be charmed with the compound, and to look rather eagerly for the Monday's paper;—Jules Janin is the man, who, not knowing a single word of the English language, as he actually professes in the preface, *has helped to translate* the *Sentimental Journey*. He is the man who, when he was married (in a week when news were slack no doubt), actually *criticised his own marriage ceremony*, letting all the public see the proof-sheets of his bridal, as was the custom among certain ancient kings, I believe. In fact, a more modest, honest, unassuming, blushing, truth-telling, gentlemanlike, J. J. it is impossible to conceive.

Well, he has fallen foul of Monsieur Dickens, this fat French moralist; he says Dickens is *immodest*, and Jules cannot abide immodesty; and a great and conclusive proof this is upon a question which the two nations have been in the habit of arguing, namely, which of the two is the purer in morals? and may be argued clear thus:—

1. We in England are accustomed to think Dickens modest, and allow our children to peruse his works.

2. In France the man who wrote the history of *The Dead Donkey and the Guillotined Woman,** and afterwards his own epithalamium in the newspaper, is revolted by Dickens.

---

* Some day the writer meditates a great and splendid review of J. J.'s work.

3. Therefore Dickens *must* be immodest, and grossly immodest, otherwise a person so confessedly excellent as J. J. would never have discovered the crime.

4. And therefore it is pretty clear that the French morals are of a much higher order than our own, which remark will apply to persons and books, and all the relations of private and public life.

Let us now see how our fat Jules attacks Dickens. His remarks on him begin in the following jocular way:—

" THÉÂTRE DE L'AMBIGU-COMIQUE.

" *Nicolas Nickleby,* Mélodrame, en Six Actes.

" A genoux devant celui-là qui s'appelle Charles Dickens ! à genoux ! Il a accompli à lui seul ce que n'ont pu faire à eux deux lord Byron et Walter Scott ! Joignez-y, si vous voulez, Pope et Milton et tout ce que la littérature Anglaise a produit de plus solennel et de plus charmant. Charles Dickens ! mais il n'est question que de lui en Angleterre. Il en est la gloire, et la joie, et l'orgueil ! Savez-vous combien d'acheteurs possède ce Dickens ; j'ai dit *d'acheteurs,* de gens qui tirent leur argent de leur bourse pour que cet argent passe de leur main dans la main du libraire ?—Dix mille acheteurs. Dix mille ? que disons-nous, dix mille ! vingt mille !—Vingt mille ? Quoi ! vingt mille acheteurs ?—Fi donc, vingt mille ! quarante mille acheteurs.—Et quoi ! il a trouvé quarante mille acheteurs, vous vous moquez de nous sans doute ?—Oui, mon brave homme, on se moque de vous, car ce n'est pas vingt mille et quarante mille et soixante mille acheteurs qu'a rencontrés ce Charles Dickens, c'est cent mille acheteurs. Cent mille, pas un de moins. Cent mille esclaves, cent mille tributaires, cent mille ! Et nos grands écrivains modernes s'estiment bien heureux et bien fiers quand leur livre le plus vanté parvient, au bout de six mois de célébrité, à son huitième cent !"

There is raillery for you ! there is a knowledge of English literature,—of " Pope et Milton, si solennel et si charmant !" Milton, above all ; his little comédie *Samson l'Agoniste* is one of the gayest and most graceful trifles that ever was acted on the stage. And to think that Dickens has sold more copies of his work than the above two eminent hommes-de-lettres, and Scott and Byron into the bargain! It is a fact, and J. J. vouches for it. To be sure, J. J. knows no more of English literature than I do of hieroglyphics,—to be sure, he has not one word of English. N'importe: he has had the advantage of examining the books of Mr. Dickens's publishers, and has discovered that they sell of Boz's works " *cent-mille pas un de moins.*" Janin will not allow of one less. Can you answer numbers? And there are our grands écrivains modernes, who are happy if they sell eight hundred in six months. Byron and Scott doubtless, " le solennel Pope, et le charmant Milton," as well as other geniuses not belonging to the three kingdoms. If a man is an arithmetician as well as a critic, and we join together figures of speech and Arabic numerals, there is no knowing what he may not prove.

"*Or*," continues J. J. :—

" Or, parmi les chefs-d'œuvre de sa façon que dévore l'Angleterre, ce Charles Dickens a produit un gros mélodrame en deux gros volumes, intitulé *Nicolas Nickleby.* Ce livre a été traduit chez nous par un homme de beaucoup d'esprit, qui n'est pas fait pour ce triste métier-là. Si vous saviez ce que peut être un pareil chef-d'œuvre, certes vous prendriez en pitié les susdits cent mille souscripteurs de Charles Dickens. Figurez-vous donc un amas d'inventions puériles, où l'horrible et le niais se donnent la main, dans une ronde infernale ; ici passent en riant de bonnes gens si bons qu'ils en sont tout-à-fait bêtes ; plus loin bondissent et blasphèment toutes sortes de bandits, de fripons, de voleurs et de misérables si affreux qu'on ne sait pas comment pourrait vivre, seulement vingt-quatre heures, une société ainsi composée. C'est le plus nauséabond mélange qu'on puisse imaginer de lait chaud et de bière tournée, d'œufs frais et de bœuf salé, de haillons et d'habits brodés, d'écus d'or et de gros sous, de roses et de pissenlits. On se bat, on s'embrasse, on s'injurie, on s'enivre, on meurt de faim. Les filles de la rue et les lords de la Chambre haute, les porte-faix et les poëtes, les écoliers et les voleurs, se promènent, bras dessus bras dessous, au milieu de ce tohubohu insupportable. Aimez-vous la fumée de tabac, l'odeur de l'ail, le goût du porc frais, l'harmonie que fait un plat d'étain

frappé contre une casserole de cuivre non étamé ? Lisez-moi
consciencieusement ce livre de Charles Dickens. Quelles plaies !
quelles pustules ! et que de saintes vertus ! Ce Dickens a réuni
en bloc toutes les descriptions de Guzman d'Alfarache et tous
les rêves de Grandisson. Oh ! qu'êtes-vous devenus, vous les
lectrices tant soit peu prudes des romans de Walter Scott?
Oh ! qu'a-t-on fait de vous, les lectrices animées de *Don Juan*
et de *Lara ?* O vous, les chastes enthousiastes de la *Clarisse
Harlowe*, voilez-vous la face de honte ! A cent mille exemplaires
le Charles Dickens !"

To what a pitch of *dévergondage* must the English ladies have
arrived, when a fellow who can chronicle his own marriage, and
write *The Dead Donkey and the Guillotined Woman,*—when
even a man like that, whom nobody can accuse of being
squeamish, is obliged to turn away with disgust at their monstrous immodesty !

J. J. is not difficult; a little harmless gallantry and trifling
with the seventh commandment does not offend him,—far
from it. Because there are no love-intrigues in Walter Scott,
Jules says that Scott's readers are *tant soit peu prudes !* There
ought to be, in fact, in life and in novels, a little, pleasant,
gentlemanlike, anti-seventh-commandment excitement. Read
The Dead Donkey and the Guillotined Woman, and you will
see how the thing may be agreeably and genteelly done.
See what he says of *Clarissa,*—it is *chaste ;* of *Don Juan,*—it is
not indecent, it is not immoral, it is only ANIMÉE ! Animée ! O
ciel ! what a word ! Could any but a Frenchman have had the
grace to hit on it ? " Animation " our Jules can pardon ; prudery
he can excuse, in his good-humoured, contemptuous way ; but
Dickens—this Dickens,—O fie ! And, perhaps, there never was
a more succinct, complete, elegant, just, and satisfactory account
given of a book than that by our friend Jules of *Nicholas
Nickleby.* "It is the most disgusting mixture imaginable of warm
milk and sour beer, of fresh eggs and salt beef, of rags and laced
clothes, of gold crowns and coppers, of rose and dandelions."

There is a receipt for you ! or take another, which is quite as
pleasant :—

II.

"The fumes of tobacco, the odour of garlic, the taste of fresh pork, the harmony made by striking a pewter plate against an untinned copper saucepan. Read me conscientiously this book of Charles Dickens ; what sores ! what pustules !" &c.

Try either mixture (and both are curious),—for fresh pork is an ingredient in one, salt beef in another; tobacco and garlic in receipt No. 2 agreeably take the places of warm milk and sour beer in formula No. 1 ; and whereas, in the second prescription, a pewter plate and *untinned* copper saucepan (what a devilish satire in that epithet *untinned !*), a gold crown and a few half-pence, answer in the first. Take either mixture, and the result is a Dickens. Hang thyself, thou unhappy writer of *Pickwick ;* or, blushing at this exposition of thy faults, turn red man altogether, and build a wigwam in a wilderness, and live with 'possums up gum-trees. Fresh pork and warm milk ; sour beer and salt b——. Faugh ! how could you serve us so atrociously ?

And this is one of the " chefs-d'œuvre *de sa façon* que dévore l'Angleterre." The beastly country ! How Jules lashes the islanders with the sting of that epigram—*chefs-d'œuvre de leur façon !*

*   *   *   *

Look you, J. J., it is time that such impertinence should cease. Will somebody—out of three thousand literary men in France, there are about three who have a smattering of the English—will some one of the three explain to J. J. the enormous folly and falsehood of all that the fellow has been saying about Dickens and English literature generally ? We have in England literary *chefs-d'œuvre de notre façon*, and are by no means ashamed to devour the same. " Le charmant Milton " was not, perhaps, very skilled for making epigrams and chansons-à-boire, but, after all, was a person of merit, and of his works have been sold considerably more than eight hundred copies. " Le solennel Pope " was a writer not undeserving of praise. There must have been something worthy in Shakespeare,—for his name has penetrated even to France, where he is not unfrequently called " le Sublime Williams." Walter Scott, though a prude, as you

say, and not having the agreeable *laisser-aller* of the author of
the *Dead Donkey*, &c., could still turn off a romance pretty
creditably. He and " le Sublime Williams" between them have
turned your French literature topsy-turvy ; and many a live
donkey of your crew is trying to imitate their paces and their
roars, and to lord it like those dead lions. These men made
chefs-d'œuvre de notre façon, and we are by no means ashamed
to acknowledge them.

But what right have you, O blundering ignoramus ! to pretend
to judge them and their works,—you, who might as well attempt
to give a series of lectures upon the literature of the Hottentots,
and are as ignorant of English as the author of the *Random
Recollections?* * Learn modesty, Jules ; Listen to good advice ;
and when you say to other persons, *lisez moi ce livre consciencieusement*, at least do the same thing, O critic ! before you
attempt to judge and arbitrate.

And I am ready to take an affidavit in the matter of this
criticism of *Nicholas Nickleby*, that the translator of Sterne, who
does not know English, has not read Boz in the original—has
not even read him in the translation, and slanders him out of
pure invention. Take these concluding opinions of J. J. as a
proof of the fact :—

"De ce roman de *Nicolas Nickleby* a été tiré le mélodrame qui
va suivre. Commencez d'abord par entasser les souterrains sur
les ténèbres, le vice sur le sang, le mensonge sur l'injure,
l'adultère sur l'inceste, battez-moi tout ce mélange, et vous
verrez ce que vous allez voir.

"Dans un comté Anglais, dans une école, ou plutôt dans une
horrible prison habitée par le froid et la faim, un nommé
Squeers entraine, sous prétexte de les élever dans la belle
discipline, tous les enfans qu'on lui confie. Ce misérable
Squeers spécule tout simplement sur la faim, sur la soif, sur les
habits de ces pauvres petits. On n'entend que le bruit des
verges, les soupirs des battus, les cris des battans, les blasphèmes

---

* James Grant, whose book entitled " Paris and its People," was very
caustically reviewed by Thackeray in *Fraser's Magazine*, December 1843,
under the title of " Grant in Paris " (reprinted in Thackeray's Works, ed.
1885, vol. xxv.).—ED.

du maître. C'est affreux à lire et à voir. Surtout ce qui fait
peur (je parle du livre en question), c'est la misère d'un pauvre
petit nommé Smike, dont cet affreux Squeers est le bourreau.
Quand parut le livre de Charles Dickens, on raconte que plus
d'un maître de pension de l'Angleterre se récria contre la
calomnie. Mais, juste ciel! si la cent millième partie d'une
pareille honte était possible ; s'il était vrai qu'un seul marchand
de chair humaine ainsi bâti pût exister de l'autre côté du détroit
ce serait le déshonneur d'une nation tout entière. Et si en
effet la chose est impossible, que venez-vous donc nous conter,
que le roman, tout comme la comédie, est la peinture des
mœurs ?

"Or ce petit malheureux couvert de haillons et de plaies, le
jouet de M. Squeers, c'est tout simplement le fils unique de
Lord Clarendon, un des plus grands seigneurs de l'Angleterre.
Voilà justement ce que je disais tout à l'heure. Dans ces
romans qui sont le rebut d'une imagination en délire, il n'y a
pas de milieu. Ou bien vous êtes le dernier des mendians
chargés d'une besace vide, ou bien, salut à vous! vous êtes
duc et pair du royaume et chevalier de la Jarretière! Ou
le manteau royal ou le haillon. Quelquefois, pour varier la
thèse, on vous met par dessus vos haillons le manteau de
pourpre.—Votre tête est pleine de vermine, à la bonne heure !
mais laissez faire le romancier, il posera tout à l'heure sur vos
immondes cheveux, la couronne ducale. Ainsi procèdent M.
Dickens et le Capitaine Marryat et tous les autres."

Here we have a third receipt for the confection of *Nicholas
Nickleby*,—darkness and caverns, vice and blood, incest and
adultery, "*battez-moi tout ça*," and the thing is done. Considering that Mr. Dickens has not said a word about darkness,
about caverns, about blood (farther than a little harmless claret
drawn from Squeers's nose), about the two other crimes mentioned by J. J.,—is it not *de luxe* to put them into the Nickleby-
receipt ? Having read the romances of his own country, and
no others, J. J. thought he was safe, no doubt, in introducing
the last-named ingredients ; but in England the people is still
tant soit peu prudes, and will have none such fare. In what a
luxury of filth, too, does this delicate critic indulge ! *votre tête*

est pleine de vermine (a flattering supposition for the French reader, by the way, and remarkable for its polite propriety). Your head is in this condition ; but never mind; let the romancer do his work, and he will presently place upon *your filthy hair* (kind again) the ducal coronet. This is the way with Monsieur Dickens, Captain Marryat, and *the others.*

With whom, in Heaven's name ? What has poor Dickens ever had to do with ducal crowns, or with the other ornaments of the kind which Monsieur Jules distributes to his friends ? Tell lies about men, friend Jules, if you will, but not *such* lies. See, for the future, that they have a greater likelihood about them ; and try, at least when you are talking of propriety and decency of behaviour, to have your words somewhat more cleanly, and your own manners as little offensive as possible.

And with regard to the character of Squeers, the impossibility of it, and the consequent folly of placing such a portrait in a work that pretends to be a painting of manners, that, too, is a falsehood like the rest. Such a disgrace to human nature not only existed, but existed in J. J.'s country of France. Who does not remember the history of the Boulogne schoolmaster, a year since, whom the newspapers called the " French Squeers ; " and about the same time, in the neighbourhood of Paris, there was a case still more atrocious, of a man and his wife who farmed some score of children, subjected them to ill-treatment so horrible that only J. J. himself, in his nastiest fit of indignation, could describe it ; and ended by murdering one or two, and starving all. The whole story was in the *Débats,* J. J.'s own newspaper, where the accomplished critic may read it.

AN EXHIBITION GOSSIP.

BY

MICHAEL ANGELO TITMARSH.

In a Letter to Monsieur Guillaume, Peintre,
A son Atelier, Rue de Monsieur, Faubourg St. Germain, Paris.

EAR GUILLAUME,—Some of the dullest chapters
that ever were written in this world—viz., those on
the History of Modern Europe, by Russell, begin with
an address to some imaginary young friend, to whom
the Doctor is supposed to communicate his knowledge. "Dear
John," begins he, quite affectionately, "I take up my pen to
state that the last of the Carlovingians "—or, "Dear John, I am
happy to inform you that the aspect of Europe on the accession
of Henry VIII, was so and so." In the same manner, and in
your famous "Lettres à Sophie," the history of the heathen gods
and goddesses is communicated to some possible young lady ;
and this simple plan has, no doubt, been adopted because the
authors wished to convey their information with the utmost
simplicity possible, and in a free, easy, honest, confidential sort
of a way.

This (as usual), dear Guillaume, has nothing to do with the
subject in hand ; but I have ventured to place a little gossip
concerning the Exhibition, under an envelope inscribed with
your respectable name, because I have no right to adopt the
editorial *we*, and so implicate a host of illustrious authors, who
give their names and aid to Mr. Ainsworth's Magazine,* in
opinions that are very likely not worth sixpence ; and because

* This paper originally appeared in *Ainsworth's Magazine*, June 1842.—
Ed.

that simple upright I, which often seems egotistical and presuming, is, I fancy, less affected and pert than "we" often is.
"I," is merely an individual; whereas, "we," is clearly somebody
else. "I," merely expresses an opinion; whereas, "we," at
once lays down the law.

Pardon, then, the continued use of the personal pronoun, as I am
sure, my dear friend, you will; because as you do not understand a
word of English, how possibly can you quarrel with my style?

We have often had great battles together on the subject of
our respective schools of art; and having seen the two Exhibitions, I am glad to be able to say that ours is the best *this* year,
at least, though, perhaps, for many years past you have had the
superiority. We have more good pictures in our 1400, than
you in your 3000; among the good, we have more *very* good, than
you have this year, (none nobler and better than the drawings of
M. Decamps); and though there are no such large canvases and
ambitious subjects as cover the walls of your salon, I think our
painters have more first-class pictures in their humble way.

They wisely, I think, avoid those great historical "parades"
which cover so much space in the Louvre. A young man has
sometimes a fit of what is called "historical painting"; comes
out with a great canvas, disposed in the regular six-feet heroical
order; and having probably half ruined himself in the painting
of his piece, which nobody (let us be thankful for it!) buys,
curses the decayed state of taste in the country, and falls to
portrait-painting, or takes small natural subjects, in which the
world can sympathise, and with which he is best able to grapple.
We have no government museums like yours to furnish;—no
galleries in chief towns of departments to adorn;—no painted
chapels, requiring fresh supplies of saints and martyrs, which
your artists do to order. Art is a matter of private enterprise
here, like everything else: and our painters must suit the small
rooms of their customers, and supply them with such subjects as
are likely to please them. If you were to make me a present
of half a cartoon, or a prophet by Michael Angelo, or a Spanish
martyrdom, I would turn the picture against the wall. Such
great things are only good for great edifices, and to be seen
occasionally;—we want pleasant pictures, that we can live with

E

—something that shall be lively, pleasing or tender, or sublime, if you will, but only of a moderate-sized sublimity. Confess, if you had to live in a huge room with the Last Judgment at one end of it, and the Death of Ananias at the other, would not you be afraid to remain alone—or, at any rate, long for a comfortable bare wall ? The world produces, now and then, one of the great daring geniuses who make those tremendous works of art ; but they come only seldom—and Heaven be thanked for it ! We have had one in our country—John Milton by name. Honestly confess now, was there not a fervour in your youth when you had a plan of an epic, or, at least, of an heroic Michael-Angelesque picture ? The sublime rage fades as one grows older and cooler ; and so the good, sensible, honest English painters, for the most part, content themselves with doing no more than they can.

But though we have no heroical canvases, it is not to be inferred that we do not cultivate a humbler sort of high art ; and you painters of religious subjects know, from the very subjects which you are called upon to draw, that humility may be even more sublime than greatness. For instance, there is in almost everything Mr. Eastlake does (in spite of a little feebleness of hand and primness of mannerism), a purity which is to us quite angelical, so that we can't look at one of his pictures without being touched and purified by it. Mr. Mulready has an art, too, which is not inferior, and though he commonly takes, like the before-mentioned gentleman, some very simple, homely subject to illustrate, manages to affect and delight one, as much as painter can. Mr. Mulready calls his picture, " The Ford " ; Mr. Eastlake styles his, " Sisters." The " Sisters " are two young ladies looking over a balcony ; " The Ford " is a stream through which some boys are carrying a girl : and how is a critic to describe the beauty in such subjects as these ? It would be easy to say these pictures are exquisitely drawn, beautifully coloured, and so forth ; but that is not the reason of their beauty : on the contrary, any man who has a mind may find fault with the drawing and colouring of both. Well, there is a charm about them seemingly independent of drawing and colouring ; and what is it ? There's no foot rule that I know of to measure it; and the very wisest lecturer on art might define and define, and be not a whit nearer the truth. I can't tell you why I like to hear a blackbird sing; it is certainly not so clever as a piping bullfinch.

I always begin with the works of these gentlemen, and look at them oftenest and longest; but that is only a simple expression of individual taste, and by no means an attempt at laying down the law, upon a subject which is quite out of the limits of all legislation. A better critic might possibly, (I say "possibly," not as regards the correctness of my own opinion, but the unquestionable merit of the two admirable artists above named;) another critic will possibly have other objects for admiration, and if such a person were to say, Pause—before you award pre-eminence to this artist or that, pause—for instance, look at those two Leslies, can anything in point of *esprit* and feeling surpass them?—indeed the other critic would give very sound advice. Nothing can be finer than the comedy of the Scene from Twelfth Night, more joyous, frank, manly, laughter-moving;—or more tender, and grave, and naïf, than the picture of Queen Catherine and her attendant. The great beauty of these pieces is the total absence of affectation. The figures are in perfectly quiet, simple positions, looking as if they were not the least aware of the spectator's presence, (a rare quality in pictures, as I think, of which little dramas, the actors, like those upon the living stage, have a great love of "striking an attitude," and are always on the look-out for the applause of the lookers-on,) whereas Mr. Leslie's excellent little troop of comedians know their art so perfectly, that it becomes the very image of nature, and the best nature, too. Some painters (skilled in the depicting of such knicknacks) overpower their pieces with "properties"—guitars, old armours, flower-jugs, curtains, and what not. The very chairs and tables in the picture of Queen Catherine have a noble, simple arrangement about them: they look sad and stately, and cast great dreary shadows—they will lighten up a little, doubtless, when the girl begins to sing.

You and I have been in the habit of accusing one of the cleverest painters of the country of want of poetry: no other than Mr. Edwin Landseer, who, with his marvellous power of

E 2

hand, a sort of aristocrat among painters, has seemed to say—I care for my dog and my gun; I'm an English country gentleman, and poetry is beneath me. He has made us laugh sometimes, when he is in the mood, with his admirable humour, but has held off as it were from poetic subjects, as a man would do who was addressing himself in a fine ball-room to a party of fine people, who would stare if any such subjects were broached. I don't care to own that in former years those dogs, those birds, deer, wild-ducks, and so forth, were painted to such a pitch of desperate perfection, as to make me quite angry—elegant, beautiful, well-appointed, perfect models for grace and manner; they were like some of our English dandies that one sees, and who never can be brought to pass the limits of a certain polite smile, and decorous, sensible insipidity. The more one sees them, the more vexed one grows, for, be hanged to them, there is no earthly fault to find with them. This, to be sure, is begging the question, and you may not be disposed to allow either the correctness of the simile, or that dandies are insipid, or that field-sports, or pictures thereof, can possibly be tedious; but, at any rate, it is a comfort to see that a man of genius who is a poet *will* be one sometimes, and here are a couple of noble poetical pieces from Mr. Landseer's pencil. The "Otter and Trout" has something awful about it; the hunted stag, panting through the water and startling up the wild-fowl, is a beautiful and touching poem. Oh, that these two pictures, and a few more of different English artists, could be carried across the Channel—say when Mr. Partridge's portrait of the Queen goes, to act as a counterpoise to that work!

A few Etties might likewise be put into the same box, and a few delightful golden landscapes of Callcott. To these I would add Mr. Maclise's "Hamlet," about whose faults and merits there have been some loud controversies; but in every Exhibition for the last five years, if you saw a crowd before a picture, it was sure to be before his; and with all the faults people found, no one could go away without a sort of wonder at the prodigious talent of this gentleman. Sometimes it was mere wonder; in the present Exhibition it is wonder and pleasure too; and his picture of Hamlet is by far the best, to my thinking, that the artist has ever produced. If, for the credit of Old England, (and I hereby humbly beg Mr. Maclise to listen to the suggestion,) it could be transported to the walls of your salon, it would shew French artists, who are accustomed to sneer at the drawing of the English school, that we have a man whose power of drawing is greater than that of any artist among you,—of any artist that ever lived, I should like to venture to say. An artist, possessing this vast power of hand, often wastes it—as Paganini did, for instance—in capriccios, and extravagances, and brilliant feats of skill, as if defying the world to come and cope with him. The picture of the play in " Hamlet" is a great deal more, and is a noble poetic delineation of the awful story. Here I am obliged to repeat, for the tenth time in this letter, how vain it is to attempt to describe such works by means of pen and ink. Fancy Hamlet, ungartered, lying on the ground, looking into the very soul of King Claudius, who writhes under the play of Gonzago. Fancy the Queen, perplexed and sad, (she does not know of the murder,) and poor Ophelia, and Polonius, with his staff, pottering over the tragedy; and Horatio, and all sorts of knights and ladies, looking wondering on. Fancy, in the little theatre, the king asleep ; a lamp in front casts a huge forked fantastic shadow over the scene—a shadow that looks like a horrible devil in the background that is grinning and aping the murder. Fancy ghastly flickering tapestries of Cain and Abel on the walls, and all this painted with the utmost force, truth, and dexterity—fancy all this, and then you will have not the least idea of one of the most startling, wonderful pictures that the English school has ever produced.

Mr. Maclise may be said to be at the head of the young men ; and though you and I, my dear Guillaume, are both old, and while others are perpetually deploring the past, I think it is a consolation to see that the present is better, and to argue that the future will be better still. You did not give up David without a pang, and still think Baron Gérard a very wonderful fellow. I can remember once, when Westall seemed really worth looking at, when a huge black exaggeration of Northcote or Opie struck me as mighty fine, and Mr. West seemed a most worthy President of our Academy. Confess now that the race

who succeeded them did better than they; and indeed the
young men, if I may be permitted to hint such a thing, do
better still—not better than individuals—for Eastlake, Mulready,
Etty, Leslie, are exhibitors of twenty years' standing, and the
young men may live a thousand years and never surpass them;
but a finer taste is more general among them than existed some
thirty years back, and a purer, humbler, truer love of nature.
Have you seen the "Deserted Village" of the "Etching Club"?
What charming feeling and purity is there among most of the
designs of these young painters, and what a credit are they to
the English school!

The designers of the "Etching Club" seem to form a little
knot or circle among themselves; and though the names of
Cope, Redgrave, Herbert, Stone, have hardly reached you as yet
in France, they will be heard of some day even there, where your
clever people, who can appreciate all sorts of art, will not fail
to admire the quiet, thoughtful, pious, delicate feeling which
characterizes the works of this charming little school. All Mr.
Cope's pictures, though somewhat feeble in hand, are beautifully
tender and graceful. "The Hawthorn-bush, with seats beneath
the shade, for talking age and whispering lovers made," is a
beautiful picture for colour, sentiment, and composition. The
old people, properly garrulous, talking of old times, or the crops,
or the Doctor's sermon; the lovers—a charming pair—loving
with all their souls, kind, hearty, and tender. The Schoolmaster
of one of his other pictures is an excellent awful portrait of
Goldsmith's pedagogue. Mr. Redgrave's "Cinderella" is very
pleasant, his landscape beautiful. Mr. Stone's "Advice" is full
of tender sentiment, and contains some frank, excellent painting;
but how vapid all such comments appear, and how can you, on
the banks of the Seine, understand from these sort of vague,
unsatisfactory praises, what are the merits or demerits of the
pieces spoken about?

We have here a delightful, *naïf* artist, Mr. Webster by name,
who has taken little boys under his protection, and paints them
in the most charming comic way—in that best sort of comedy,
which makes one doubt whether to laugh or to cry. His largest
picture this year represents two boys bound for school. Break-

fast is hurried over, (a horrid early breakfast;) the trunk is packed; papa is pulling on his boots; there is the coach coming down the hill, and the guard blowing his pitiless horn. All the little girls are gathered round their brothers: the elder is munching a biscuit, and determined to be a man; but the younger, whom the little sister of all has got hold of by the hand, can't bear the parting, and is crying his eyes out.

I quarrel with Mr. Webster for making one laugh at the boy, and giving him a comic face. I say no man who has experienced it, has a right to laugh at such a sorrow. Did you ever, in France, look out for the diligence that was to take you to school, and hear a fatal conducteur blowing his horn as you waited by the hill side—as you waited with the poor mother, turning her eyes away—and slowly got off the old pony, which you were not to see for six months—for a century—for a thousand miserable years again? Oh, that first night at school! those bitter, bitter tears at night, as you lay awake in the silence, poor little lonely boy, yearning after love and home. Life has sorrows enough, God knows, but, I swear, none like that! I was thinking about all this as I looked at Mr. Webster's picture, and behold it turned itself into an avenue of lime-trees, and a certain old stile that led to a stubble-field; and it was evening, about the 14th of September, and after dinner, (how that *last* glass of wine used to choke and burn in the throat!) and presently, a mile off, you heard, horribly distinct, the whirring of the well-known Defiance coach wheels. It was up in a moment—the trunk on the roof; and—bah! from that day I can't bear to see mothers and children parting.

This, to be sure, is beside the subject; but pray let Mr. Webster change the face of his boy.

Letters (except from young ladies to one another) are not allowed to go beyond a certain decent length; hence, though I may have a fancy to speak to you of many score of other good pictures, out of the fourteen hundred here exhibited, there are numbers which we must pass over without any notice whatever. It is hard to pass by Mr. Richmond's beautiful water-colour figures, without a word concerning them; or Mr. Charles Landseer's capital picture of " Ladies and Cavaliers "; or not to

have at least half a page to spare, in order to make an onslaught
upon Mr. Chalon and his ogling beauties: he has a portrait of
Mdlle. Rachel, quite curious for its cleverness and unlikeness,
and one of the most chaste and refined of our actresses, Mrs.
Charles Kean, who is represented as a killing coquette; and so
Mr. Kean may be thankful that the portrait does. not in the
least resemble his lady.

There is scarce any need to say that the oil portrait-painters
maintain their usual reputation and excellence: Mr. Briggs,
Mr. Pickersgill, Mr. Grant, shew some excellent canvases: the
latter's ladies are beautiful, and his "Lord Cardigan" a fine
painting and portrait; Mr. Briggs' "Archbishop" is a noble
head and picture; Mr. Pickersgill has, among others, a full-
length of a Navy Captain, very fine; Mr. Linnell's portraits are
very fine; and Mr. S. Lawrence has one (the Attorney-General),
excellently drawn, and fine in character. This year's picture of
her Majesty is intended for *your* Majesty, Louis Philippe—
perhaps the French court might have had a more favourable
representation of the Queen. There is only one "Duke of
Wellington" that I have remarked—(indeed it must be a weary
task to the good-natured and simple old nobleman to give up
to artists the use of his brave face, as he is so often called upon
to do)—at present he appears in a group of red-coated brethren
in arms, called the "Heroes of Waterloo." The picture, from
the quantity of requisite vermilion, was most difficult to treat,
but is cleverly managed, and the likeness very good. All the
warriors assembled are smiling, to a man; and in the background is a picture of Napoleon, who is smiling too—and this
is surely too great a stretch of good nature.

What can I say of the Napoleon of Mr. Turner? called (with
frightful satire) the "Exile and the *Rock-limpet*." He stands in
the midst of a scarlet tornado, looking at least forty feet high.

Ah! says the mysterious poet, from whom Mr. Turner loves
to quote,—

"Ah! thy tent-formed shell is like
The soldier's nightly bivouac, alone
Amidst a sea of blood ——
—— but you can join your comrades."
FALLACIES OF HOPE.

These remarkable lines entirely explain the meaning of the picture; another piece is described by lines from the same poem, in a metre more regular:—

> "The midnight-torch gleam'd o'er the steamer's side
> And *merit's corse* was yielded to the tide."

When the pictures are re-hung, as sometimes I believe is the case, it might perhaps be as well to turn these upside down, and see how they would look *then ;* the Campo Santo of Venice, when examined closely, is scarcely less mysterious; at a little distance, however, it is a most brilliant, airy, and beautiful picture. O for the old days, before Mr. Turner had lighted on " The Fallacies," and could see like other people !

Other landscape-painters, not so romantic, are, as usual, excellent. You know Mr. Stanfield and Mr. Roberts, in France, as well as we do: I wish one day you could see the hearty, fresh English landscapes of Lee and Creswick, where you can almost see the dew on the fresh grass, and trace the ripple of the water, and the whispering in the foliage of the cool, wholesome wind.

*   *   *   *   *

There is not an inch more room in the paper ; and a great deal that was to be said about the Water-colour Societies and Suffolk-street must remain unsaid for ever and ever. But I wish you could see a drawing by Miss Setchel, in the Junior Water-colour Society, and a dozen by Mr. Absolon, which are delightful in grace and expression, and in tender, pathetic humour.

M. A. T.

LETTERS ON THE FINE ARTS.

No. 1.—THE ART UNIONS.

From M. A. Titmarsh, Esq., to Sanders M'Gilp, Esq.

Y DEAR SANDERS, — I have always had the highest confidence in your judgment, and am therefore pretty certain that your picture is one of vast merit. The value, you say, is two hundred guineas, and you have, I hope, with laudable prudence, induced your relatives, your grandmother, your confiding aunts, the tradesmen with whom you have little accounts, and the friends with whom you are occasionally kind enough to go and dine, to subscribe to the Art Union, in hopes that one or other of them may gain the principal prize, when their taste, as well as their friendship (and where can friendship be better bestowed?) will induce them to purchase your work. To your relatives affection alone would dictate the acquisition of your picture; to your tradesmen you offer, if possible, a still stronger inducement. " I owe you 40*l.*" you can say to Mr. Snip, your respected tailor: " I cannot pay those 40*l.* ; but gain the first prize, and you have my picture for 200 guineas, which in reality is worth 500, plus the payment of your bill, the amount of which you can deduct from the sum due to myself." Thus Mr. Snooks gets

	£	s.	d.
A picture (valued at 500 guineas)...	525	0	0
The payment of his bill	40	0	0
And costs of writ	2	2	0
	£567	2	0

in return for a single sovereign subscribed to the Union.

The advantage of Art Unions has never before, I believe, been considered in this light; and if every artist would but go round to his tradesmen and represent the truth to them as here laid down, no doubt great numbers of additional patrons would be found for the noble art you practise. How many a man, for instance, has not one but half-a-dozen tailors in the category in which I have placed Mr. Snip. Well; let them all subscribe;—the more the merrier. "If one win, gentlemen," you say, "remember I am in a condition to pay all the rest their accounts." And thus is an interest for Art brought home to the bosoms and boards of six deserving families.

Is, or is not, the principle a good one? Are, or are not, tradesmen to be paid? Are, or are not, artists to be well-clothed? And would, or would not, the diffusion of their divine science enlarge the heart and soften the rude manners of the million? What, on this head, does Hesiod observe? The Teian bard nobly remarks,*

Ινγεννας διδικισσε φιδηλιτερ αρτης,
Ημολλιτ μωρης νεκ σινιτ εσσε φερως.

And if the principle be a good one, I say it should be universal. Say (as an encouragement) to the collector who comes for your rate, "I'll pay you if you take a ticket in the Art Union!" Remark to your butcher, in a pleasant way, "Mr. Brisket, I desire from you, for your own advantage, one stake more." "From the loin, or where?" says he. "No," say you, laughingly interrupting him, "a stake in the Art Union." And point out to your washerwoman what an ennobling and glorious thing it would be—a holy effluence, a bright and beaming radiance woven into the dark chain of her existence—(or other words of might and poesy suited to her capacity), point out, I say, what a pleasure it would be to her to be able to exclaim, "I wash Mr. M'Gilp's shirts—and look! one of his five hundred guinea master-pieces hangs yonder, over my mangle."

It is in his power, it is in any body's power. The very

---

* We suspect that Mr. Titmarsh is here attempting to mystify the unlearned reader. Anacreon, not Hesiod, was "the Teian bard," and it is neither Hesiod nor Anacreon, but Ovid, who (in Latin not in Greek verse) "remarks":—

—— ingenuas didicisse fideliter artes,
Emollit mores, nec sinit esse feros.   ED.

Malay sweeper who shivers at the corner of your street and acts as your model, may easily save money enough to take a ticket, and have his portrait, as Othello, to decorate his humble place of abode.

You may fancy, my friend, that there is some caricature in this, and possibly you are right. You will never stoop to Mr. Snip in the manner pointed out by me : you are above entreating your washerwoman, cutting jokes with your butcher, or cajoling the respectable gentleman who calls for your contributions once a quarter. Art, say you, is above paltry speculation and mean ideas of gain. An artist never stoops to intrigue, or chaffers for money. He is the priest of nature, called to worship at her glorious altar, by special vocation ; one chosen out of the million, and called up to the high places ; in short, you will make a speech, crammed with fine words, proving your disinterestedness and the awful poetical nature of your calling.

Psha ! my good friend, let us have no more of this stale talk. You are a tradesman as well as my lord on the woolsack, or Mr. Smith selling figs, or General Sones breathing freely and at his ease in an atmosphere of cannon-balls. You each do your duty in your calling, and according to your genius, but you want to be paid for what you do. You want the best pay and the greatest share of reputation you can get. You will do nothing dishonest in the pursuit of your trade ; but will you not yield a little " to the exigencies of the public service ? " General Sones, though he may have his own opinion of the Chinese war, will attack mandarins without mercy ; my Lord Chancellor has pleaded many a queer cause before he reposed on yonder woolsack ; Smith has had recourse to many little harmless tricks to get a sale for his figs and treacle ; and you (as I take it) are not a whit better than they. Did you ever paint a lady in her portrait handsomer than nature made her ? Did you ever, when your immense genius panted to be at work on some vast historical piece, crush your aspirations so far as to sit down and depict a plain gentleman in a buff waistcoat and a watch-chain, for the sake of the twenty guineas which were to be elicited from his ample pepper-and-salt pantaloons ? You have done all this ; and were quite right in doing it too. How else are the little M'Gilps to get their dinners, or your lady the means of discharging her weekly bills ?

And now you will begin, I trust, to perceive that the ridicule cast upon the Art Union system in the first sentences of this letter, is not in reality so very severe : it is the sort of sneering language which the enemies of those establishments are in the habit of indulging in, though expressed as high, no doubt you will think in a far more satiric and witty manner than most of the Anti-Unionists have at command. Hear for instance, the " Athenæum." " So early," says that journal, " as 1837, we put on record our opinion that the Art Union would and must of necessity tend to the still further degradation of Art. Any man," we observed, " who purchases pictures may be presumed to have a love for, and this will in the end generate a knowledge of, Art. But there will be many subscribers who desire only a little gambling—to risk a pound for the chance of winning a hundred—and who would quite as soon join in a raffle for a horse or a snuff-box, or a pipe of port wine, as for a picture. The motive of the subscriber is of no consequence, so long as others have to dispose of the money ; but the Art Union proposes that each subscriber ' shall select for himself.' Now, is it not certain that such patronage must tend to degrade Art ? The scheme may be beneficial to the lowest class of artists, but utterly ruinous to Art itself. When every individual, be he *whom* he may, is allowed to follow his own judgment in the disposal of his prize-money, the best results can be but an irresponsible indulgence of individual whim and caprice —the worst and certain is the degradation of Art. Men who paint to live, instead of working with all their power, be it more or less, up to the best and highest judgments, must solicit the sweet voices of the uninformed, the chance prize-holders, and therefore purchasers of the Art Unions."

So writes the " Athenæum," and you will at once perceive the truth of my previous assertions :—1. That the " Athenæum's " arguments resemble those employed at the commencement of this letter. 2. That the arguments at the beginning of this letter are far more cleverly and wickedly put.

Let us now proceed to demolish the one and the other ; and

we will, if you please, take the dicta of the "Athenæum" in
the first place into consideration.

"Every man" (says the 'Athenæum') "who purchases pictures, may be presumed to have a love for, and this will in the
end generate a knowledge of, Art."

"But this Art Union is joined by many for the sake of gambling, and who would *quite as soon* join in a raffle for a horse, or
a snuff-box, or a pipe of port wine, as for a picture."

Why quite as soon ?   A man who wants a pipe of port wine
does not, we presume, raffle for a horse ; or being exceedingly
desirous of a snuff-mull, he does not raffle for a pipe of port
wine.   There are certainly in the world many "uninformed"
persons, as the insinuating "Athenæum" remarks ; let us say
at once there are fools, but not such tremendous fools as our
misanthropic contemporary would discover.

No, no.   A man raffles for a horse because the dealers or the
knackers will give him a price for it, or because his wife wishes
to be driven out in the gig, or because he has a mind to cut a
dash in the ring.   A man raffles for a gold snuff-box because he
is fond of Macabau, or because he likes to sport such a box
after dinner, or because he wishes to make it a present to Mr.
Boys when he brings out any more of his relative's lithographs,
or for some other simple and equally apparent reason.   And so
for a pipe of port wine, a man risks his money in order to gain it,
because he likes port wine, or because he can sell it, or because
he wishes to present a few dozens to a friend.

I wish, for my part, I had a friend who desired to dispose of
either of the three articles ; but that is a mere personal ejaculation, and nothing to the point.   The point is, that a man bids
money for a horse because he wants it, and for a picture because he would like to have a picture.   Common charity must
admit so much good sense in the world.

Well, then, it is granted that a man joins in a raffle for a
set of pictures because he is interested in pictures ; that is, *he
may be presumed to have a love for Art.*   And a love for Art in
the end, says the "Athenæum," with much sagacity, *will generate
a knowledge of Art.*   Amen.   In that case the excellence of
Art Unions is established at once.

But no, says the philosopher who argues every week from under the columns of the temple of Minerva : this love which generates knowledge is only conceded to men who purchase pictures, not to those who rattle for them. Is not this a little hard ? How much income tax must a man pay in order to have a decent love of Art ; a love that shall be potent enough to become the father of a future knowledge ? I may say, without exaggeration, that Sir Robert Peel is richer than I am ; but does it follow that he loves Art better ? It may be, or not ; but, at least, the right honourable baronet's income does not establish the superiority of his taste. Let any gentleman go into a pastry-cook's and eat raspberry tarts ; ten to one, pressed against the window of the shop you will see the blue nose of a penniless urchin, who is looking at the good things with all his might. Would one say that Dives, because he eats the tarts, loved them better than little Lazarus who yearned after them ? No, even the " Athenæum " would not say that ; the cruel, cruel " Athenæum."

Now, suppose that round that shop-window, and allured by the same charming prospect which has brought their comrade thither, other little Lazaruses should assemble : they love tarts ; they are penniless ; but still not altogether without coin. Say they have a farthing apiece ; and clubbing together their wealth, or poverty rather, these rascally young gamblers make a lottery in the cap of one of them, and what is the consequence ? the winner of the prize steps in and takes a raspberry tart from the very same tray at which great Dives himself has been gormandising. It is gambling, certainly ; but I suspect the pastrycook (considering its result) will look upon the crime rather justly —she might never have sold her wares but for that TART UNION.

I shall resume this subject next week with philosophical considerations upon Polytechnic societies, upon the lunar prospectus (or that of Mr. Moon), and upon the puerile distribution (or that of Mr. Boys).

Meanwhile, dear M'Gilp, I remain,

Your very humble servant,

MICHAEL ANGELO TITMARSH.

No. 2.—THE OBJECTIONS AGAINST ART UNIONS.

M. A. Titmarsh, Esq., to Sanders M'Gilp, Esq.

My dear Sanders,—The Tart Union alluded to last week has been appreciated; and I am given to understand that several young gentlemen about Covent Garden and the foundation colleges in the city (where the youthful students wear leather breeches, and green coats, and caps famous for their similarity in shape to the muffin) have put the scheme into practice, and are very eager in borrowing or begging farthings for the pastrycook's interest and their own.

That the scheme will benefit the former is clear : and should any of them be inclined, by way of gratitude, to forward to the office of the paper a *proof plate* of their tarts, there are several juvenile persons about the premises who will gladly give an opinion of their merits. One of the union or distribution schemes mentioned in our last has forwarded proofs of its claims to public favour, proofs of its puffs we would say, but that is a pun, and the truth must be told, let what will come - of it, and we are now solemnly met, my brave M'Gilp, to discuss it.

The fact is, that the goodness or badness of the prints in question does not, at least for the sake of the argument, matter a fig. Suppose a man (by means of the electrotype of course) were enabled to reproduce a series of copies from the vignettes to Mr. Catnach's ballads, and charge a guinea, two guineas— a thousand pounds ; three farthings, for whitey-brown proofs of the same. He is quite free to do so. Nobody need buy unless they like. Or suppose he could (always by means of the electrotype) produce India paper proof plates of all the Cartoons, and sell them for a halfpenny. He is quite as much at liberty to do the one as the other ; and I do believe that the reason of fair dealing and moderate prices in the world has been not so much the honesty as the selfishness of our nature. We sell cheap because no one will buy else. We are honest because no one *will* trust us unless they *can* trust us. In a doubtful commerce with few concurrents and uncertain gains, men do not unfrequently cheat. But competition hustles roguery pretty quickly out of the market; the swaggering, swindling, lying impostor has no chance against the burly good sense of the public.

And I must confess, for my part, that if a man has a thirty guinea watch to raffle for, and thirty persons are willing to subscribe so much amongst them, and try the chance of winning it, I see no much greater harm in this "union" than in many other speculations where (of course) chances exist of losing or winning. But to moralise on the Art Union case because of this little harmless peddling with guineas, and to say that it provokes a spirit of gambling, is too hard. Is it altogether sinful to play a rubber of whist at shilling points? Does it imply an abominable desire of gain and a frightful perversion in the individual who bets half-a-crown on the rubber? Are we basely cast down because we lose, or brutally exultant because we win, half a score shillings? If it be a deadly sin, heaven help our grand-fathers and grandmothers, who played cards every night of their lives, and must be anything but comfortable now. But let us hope that with regard to the criminalty of the proceeding the "Athenæum" is wrong. Many of us have tried a raffle at Margate, and slept no worse for it. Once, at school, I drew lots with two other boys, and the prize was a flogging; and it does not much matter which of us won: but the others were not very sorry about it, depend on that. No; let this harmless little sin pass. As long as it provokes no very evil passions, as long as the pleasure of winning is great, and the pain of losing small, let gentlemen and ladies have their sport, and bet their bet, and our moralists not altogether despair. You cannot say that the Art Union supporters are actuated by a violent or unwholesome love of gambling; they don't injure their properties by the subscription of their guinea; they don't absent them-selves from home, contract dissipated habits, bring their wives and families to ruin. They give a guinea, and are not much the better or the worse for the outlay. This is an encourage-ment of lotteries, the Athenæum may say, presently; but indeed the objection is not worth a fig. The old lotteries were undisguised robberies. The Art Unions are none. The old

F

lotteries lived upon atrocious lies and puffs, encouraged silly people with exaggerated notions of gain. The Art Union offers but to purchase pictures with the aggregate of your money, and to distribute the pictures so bought. There are no falsehoods told, and no absurd lying baits held out.

A country book-club is a lottery, a wicked gambling transaction, in which squires and parsons take a part. A house or life assurance is a lottery. You take the odds there to win in a certain event; and may by very strait-laced moralists be accused of "gambling," for so providing against fortune; but the Parliament has sanctioned this gambling, and the State draws a considerable profit from it. An underwriter gambles when he insures a ship; calculating that he has a profit on the chances. A man gambles when he buys stock to sell afterwards, or a newspaper, or a house, or any other commodity upon which profit or loss may accrue. In the latter cases, perhaps, he gambles as he does at whist, knowing himself to be a good player, and trusting to skill and chance for his success. But in the former cases the underwriter of the ship or house has no security; it is sheer luck; dependent on a fire or a gale of wind, with the *pull* of the chances in his favour.

In a commercial country, then, where there is so much authorised gambling for profit, a little gambling for mere amusement's and kindness's sake may be tolerated. Let it be allowed at any rate that there is no great criminality in the Art Union species of gambling, and so quietly pass over the moral objection to the scheme. Then there has been lately mooted in the papers a legal objection; but that is not a very frightful one. Both of the learned gentlemen who have been consulted and have pronounced for and against Art Unions, have allowed that there is no danger of prosecution, and that poor bugbear will frighten honest folks no more.

But the strong objection is that on the part of some artists of the old school, who say that the Art Union system deteriorates art; that it sets painters speculating upon fancy pieces to suit the tastes of the prize-holders; that they think this will be a taking two hundred guinea subject, or that a neat gaudy piece that will be sure to hook something; and they paint accordingly.

Now, let any man who has looked at English picture-galleries for the last ten or twenty years be called upon to say from his heart, whether there has not been a great, a noble improvement?—whether there is not infinitely more fancy, feeling, poetry, education among artists as a body now than then? Good Heavens! if they do paint what are called *subjects*, what is the harm? If people do like fancy pieces, where is the great evil? If I have no fancy to have my own portrait staring me in the face in the dining-room, and would rather have Mr. Stone's "one particular star," for instance, (and it is a charming picture,) am I such a degraded wretch? This is but cant on the part of humbugs on one side, and on the other ultra-ticklishness of too susceptible minds.

What does the charge amount to? That the artist tries by one means or other to consult the taste of the public. The public is ignorant; therefore its choice is bad: therefore the artists paint bad pictures: therefore the taste grows worse and worse: therefore the public and artist are degraded by a desperate helpless arithmetical progression, out of which as one fancies there is no escape.

But look what the real state of the case is, as it has been recited by a weekly paper (the "Age")—that too moans over the degeneracy of its namesake, and prophesies a most pathetic future for Englishmen, because they have been lately seized with a love for illustrated books. First, says the "Age," came the "Observer," with its picture of Thurtell's cottage, then the "Hive," then the "Mirror," then this and that, then the "Illustrated London News," then the "Pictorial Times." Well, *après?* as the French say. The "Hive" was better than Thurtell's cottage, the "Mirror" was better than the "Hive," the "News" better than the "Mirror," and the "Times" better than the "News," and (though the "Times" readers may fancy the thing impossible) the day will come when something shall surpass even the "Times," and so on to the infinity of optimism. And so with pictures as with prints. The public is not used to having the former yet, but wait a while and it will take them; and take them better and better every day. The commercial energy of our hearty country is such, that where there is a small demand dealers well know how to raise it to be a great one ; and raise fresh wants by fresh supplies ingeniously insinuated, and by happy inventions in advance. As for GENIUS, that is not to be spoken of in this way ; but Genius is rare ; it comes to us but once in many many years ; and do you think the genius of painting less likely to flourish in our country because people are buying (by means of these Art Unions) five hundred little fancy pictures per annum, in addition to the ten thousand portraits they bought before ?

As for aristocratic patronage of Art only let us ask in what state was Art here before Art Unions began ? Did artists complain or not ? Did they say that there was no opportunity to cultivate their poetical feelings, and that they must paint portraits to live ? I am sure the people of England are likely to be better patrons of art than the English aristocracy ever were, and that the aristocracy have been tried and *didn't* patronise it; that they neither knew how to value a picture nor an artist: what artist ever got so good a place as a tenth-rate lawyer, or as a hundredth-rate soldier, or as a lucky physician, or as an alderman who had made a good speculation, or a country squire who had a borough ? The aristocracy never acknowledged the existence of art in this country, for they never acknowledged the artist. They were the handsomest men and women in the world, and they had their simpering faces painted: but what have they done for art to honour it ? No, no. *They* are not the friends of Genius: that day is over: its friends lie elsewhere ; rude and uncultivated as yet, but hearty, generous and eager. It may put up with rough fare; but it can't live in ante-chambers with lackeys, eating my lord's broken meat: equality is its breath, and *sympathy* the condition of its existence. What sympathy did my lords ever give it ? No : the law, the sword, the alderman's consols, and the doctor's pill, they can stomach ; they can reconcile these to their lordly nature, and infuse them into their august body.

But the POET had best come lower. What have their lordships to do with *him* ? He has never been one of their intimates. In the old song of Schiller, Love bids the poet, now that the earth is partitioned among the strong and wealthy, to come to Heaven in his distress, in which there will always be a place for him : but he has to try the people yet—the weak and poor ; and they, whose union makes their strength, depend on it, have a shelter and a welcome for him.

And so, though the taste of the public might be better than it is now (of which there is no question), I think we have every right to hope that it *will* be better. There are a thousand men read and think to-day, for one who read on this same day of April, 1743. The poet and artist is called upon to appeal to the few no longer. His profit and fame are with the many ; and do not let it be thought irreverence to put the profit and fame together. Nobody ever denies the Duke of Wellington's genius, because his Grace receives twenty thousand a year from his country in gratitude for the services rendered by him : and if the nation should take a fancy to reward poets in the same way, we have similarly no right to quarrel with the verdict.

The dukedoms, twenty-thousands-a-year, Piccadilly-palaces, and the like are not, however, pleaded for here. Miss Coutts or Mr. Rothschild have the like (or may, no doubt, for the asking), and nobody grudges the wealth, though neither ever were in the battle of Waterloo that I know of. But let us ask, as the condition of improvement in art, if not fame and honour, at least sympathy, from the public for the artist. The refinement of taste will come afterwards ; and as every man a little conversant with the art of painting, or any other art, must know how his judgment improves, and how by degrees he learns to admire justly, so the public will learn to admire more and more wisely every day. The sixpenny prints they buy twenty years hence will be better than the sixpenny prints now : the Art Union pictures they select better than those which frighten the desponding susceptibilities of our philosophers now-a-days. Away with these prophets of ill, these timid old maids of Cassandras, who lift up their crutches and croak, and cry, "Woe !" It is the nature of the old bodies to despond, but let "us youth" be not frightened by their prate. If any publisher could find it worth his while to bring out a hundred beautiful engravings for a penny, depend on it art would not retrograde in the country.

If a hundred thousand people chose to subscribe to the Art Union, the interest for art would be so much the greater, the encouragement to artists so much the greater; and if you interest the people and encourage the artists, it is absurd to suppose that one or the other would go back.

But this, as you will doubtless observe, has nothing to do with the lunatic prospectus (or that of Mr. Moon), or with the puerile distribution (or that of Mr. Boys). Let us consider the sham Art Unions on another day. What I wish to urge in the above sentences is, that the people are the artist's best friends; that for his reputation and profit henceforth he had best look to them; and rather than work for a class of *patrons*, he had better rely for support on his friends. If you have something that is worth the telling,—something for the good of mankind,—it is better to be able to take it to a hundred tailors or tinkers than to one duke or two dandies (speaking with perfect respect of both); and as an actor would rather have a hundred people in the pit for an audience than but one hearer who had paid ten pounds for a private box, an artist need have no squeamish objections to the same popularity, and will find a more sure and lasting profit in it. Many men of genius will say, " No ; we do not want the applause of the vulgar ; give us the opinion of the few." Who prevents them ? They *have* these few as before ; but because the artist of a lower walk changes his patron, and, instead of catering for the private boxes, appeals to the pit, there is no harm done. The pit, it is my firm belief, knows just as much about the matter in question as the boxes know ; and now you have made art one of the wants of the public, you will find the providers of the commodity and its purchasers grow more refined in their tastes alike ; and the popular critic of a few years hence calling for good pictures, when now bad ones please him.

How should he know better as yet ? His betters have taught him to admire Books of Beauty, trashy, flashy, coronation pictures, and the like tawdry gimcracks, which please a feeble intellect and a debauched taste. Give him time, and he will learn to like better things. And for the artist himself, will he not gain by bringing to the public market the article which he was obliged before to prepare for individual patronage? He has made many more sacrifices to the latter, than ever he will be called upon to do for the former. His independence does not suffer by honest barter in the public place, any more than an author's does who takes his wares to the bookseller or newspaper, and asks and gets his price. The writer looks to my lord no longer, but has found a better and surer friend: and so for art; I would like to see Art Unions all over England, from London to Little Peddlington: every one of the subscribers become interested in a subject about which he has not thought hitherto, and which was kept as the exclusive privilege of his betters.

The "Spectator" has an excellent suggestion with regard to Art Unions, I think; which is, that a committee should purchase pictures with the funds of the Union, and that the prize-holder should then choose. Bad pictures would not, probably, be bought in this way, and the threatened degradation of art would then be averted. Perhaps the majority of the present Unionists, however, would not accede to this plan, and prefer to choose their pictures for themselves. Well: let them keep to the old plan, and let us have another Art Union as the new. The more the better—the more *real* Unions: as for the sham ones, we will discourse of these anon.

Yours, my dear M'Gilp,

M. A. Titmarsh.

P.S. I hope your Cartoon is in a state of forwardness: we shall see in a month or two what the giants of art can do. But meanwhile do not neglect your little picture out of Gil Blas or the Vicar of Wakefield (of course it is from one or the other). Let those humble intellects which can only understand common feeling and every-day life have too their little gentle gratifications. Why should not the poor in spirit be provided for as well as the tremendous geniuses? If a child take a fancy to a penny theatrical print, let him have it; if a workman want a green parrot with a bobbing head to decorate his humble mantel-piece, let us not grudge it to him; and if an immense supereminent intelligence cannot satisfy his poetical craving with anything less sublime than Milton, or less vast than Michael Angelo,—all I can say for my part is, that I wish he may get it. The kind and beneficent Genius of Art has pleasures for all according to their degree ; and spreads its harmless happy feast for big and little—for the Titanic appetite that can't be satisfied with less than a roasted elephant, as well as for the small humble cock-robin of an intellect that can sing its little grace and make its meal on a bread-crumb.

No. III.—THE ROYAL ACADEMY.

My dear M'Gilp,

I think every succeeding year shows a progress in the English school of painters. They paint from *the heart* more than of old, and less from the old heroic, absurd, incomprehensible, unattainable rules. They look at Nature very hard, and match her with the best of their eyes and ability. They do not aim at such great subjects as heretofore, or at subjects which the world is pleased to call great, viz. tales from Hume or Gibbon of royal personages under various circumstances of battle, murder and sudden death. Lemprière, too, is justly neglected ; and Milton has quite given place to Gil Blas and the Vicar of Wakefield.

The heroic, and peace be with it ! has been deposed ; and our artists, in place, cultivate the pathetic and the familiar. But a few, very few, worshippers of the old gods remain. There are only two or three specimens in the present exhibition of the grand historic style. There is a huge dun-coloured picture in the large room, by an Academician probably ; but I have neither the name nor the subject : there is Mr. Haydon's history-piece of the Maid of Saragossa—a great, coarse, vulgar, ill-drawn, ill-painted caricature ; and an allegory or two by other artists, in the oldfashioned style.

The younger painters are content to exercise their art on subjects far less exalted : a gentle sentiment, an agreeable, quiet incident, a tea-table tragedy, or a bread-and-butter idyl suffices for the most part their gentle powers. Nor surely ought one to quarrel at all with this prevalent mode. It is at least natural, which the heroic was not. Bread and butter can be digested by every man; whereas Prometheus on his rock, or Orestes in his strait-waistcoat, or Hector dragged behind Achilles' car, or "Britannia, guarded by Religion and Neptune, welcoming General Tomkins in the Temple of Glory"—the ancient heroic, allegorical subjects—can be supposed deeply to interest very few of the inhabitants of this city or kingdom. We have wisely given up pretending that we were interested in such, and confess a partiality for more simple and homely themes.

The Exhibition rooms are adorned with numberless very pleasing pictures in this quiet taste. Mr. Leslie offers up to our simple household gods a Vicar of Wakefield; Mr. Maclise presents a Gil Blas; Mr. Redgrave gently depicts the woes of a governess who is reading a black-edged note, and the soft sorrows of a country-lass going to service; Mr. Stone has the last appeal of a rustic lover; Mr. Charles Landseer has a party drinking comfortably under the trees; Mr. Macnee shows us a young person musing in a quiet nook, and thinking over her love.

All these subjects, it will be observed, are small subjects; but they are treated, for the most part, with extraordinary skill. As for Lady Blarney, in Mr. Leslie's picture, with that wonderful leer of her wicked, squinting, vacant eyes, she is as good as the very best Hogarth; her face is the perfection of comedy; and the honest Primrose countenances round about, charming for their simplicity and rich, kindly humour. The Malade Imaginaire is no less excellent; more farcical and exaggerated in the arrangement; but the play is farcical and exaggerated; and the picture, as the play, is full of jovial, hearty laughter. No artist possesses this precious quality of making us laugh kindly, so much as Mr. Leslie. There is not the least gall or satire in it, only sheer, irresistible, good humour.

Now in the tableau by Mr. Maclise, many of the principal personages are scowling, or ogling, or grinning, and showing their teeth, with all their might; and yet the spectator, as I fancy, is by no means so amused as by those more quiet actors in Mr. Leslie's little comedies. There is, especially in Mr. Maclise's company, one young fellow who ought to be

hissed, or who should have humble parts to act, and not be
thrust forward in the chief characters as he has been of late years,
with his immense grinning mouthful of white teeth and knowing, leering eyes.   The ladies we have seen, too, repeatedly,
and it must be confessed they are not of the high comedy sort.
The characters appear to be, as it were, performing a tableau
from Gil Blas, not the actual heroes or heroines of that easy
jovial drama.

As for the "properties" of the piece, to use the dramatic
phrase, they are admirably rich and correct.   The painter's skill
in representing them is prodigious.   The plate, the carvings,
the wine-flasks, the poor old melancholy monkey on his perch,
the little parrots, the carpet, are painted with a truth and dexterity quite marvellous, and equal the most finished productions
of the Dutch schools.   Terburg never painted such a carpet;
every bit of plate is a curiosity of truthful representation.
This extraordinary power of minute representation is shown in
another picture by Mr. Maclise, the Cornish Waterfall, round
which every leaf in every tree is depicted, and in which the
figure of the girl is a delightful specimen of the artist's graphic
power.

Mr. Redgrave's "Going to Service," is not so well drawn as
his pictures of former years.   An old lady in an arm chair, two
young sisters embracing each other, a brother very stiff and
solemn in a smock-frock, and a waggon waiting outside, tell the
story of this little domestic comedy.   It has a milk-and-watery
pathos.   The governess has her bread-and-butter by her side
too ; but the picture is much better, the girl's figure extremely
beautiful and graceful, and the adjuncts of the picture are
painted with extreme care and skill.

Mr. Stone's "Last Appeal" is beautiful.   It is evidently the
finish of the history of the two young people who are to be seen
in the Water-Colour Exhibition.   There the girl is smiling and
pleased, and there is some hope still for the pale, earnest young
man who loves her with all his might.   But between the two
pictures, between Pall Mall and the Trafalgar Column, sad
changes have occurred.   The young woman has met a great big
life-guardsman probably, who has quite changed her views of

things : and you see that the last appeal is made without any hope for the appellant. The girl hides away her pretty face, and we see that all is over. She likes the poor fellow well enough, but it is only as a brother; her heart is with the life-guardsman, who is strutting down the lane at this moment with his laced cap on one ear, cutting the buttercups' heads off with his rattan cane. The whole story is told, without, alas ! the possibility of a mistake, and the young fellow in the grey stockings has nothing to do but to jump down the well, at the side of which he has been making his appeal.

The painting of this picture is excellent : the amateur will not fail to appreciate the beauty of the drawing, the care, and at the same time freedom, of the execution, and a number of excellencies of method which are difficult to be described in print, except in certain technical terms that are quite unsatis-factory to the general reader.

Mr. Charles Landseer's *Monks of Rubrosi* is the best, perhaps, of his pictures. The scene is extremely cheerful, fresh, and brilliant ; the landscape almost as good as the figures, and these are all good. Two grave-looking, aristocratic fathers of the abbey have been fly-fishing ; a couple of humbler breth-ren in brown are busy at a hamper of good things ; a gallant young sportsman in green velvet lies on the grass and toasts a pretty lass that is somehow waiting upon their reverences. The picture is not only good, but has the further good quality of being *pleasant ;* and some clever artist will do no harm in condescending so far to suit the general taste. There is no reason after all why a man should not humble himself to this extent, and make friends with the public patron.

For instance, take Mr. Poole's picture of Solomon Eagle and the Plague of London. It is exceedingly clever ; but who would buy such a piece ? Figures writhe over the picture blue and livid with the plague—some are dying in agony—some stupid with pain. You see the dead-cart in the distance ; and in the midst stands naked Solomon, with bloodshot eyes and wild maniacal looks, preaching death, woe, and judgment. Where should such a piece hang ? It is too gloomy for a hospital, and surely not cheerful enough for a dining-room. It is not a religious picture that would serve to decorate the walls of a church. A very dismal gloomy conventicle might perhaps be a suitable abode for it; but would it not be better to tempt the public with something more good-humoured ?

Of the religious pieces Mr. Herbert's " Woman of Samaria " will please many a visitor to the Exhibition, on account of the beauty and dignity of the head and figure of the Saviour. The woman, as I thought, was neither beautiful nor graceful. Mr. Eastlake's " Hagar " is beautiful as everything else by this accomplished artist ; but here, perhaps, the beauty is too great, and the pain not enough. The scene is not represented with its actual agony and despair ; but this is, as it were, a sort of limning to remind you of the scene ; a piece of mystical poetry with Ishmael and Hagar for the theme. I must confess that Mr. Linnell's " Supper at Emmaus " did not strike me as the least mystical or poetical, and that Mr. Etty's " Entombment " was anything but holy and severe. Perhaps the most pious and charming head in the whole Exhibition is that of the Queen, by Mr. Leslie, in his Coronation picture, it has a delightful modesty and a purity quite angelical.

Mr. Etty's pictures of the heathen sort are delightful ; wonderful for a gorgeous flush of colour, such as has belonged, perhaps, to no painter since Rubens. But of these we will discourse next week.

M. A. TITMARSH.

No. IV.—THE ROYAL ACADEMY (SECOND NOTICE).

My dear M'Gilp,—If Her Majesty is the purchaser of all the royal pictures by Parris, by Hayter, by Leslie, by Landseer, —of all the royal portraits, by these and a score more, in and out of the Academy,—there must be a pretty large gallery at Buckingham Palace by this time, and, let it be said with respect, a considerable sameness in the collection. The royal face is a very handsome one, and especially in the medallion-shape, in gold. I would like to look at thousands of them every week for my part, and would never tire in extending my cabinet.

But confess, my dear Sir, are we not beginning to have enough of royal-parade pictures? And are not the humbler classes somewhat tired of them? Only the publishers and the grandees, their enlightened patrons, still continue to admire. Dark rooms are still prepared for such; gas-jets and large subscription books artfully laid on and out. The Court Guide still goes to see Winterhalter's portrait of the Queen ("I wish they may get it," as the D—ch—ss of —— observes; the picture is not painted by Winterhalter: but what do *they* know, whether it be good or bad?). The Court Guide still buys huge proofs of her Majesty's marriage, or the Princess's christening, or the real authorised Coronation picture (every one of the half dozen are real authorised Coronation pictures), and is content therewith. Ah! Heaven bless that elegant aristocracy of England; that wise, that enlightened, that noble class of our betters! The subject of these pictures is worthy of their noble souls—fit for their vast comprehensions; and as the poor workman buys his prints of the Prodigal Son's progress, the young cockney-buck his portrait of Mrs. Honey, or some other beauty with long ringlets and short petticoats, the sporting man his varnished hunting-piece, so the great have their likings, and we judge them by what they admire.

And what an admiration theirs is! There's her Majesty in state! what a lovely white satin! and the velvet, my dear, painted to the very life. Every single jewel's a portrait, I give you my honour; and Prince Albert's own star and garter sat to the artist; the archbishop's wig is done to a hair; and was there ever a more wonderful piece of art than that picture of the duke in his orders and his epaulets, and his white kersey-mere pantaloons? Round the Sovereign are all the maids of honour; round the maids of honour all the officers of state; round the officers of state all the beef-eaters and gentlemen-at-arms: and on these magnificent subjects our best painters are continually employed. Noble themes for the exercise of genius! brilliant proofs of enlightened public taste! The court-milliners must be proud to think that their works are thus immortalised, and the descendants of our tailors will look at these pieces with a justifiable family pride.

Mr. Leslie has had to chronicle coats and satin-slips in this way, and has represented *his* sense in the drama of the coronation (how many more episodes of the same piece have been represented, and by how many more painters I don't know), and his picture is so finely done, so full of beauty and grandeur, that for once a court picture has been made interesting. I have remarked on the principal feature before—the exquisite grace and piety represented in the countenance and attitude of the Queen; but the judgment of the quality, as far as I have been able to gather it (and it is good to this end to play the spy's part, and overhear the opinions of the genteel personages who come to see the Exhibition),—the genteel judgment is decidedly against the painter, and his portraits are pronounced to be failures, and his picture quite inferior to many others by other hands. Let us hope the opinion will be so general, that this charming painter shall never be called upon to paint a court ceremony again. I would rather see honest Mrs. Primrose's portrait by him, than that of the loveliest lady of honour; and the depicting of uniforms, and lappets, and feathers left to those politer artists whose genius is suited to subjects so genteel.

There is no Prince Albert this year, I regret to say; but we have two portraits of her Majesty, in trains, velvets, arm-chairs, &c.—one by the President and one by Mr. Grant, and neither worth a crown-piece. One of the most exquisite and refined little sketches ever seen is the portrait of Lady Lyttelton by the latter artist; it is a delightful picture of a beautiful and high-bred maiden. Mr. Chalon's aristocracy does not ogle and simper quite so much as in former years; and their ladyships are painted with all the artist's accustomed skill. Mr. Richmond's heads are excellent as usual; and there is a rival to these gentlemen, who has given us a water-colour portrait of the Bishop of Exeter, in which the amiable and candid features of that learned prelate are depicted with great fidelity and talent. Mr. Carrick's men-miniatures are perhaps the best among those pleasing performances: the likeness of a former secretary for Ireland will especially please those who know his lordship's countenance, and those who do not, by its resemblance to an eminent comedian whose absence from the stage all regret.

Mr. Thorburn cultivates more, perhaps, than any other miniature painter, the poetry of his art. The gallant knights Sir Ross and Sir Newton are as victorious as usual ; and Mr. Lover's head of Mr. Lever deserves praiseworthy mention : it will be looked at with interest by Harry Lorrequer's English readers, and by those who had the opportunity of seeing him in the body, and hearing his manly and kind-hearted speech at the Literary Fund the other day.

Of Mr. Etty's colour pieces what words can give an idea ? Many lovers of Titian and Rubens will admit that here is an English painter who almost rivals them in his original way, and all will admire their magnificent beauty. Mr. Turner, our other colourist, is harder to be understood. The last time the gentle reader received a black eye at school, and for a moment after the delivery of the blow, when flashes of blue, yellow and crimson lightning blazed before the ball so preternaturally excited, he saw something not unlike the Moses of Mr. Turner. His picture of Cleopatra meeting Alexander the Great at Moscow the Morning before the Deluge (perhaps this may not be the exact title, but it will do as well as another), is of the most transcendental sort. The quotations from the " Fallacies of Hope " continue still in great force : as thus—

> " The ark stood firm on Ararat : the returning Sun
> Exhaled Earth's humid bubbles, and, emulous of light,
> Reflected her lost forms, each in prismatic guise,
> Hope's harbinger, ephemeral as the summer fly,
> Which rises, flits, expands, and dies."
>
> *Fallacies of Hope.*

The artist has done full justice to these sweet lines.

We are given to understand by cognoscenti that the Italian skies are always of the bluest cobalt : hence many persons are dissatisfied with Mr. Stanfield's Italian landscapes as unfaithful, because deficient in the proper depth of ultramarine. On this subject let proper judges speak ; but others less qualified will find the pictures beautiful, and more beautiful for their quiet and calm. Who can praise Mr. Creswick sufficiently ? The Welsh girl will, one of these days, fetch a sum of money as great as ever was given for Hobbima or Ruysdael ; and Evening is an English

Claude.   Mr. Lee's fresh country landscapes will find hundreds
of admirers ; and perhaps there are no two prettier little pictures in the gallery than Mr. Linton's Sorrento and Mr. Jutsum's
Tintern.

In walking round the vault in which the sculpture is en-
tombed, I did not see anything especially worthy of mark,
except a bust of Count d'Orsay, who has himself broken ground
as an artist, and whose genius will one day no doubt make its
way.   Why have we not our common share of the admirable
pictures of Mr. Edwin Landseer ?   It can't be that a man of his
facility has painted but three pictures in a year, and picture-
lovers wonder where the rest are.

M. A. TITMARSH.

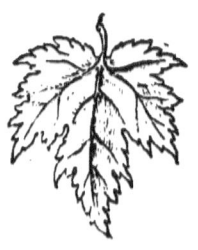

THE PARTIE FINE.

By LANCELOT WAGSTAFF, ESQ.

OLONEL GOLLOP'S dinner in Harley-street (the colonel is an East-India director, and his Mulligatawney the best out of Bengal) was just put off, much to my disappointment, for I had no other engagement; Mrs. Wagstaff was out of town with her mother at Bognor; and my clothes had been brought down to the club to dress—all to no purpose.

I was disconsolately looking over the bill of fare, and debating between Irish stew and the thirteenth cut at a leg of lamb (of which seven barristers had partaken, each with his half pint of Marsala), when Jiggins, the waiter, brought me in a card, saying that the gentleman was in the hall, and wished to see me.

The card was Fitzsimons's;—a worthy fellow, as I dare say my reader knows. I went out to speak to him. "Perhaps," thought I, "he is going to ask me to dine."

There was something particularly splendid in Fitz's appearance, as I saw at a glance. He had on a new blue-and-white silk neckcloth, so new that it had never been hemmed; his great gold jack-chain, as I call it, was displayed across his breast, showing off itself and a lace-ruffle a great deal too ostentatiously, as I thought. He had lemon-coloured gloves; French polished boots, with deuced high heels; his hair curled (it is red, but oils to a mahogany colour); his hat extremely on one side; and his moustache lacquered up with, I do believe, the very same varnish which he puts to his boots. I hate those

G

varnished boots, except for moderns, and Fitz is three-and-forty if he is a day.

However, there he stood, whipping his lacquered boots with a gold-headed stick, whistling, twirling his moustache, pulling up his shirt-collar, and giving himself confoundedly dandified airs in a word, before the hall-porter and the club message-boy in brass buttons.

"Wagstaff, my boy," says he, holding out a kid glove, in a most condescending manner, "I have something to propose to you."

"What is it, and what's your hour?" said I, quite playfully.

"You've guessed it at once," answered he. "A dinner is what I mean—Mrs. Wagstaff is out of town, and ——"

Here he whispered me.

* * * * * *

Well? why not?—After all there may be some very good fun. If my mother-in-law heard of it she would be sure to make a row. But she is safe at Bognor (may she stay there for ever!). It is much better that I should have some agreeable society than dine alone at the club, after the seven barristers, on the leg of lamb. Of course it was not to be an expensive dinner—of course not, Fitzsimons said,—no more it was to *him* —hang him—as you shall hear.

It was agreed that the dinner-hour should be seven: the place, Durognon's in the Haymarket; and as I rather pique myself on ordering a French dinner, that matter was to be consigned to me. I walked down to Durognon's, looked at the room, and ordered the dinner for four persons—the man asked how much champagne should be put in ice? which I considered rather a leading question, and giving a vague sort of reply to this (for I determined that Fitzsimons should treat us to as much as he liked), I walked away to while away the hour before dinner.

After all, I thought, I may as well dress: the things are ready at the club, and a man is right to give himself every personal advantage, especially when he is going to dine with—with LADIES. There—the secret is out. Fitz has invited me to make a fourth in a *petit dîner* given to Madame Nelval of the

French theatre, and her friend Mademoiselle Delval. I had seen Madame Nelval from a side-box a few evenings before—and, *parbleu, homo sum ;* I meant no harm ; Gollop's dinner was off ; Mrs. Wagstaff was out of town ; and I confess I was very glad to have an opportunity of meeting this fascinating actress, and keeping up my French. So I dressed, and at seven o'clock walked back to Durognon's, whither it was agreed that Fitz was to bring the ladies in his Brougham ;—the deuce knows how he gets the money to pay for it by the way, or to indulge in a hundred other expenses far beyond any moderate man's means.

As the St. James's clock struck seven, a gentleman—past the period of extreme youth it is true, but exhibiting a remarkably elegant person still in a very becoming costume, might have been seen walking by London House, and turning down Charles-street to the Haymarket. This individual, I need not say, was myself. I had done my white tie to a nicety, and could not help saying, as I gazed for a moment in the great glass in the club drawing-room—" *Corblen,* Wagstaff, you are still as *distingué* a looking fellow as any in London." How women can admire that odious Fitzsimons on account of his dyed moustaches, I for one never could understand.

The dinner-table at Durognon's made a neat and hospitable appearance ; the plated candlesticks were not more coppery than such goods usually are at taverns ; the works of art on the wall were of tolerable merit ; the window-curtains, partially drawn, yet allowed the occupant of the room to have a glimpse of the cab-stand opposite, and I seated myself close to the casement, as they say in the novels, awaiting Captain Fitzsimons's arrival with the two ladies.

I waited for some time—the cabs on the stand disappeared from the rank, plunged rattling into the mighty vortex of London, and were replaced by other cabs. The sun, which had set somewhere behind Piccadilly, was now replaced by the lustrous moon, the gas lamps, and the red and blue orbs that flared in the windows of the chemist opposite. Time passed on, but no Fitzsimons's Brougham made its appearance. I read the evening paper, half an hour was gone and no company come.

At last, as the opera carriages actually began to thunder down
the street, "a hand was on my shoulder," as the member for
Pontefract * sings.   I turned round suddenly from my reverie—
that hand, that yellow kid-glove-covered hand was Fitzsimons's.

"Come along, my boy," says he, " we will go fetch the ladies
—they live in Bury-street, only three minutes walk."

I go to Bury-street ?   I be seen walking through St. James's-
square, giving an arm to any other lady in Europe but my
Arabella, my wife, Mrs. Wagstaff ?   Suppose her uncle, the
dean, is going to dine at the bishop's, and should see me ?—me,
walking with a French lady, in three quarters of a bonnet !   I
should like to know what an opinion he would have of me, and
where his money in the funds would go to ?

"No," says I, "my dear Fitzsimons, a joke is a joke, and I
am not more strait-laced than another ; but the idea that Mr.
Lancelot Wagstaff should be seen walking in St. James's-
square with a young French actress, is a *little* too absurd.   It
would be all over the city tomorrow, and Arabella would tear
my eyes out."

"You sha'n't walk with a French actress," said Fitz.   "You
shall give your arm to as respectable a woman as any in Baker-
street—I pledge you my honour of this—Madame la Baronne
de Saint Ménéhould, the widow of a General of the Empire—
connected with the first people in France.   Do you mean to
say that she is not equal to any of your sugar-baking family ?"
I passed over Fitz's sneer regarding my family ; and as it was a
baroness, of course agreed to walk with Fitzsimons in search
of the ladies.

"I thought you said Madame Delval this morning,"
said I.

"Oh, the baroness is coming too," answered Fitzsimons, and
ordered a fifth cover to be laid.   We walked to Bury-street, and
presently after a great deal of chattering and clapping of doors
and drawers, three ladies made their appearance in the drawing-
room, and having gone through the ceremony of an introduction

* Richard Monckton Milnes.—Ed.

in an entire state of darkness, the order of march was given. I offered my arm to the Baroness de Saint Ménéhould, Fitz leading the way with the other two ladies.

We walked down Jermyn-street; my heart thumped with some uneasiness as we crossed by the gambling-house in Waterloo-place, lest any one should see me. There is a strong gas-lamp there, and I looked for the first time at my portly companion. She was fifty-five if a day—five years older than that Fitzsimons. This eased me, but somehow it didn't please me. I can walk with a woman of five-and-fifty any day—there's my mother-in-law, my aunts, and the deuce knows how many more I could mention. But I was consoled by the baroness presently saying, that she should, from my accent, have mistaken me for a Frenchman—a great compliment to a man who has been in Paris but once, and learned the language from a Scotch usher, never mind how many years ago, at Mr. Lord's Academy, Tooting, Surrey.

But I adore Paul de Kock's novels, and have studied them so rapturously that no wonder I should have made a proficiency in the language. Indeed Arabella has often expressed herself quite jealous as I lay on the sofa of an evening, laughing my waistcoat-strings off, over his delightful pages. (The dear creature is not herself very familiar with the language, and sings *Flore dew Tage, Partong pour Syric,* &c., with the most confirmed Clapham accent.) I say she has often confessed herself to be jealous of the effect produced on my mind by this dear, delightful, wicked, odious, fascinating writer, whose pictures of French society are so admirably ludicrous. It was through Paul de Kock that I longed to know something about Parisian life, and those charming *sémillantes, frétillantes, pétillantes* grisettes, whose manners he describes. "It's Paul de Kock in London by Jove," said I to myself, when Fitz proposed the little dinner to me; "I shall see all their ways and their fun."—And *that* was the reason why, as Mrs. Wagstaff was out of town, I accepted the invitation so cordially.

Well; we arrived at Durognon's at a quarter-past-eight, we five, and were ushered at length into the dining-room,

where the ladies flung off their cloaks and bonnets, and I
had an opportunity of seeing their faces completely.

Madame Nelval's was as charming a face as I ever looked
upon ; her hair parted meekly over the forehead, which was
rather low ; the eyes and eyebrows beautiful ; the nose such as
Grecian sculptor scarce ever chipped out of Parian stone ; the
mouth small, and, when innocently smiling, displaying the
loveliest pearly teeth, and calling out two charming attendant
dimples on each fresh cheek ; the ear a perfect little gem of an
ear. (I adore ears—unadorned ears without any hideous ornaments dangling from them—pagodas, chandeliers, bunches of
grapes, and similar monstrosities, such as ladies will hang from
them—*entr' autres* my own wife, Mrs. W., who has got a pair
of earrings her uncle, the dean, gave her, that really are as big
as boot-jacks almost.) She was habited in a neat, closely-fitting
silk dress of Parisian tartan silk, which showed off to advantage a figure that was perfect, and a waist that was ridiculously
small. A more charming, candid, distinguished head it was
impossible to see.

Mademoiselle Delval was a modest, clever, pleasing person,
neatly attired in a striped something, I don't know the proper
phrase ; and Madame la Baronne was in a dress which I should
decidedly call gingham.

When we sat down to the Potage Printanière, and I helped
the baroness naturally first, addressing her respectfully by her
title, the other two ladies began to laugh, and that brute, Fitzsimons, roared as if he was insane. "La Baronne de Saint
Ménéhould !" cried out little Madame Nelval; "o par exemple!
c'est maman, mon cher monsieur!" On which (though I was
deucedly nettled, I must confess,) I said, that to be the mother
of Madame Nelval, was the proudest title any lady could have,
and so sneaked out of my mortification with this, I flatter
myself, not inelegant compliment. The ladies, one and all,
declared that I spoke French like a Parisian, and so I ordered
in the champagne ; and very good Durognon's Sillery is too.

Both the young ladies declared they detested it, but Madame
Nelval, the elder, honestly owned that she liked it ; and indeed
I could not but remark that, in our favour doubtless, the two

younger dames forgot their prejudices, and that their glasses were no sooner filled than they were empty.

Ah, how charming it was to see the shuddering, timid, nervous way in which the lovely Nelval, junior (let me call her at once by her Christian name of Virginie), turned away her little shrinking head as the waiter opened the bottles, and they went off with their natural exhilarating pop and fizz. At the opening of the first bottle, she flew into a corner: at the opening of the second, she ran to her mother's arms (*hinnuleo similis quærenti pavidam montibus aviis matrem,** as we used to say at Tooting), sweet sensibility! charming, timorous grace! but she took the liquor very kindly when it *was* opened, saying, as she turned up her fine eyes to Heaven, "Il n'y a rien qui m'agaçe les nerfs comme cela!" Agaçer les nerfs! What a delicate expression! The good old lady told her to be calm, and made light of her terror.

But though I had piqued myself on ordering the dinner, the little coquette soon set me down. She asked for the most wonderful things—for instance, she would have a salad of dandelion—the waiter was packed off to Covent Garden to seek for it. When the fish came, she turned to the waiter and said, "Comment? vous n'avez point de moules?" with the most natural air in the world, and as if mussels were always served at Parisian dinners, which, I suppose is the case. And then at dessert, what must she remark but the absence of asparagus, which, I must confess, I had not ordered.

" What," she said, turning round to my companion, " are there no asparagus, monsieur?—No asparagus! ah, monsieur! c'est ma vie, mon bonheur, que les asperges! J'en suis folle—des asperges. Je les adore—les asperges! Je ne mange que cela,— il me les faut, Monsieur Fitzsimons. Vite, garçon! des asperges —des asperges à l'huile, entendez vous?"

[* " *Vitas hinnuleo me similis, Chlöe,*
Quærenti pavidam montibus aviis
Matrem."—HOR. *Carm. lib.* I. *od.* 23.
Thackeray knew his Horace by heart, and was fond occasionally of showing a familiarity which few college men even retain on into middle life.—ED.]

We were both very much alarmed by this manifest excitement of Virginie's nerves ; and the asparagus was sent for.   O
woman! you are some of you like the animals of the field in
so far as this, that you do not know your power.   Those who
do can work wonders over us.   No man can resist them.   We
two were as timid, wretched, and trembling, until the asparagus
came, as any mortal could be.   It seemed as if we had committed a crime in not ordering the asparagus that Virginie
adored.   If she had proposed a pint of melted pearls, I think
Fitz was the man to send off to Storr and Mortimer's, and have
the materials bought.   They (I don't mean the pearls, but the
vegetables) came in about half an hour, and she ate them cold,
as she said, with oil and vinegar; but the half hour's pause was
a very painful one, and we vainly endeavoured to fill the odious
vacuum with champagne.   All the while, Fitzsimons, though he
drank and kept nervously helping his neighbours right and left,
was quite silent and frightened.   I know which will be the
better horse (as the phrase is) if *he's* ever married.   I was of
course collected, and kept putting in my jokes as usual, but I
cannot help saying that I wished myself out of the premises,
dreading to think what else Madame Virginie might ask for,
and saying inwardly, " What would my poor Arabella say if she
knew her scoundrel of a Lancelot was in such company ? "

Well—it may have been the champagne, or it may have been
the asparagus,—though I never, I confess, remarked such a
quality in the vegetable,—it may, I say, have been the asparagus
which created—what do you think ?—a reconciliation between
Virginie and Héloïse—the Madame Delval before mentioned.
This is a delicate matter, but it appeared the ladies had had a
difference in the morning about a ribbon, a fichu, or some such
matter doubtless, and they had not spoken all dinner time.

But after a bottle of sherry, four of Sillery (which we all took
fairly, no flinching, no heel-taps, glass and glass about), after
coffee and curaçoa, and after the asparagus, a reconciliation
took place, Héloïse looked at Virginie, Virginie looked at
Héloïse, the latter rose from her chair, tottered towards her
friend, and they were in each other's arms in a minute.   Old
Madame Nelval looked quite pleased at the scene, and said,

smiling, to us, "*Elle a si bon cœur, ma fille!*" Oh those
mothers! they are all the same. Not that she was wrong in
this instance. The two young ladies embraced with the warmest
cordiality, the quarrel about the ribbon was forgotten, the two
young hearts were united once more; and though that selfish
brute, Fitzsimons, who has no more heart than a bed-post,
twiddled his eternal moustache, and yawned over the scene, I
confess I was touched by this little outbreak of feeling, and this
glimpse into the history of the hearts of the young persons, and
drank a glass of curaçoa to old Madame Nelval with a great
deal of pleasure.

But, oh! fancy our terror, when all of a sudden Héloise,
weeping on her friend's neck, began to laugh and to cry, and
burst out shrieking into a fit of hysterics! When women begin
hysterics a tremor seizes me—I become mad myself—I have
had my wife and mother-in-law both in hysterics on the same
rug, and I know what it is—the very sound of the whoo—oo—oo
drives me wild. I have heard it imitated in theatres, and have
rushed out in a frenzy. "Water! water!" gasped Virginie (we
had somehow not had any all dinner-time), I tumbled out
of the room, upsetting three waiters who were huddled at the
door (and be hanged to them); "water," roared I, rushing down
stairs, upsetting boots, and alarmed chamber-maids came panting in with a jug.

"What will they think of us?" thought I, trembling with
emotion—"they will think we have murdered the poor young
lady, and yet on my honour and conscience I—Oh why did I
come—what *would* Arabella say if she knew?" I thought of
the police coming in, of paragraphs in the paper beginning,
"Two ruffians of gentlemanly exterior were brought before Mr.
Jardine," &c., it was too horrible—if I had had my hat I would
have taken a cab off the stand, and driven down to my wife
at Bognor that minute; but I hadn't — so I went up to
fetch it.

Héloise was lying on the sofa now, a little calmer; Madame
Delval and the chamber-maid were being kind to her: as for
that brute, Fitzsimons, he was standing in one of the windows,
his legs asunder, his two fists thrust into the tail pockets of his

brass buttoned coat, whistling, " Suoni la Tromba," the picture of
heartless, shameless, indifference.

As soon as the maid was gone, and I was come in, Madame
Virginie must of course begin hysterics too—they always do,
these women. She turned towards me with an appealing look
(she had been particularly attentive to me at dinner, much more
than to Fitzsimons, whom she *bullied* the whole time)—she gave
me an appealing look—and struck up too.

I couldn't bear it. I flung myself down on a chair, and beginning to bang my forehead, gasped out " Oh Heavens ! a cab,
a cab !"

" We'll have a coach. Go back with them," said Fitz, coming
swaggering up.

" *Go back* with them ? " said I, " I'll never see them again as
long as I live." No more I *would* go back with them. The
carriage was called (the hysterics ceased the very moment Fitz
flung open the window and the cab-stand opposite could hear)—
the ladies went out. In vain good old Madame Nelval looked
as if she expected my arm. In vain Virginie cast her
appealing look. I returned it them with the most stony indifference, and falling back upon my chair, thought of my
poor Arabella.

The coach drove off. I felt easier as the rattle of the departing wheels died away in the night, and I got up to go. " How
glad I am it's over," thought I, on the stair ; " if ever I go to a
partie fine again may I   *   *

" I beg your parding, sir," said the waiter, touching my elbow
just as I was at the hotel door.

" What is it ? " says I.

" The bill, sir," says he, with a grin.

" The bill, sir ? " I exclaimed ; why it's Captain Fitzsimons's
dinner !"

" I beg your parding, sir, you ordered it," answered the
man.

" But, good Heavens ! you know Captain Fitzsimons ? "

" We do, sir, precious well too. The capting owes master two
underd pound," answered the wretched official, and thrust the
document into my hand.

No. 24.   *To Anatole Durognon.*

	£	s.	d.
5 Dinners	1	15	0
Sherry	0	6	0
Sillery champagne (4 bottles) ...	2	0	0
Asparagus	0	5	0
Coffee and liqueurs	0	7	6
Wax-lights and apartment	0	5	0
	£4	18	6

And I must say that the bill, considered as a bill, was moderate, but I had better have dined off that Irish stew at the club.

ARABELLA;

OR, THE MORAL OF THE "PARTIE FINE."

HEN the news came to Wagstaff that he had made a public appearance in the *New Monthly Magazine*, he affected to be in great wrath that his peccadilloes should have been laid bare to the whole nation; and was for sacrificing the individual who had held him up to ridicule. Luckily, that person was out of town for some days, so his anger had time to cool if it were real; but the truth must be told, that Lancelot Wagstaff was in heart quite delighted at being shown up for a *séducteur*, and has ordered some new waistcoats, and affects to talk very big about the French play, and has been growing a tuft to his chin ever since. Mrs. Wagstaff still continues at Bognor. Poor soul! *She* will never know whose was the portrait which figured last month in this Miscellany under the pseudonym of Wagstaff: it is only the coincidence of the new waistcoats and the sudden growth of that tuft that can by any possibility betray him.

Some critics have hinted that the scene described was immoral. So it was, there's not a doubt of it; but so is a great deal of life immoral: so are many of Hogarth's pictures immoral, if you don't choose to see their moral tendency;—nor indeed are critics to be very much blamed for not perceiving the moral of the brief tract called the Partie Fine, seeing, as it were, that it was not yet in sight. No: it was purposely kept back, as a surprise for the June number of the Magazine. This is going to be the moral paper: and I hope to goodness that Mr. Colburn's editor will not refuse it, or I shall be set down, in spite of myself, as a writer of a questionable tendency. I solemnly demand the insertion of this paper, in order to set a well-meaning man right with a public he respects. Yes, ladies, you yourselves, if you peruse these few, these very few pages, will say, " Well, although he shocked us, the man *is* a moral man after all." He is, indeed he is. Don't believe the critics who say the contrary.

The former history described to you the conduct of Wagstaff abroad. Ah, ladies! you little knew that it was preparatory to showing the monster up when *at home*. You would not have understood the wretch had you not received this previous insight into his character. If *this* be not morality, I know not what is.

Those people who at the club and elsewhere are acquainted with Mr. W. declare he is the most generous and agreeable creature that ever turned out of the city. He arrives, his jolly face beaming with good nature. He has a good word for every body, and every man a good word for him. Some Bachelor says, " Wag, my boy, there is a white-bait party at Greenwich; will you be one?" He hesitates. " I promised Mrs. Wagstaff to be home to dinner," says he; and when he says *that*, you may be sure he will go. If you propose to him a game of billiards in the afternoon, he will play till dinner, and make the most ludicrous jokes about his poor wife waiting till his return. If you ask him to smoke cigars, he will do so till morning, and goes home with a story to Mrs. W., which the poor soul receives with a desperate credulity. Once she used to sit up for him; but to continue that practice would have killed her. She goes to bed now, and Wagstaff reels in when he likes.

He is not ill-humoured. Far from it. He never says an unkind word to the children, or to the cook, or to the boy who blacks his boots, or to his wife. She wishes he would. He comes down stairs exactly three minutes before office time. He has his tea and his newspaper in bed. His eldest daughter brings the paper in, and his poor wife appears with the tea. He has a kind word for both, and scrubs the little girl's fresh cheek with his bristly beard, and laughs at the joke, and professes a prodigious interest in her lessons, and in knowing whether Miss Wiggles, the governess, is satisfied with her; and before she finishes her answer, he is deep in the folios of the *Times*, and does not care one farthing piece what the little girl says. He has promised to take the child to Astley's any time these four years. She could hardly speak when he promised it. She is a fine tall lass, and can read and write now: and though it was so long ago, has never forgotten the promise about Astley's.

When he is away from home, Wagstaff talks about his family with great affection. In the long, long days when he is away, their mother, God help her! is telling them what a good man their papa is—how kind and generous—and how busy he is—what a pity! he is obliged to work so hard and stay away from home! Poor creature, poor creature! Sure Heaven will pardon her these lies if any lies are pardonable. Whenever he says he will walk with her, Arabella dresses herself in the gown he likes, and puts on her pink bonnet, and is ready to the very minute, you may be sure. How often is it that *he* is ready at the minute? How many scores and scores of times has he left the heart-sick girl?—not forgetting her in the least—but engaged elsewhere with a game of billiards, or a jolly friend and a cigar—and perhaps wishing rather to be at home all the time—but he is *so* goodnatured, such a capital fellow! Whenever he keeps his appointment—Heaven help us! she brightens up as if it were Paradise coming to her. She looks with a triumphant air at the servant who opens the door, and round about at the neighbours' windows, as if she would have all the world know that she is walking with her husband. Every now and then as she walks (if it is but twice or thrice in a year, for Wagstaff has his business on week-days, and never gets up till one of a Sunday); every now and then as she walks with him, the delighted creature gives a skip, and squeezes his arm, and looks up in his face, she is so happy. And so is he too, for he is as goodnatured a fellow as ever breathed—and he resolves to take her out the very next Sunday—only he doesn't. Every one of these walk-days are noted down in the poor soul's little Calendar of Home as saint's days. She talks of them quite fondly; and there is not one of her female friends whom she won't visit for weeks after, and to whom she will not be sure to find some pretext for recounting the wonderful walk.

Mon dieu, ladies—all the time I was describing that affair at Durognon's, those odious French women, and their chatter, and their ogling, and their champagne, I was thinking of Arabella far away in the distance and alone—I declare, upon my honour, she was never out of my thoughts for a single minute. *She* was the moral of the Partie Fine—the simple, white-robed, spotless, meek-eyed angel of a wife—thinking about her husband—and he among the tawdry good-for-nothings, yonder! Fizz! there goes the first champagne cork, Mr. Wagstaff is making a tender speech to Madame Virginie.

At that moment Arabella is upstairs in the nursery, where the same moon is shining in, and putting her youngest boy to bed.

Bang! there goes the second cork. Virginie screams—Fitz-simons roars with laughter—Wagstaff hob-nobs with the old lady, who gives a wink and a nod. They are taking away the fish and putting down the *entrées.*

At that moment Arabella has her second child between her knees (the little one is asleep with its thumb in its mouth, and the elder even is beginning to rub her eyes over her favourite fairy tale, though she has read it many scores of times). Arabella has the child between her knees, and just as Wag is clinking his glass with the old lady in London, his wife at Bognor says something to the child, who says after her,

"*Dod bless my dear papa:*" and presently he is in bed too, and sleeps as soundly as his little sister.

And so it is that these pure blessings are sent—yearning after that fellow over his cups. Suppose they reach him? Why, the spotless things must blush and go out again from the company in which they find him. The drinking goes on, the jokes and fun get faster and faster. Arabella by this time has seen the eldest child asleep in her crib, and is looking out at the moon in silence as the children breathe round about her a soft chorus of slumber. Her mother is down stairs alone, reading " Blair's Sermons,"—a high-shouldered, hook-nosed, lean, moral woman. She wonders her daughter don't come down to tea—there is her cup quite cold, with the cream stagnant on the surface, and her work-basket by its side, with a pair of man's slippers nearly done, and one lazy scrawl from her husband, four lines only, and ten days old. But Arabella keeps away thinking, thinking, and preferring to be alone.   The girl has a sweet soft heart, and little sympathy with the mother's coarse, rigid, strong-minded nature.   The only time they quarrel is, when the old lady calls her son-in-law a brute: *then* the young one fires up and defends her own like a little Amazon.

What is this secret of love? How does it spring? How is it that no neglect can kill it? In truth, its origin and endurance are alike, utterly absurd and unreasonable.   What secret power was it that made this delicate-minded young creature; who had been bred up upon the purest doctrines of the sainted Mrs. Chapone; who had never thought about love; who, simple soul, had been utterly absorbed in her little daily duties, her pianoforte practice, her French lesson, her use-of-the-globes, her canary bird, and her Mangnall's questions—what, I say is it, that makes this delicate girl all of a sudden expand into a passion of love for a young sugar-baker, simply because she meets him three times riding a gray mare on Clapham Common, and afterwards (the sly rogue!) on half-a-dozen occasions at her aunt's at tea? What is it that makes her feel that that young sugar-baker is the fatal man with whom her existence is bound up: go through fire and water to marry him: love him in spite of neglect and indifference: adore him so absurdly, that a half-hour's kindness from him more than balances a month's brutality! O, mystery of woman's heart! I declare all this lies in the moral of the *Partie Fine.*

Wagstaff, so splendid with his dinners and so generous on himself, is not so generous at home. He pays the bills with only a few oaths; but somehow he leaves his wife without money. He will give it to anybody rather than to her: a fact of which he himself is, very likely, unaware at this minute, or of the timidity of his wife in asking for it.   In order to avoid this asking, the poor girl goes through unheard of economies, and performs the most curious tricks of avarice. She dresses herself for nothing, and she dresses her children out of her own frocks.   Certain dimities, caps, pinafores, and other fallals have gone through the family; and Arabella, though she sees ever such a pretty thing in a shop-window, will pass on with a sigh; whereas her Lancelot is a perfect devourer of waistcoats, and never sets his eyes on a flaring velvet that strikes his fancy, but you will be sure to behold him the next week swaggering about in the garment in Pall Mall. Women are ever practising these petty denials, about which the Lords of the Creation never think.

I will tell you what I once saw Arabella doing. She is a woman of very high breeding, and no inconsiderable share of family pride: well, one day on going to Wagstaff's house, who had invited a party of us to Blackwall, about a bet he had lost, I was, in the master's absence, ushered into the drawing-room, which is furnished very fine, and there sat the lady of the house at her work-table, with her child prattling at her knee.

I could not understand what made Mrs. Wagstaff blush so— look so entirely guilty of something or other—fidget, answer *à travers*, and receive an old friend in this strange and inhospitable way.

She, the descendant of the Smiths of Smithfield, of the Browns of Brown Hall, the proud daughter of the aristocracy, *was making a pair of trousers for her eldest son.* She huddled them away hastily under a pillow—but bah! we have keen eyes —and from under that pillow the buttons peeped out, and with those buttons the secret—they were white ducks—Wagstaff's white ducks—his wife was making them into white ducklings for little Fred.

The sight affected me. I should like to have cried, only it is unmanly; and to cry about a pair of little breeches!—I should like to have seized hold of Mrs. Wagstaff and hugged her to my heart: but she would have screamed, and rung for John to show me down stairs; so I disguised my feelings by treading on the tail of her spaniel dog, whose squealing caused a diversion.

But I shall never forget those breeches. What! Wagstaff is flaunting in a coat of Nugee's, and his son has that sweet, humble tailor. Wagstaff is preparing for Blackwall, and here is his wife plying her gentle needle. Wagstaff feasts off plate and frothing wine; and Arabella sits down to cold mutton in the nursery, with her little ones ranged about her. Wagstaff enjoys,

Arabella suffers. He flings about his gold; and she tries to stave off evil days by little savings of meek pence. Wagstaff sins and she forgives—and trusts, and loves, and hopes on in spite of carelessness, and coldness, and neglect, and extravagance, and—and *Parties Fines.*

This is the moral of the last story. O, ye Wagstaffs of this world, profit by it. O, ye gentle, meek angels of Arabellas, be meek and gentle still. If an angel can't reclaim a man, who can? And I live in hopes of hearing that by the means of that charming mediation, the odious Lancelot has become a reformed character.

TITMARSH.

CARLYLE'S FRENCH REVOLUTION.*

[1837.]

INCE the appearance of this work, within the last two months, it has raised among the critics and the reading public a strange storm of applause and discontent. To hear one party you would fancy the author was but a dull madman, indulging in wild vagaries of language and dispensing with common sense and reason, while, according to another, his opinions are little short of inspiration, and his eloquence unbounded as his genius. We confess, that in reading the first few pages, we were not a little inclined to adopt the former opinion, and yet, after perusing the whole of this extraordinary work, we can allow, almost to their fullest extent, the high qualities with which Mr. Carlyle's idolators endow him.

But never did a book sin so grievously from outward appearance, or a man's style so mar his subject and dim his genius. It is stiff, short, and rugged, it abounds with Germanisms and Latinisms, strange epithets, and choking double words, astonishing to the admirers of simple Addisonian English, to those who love history as it gracefully runs in Hume, or struts pompously in Gibbon—no such style is Mr. Carlyle's. A man, at the first onset, must take breath at the end of a sentence, or, worse still, go to sleep in the midst of it. But these hardships become lighter as the traveller grows accustomed to the road, and he speedily learns to admire and sympathise; just as he would

---

* *The French Revolution: A History.* In three volumes. By Thomas Carlyle. London : James Fraser, 1837.

admire a Gothic cathedral in spite of the quaint carvings and hideous images on door and buttress.

There are, however, a happy few of Mr. Carlyle's critics and readers to whom these very obscurities and mysticisms of style are welcome and almost intelligible ; the initiated in metaphysics, the sages who have passed the veil of Kantian philosophy, and discovered that the "critique of pure reason" is really that which it purports to be, and not the critique of pure nonsense, as it seems to worldly men : to these the present book has charms unknown to us, who can merely receive it as a history of a stirring time, and a skilful record of men's worldly thoughts and doings. Even through these dim spectacles a man may read and profit much from Mr. Carlyle's volumes.

He is not a party historian like Scott, who could not, in his benevolent respect for rank and royalty, see duly the faults of either : he is as impartial as Thiers, but with a far loftier and nobler impartiality.

No man can have read the admirable history of the French ex-Minister who has not been struck with this equal justice which he bestows on all the parties or heroes of his book. He has completely mastered the active part of the history : he has no more partiality for court than for regicide—scarcely a movement of intriguing king or republican which is unknown to him or undescribed. He sees with equal eyes Madame Roland or Marie Antoinette—bullying Brunswick on the frontier, or Marat at his butcher's work or in his cellar—he metes to each of them justice, and no more, finding good even in butcher Marat or bullying Brunswick, and recording what he finds. What a pity that one gains such a complete contempt for the author of all this cleverness ! Only a rogue could be so impartial, for Thiers but views this awful series of circumstances in their very meanest and basest light, like a petty, clever statesman as he is, watching with wonderful accuracy all the moves of the great game, but looking for no more, never drawing a single moral from it, or seeking to tell aught beyond it.

Mr. Carlyle, as we have said, is as impartial as the illustrious Academician and Minister ; but with what different eyes he looks upon the men and the doings of this strange time ! To

the one the whole story is but a hustling for places—a list of
battles and intrigues—of kings and governments rising and
falling; to the other, the little actors of this great drama are
striving but towards a great end and moral. It is better to
view it loftily from afar, like our mystic poetic Mr. Carlyle, than
too nearly with sharp-sighted and prosaic Thiers. Thiers is the
valet de chambre of this history, he is too familiar with its dis-
habille and off-scourings: it can never be a hero to him.

It is difficult to convey to the reader a fair notion of Mr.
Carlyle's powers or his philosophy, for the reader has not grown
familiar with the strange style of this book, and may laugh
perhaps at the grotesqueness of his teacher: in this some honest
critics of the present day have preceded him, who have formed
their awful judgments after scanning half a dozen lines, and
damned poor Mr. Carlyle's because they chanced to be lazy.
Here, at hazard, however, we fall upon the story of the Bastille
capture; the people are thundering at the gates, but Delaunay
will receive no' terms, raises his drawbridge and gives fire.
Now, cries Mr. Carlyle with an uncouth Orson-like shout :—

" Bursts forth Insurrection, at sight of its own blood, into
endless explosion of musketry, distraction, execration;—and
over head, from the Fortress, let one great gun go booming, to
shew what we *could* do. The Bastille is besieged !

" On, then, all Frenchmen that have hearts in their bodies !
Roar with all your throats, of cartilage and metal, ye Sons of
Liberty; stir spasmodically whatsoever of utmost faculty is in
you, soul, body, or spirit; for it is the hour ! Smite, thou Louis
Tournay, cartwright of the Marais, old-soldier of the Regiment
Dauphiné; smite at that Outer Drawbridge-chain, though the
fiery hail whistles round thee ! Never, over nave or felloe, did thy
axe strike such a stroke. Down with it, man; down with it to
Orcus : let the whole accursed Edifice sink thither, and Tyranny
be swallowed up for ever ! Mounted, some say, on the roof of
the guard-room, Louis Tournay smites, brave Aubin Bonnemère
(also an old soldier) seconding him : the chain yields, breaks;
the huge Drawbridge slams down, thundering. Glorious: and yet,
alas, it is still but the outworks. The Eight grim Towers, with
their Invalides, musketry, their paving stones and cannon-mouths,

still soar aloft intact ;—Ditch yawning impassable, stone-faced ; the inner Drawbridge with its *back* towards us : the Bastille is still to take !"

Did " Savage Rosa" ever " dash" a more spirited battle sketch ? The two principal figures of the pieces, placed in skilful relief, the raging multitude and sombre fortress admirably laid down ! In the midst of this writhing and wrestling, "the line too labours (Mr. Carlyle's line labours perhaps too often), and the words move slow." The whole story of the fall of the fortress and its defenders is told in a style similarly picturesque and real.

" The poor Invalides have sunk under their battlements, or rise only with reversed muskets : they have made a white flag of napkins ; go beating the *chamade*, or seeming to beat, for one can hear nothing. The very Swiss at the Portcullis look weary of firing ; disheartened in the fire-deluge ; a porthole at the draw-bridge is opened, as by one that would speak. See Huissier Maillard, the shifty man ! On his plank, swinging over the abyss of that stone-Ditch ; plank resting on parapet, balanced by weight of Patriots,—he hovers perilous : such a Dove towards such an Ark ! Deftly, thou shifty Usher : one man already fell ; and lies smashed, far down there against the masonry ! Usher Maillard falls not : deftly, unerring he walks, with out-spread palm. The Swiss holds a paper through his porthole ; the shifty Usher snatches it, and returns. Terms of surrender : Pardon, immunity to all ! Are they accepted ? ' *Foi d'officier*, on the word of an officer,' answers half-pay Hulin,—or half-pay Elie, for men do not agree on it, " they are." Sinks the drawbridge,— Usher Maillard bolting it when down ; rushes-in the living deluge : the Bastille is fallen ! *Victoire ! La Bastille est prise !*"

This is prose run mad—no doubt of it—according to our notions of the sober gait and avocations of homely prose ; but is there not method in it, and could sober prose have described the incident in briefer words, more emphatically, or more sensibly ? And this passage, which succeeds the picture of storm and slaughter, opens (grotesque though it be), not in prose, but in noble poetry, the author describes the rest of France during the acting of this Paris tragedy—and by this peaceful image admirably heightens the gloom and storm of his first description :—

"O evening sun of July, how, at this hour, thy beams fall slant on reapers amid peaceful woody fields ; on old women spinning in cottages ; on ships far out in the silent main ; on Balls at the Orangerie of Versailles, where high-rouged Dames are even now dancing with double-jacketted Hussar-Officers, and also on this roaring Hell-porch of a Hôtel-de-Ville ! One forest of distracted steel bristles, in front of an Electoral Committee ; points itself, in horrid radii, against this and the other accused breast. It was the Titans warring with Olympus ; and they, scarcely crediting it, have *conquered*." The reader will smile at the double-jackets and rouge, which never would be allowed entrance into a polite modern epic, but, familiar though they be, they complete the picture, and give it reality, that gloomy rough Rembrandt-kind of reality which is Mr. Carlyle's style of historic painting.

In this same style Mr. Carlyle dashes off the portraits of his various characters as they rise in the course of the history. Take, for instance, this grotesque portrait of vapouring Tonneau Mirabeau, his life and death ; it follows a solemn, almost awful picture of the demise of his great brother :—

"Here, then, the wild Gabriel Honoré drops from the tissue of our History ; not without a tragic farewell. He is gone : the flower of the wild Riquetti kindred ; which seems as if in him it had done its best, and then expired, or sunk down to the undistinguished level. Crabbed old Marquis Mirabeau, the Friend of Men, sleeps sound. Barrel Mirabeau gone across the Rhine ; his Regiment of Emigrants will drive nigh desperate. 'Barrel Mirabeau,' says a biographer of his, 'went indignantly across the Rhine, and drilled Emigrant Regiments. But as he sat one morning in his tent, sour of stomach doubtless and of heart, meditating in Tartarean humour on the turn things took, a certain Captain or Subaltern demanded admittance on business. Such Captain is refused ; he again demands, with refusal ; and then again, till Colonel Viscount Barrel-Mirabeau, blazing up into a mere brandy barrel, clutches his sword and tumbles out on this *canaille* of an intruder,—alas, on the *canaille* of an intruder's sword's point, who had drawn with swift dexterity; and dies, and the Newspapers name it *apoplexy* and *alarming accident.* So die the Mirabeaus."

Mr. Carlyle gives this passage to "a biographer," but he himself must be the author of this History of a Tub; the grim humour and style belong only to him. In a graver strain he speaks of Gabriel:—

"New Mirabeaus one hears not of: the wild kindred, as we said, is gone out with this its greatest. As families and kindreds sometimes do; producing, after long ages of unnoted notability, some living quintessence of all they had, to flame forth as a man world-noted; after whom they rest, as if exhausted; the sceptre passing to others. The chosen Last of the Mirabeaus is gone; the chosen man of France is gone. It was he who shook old France from its basis; and, as if with his single hand, has held it toppling there, still unfallen. What things depended on that one man! He is as a ship suddenly shivered on sunk rocks: much swims on the waste waters, far from help."

Here is a picture of *the* heroine of the Revolution :—"Radiant with enthusiasm are those dark eyes, is that strong Minerva-face, looking dignity and earnest joy; joyfullest she where all are joyful. Reader, mark that queen-like burgher-woman : beautiful, Amazonian-graceful to the eye; more so to the mind. Unconscious of her worth (as all worth is), of her greatness, of her crystal clearness; genuine, the creature of Sincerity and Nature in an age of Artificiality, Pollution, and Cant ; there, in her still completeness, in her still invincibility, *she,* if thou knew it, is the noblest of all living Frenchwomen,—and will be seen, one day."

The reader, we think, will not fail to observe the real beauty which lurks among all these odd words and twisted sentences, living, as it were, in spite of the weeds ; but we repeat, that no mere extracts can do justice to the book ; it requires time and study. A first acquaintance with it is very unprepossessing; only familiarity knows its great merits, and values it accordingly.

We would gladly extract a complete chapter or episode from the work—the flight to Varennes, for instance, the huge coach bearing away the sleepy, dawdling, milk-sop royalty of France ;

fiery Bouillé spreading abroad his scouts and Hussars, "his
electric thunder-chain of military out-posts," as Mr. Carlyle
calls them with one of his great similes. Paris in tremendous
commotion, the country up and armed, to prevent the King's
egress, the chance of escape glimmering bright until the last
moment, and only extinguished by bewildered Louis himself,
too pious and too out-of-breath, too hungry and sleepy, to make
one charge at the head of those gallant dragoons—one single
blow to win crown and kingdom and liberty again! We never
read this hundred-times told tale with such a breathless interest
as Mr. Carlyle has managed to instil into it. The whole of the
sad story is equally touching and vivid, from the mean ignominious return down to the fatal 10th of August, when the
sections beleaguered the King's palace, and King Louis, with arms,
artillery, and 2,000 true and gallant men, flung open the Tuileries
gates and said *"Marchons! marchons!"* whither? Not with
vive le Roi, and roaring guns, and bright bayonets, sheer through
the rabble who barred the gate, swift through the broad Champs
Elysées, and the near barrier,—not to conquer or fall like a
King and gentleman, but to the reporters' box in the National
Assembly, to be cooped and fattened until killing time; to die
trussed and tranquil like a fat capon. What a son for St. Louis!
What a husband for brave Antoinette!

Let us, however, follow Mr. Carlyle to the last volume, and
passing over the time, when, in Danton's awful image, "coalized
Kings made war upon France, and France, as a gage of battle,
flung the head of a King at their feet," quote two of the last
scenes of that awful tragedy, the deaths of bold Danton and
"sea-green" Robespierre, as Carlyle delights to call him.

"On the night of the 30th of March, Juryman Pâris came
rushing in; haste looking through his eyes: a clerk of the *Salut*
Committee had told him Danton's warrant was made out, he is to
be arrested this very night! Entreaties there are and trepida-
tion, of poor Wife, of Pâris and Friends: Danton sat silent for a
while; then answered, '*Ils n'oseraient*, They dare not'; and
would take no measures. Murmuring 'They dare not,' he
goes to sleep as usual.

"And yet, on the morrow morning, strange rumour spreads

over Paris city : Danton, Camille, Phélippeaux, Lacroix, have been arrested over night ! It is verily so : the corridors of the Luxembourg were all crowded, Prisoners crowding forth to see this giant of the Revolution enter among them. 'Messieurs,' said Danton politely, 'I hoped soon to have got you all out of this: but here I am myself ; and one sees not where it will end.'— Rumour may spread over Paris : the Convention clusters itself into groups ; wide-eyed, whispering, 'Danton arrested !' Who then is safe ? Legendre, mounting the Tribune, utters, at his own peril, a feeble word for him ; moving that he be heard at that Bar before indictment ; but Robespierre frowns him down : ' Did you hear Chabot, or Bazire ? Would you have two weights and measures ? ' Legendre cowers low ; Danton, like the others, must take his doom.

" Danton's Prison-thoughts were curious to have ; but are not given in any quantity : indeed few such remarkable men have been left so obscure to us as this Titan of the Revolution.   He was heard to ejaculate : 'This time twelvemonth, I was moving the creation of that same Revolutionary Tribunal. I crave pardon for it of God and man. They are all Brothers Cain : Briscot would have had me guillotined as Robespierre now will. I leave the whole business in a frightful welter (*gâchis épouvantable*) : not one of them understands anything of government. Robespierre will follow me ; I drag down Robespierre. O, it were better to be a poor fisherman than to meddle with governing of men.'—Camille's young beautiful Wife, who had made him rich not in money alone, hovers round the Luxembourg, like a disembodied spirit, day and night. Camille's stolen letters to her still exist ; stained with the mark of his tears. 'I carry my head like a Saint-Sacrament ? ' So Saint Just was heard to mutter : ' Perhaps he will carry his like a Saint-Dennis.'

" Unhappy Danton, thou still unhappier light Camille, once light *Procureur de la Lanterne*, ye also have arrived, then, at the Bourne of Creation, where, like Ulysses Polytlas at the limit and utmost Gades of his voyage, gazing into that dim Waste beyond Creation, a man does see *the Shade of his Mother*, pale, ineffectual; —and days when his Mother nursed and wrapped him are all-too sternly contrasted with this day ! Danton, Camille, Hérault,

Westermann, and the others, very strangely massed up with Bazires, Swindler Chabots, Fabre d'Eglantines, Banker Freys, a most motley Batch, ' *Fournée* ' as such things will be called, stand ranked at the bar of Tinville.   It is the 2d of April 1794.   Danton has had but three days to lie in Prison ; for the time presses.

" ' What is your name ? place of abode ? ' and the like, Fouquier asks ; according to formality.   ' My name is Danton,' answers he ; 'a name tolerably known in the Revolution : my abode will soon be Annihilation (*dans le Néant*) ; but I shall live in the Pantheon of History.'   A man will endeavour to say something forcible, be it by nature or not !   Hérault mentions epigrammatically that he ' sat in this Hall, and was detested of Parlementeers.'   Camille makes answer, ' My age is that of the *bon Sansculotte Jésus* ; an age fatal to Revolutionists.'   O Camille, Camille !   And yet in that Divine Transaction, let us say, there did lie, among other things, the fatallest Reproof ever uttered here below to Worldly Right-honourableness ; ' the highest Fact,' so devout Novalis calls it, ' in the Rights of Man.'   Camille's real age, it would seem, is thirty-four.   Danton is one year older.

" Some five months ago, the Trial of the Twenty-two Girondins was the greatest that Fouquier had then done.   But here is a still greater to do ; a thing which tasks the whole faculty of Fouquier ; which makes the very heart of him waver.   For it is the voice of Danton that reverberates now from these domes ; in passionate words, piercing with their wild sincerity, winged with wrath. Your best Witnesses he shivers into ruin at one stroke.   He demands that the Committee-men themselves come as Witnesses, as Accusers ; he ' will cover them with ignominy.'   He raises his huge stature, he shakes his huge black head, fire flashes from the eyes of him,—piercing to all Republican hearts : so that the very Galleries, though we filled them by ticket, murmur sym- pathy ; and are like to burst down, and raise the People, and deliver him !   He complains loudly that he is classed with Chabots, with swindling Stockjobbers ; that his Indictment is a list of platitudes and horrors.   ' Danton hidden on the Tenth of August ? ' reverberates he, with the roar of a lion in the toils : ' Where are the men that had to press Danton to shew himself,

that day? Where are these high-gifted souls of whom he
borrowed energy? Let them appear, these Accusers of mine: I
have all the clearness of my self-possession when I demand
them. I will unmask the three shallow scoundrels,' *les trois plats
coquins*, Saint-Just, Couthon, Lebas, 'who fawn on Robespierre,
and lead him towards his destruction. Let them produce themselves here; I will plunge them into Nothingness, out of which
they ought never to have risen.' The agitated President agitates
his bell; enjoins calmness, in a vehement manner : 'What is it
to thee how I defend myself?' cries the other; 'the right of
dooming me is thine always. The voice of a man speaking for
his honour and his life may well drown the jingling of thy bell!'
Thus Danton, higher and higher; till the lion voice of him 'dies
away in his throat:' speech will not utter what is in that man.
The Galleries murmur ominously; the first day's Session is over."

*   *   *   *   *

"Danton carried a high look in the Death-cart. Not so
Camille: it is but one week, and all is so topsy-turvied; angel
Wife left weeping; love, riches, Revolutionary fame, left all at
the Prison-gate; carnivorous Rabble now howling round. Palp-
able, and yet incredible; like a madman's dream! Camille
struggles and writhes; his shoulders shuffle the loose coat off
them, which hangs knotted, the hands tied : 'Calm, my friend,'
said Danton, 'heed not that vile canaille (*laissez là cette vile
canaille*).' At the foot of the Scaffold, Danton was heard to
ejaculate, 'O my Wife, my well-beloved, I shall never see thee
more then!'—but, interrupting himself : 'Danton, no weakness!'
He said to Hérault-Séchelles stepping forward to embrace him :
'Our heads will meet *there*,' in the Headsman's sack. His last
words were to Samson the Headsman himself, 'Thou wilt shew
my head to the people; it is worth shewing.'

"So passes, like a gigantic mass, of valour, ostentation, fury,
affection, and wild revolutionary manhood, this Danton, to his
unknown home. He was of Arcis-sur-Aube; born of 'good
farmer-people' there. He had many sins; but one worst sin
he had not, that of Cant. No hollow Formalist, deceptive and
self-deceptive, *ghastly* to the natural sense, was this; but a very
Man : with all his dross he was a Man; fiery-real, from the great

fire-bosom of Nature herself. He saved France from Brunswick ; he walked straight his own wild road, whither it led him. He may live for some generations in the memory of men."

This noble passage requires no comment, nor does that in which the poor wretched Robespierre shrieks his last shriek, and dies his pitiful and cowardly death. Tallien has drawn his theatrical dagger, and made his speech, trembling Robespierre has fled to the Hôtel de Ville, and Henriot, of the National Guard, clatters through the city, summoning the sections to the aid of the people's friend.

"About three in the morning, the dissident Armed-forces have *met.* Henriot's Armed Force stood ranked in the Place de Grève ; and now Barras's, which he has recruited, arrives there ; and they front each other, cannon bristling against cannon. Citoyens! cries the voice of Discretion loudly enough, Before coming to bloodshed, to endless civil-war, hear the Convention Decree read :—' Robespierre and all rebels Out of Law!' Out of Law? There is terror in the sound : unarmed Citoyens disperse rapidly home ; Municipal Cannoneers range themselves on the Convention side, with shouting. At which shout, Henriot descends from his upper room, far gone in drink as some say ; finds his Place de Grève empty ; the cannons' mouth turned *towards* him ; and, on the whole,—that it is now the catastrophe!

"Stumbling in again, the wretched drunk-sobered Henriot announces: 'All is lost!' '*Misérable!* it is thou that hast lost it,' cry they; and fling him, or else he flings himself, out of window : far enough down ; into masonwork and horror of cesspool ; not into death but worse. Augustin Robespierre follows him ; with the like fate. Saint-Just called on Lebas to kill him ; who would not. Couthon crept under a table ; attempting to kill himself ; not doing it.—On entering that Sanhedrim of Insurrection, we find all as good as extinct ; undone, ready for seizure. Robespierre was sitting on a chair, with pistol-shot blown through, not his head, but his under jaw ; the suicidal hand had failed. With prompt zeal, not without trouble, we gather these wrecked Conspirators ; fish up even Henriot and Augustin, bleeding and foul ; pack them all, rudely enough, into carts; and shall, before sunrise, have them safe under lock and key. Amid shoutings and embracings.

"Robespierre lay in an anteroom of the Convention Hall, while his Prison-escort was getting ready; the mangled jaw bound up rudely with bloody linen : a spectacle to men. He lies stretched on a table, a deal-box his pillow; the sheath of the pistol is still clenched convulsively in his hand. Men bully him, insult him : his eyes still indicate intelligence; he speaks no word. 'He had on the sky-blue coat he had got made for the Feast of the *Être Suprême*'—O reader, can thy hard heart hold out against that ? His trousers were nankeen; the stockings had fallen down over the ancles. He spake no word more in this world."

*   *   *   *   *

"The Death-tumbrils, with their motley Batch of Outlaws, some Twenty-three or so, from Maximilien to Mayor Fleuriot and Simon the Cordwainer, roll on. All eyes are on Robespierre's Tumbril, where he, his jaw bound in dirty linen, with his half-dead Brother, and half-dead Henriot, lie shattered, their 'seventeen hours' of agony about to end. The Gendarmes point their swords at him, to shew the people which is he. A woman springs on the Tumbril; clutching the side of it with one hand; waving the other Sibyl-like; and exclaims, 'The death of thee gladdens my very heart, *m'enivre de joie;*' Robespierre opened his eyes; '*Scélérat*, go down to Hell, with the curses of all wives and mothers !'—At the foot of the scaffold, they stretched him on the ground till his turn came. Lifted aloft, his eyes again opened ; caught the bloody axe. Samson wrenched the coat off him ; wrenched the dirty linen from his jaw : the jaw fell powerless, there burst from him a cry ;—hideous to hear and see. Samson, thou canst not be too quick !

"Samson's work done, there bursts forth shout on shout of applause. Shout, which prolongs itself not only over Paris, but over France, but over Europe, and down to this Generation. Deservedly, and also undeservedly. O, unhappiest Advocate of Arras, wert thou worse than other Advocates ? Stricter man, according to his Formula, to his Credo, and his Cant, of probities, benevolences, pleasures-of-virtue, and such like, lived not in that age. A man fitted, in some luckier settled age, to have become one of those incorruptible barren Pattern-Figures, and have had marble-tablets and funeral-sermons! His poor landlord, the Cabinet-maker in the Rue Saint-Honoré, loved him; his Brother died for him. May God be merciful to him, and to us!"

The reader will see in the above extracts most of the faults, and a few of the merits, of this book. He need not be told that it is written in an eccentric prose, here and there disfigured by grotesque conceits and images; but, for all this, it betrays most extraordinary powers—learning, observation, and humour. Above all, it has no CANT. It teems with sound, hearty, philosophy (besides certain transcendentalisms which we do not pretend to understand), it possesses genius, if any book ever did. It wanted no more for keen critics to cry fie upon it! Clever critics who have such an eye for genius, that when Mr. Bulwer published his forgotten book concerning Athens, they discovered that no historian was like to him; that he, on his Athenian hobby, had quite out-trotted stately Mr. Gibbon: and with the same creditable unanimity they cried down Mr. Carlyle's history, opening upon it a hundred little piddling sluices of small wit, destined to wash the book sheer away; and lo! the book remains, it is only the poor wit which has run dry.

We need scarcely recommend this book and its timely appearance, now that some of the questions solved in it seem almost likely to be battled over again. The hottest Radical in England may learn by it that there is something more necessary for him even than his mad liberty—the authority, namely, by which he retains his head on his shoulders and his money in his pocket, which privileges that by-word " liberty " is often unable to secure for him. It teaches (by as strong examples as ever taught any thing) to rulers and to ruled alike moderation, and yet there are many who would react the same dire tragedy, and repeat the experiment tried in France so fatally. " No Peers—no Bishops—no property qualification—no restriction of suffrage." Mr. Leader bellows it out at Westminster and Mr. Roebuck croaks it at Bath. Pert quacks at public meetings joke about hereditary legislators, journalists gibe at them, and moody starving labourers, who do not know how to jest, but can hate lustily, are told to curse crowns and coronets as the origin of their woes and their poverty, and so did the clever French spouters and journalists gibe at royalty, until royalty fell poisoned under their satire; and so did the screaming hungry French mob curse royalty until they overthrew it: and to what end ? To bring tyranny and leave starvation, battering down Bastilles to erect guillotines, and murdering kings to set up emperors in their stead.

We do not say that in our own country similar excesses are to be expected or feared; the cause of complaint has never been so great, the wrong has never been so crying on the part of the rulers, as to bring down such fearful retaliation from the governed. Mr. Roebuck is not Robespierre, and Mr. Attwood, with his threatened legion of fiery Marseillois, is at best but a Brummagem Barbaroux. But men alter with circumstances; six months before the kingly *déchéance*, the bitter and bilious advocate of Arras spake with tears in his eyes about good King Louis, and the sweets and merits of constitutional monarchy and hereditary representation : and so he spoke, until his own turn came, and his own delectable guillotining system had its hour. God forbid that we should pursue the simile with Mr. Roebuck so far as this; God forbid, too, that he ever should have the trial.

True; but we have no right, it is said, to compare the Republicanism of England with that of France, no right to suppose that such crimes would be perpetrated in a country so enlightened as ours. Why is there peace and liberty and a republic in America ? No guillotining, no ruthless Yankee tribunes retaliating for bygone tyranny by double oppression ? Surely the reason is obvious—because there was no hunger in America; because there were easier ways of livelihood than those offered by ambition. Banish Queen, and Bishops, and Lords, seize the lands, open the ports, or shut them, (according to the fancy of your trades' unions and democratic clubs, who have each their freaks and hobbies,) and are you a whit richer in a month, are your poor Spitalfields men vending their silks, or your poor Irishmen reaping their harvests at home ? Strong interest keeps Americans quiet, not Government; here there is always a party which is interested in rebellion. People America like England and the poor weak rickety republic is jostled to death in the crowd. Give us this republic to-morrow and it would share no better fate ; have not all of us the power, and many of us the interest, to destroy it ?

ELIZABETH BROWNRIGGE: A TALE.

DEDICATED TO THE AUTHOR OF " EUGENE ARAM, A NOVEL."

Φεῦ, φεῦ τι προσδερξεσθε μ᾽ ὄμμασιν, τεκνα ;
Τι προσγελᾶτε τον παννστατον γεδων
Αἰ, αἰ, τι δρασω ;   *   *   *
᾽Εασον αἰτας, ὦ ταλαν, φεῖσαι τεκνων.

EURIPIDIS Medea.

DEDICATION.

To the Author of " Eugene Aram."

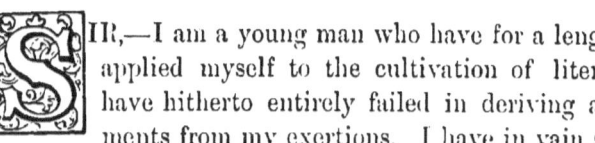

IR,—I am a young man who have for a length of time applied myself to the cultivation of literature, and have hitherto entirely failed in deriving any emoluments from my exertions. I have in vain supplicated the magnates of every theatre in the metropolis with the offerings of my tragedies and comedies, my operas and farces ; and I have suffered reiterated rejections of my novels, poems, and romances, from every publisher who flourishes between the two opposite points of Paternoster Row and Albemarle Street. In despair of ever finding a vent for my lucubrations, and alarmed at the heaps of unprofitable MSS. which have been daily growing larger and larger upon my shelves, I sat myself down one evening about a fortnight ago, and spread out before me all the many cold and civil letters of refusal which I had received from different managers and booksellers, with a view of comparing their contents, and endeavouring to elicit the cause to which the universally unfavourable reception of my works was to be ascribed. As my eyes glanced along the ranks of the letters which I had disposed in parade order on my writing-table, I was surprised to find that the very identical phrase occurred in every one of ·them : managers of major or of minor theatres, publishers of every grade of fashion, and of every quarter of the metropolis, were all unanimous in expressing their approbation of the talent exhibited in my productions. My dramatic efforts, whether in five acts or in two, would doubtless have succeeded some ten years ago; but, unhappily, they were not of a "*popular description;*"—my poems were classical, pure in taste, perfect in diction; but most unhappily, were not, at present, of a "*popular description;*"—my novels were "just in character, interesting in plot, pathetic, unexcep-tionable in sentiment; but, unhappily, they were not of a *popular description.*" The letters, in fact, informed me that my literary exertions possessed every merit, except the one essential and only merit which is really valued by the dealer in such commodities—the merit of suiting the reigning taste of the public. Having arrived at this discovery, my hopes revived. "Those who write to live," I exclaimed, "must write to please!" I resolved to apply myself, on the instant, to the reformation of my mode of composition. I tied up my former works in separate parcels, and deposited them in my trunks and closets, to await a change of fashion in the reading world; and sending my laundress to the circulating library for the last most popular novel, I deter-mined to study its style and manner, to investigate the principles on which it was written, to imbibe its spirit, and to compose my next new work as nearly as possible upon its model. Sir, the volumes which were brought to me were those of *Eugene Aram.*

Before I had read a hundred pages of that most extraordinary production, the errors and defects of my own efforts were made apparent to me. From the frequent perusal of older works of imagination, I had learnt so to weave the incidents of my story as to interest the feelings of the reader in favour of virtue, and to increase his detestation of vice. I have been taught by *Eugene Aram* to mix vice and virtue up together in such an inextricable confusion as to render it impossible that any preference should be given to either, or that the one, indeed,

should be at all distinguishable from the other. I had hitherto
sought to give an agreeable view of life, to inspire contented
dispositions towards the existing institutions of society, and to
leave a calm and pleasing impression upon the mind. But I
have been wrong: this was evidently an *unpopular* proceeding;
for nothing can be more painful than the recollections that
remain after the perusal of your volumes, in which " whatever
is " is sneered at as being wrong, and nothing is eulogised but
" what is *not.*"   I had, in all my former works, endeavoured to
draw my characters in correspondence with the general principles
of nature, and the ordinary effects of education and circumstances upon them ; but you, sir, I perceive, have taken a course
diametrically opposite to this, and delight in imagining and
representing the exceptions.   A learned friend of mine has
considered you as an eminent disciple of the " intensity school "
of novel-writers ; but in this I cannot agree with him.   *Eugene
Aram* has certainly many qualities in common with the Anglo-
German style of Mr. Godwin's followers ; but I cannot help
thinking that your rank in literature is of a higher grade than
that which any mere disciple can ever hope to reach.   I am
inclined to regard you as an original discoverer in the world of
literary enterprise, and to reverence you as the father of a new
" *lusus naturæ* school."   There is no other title by which your
manner could be so aptly designated.   I am told, for instance,
that in a former work, having to paint an adulterer, you described
him as belonging to the class of country curates, among whom,
perhaps, such a criminal is not met with once in a hundred
years; while, on the contrary, being in search of a tender-
hearted, generous, sentimental, high-minded hero of romance,
you turned to the pages of *The Newgate Calendar*, and looked
for him in the list of men who have cut throats for money,
among whom a person in possession of such qualities could
never have been met with at all.   Wanting a shrewd, selfish,
worldly, calculating valet, you describe him as an old soldier,
though he bears not a single trait of the character which might
have been moulded by a long course of military service, but, on
the contrary, is marked by all the distinguishing features of a
bankrupt attorney or a lame duck from the Stock Exchange.

Having to paint a cat, you endow her with the idiosyncrasies of a dog.

In the following tale I have attempted to pursue the same path—*longo intervallo*, certainly—and to class myself as a diligent and admiring disciple of "the *lusus naturæ* school." It will be my sole ambition to impart to my future efforts some portion of the intense interest that distinguishes your works, and to acquire the fame which the skilful imitation of so great a master as yourself may hope to receive from the generosity of an enlightened and delighted public. In taking my subject from that walk of life to which you had directed my attention, many motives conspired to fix my choice on the heroine of the ensuing tale : she is a classic personage—her name has been already "linked to immortal verse" by the muse of Canning.* Besides, it is extraordinary that, as you had commenced a tragedy under the title of *Eugene Aram*, I had already sketched a burletta with the title of *Elizabeth Brownrigge*. I had, indeed, in my dramatic piece, been guilty of an egregious and unpardonable

---

* In the "Inscription for the door of the cell in Newgate, where Mrs. Brownrigg, the Prentice-cide, was confined previous to her execution," published in the *Poetry of the Anti-Jacobin* :—

> " For one long term, or ere her trial came,
> Here Brownrigg linger'd. Often have these cells
> Echo'd her blasphemies, as with shrill voice
> She scream'd for fresh geneva. Not to her
> Did the blithe fields of Tothill, or thy street,
> St. Giles, its fair varieties expand,
> Till at the last, in slow-drawn cart, she went,
> To execution. Dost thou ask her crime ?
> SHE WHIPP'D TWO FEMALE PRENTICES TO DEATH,
> AND HID THEM IN THE COAL-HOLE."

Then follow the lines quoted as one of the headings to Chapter III. (*infra*, p. 141), and the " Inscription " thus concludes :—

> " For this act
> Did Brownrigg swing. Harsh laws ! But time shall come,
> When France shall reign, and laws be all repeal'd !"

The lines, which were the joint production of Canning and Frere, originally appeared in the first number of the *Anti-Jacobin*, Nov. 20, 1797.

ED.

error: I had attempted to excite the sympathies of the audience
in favour of the murdered apprentices, but your novel has disabused me of so vulgar a prejudice, and, in my present version
of her case, all the, interest of the reader and all the pathetic
powers of the author will be engaged on the side of the murderess.   I have taken a few slight liberties with the story, but
such alterations have the sanction of your example and the
recommendation of your authority.   As you have omitted any
mention of the wife of your Eugene, I have not thought it
necessary to recall the reader's attention to the husband and
children of my Elizabeth.   As you have given your hero more
learning and virtue than he possessed, and converted the usher
of a grammar-school at Hayes, whom the boys used to irritate
for their amusement by whistling behind his back, into the
solitary student of a lone and romantic tower in a distant
county ; I have presumed to raise the situation of my heroine,
and, instead of portraying her as the wife of a saddler in Fleur-
de-lis Court, and mid-wife of the poor-house, I have represented
her in my tale as a young gentlewoman of independent fortune,
a paragon of beauty, a severe and learned moral philosopher,
and the Lady Bountiful of the village of Islington.   As your
Jacobina, the cat, is endowed with all the properties of a dog, I
have not scrupled, where the urgency of the case required it, to
transfer to my Muggletonian, the dog, the instincts that are
peculiar to a cat.   With a single exception, I have endeavoured
to follow your steps, sir, as an humble votary of the *lusus naturæ*
school ; but in *one* case, I have found myself compelled to disregard the example of my great prototype : it was necessary, in
the progress of my plot, to introduce the character of a kind
and affectionate parent.   You will excuse the lingering prejudices of early education ;—I have not made him, in imitation
of your Houseman, a person of low life and ferocious manners, a
housebreaker and a *cut-throat*, but a gentleman, a magistrate, and
a Christian.

But enough of this.   It is not the design, but the execution
of my work that you and the world will judge me by.   Should
it be thought to bear any even the slightest resemblance to your
celebrated production, I shall be content; and, with every due

sentiment of respect for your talents, and admiration of your ingenious application of them, I beg leave to lay the tale of *Elizabeth Brownrigge* as an humble offering on the shrine of that genius to which we are indebted for the novel of *Eugene Aram*.

THE AUTHOR.

BOOK I.

CHAPTER I.

Islington : the Red Cabbage — Specimen of Lusus Naturæ — Philosophers of the Porch— Who is she ?

> " Yet about her
> There hangs a mystery ever. She doth walk,
> Wrapt in incomprehensibility ;
> Lovely but half-reveal'd, as is the moon
> Shrouded in mists of evening, or the rose
> Veil'd by its mossy coverture, and bathed
> In heavy drops of the past thunder-shower."
>
> *From Elizabeth Brownrigge, a MS. Burletta.*

SOME twenty years ago the now populous suburb of Islington stood, in the midst of its meadows and its corn-fields, a romantic but inconsiderable hamlet. The cottages of its simple and innocent peasantry, each standing in its little enclosure of neatly-cultivated garden-ground, overgrown with honeysuckle and jasmine, and sheltered by the protection of a grove of stately oaks, were scattered thickly but irregularly around the parish church, while here and there appeared among them a few houses of more extended dimensions, the villas of certain wealthier citizens, who delighted to find in this secluded spot that repose from the distractions of business, and quiet from the din of men, which was denied them in the neighbourhood of Fleet Street or Cheapside. In those days, the only inn of Islington was the Red Cabbage—a name which it had gradually acquired from the imperfect skill of the village artist who had undertaken to delineate the red rose upon its sign. The house had, two centuries before, been a royal residence ; at which time it was honoured as a favourite hunting-seat of the virgin daughter of the eighth Henry. But it had now " fallen, sadly fallen, from its high estate." Desolation had marked it for its own : its corniced gables were dilapidated, its massive window-frames were despoiled of the richly-pictured light that had once emblazoned them, and the numerous windows were either altogether fortified with brick and mortar against the demands of the tax-gatherer, to the vast abridgement of his majesty's revenue, or were disfigured by the adoption of various expedients to supply the loss of their deficient or shattered panes of glass without having recourse to the glazier. The whole of the centre and left wing of the building were overgrown with ivy, of which the branches had insinuated themselves into the fissures of the masonry, and were rapidly accelerating the work of time by increasing the ruin which their foliage concealed. The right wing was no longer habitable ; the roof had been crushed by the fall of a stack of chimneys in the high wind of January 1670, and had never afterwards been repaired. Indeed, but few traces of the ancient magnificence of the building now remained, except the ample and grotesquely-ornamented porch ; and even of this the beauty was eclipsed, for the high north road had, at that spot, been raised so many feet as to form a complete breastwork in its front, and the entrance was now reached by descending as many steps as in prouder days it had stood elevated at the summit of. But still, faded as are the glories—waned as is the light of that once royal palace—I never approach the place, and see the sign of the red cabbage hanging aloft from the projecting branch of the aged elm by which that venerable and mouldering porch is overshadowed, but a world of historic and poetic associations are awaked in my mind ; my memory reverts to the personages and the incidents of other times—to Queen Elizabeth and Queen Mary, to Lord Bacon and Lord Burleigh— to the success of the Protestant Reformation, and the defeat of the Spanish Armada.

It was somewhere about twelve o'clock on a fine, bright, sunny day, 25th of June, 1765, that Timothy Hitch and Giles Fillup were conversing together, and taking the air and the dust, their beer and their pipes, within the shady area of the porch in question. Timothy Hitch was a young man of some six-and-twenty years of age ; but his ever-laughing eye, his ruddy complexion, his loosely flowing, flaxen-coloured curls, and his thoughtless expression of countenance, might have led the superficial spectator into a belief that he had as yet scarcely passed his teens. He was dressed in the first style of elegance, according to the fashion of the time. His coat and inexpressibles were of fawn-coloured camlet, trimmed at the edge, and worked at the button-holes with silver galloon; his waistcoat was of pink satin, flowered over with a large spreading pattern of silver ranunculuses, and surrounded with a broad silver lace; on his head, placed carelessly on one side, was a small three-cornered hat, which was graced by a cockade, and in correspondence with the rest of his apparel, edged with silver. Thus attired, conscious of the attractions of his dress and person, he stood in an easy, lounging attitude, with his back resting against the pillar of the porch of the Red Cabbage, and looked laughingly down upon the long, spare figure, and the grim and sallow face, of Giles Fillup the host, who was seated on the opposite bench, as they exchanged the following brief sentences of talk, intermixed with copious draughts of ale and puffs of tobacco-smoke.

" It's all a fallacy—it's all a fallacy," sighed forth the melancholy Giles; " life's a vale of tears."

" Pshaw! nonsense!" replied Timothy: " a vale of beer, you mean, man!"

" All labour and sorrow—eating and growing hungry again, drinking and becoming dry!"

" *Dry!* what, already? Why, man, you were *wet* enough last night when I pulled you dead drunk out of the gutter."

"Timothy Hitch, don't be so profane! *Dead* drunk!—*dead!* I wonder that a man of your trade"—

" Profession, Giles, my boy! Zooks, profession!"

" Well, of your profession, then—I'm astonished, I say, that you, who pick all the bread you eat out of dead men's mouths, and haven't a shirt belonging to you but was pilfered from a dead man's back, can bear even to give utterance to the word without a shudder."

" No reflection upon my profession, Master Fillup. What! isn't it the last and most honourable branch of the law?"

" Most honourable ! "

" Ay, to be sure it is.   I say it again,—*most* honourable."

" Prove it, Timothy—prove it."

" Why, with us gentlemen of the law, isn't the order of precedency reversed, as it were, by general consent ?"

" How do ye mean ?   I don't know.   Is it ?"

" As certainly as I stand here.   Why, is not the constable more honourable than the thief ?"

" Why yes."

" And the attorney that compounds the brief against him more honourable than the constable ?"

" Perhaps he is."

" And the counsellor that pleads out of the brief more honourable than the attorney ?"

" There's no denying it."

" And is not the judge, again, more honourable than the counsellor ?   Zooks !   Giles Fillup, I say, are not all these things true ?"

" I think they are."

" Well, then, by parity of reasoning, must not I, Timothy Hitch, his majesty's hangman, and last executor of the laws of this great kingdom, be as much more honourable than the judge, who only utters the sentence of the law, as he is than the counsellor, or the counsellor than the attorney, or the attorney than the constable, or the constable than the thief ?   Why, the point's as clear as day.—My pipe's out, though.—But doesn't it stand to common sense ?—Isn't it reason, Master Fillup ?"

" Say what you will, it's a dark and melancholy office, Timothy."

" Melancholy !—why ?   Haven't I plenty of leisure, plenty of money, plenty of victuals, and plenty of the best apparel ?   Then for variety !   Don't I travel, whenever a job's required to be neatly done, from one end of England to the other, half a dozen times in the course of the circuit ?   And for sights !   Zounds !   who ever gets so many, or finer ?   Shew me a finer sight anywhere than a fine execution !   And where's the man that ever sees so many of them as I do ?"

" Your heart's as hard as a stone, Timothy !   Timothy,

you've no fellow-feeling for the poor, guilty creatures you help
to put out of the world."

"No, no, Fillup!—don't say that," replied the young, the
fair-faced, and the light-spirited companion of mine host, while
his fine jocund countenance assumed a cast of unwonted sad-
ness, and the tear of sensibility, which rose involuntarily in his
usually laughing eye, for a moment dimmed its brightness—
"No!—don't say so!—I do pity the poor creatures, Giles, with
my whole soul I pity them ; and always tie them up as tenderly
as if they were my dearest relations. But, pshaw ! this is folly."

He here made a strong effort to suppress the rising emotions
of his heart ; and having dashed away the falling drops from
his eyelid with the back of his hand, whilst the sunny light of
his soul burst forth again, and dispersed the clouds which had
gathered about his brow, he exclaimed, in his usual tone of
vivacity, " But come, my boy ! Zooks ! fill me another pipe ; and
I'm not the fellow that would make any objection to a second
pot of porter.—What !" he continued to the host, who had now
returned, bearing a pewter vessel full of the generous and
frothy beverage in his hand—" What ! does Miss Elizabeth
Brownrigge live here still !"

" Yes ; at the new house in the village, with the green railing
before it."

" And as beautiful as ever ?"

" Beauty is but a fading flower," sighed Giles ; " 'tis but as
the grass of the field—here to-day and gone to-morrow ! But,
to be sure, she is wonderfully fair—a lily of Sharon, my friend
Timothy—fair as a lily and as upright as a lily ?"

" Well, who could have thought it ? Not married yet ! Such
a beautiful girl !"

" Ay, and so virtuous withal ! Why, she has founded in
the village a lying-in hospital for married women only. She
attends the poor creatures herself, and feeds, washes, and lodges
them all at her own expense."

" So good and so beautiful, and not married !" exclaimed the
enthusiastic hangman. " Why, the bachelors of these parts
have no taste, no soul, no sense of what is really lovely and
exquisite in human nature !"

"I don't know; I should not like to have it said that it came from me, but"—and Giles Fillup lowered his voice to an audible whisper as he added, "according to my notions, that young Master Alphonso Belvidere, the son of the rich banker that has just purchased the manor house and park at the end of the village, is casting a sheep's eye at Miss Elizabeth Brownrigge."

"Well done, Master Alphonso Belvidere!" cried Timothy Hitch; "I would not wish any man a better fortune. Here's a health to him and to Miss Elizabeth Brownrigge. Here, Fillup, my old fellow:—"

"Not so old either, Master Hitch; only sixty last Martinmas."

"My young fellow, then?"

"Not so young either."

"Well, my middle-aged fellow, then—we'll not quarrel about an epithet—here, take a draught to the health of Miss Elizabeth Brownrigge."

"Long life and happiness," uttered Giles, with the deep-drawn breath, the demure air, and the earnest tone of one making a most important effort of volition, while, by a dexterous turn of his hand, he imparted a slow circuitous motion to the contents of the porter pot—"Long life and every earthly happiness to the good and beautiful Elizabeth Brownrigge!"

"Elizabeth Brownrigge! Ah! ah!" shrieked a voice at the top of the steps which descended from the high road to the porch of the Red Cabbage—"who speaks of Elizabeth Brownrigge?"

Timothy Hitch started at the frightful vehemence of the sound—the porter pot was suddenly arrested on its way to the mouth of Giles Fillup—both motionless as statues, stood rivetted to the spot on which the unexpected and soul-appalling words had fixed them, with their eyes turned in astonishment towards the wild and strangely attired female figure from whom they had proceeded.

The person who met their view appeared somewhat less than sixteen years of age. In her sunken and harassed eyes, which were red and bloodshot from fatigue and want of sleep, the traces of many cares were deeply printed. Her young features, though of the most delicate contour, and such as a sculptor might have studied to refine his views of ideal beauty, were emaciated from want and illness; yet the cheeks and lips were thickly coated with red paint, which the course of her tears and the dews of perspiration had fretted into stripes, and showered in ruddy drops upon the dusty and disarranged buffon, which, extended upon a wire framework, formed a swelling semicircle on either side her neck. Her bright chestnut hair appeared to have been most elaborately dressed and powdered, but had escaped from the confinement of its black pins and pomatum, and was straggling at large over her face and shoulders. The gauze cap, that crowned the summit of the lofty cushion over which her locks had been curled, and craped, and plastered, was torn as in a midnight broil; and the artificial flowers, and tips of variously-coloured ostrich feathers that had adorned it, were hanging about her head in loose and most-admired disorder. Her richly embroidered sack and petticoat were empurpled with several large stains of port wine, soiled with the mud of London and the dust of the country, and disfigured by many a wide and recent rent. As she stood upon the steps, raising her large hoop out of the way of her high-heeled satin shoes with her left hand, to facilitate her descent, and tossing her right arm aloft above her head, a gust of wind suddenly arising gave a fluttering motion to her streaming hair, to the shattered ornaments of her head-gear, and to her long pendant ruffles of Brussels point, which admirably harmonised with the agitated expression of her countenance and the wild character of her figure. The men were awed—they feared and pitied her—they knew not whether to retire or to advance—they wished, yet dreaded, to address her.

But while they paused, all further hesitation on their part was effectually put an end to by the unknown visitor herself, who, looking down upon them with an eye of shrewd severity, and a laugh of piercing bitterness and contemptuous derision, cried, "And so it's Elizabeth Brownrigge you're praising! Well, well! that's as it should be."

She here tottered into the porch in which the men were

standing, and fell down upon the nearest seat, exhausted with weakness and fatigue. The young and gentle-hearted Timothy, losing the feeling of astonishment in commiseration of her evident state of destitution, immediately hastened to the side of the wanderer, and was most earnest in offering, and most anxious to administer assistance. After the pause of a few moments the faintness seemed to leave her; and waving him away with the air of a woman of quality, after many abortive efforts to deliver herself with calmness and precision, she said, " You must be surprised, gentlemen, at seeing me here at this hour of the day—alone, too, and without my chariot. Ten thousand pardons for this intrusion ;—but servants are so slow. You were speaking of Miss Brownrigge —Elizabeth, I think, you said. Ah ! ah ! ah !"

A little affected laugh here interrupted the voluble but bewildered flow of her rhetoric, which was succeeded by—" I declare I feel quite faint and weak. So !—Good and beautiful ! —Very extraordinary where this coachman of mine can be loitering—at the alehouse, I'll warrant. Pray, has she any apprentices now ? "

" Whom do you speak of, madam ? " demanded Timothy Hitch, with an air of gentleness and respect, which intimated his sympathy in the distress, rather than consideration for the apparent condition, of the person he was addressing.

" Speak of !" cried the unknown female, looking wildly in his face—" speak of !—But, alas ! alas ! you here again ! That voice—that look ! Oh ! it haunts me by day—every day, and all day long. At night I see it in my dreams—it's a shadow always near me ! Light won't dissipate it—darkness cannot hide it ! Away ! away ! Let me be mocked at by the shadow only, not tortured thus by the terrible reality of your presence. I say, for mercy's sake, away !"

" Why, lady, do you shudder at the presence of a friend ? Indeed, you cannot have seen me before."

" Hush ! hush !—No more ! no more ! "

" Be assured I never injured you."

" Silence ! oh, silence ! Those words are sharp and envenomed as the pointed tongues of scorpions—they sting the core of my heart, and penetrate the marrow of my brain." Then, dropping her voice to a tone, low, solemn, and scarcely audible, grasping the left wrist of Timothy Hitch with her right hand, and holding him at the distance of her extended arm, she added, " Where were you, think ye, when my mother and my brother died ? "

" I, madam !—where was *I* when they died ! "

" Dear me ! where is this chariot of mine ?—In a very different carriage from that did they, poor souls, take their last drive in this world :—But, then, it cost them nothing—that was some advantage ; and 'tis not every cart that goes through Tyburn turnpike without paying toll as it passes.—But, oh ! my aching head, my aching head ! "

Overpowered by the energy of these strong emotions, acting upon a weakened and debilitated frame, the poor wretch here made a second attempt to conceal her misery by an affected laugh, and then went off into a violent hysteric. Giles Fillup and Timothy Hitch exerted themselves with all the interest of sincere and unsophisticated benevolence in effecting her restoration. In the course of their endeavours, some nourishment and cordials were administered, which were of essential service to the unhappy girl, and supplied the inanition, which was one of the immediate causes of the distress she laboured under. On recovering herself, she reverted to the subject of Miss Brownrigge, and studiously avoiding the sight of Timothy, she repeated to Giles Fillup her former question : " Has she any 'prentices now ? "

" She has," answered mine host of the Red Cabbage, " two young girls, as handmaids, who attend upon her, and who are apprenticed to her for seven years by the parish officers of White Friars."

" Their names are—"

" Mary Mitchel and Mary Clifford."

" Poor things ! poor things ! How I pity them ! "

" Pity them ! " exclaimed mine host ; " where could the orphan and the indigent ever hope to find so kind a guardian, or so happy an asylum as in the house of that good lady ? Pity them ! Why, they are the envy of all the young girls of the

village, as they walk to the parish church, once every
Wednesday and Friday, and twice every Sunday, in their neat
blue cloth gowns, their little, tidy, white caps, aprons, bibs and
tuckers, and each with her Bible and prayer-book under her
arm. Pity them! Oh!" said Giles, devoutly casting up his
eyes as he uttered the ejaculation, "Oh! it were a blessed
thing if every mother's daughter were trained, as they are, in
the paths of virtue from their youth."

"And," muttered the stranger, abstractedly, "both *their* names
are Mary, too."

"See there!" interrupted Giles, pointing to a thin, graceful,
and elegant young lady, who now appeared from the opening of
a green lane in the distance, accompanied by a tall, finely-
formed, patrician-looking youth; "see there is Miss Brownrigge, and Master Alphonso Belvidere along with her, as sure
as I'm alive!"

"Where! where!" said the stranger; "I'll see her—I'll
speak to her—though pestilence should strike me dead before
her, and hell should yawn and swallow me at her feet!"

So saying, she rushed wildly forth from the porch of the inn,
and fled with the speed of lightning toward the spot where
Elizabeth and Alphonso had appeared. But before she had
completely reached them, she was seen to slacken her pace—
to stop—to pause an instant, and then turn suddenly round, as
if her resolution failed her, and fly as rapidly away down a
path in the opposite direction.

At the sight of this unexpected apparition, Elizabeth started,
trembled and drew nearer to the side of Alphonso. Her alarm,
however, was but momentary. Before Timothy Hitch had time
to say, "Where the deuce could that strange woman come
from?" the agitation of Miss Brownrigge had completely
passed away; and before Giles Fillup had responded, "A poor
mad creature, I take it; but who can she be?" the lady, moving
on with her wonted air of firm and delicate composure, had led
her lover out of view of the inn.

CHAPTER II.

Portraits : a Pair of Lovers—A Dinner at Noon—Table-Talk.

" Sure such a pair were never seen,
So aptly framed to meet by nature."—
SHERIDAN.

"Gentleman, welcome ; 'tis a word I use—
From me expect no further compliment.
Nor do I name it often at our meeting.
Once spoke, to those that understand me best,
And know I always purpose as I speak,
Hath ever yet sufficed : so let it you.
Nor do I love that common phrase of guests,
As ' we make bold,' or ' we are troublesome,'
' We take you unprovided,' and the like.
I know you understanding, gentlemen,
And knowing me, cannot persuade yourselves
With me you shall be troublesome or bold."—HEYWOOD.

" Hell hath no fury like a woman scorn'd."—LEE, *Rival Queens.*

THE pair who retired from the admiring gaze of Timothy Hitch and Giles Fillup, at the conclusion of the last chapter, were formed in the very prodigality of nature. Each seemed to have been created, rich in every personal endowment, as the worthy counterpart of the other. Young they were ; but in them youth was blooming with all its freshness, and devoid of all its frivolities. Beautiful they were ; but the beauty which rendered them the delight and admiration of the eyes of others, was held of no estimation in their own. Alphonso, who stood six feet two without his shoes, united, in the compact and slender structure of his person, the vigour of the Hercules with the elegance of the Apollo. His features, which were cast in the perfect mould of the Antinous, were coloured with a deep, rich sunniness of tone, which no pencil inferior to that of Titian could ever have aspired to imitate ; while the breadth of his forehead bespoke the intellectual powers of a Newton or a Locke ; and the bright, lambent, and innocuous fires of his unfathomable eye beamed with the gentle virtues of a martyred saint. As his figure was characterised by strength and grace, so was his

K

countenance by intelligence and humility. He was distinguished
among literary men as the editor of a new monthly magazine ;
and his attire was of that simple style of elegance which accorded
well with the cast of his person, the expression of his countenance, and the gravity of his pursuits. He wore a plain black
hat, of which the somewhat expansive brim was slightly turned
up at the sides; his coat, waistcoat, and nether garments, were
formed *en suite* of snuff-coloured broad cloth ; his stockings
were of white silk, variegated with horizontal stripes of blue;
and his only ornaments were the silver buckles that glistened,
with a modest and a moon-like lustre, at his knees, on his shoes,
and in the front of his hat.

Of Elizabeth, the virgin philanthropist, the youthful bene-
factress of the village, who, when at home in the elegant apartment of her romantic cottage, occupied all her solitary hours in
making garments for the naked, and who rarely passed beyond
the green and trellised boundaries of her garden but to administer
to the sick or hungry some healing or savoury consolation—of
Elizabeth, the height was above the middle size, and the slimness
of her figure would have conveyed an idea of weakness and
fragility to the mind of the spectator, but for the upright bearing
of her person, and the firm and decided step with which she
moved. Many engravings of her are in circulation ; but, though
they all owe their origin to a miniature by a celebrated painter,
which Alphonso constantly wore about him, the likeness has
sadly suffered from being submitted to the hands of inferior
artists ; and there is no print with which I am acquainted that
affords the faintest hint of the exquisite beauty with which she
was endowed. There are some, perhaps, which convey a slight
intimation of the elevated cast of her features, but they do
nothing more. What hand, indeed, however skilful, could give
an adequate representation of that high towering forehead,
which bespoke a more than female reach of thought ; of those
large blue and finely-opened eyes, with the silken lashes that
overshadowed them ; of that aquiline but feminine nose, with
its delicately-chiselled nostrils ; of that mouth, with its curling
lips, distinctly cut and closely meeting, the sure symbols of
moral and intellectual energy ; of that well-proportioned chin,

or of the eloquent tincture of that complexion, which, bearing
in its general hue the fair, polished, and transparent whiteness
of the purest alabaster, was, from time to time, suffused with a
fainter or deeper glow of vermilion, corresponding with the
strength of the emotions that were swaying in her breast. Kind
and gentle as every feature of her face proclaimed her to be, the
prevailing expression of her countenance was that of fixedness
and determination. She looked the image of a virtue which
could never err; or, which, if it erred, was lost for ever, and
would never again recover its first state.

Such was Elizabeth Brownrigge; such she now stood at the
garden gate, which Alphonso was opening for her, attired
according to the costume she is represented as wearing in her
pictures. Over a gown of flowered Indian chintz she had on a
black mode cloak, richly trimmed with lace, and lined with rose-
coloured satin. Her dark glossy hair, which she wore without
powder, was turned up behind, and smoothed simply in front
over a moderately-sized cushion; a lace cap, neatly plaited,
covered her ears; above which, somewhat inclined, so as to
shade the eyes, and secured by long pins that projected from
both sides of her head, was a small black satin gipsy-hat,
trimmed round the crown with a puffing of rose-coloured riband
to match the lining of her cloak. As the lovers thus stood
together, at the entrance of the small garden that fronted the
dwelling of Elizabeth, protracting to the utmost, the moment
of separation, and fearing to utter the " farewell " that trembled
upon their lips, Alphonso, taking the hand of his mistress, and
regarding her with a look of tenderness, said,—

" I depend, then, on seeing you again! You'll walk with me
in the cool of the evening?"

" I have promised," replied Elizabeth. " Do you remember
any instance of my neglecting an engagement, that you seem
thus inclined to doubt me?"

" No! oh, no! Imagine it not. I am incapable of any feeling
towards thee but that of the most implicit confidence. But, my
dearest——"

" Tush!" interrupted Elizabeth. " I like not these professions;
strong actions please me better than strong words. How fre-

K 2

quently have I enjoined, Alphonso, that these superlative terms of affection should neither be uttered in my presence, nor find a place in any letter you address to me. Dearest! Absurd! The expression is as foolish as it is profane. Let our attachment be restrained within the bounds, and declared according to the rules, of reason. Nay, look not down, good Alphonso; I pardon you this error."

"Kindest, sweetest!"

"Again!"

"Impose not my own Elizabeth, this severe restriction upon the suggestions of my heart! Why interdict my tongue from delivering the sentiments which are prompted by the warm, fresh-springing, and genuine emotions of my soul?"

"I would have all men speak the truth, Alphonso,—the exact, simple, and invariable truth; not only that which they may imagine to be true for the moment, but that which was true in time past, and will be true in all time to come. It is possible, and I do not doubt it, that your present affection towards me is as devoted as your words describe; but was it so last year? can you be sure that it will be so in the next? No! What connexion, then, have these protestations of attachment with that eternal and immutable truth which should be the paramount object and the ruling principle of all intercourse of conversation between man and man?"

"Sweet monitress, your wisdom shall be the pole-star of my mind!"

"So be it, then, if you will deal in such idle metaphors and poetic exaggerations; but now betake you to your home. In five minutes the church clock will strike: it will take you *four* to reach the manor-house; and, as your father dines punctually at two, you'll have but *one* minute to spare. So away, Alphonso!"

"Why will you not accompany me? My father desired, requested, implored your presence!"

"It cannot be! I have an important and a painful duty to despatch within. This is the hour; it cannot be dispensed with; it must not be deferred. And so farewell till evening!"

"Till seven!"

"Till seven precisely," rejoined Elizabeth; and accompanied

by her little dog, Muggletonian, which had stood beside her, fondly rubbing his head against her gown during the whole of the previous conversation, she retired up the gravel walk which led to the trellised entrance of her ornamented cottage.

Alphonso gazed tenderly after her as she withdrew, and then turned his hurried steps towards his father's. He had not, however, proceeded many yards, when, having reached an eminence that afforded a view of the windows of his love, he stopped and cast a " longing, lingering look behind" him, with the hope of catching yet another glimpse of her at the em-bowered lattice, or among the flowers of her garden.

His eye was disappointed; but, as he stood silently gazing upon the casket in which was garnered up the joy and treasure of his soul, his ear was startled by the sound of two piercing shrieks in the distance : they were evidently those of a child in torture. He listened, with the fullest stretch, and most eager exertion of his faculty, to catch a repetition of the cry. For a time, all was silent ; but after the lapse of a few seconds, the same appalling expressions of agony struck upon his sense, in a fainter tone, but of a more protracted continuance than before. Whence could they proceed ? The cries appeared to issue from that part of the village in which the dwelling of the good and beautiful Elizabeth was situated. But, no—that was impossible ! Mr. Deacon, the apothecary, whose house stood next her cottage, was not a father. There were no children residing in the neigh-bourhood but those two little handmaidens to whom his beloved was so tenderly attached, and whose education she so diligently directed. That they should suffer any severity, or that they ever should have cause to give utterance to such an expression of pain, was too incredible a supposition to find an instant's lodgment in his mind. What, those little girls unhappy ? blest as they were, living in the sight, and under the care, and beneath the same roof with his Elizabeth ? It could not be ! Alphonso paused yet another moment ; the sounds returned no more ; and, convinced that he had been deceived by some auricular delusion, as the clock of Islington church struck two he hastily started from the spot, and did not relax his speed till he deposited his hat on the marble table of his father's hall.

On reaching the manor-house, he found Mr. Belvidere already seated at dinner, with Mr. and Mrs. Deacon. The name of Deacon has before been mentioned. He was the next-door neighbour of Miss Brownrigge, and the highly-judicious and very respectable medical friend of the wealthier inhabitants of Islington and its vicinity. He was a corpulent gentleman, between forty and fifty. His wife, with whom he had for several years been united in the bonds of an unfruitful, but most happy wedlock, was of no particular age: she still retained the prominent and well-rounded graces of what is generally considered a fine woman, in the unimpaired perfection of their bloom; and she was content that her time of life should be left problematical, as a matter of speculation among her friends, rather than fixed by any information of her own. Mrs. Deacon, ever since Mr. Belvidere had taken up his residence at the manor-house, had entertained the deepest sense of the exalted merits of his son. She had, indeed, ventured to express her approbation of them in so candid a manner as somewhat to distress the modesty of Alphonso, and induce a slight disinclination for her society. With that intuitive view into the recesses of the heart for which the sex is so particularly distinguished, the lady very quickly apprehended the unfavourable disposition of his feelings towards herself; while the proximity of their dwellings afforded her the opportunity of observing his frequent visits to Elizabeth, she was not long in becoming equally well-informed with regard to his sentiments in another quarter. Though Mrs. Deacon was the most irreproachable of wives; though she would not for the world have been guilty of a thought of connubial infidelity; though, indeed, her principles were so strict on this particular, that she had been the means of compelling her husband's rival apothecary to leave the village, and seek the patronage of a less scrupulous neighbourhood, because his wife had been exposed to the vague rumour of a suspected flirtation;—still, rigid as Mrs. Deacon was on the score of her matrimonial duties, she could not witness Alphonso's want of interest in her friendship, and his attachment to Elizabeth, without experiencing some degree of exasperation. She was vexed at the slight to which she was subjected. "It was not," as she continually repeated to herself, "that she was in love with the lad ; but it was enough to provoke a saint, when she had condescended to shew him so much favour, to see him prefer a pale, tame, thread-paper slip of a girl, like Elizabeth Brownrigge, to so personable a woman as herself." She conceived that an injustice was committed against her charms ; and she could not help resenting it. Her indignation found its vent in availing herself of every opportunity of depreciating her favoured rival in the presence of Alphonso. On entering the dining-room, our hero, finding that Mr. Deacon had, in his absence, taken possession of the bottom of the table, made a slight inclination to his father and his guests, and slipped quietly into the vacant seat of the *partie quarrée,* opposite Mrs. Deacon.

" You are late to-day, my boy," said his father; "you are not apt to be out of the way at pudding-time."

" I was detained longer than I expected," replied Alphonso ; " but I made the best speed I could."

" Nothing wrong in the city, I hope ? "

" No ; a mere accidental miscalculation of the time," rejoined the son ; and applied himself to the venison pasty with the determined air of a person who had completed his explanation, and with whom all attempt at any further inquiry would be bootless.

" Did you meet Miss Brownrigge to-day," demanded Mrs. Deacon, " by chance or by appointment ? "

" Which time to-day do you mean, madam ? " replied our hero. " I have had the happiness of seeing that young lady twice; in the morning when I called to convey my father's invitation to dinner, and lately, since my return from town."

" Oh ! then it was, I presume, by agreement that you met, about an hour since, opposite her new-fangled lying-in charity establishment ? "

" On the contrary, that rencontre was merely a most fortunate accident. The appointment we made this morning was for a walk towards Hampstead in the cool of the evening."

Mrs. Deacon looked utterly disconcerted ; and in her turn, applied herself to the venison pasty.

" What a beautiful creature Miss Brownrigge is ! " exclaimed old Mr. Belvidere, after a pause. " An old fellow like myself might almost wish to be young again, Deacon, to have the chance of winning the heart of such a girl."

" She's too pale," said the ruddy Mr. Deacon, casting an approving glance on the damask and full-blown beauties of his spouse.

" And far too thin," rejoined the lady, looking round with a complacent, downward glance upon that wide circumference of self to which her head formed the centre.

" Neither one nor the other, to my mind ; but every man according to his taste : *quot homines tot sententiæ*—and so let us have a glass of wine. Come, come : a general breeze ! Robin," continued the warmhearted and hospitable old gentleman, to the grey-haired butler, who was always close to his elbow,— sometimes standing, sometimes leaning, behind his chair,— " Robin, a bumper of Madeira all round !"

" However beautiful she may be," persisted Mrs. Deacon, after swallowing the contents of her capacious glass, " one thing is quite certain,—Miss Brownrigge has a most intolerable and tyrannical disposition."

As she uttered this sentence, the colour of her cheek mounted to the very top of her forehead, indicating, as exactly as the rising mercury of a thermometer does the state of the atmosphere, the blood-heat condition of her temper ; while bridling up, with a little air of malignant triumph, she fixed her eyes full upon those of her opposite neighbour.

" Disposition ! oh, she's a perfect virago !" ejaculated the uxorious apothecary. " Oh, dear ! oh, dear ! What a devil of a life she leads those two poor little parish-apprentices. I wonder ——"

" Sir !" exclaimed Alphonso, whose indignation was now raised to the extreme of endurance ;—" Sir, however I may quell my spirit, and tolerate those base and calumnious insinuations which envy of the superior merits of Elizabeth Brownrigge may incite the unworthy of the other sex to propagate,—however silently and contemptuously I may regard the petty malice of a woman,—when I hear a man ——"

" My dear Alphonso !" interrupted his father.

" Oh, sir !" interrupted Mrs. Deacon, " pray let the gentleman proceed! I beg you'll not think of stopping him. Petty malice! Unworthy! Contempt! I can tell you, Mr. Alphonso Bel——"

"My love! my love!" interrupted Mr. Deacon, in his turn, "only allow me to explain. Do not permit yourself, my lamb, to be thus run away with by the strength of your emotions. There is no cause whatever for this disturbance of the harmony of the company. I can assure, my young friend, that I never, for a moment, contemplated the possibility of occasioning him any offence. My respect for the virtues of Miss Brownrigge is fully equal to, and cannot be surpassed by, his own. My admiration of her beauty is unbounded. Perhaps she may be, according to my taste, just a thought too pale, or a thought too thin ; but what of that ? Surely, such good friends as we have ever been, are far too wise to fall into dispute upon a mere matter of private fancy ! And as to temper—I most solemnly declare that I have no personal knowledge of the matter whatever; I speak only from report. I have heard, indeed, from Mrs. Crips, and the Misses Budgdell, and Miss Hicks, and several other respectable and credible ladies of our acquaintance, that Miss Brownrigge's temper is not quite so gentle as her friends might wish ; but they have, unquestionably, been deceived. I have not a doubt but that the lady is, in every respect, the angel that she looks. Should my words appear to have implied the least intimation to the contrary, I implore Mr. Alphonso to believe that nothing could be further from my thoughts, and that my intentions have been entirely misunderstood."

So spoke the fluent apothecary : our hero received his most veritable and highly parliamentary explanation with a faint smile of contemptuous acknowledgment ; and kind old Mr. Belvidere, taking upon himself the part of chorus to the dialogue, and moralising on the subject matter of the scene, observed,

"Well, well! it's a good thing these idle and silly women do not presume to say anything worse. Never, my boy, attempt to justify so fair and excellent a being as Elizabeth against the charge of a defective temper. The mischievous and talking world will never be satisfied unless they have some error to allege against every meritorious and highly-gifted individual. If they cannot find, they will always invent, a fault to exercise their tongues upon; and a judicious friend should be content to leave them the undisturbed discussion of a weakness, lest, in the absence of such a theme, they should venture to impute a crime."

"But, sir! Mr. Belvidere! Gracious me! why you talk," cried Mrs. Deacon, "as if we only accused Miss Brownrigge of being, every now and then, a little peppery or so, like the rest of our acquaintance; but that's not it in the least."

"Then pray, madam," demanded Alphonso, calmly but severely, "may I be allowed to inquire what it is you do accuse that lady of?"

"Accuse her of? Tyranny—brutality! Oh, if you should only chance to be near our house at flogging-time!"

"Flogging-time!" exclaimed Alphonso.

"Ay, flogging-time. Almost every day, just a few minutes before two, if either of the poor children have done anything in the least wrong, this sweet, mild, fair, amiable Miss Elizabeth Brownrigge, whom you gentlemen all admire so much, administers what she calls her dose of salutary chastisement; and it's quite terrible—it absolutely shatters one's nerves for the rest of the day—to hear the shrieks of the infants."

"I don't believe it, madam!" cried old Mr. Belvidere,—his whole soul swelling with indignation at what he deemed an unjust aspersion on the fair fame of his adopted daughter-in-law. "Madam, I beg your pardon a thousand times for contradicting you so abruptly; but, my life on it, you are deceived."

"It must be impossible," said Alphonso; but the tone of his voice was far lower and humbler than his father's, and his manner was not expressive of so implicit a confidence; for his heart misgave him; and he thought of the shrieks which he had so lately heard in the direction of Elizabeth's cottage.

"Well, gentlemen, as you please! but what I know, I know; and what I see, I see; and what I *hear*, I *hear*!"

"Surely," cried Alphonso, "there must be some strange misapprehension here!"

The dinner was now concluded ; and Mr. Belvidere proposed that the wine, punch, and dessert, should be carried to a summer-house at the end of the bowling-green, where he and Mr. Deacon might each enjoy his pipe, in an airy situation, without incommoding the lady, at her chain and satin-stitch, by the condensation of their tobacco smoke.

Having seen the trio thus quietly deposited for the afternoon, and drank one small glass of that well-concocted beverage for which the grey-headed butler was very widely celebrated, our hero, disgusted with the malice of the lady, loathing the syco-phancy of the husband, and impatient for an explanation with Elizabeth, invented some slight pretext for returning into the house, as the readiest mode of making his escape from the persecution of such unworshipful society, without incurring the formality of a regular leave-taking. Intending that his returning to them again should remain in doubt, he first ran up stairs to his chamber, with the view of making such little adjustments in his dress as even those who are least curious about their personal appearance seldom fail regarding as indispensable preliminaries to visiting the lady of their love, and then descended to the hall for his hat and cane. Close to the marble slab on which they lay stood Mrs. Deacon. A spectre from the grave could not have startled him more, or been more offensive to his sight. She had divined his purpose ; and, acting with the promptitude of strongly-excited jealousy, had resolved to intercept him. As he approached the table, the lady, forgetting her accustomed deference to the rules of propriety, moved with a rapid step towards him, and, making a violent seizure of his hand, exclaimed with impassioned earnestness,—

" My fears have not deceived me—you are then already weary of our society—I was convinced that you meant to leave us ! Oh, Alphonso !" and, in an agony of tears, she hid her head upon the arm of the hand she held. " Oh, Alphonso! you have no thought, no consideration, for the feelings of the best of friends !"

" I can consider no person, madam, as a friend of mine, who avows herself the enemy of Miss Brownrigge," answered Belvi-dere, coldly and formally, endeavouring in vain to deliver himself from the grasp by which he was detained.

" One word, Alphonso ! Hear me ! answer me this one single question."

" Well, madam ? "

" Are you going to the cottage of that detested girl ? "

" The wife of Mr. Deacon ought to have no interest in the movements of any other man than her husband ; and I, on my part, might without discourtesy refuse replying to an inquiry which, on your own part, is not made without disgrace : but I am perfectly willing that the whole world should be acquainted with the course of my proceedings. I have no hesitation in acknowledging, that it is my immediate purpose to seek the cottage of Miss Brownrigge."

" You are going there ! and you have the barbarity to own it ! Oh, Alphonso ! cruel, cruel man ! Oh ! you will break my heart."

" For shame, Mrs. Deacon !—this language to *me* from a married woman ! Madam ! madam ! think of your affectionate and confiding husband, and allow me to depart."

" Is it then come to this ? He scorns my tenderness—my devotion ! "

" For pity's sake, madam, forbear ! If the ties of duty, and a sense of matronly decorum, are too weak to restrain these idle demonstrations of your folly, only consider the disparity of our years. If you have no horror of being vicious, at least forbear to render yourself ridiculous. Remember, madam, I am young enough to be your son—your grandson ! Why, my good lady, I was only twenty last February, and I'll be sworn that you can't be much under fifty-six ! "

" Sir ! " cried Mrs. Deacon, flinging Alphonso's hand away from her in a paroxysm of wrath, while every inch of her person that was visible assumed a hue of the deepest crimson, and her eyes flashed with the fire of the furies as she spoke ;—" Sir, you're not a gentleman ! Sir, I defy and scorn you ! Sir, you've insulted a weak and defenceless woman ! The age of chivalry is gone ! You have none of that gallant consideration which is due to the female sex ! I hate and I despise you. But beware, Mr. Alphonso Belvidere,—I warn you to beware in time. Remember that you've roused a lioness, which, insignificant as you may think her power, will neither sleep nor rest till she have found an opportunity for working the accomplishment of her revenge!"

With these words the lady sailed away, muttering malice to herself, to resume her chain and satin-stitch, by the side of her husband, in the summer-house; while our hero, having gained possession of his hat and cane, departed in an opposite direction towards the house of his Elizabeth, saying, in audible soliloquy, as he quitted the hall, "What a towering passion that elderly gentlewoman has put herself into!"

CHAPTER III.

Old Acquaintance — Thoughts on Education — Benefits of the Sovereignty of the People.

"Shall I not take mine ease in mine inn?"--SHAKESPEARE.

"For her mind
Shaped strictest plans of discipline; sage schemes,
Such as Lycurgus taught, when at the shrine
Of the Orthyan goddess he bade flog
The little Spartans; such as erst chastised
Our Milton, when at college."—CANNING.

"Hubble bubble, toil and trouble."—SHAKESPEARE.

SEVERAL hours had now elapsed—noon and afternoon had passed away—evening was coming on, but Timothy Hitch and Giles Fillup still retained their station in the porch of the Red Cabbage. The light heart of our friend Timothy was now rendered considerably lighter by frequent application to the flowing can of mine host's home-brewed; which can, for some reason or other—either because the weather was so sultry, or because he was getting dry, or because he wanted to wash the dust out of his throat, or because he would pledge some old companion who chanced to join them, or because he would drink to the better acquaintance with some casual stranger who stopped to refresh himself, or for some pretext of an equally weighty description—he constantly found occasion for emptying, and as constantly for having filled again. Seven o'clock struck, and found the young and merry-hearted hangman in a highly communicative state of mind, his conversational powers in active play, holding "discourse of reason" with an elderly woman, in the dress of a villager, who was resting herself in the porch after the fatigues of a long day's travel. "My good lady," said the kind Timothy, with a gentle and supplicating tone, "let me entreat you to take another taste of the fourpenny; depend upon it, you'll find yourself the better for it. After a long day's journey, according to my mind, there's nothing so refreshing as a draught of good, strong, home-brewed ale. Some people prefer purl; but I count them as little better than mere ignoramuses in the article of tipple."

"Well, sir, I *do* like a glass of good ale myself."

"My good madam, you're a woman of sense;—and so you're Hertfordshire, you say, by birth."

"No, sir,—Hampshire; from the other side of Alton, down away by Basingstoke."

"You don't say so! That's wonderful. So am I! And what the devil brought you to Islington?"

"A fool's errand, I am afraid."

"Ay, that's the reason most people leave home upon. And pray may I ask what it was?"

"Why, you must know, my husband's first wife was a widow; she was daughter of one Nash, a baker at Clapton, and had married a person of the name of Clifford, who——"

"O, confound the family pedigree! Here, take another pull to wet your whistle, and come at once to the point."

"Well, then, my husband, Martin Jukes, had a daughter-in-law named Mary Clifford: she was but a little thing when her mother died, about two years old or so; and when her father-in-law married me, why, as she had no claim upon either of us, as Jukes and I were going to settle on my bit of a farm in Hampshire, and as we expected to have a large family of our own, we thought it better for ourselves to leave little Moll with her mother's friends in London. Well, nine years passed away, and not a child have we had to bless us. I very often used to think with myself that it was all a judgment from Heaven upon our hardheartedness for turning the poor, helpless, little creature out of our own doors, when we had enough for all of us, and to spare besides. Well, sir, at last my master got the ague, and then, when the cold and fever fits were on him, he fell a-thinking of Molly too ; and nothing would satisfy him but he must see the child once more ; and so, after a deal of talking and thinking upon the matter, off I set in the waggon, and came up to London to find her out, and bring her home to her father-in-law's again."

"Well done, old lady ! I like you the better for it ; so here's to your health, and to the better health of your master too, as you call him ! You're really kind, warm-hearted people, like myself, that have a proper feeling for the sorrows of a fellow-creature ; and that's what I admire, whether in man, woman, or child." So saying, Timothy handed Dame Jukes the tankard with his right hand, and wiped away the starting tear of sensibility with the left. "But," he added, after a pause, "you've found the little dear, I hope ? "

" I have, and I have not : I've found out where she is," replied the good woman, with a sigh, " but, alas ! I'm not even allowed to have a sight of her."

"Not a sight of her ! What ! in this free country shut up a child from her own flesh and blood, as you are—that is to say, her own flesh and blood by marriage ! O, it can't be !—the thing's impossible ! "

" It may be impossible, but it's very true, nevertheless."

" How can that be, my good woman ? but are not you her relation, and haven't you a right in her ? "

" Lord, no, sir ! not now, they tell me ; for, you must know, she's bound an apprentice."

" Bound an apprentice ? "

" Ay ! her mother's friends, it seems, got tired of the sweet baby, and sent her to the workhouse ; and there the overseers, I suppose, got tired of her too, and bound her an apprentice, for seven years, up here, at a house hard by in the village."

" Well, and have you been to the house ? "

" To be sure I have."

" And what did they say to you ? "

" Just told me to get about my business ; that I'd no right to

meddle or make with the child; and that, if I occasioned any
disturbance, or even presumed to come near the house again
before the seven years were out, they'd certainly send for a
constable, and have me taken before a magistrate."

"The devil!" cried Timothy Hitch, following his ejaculation
with a shrill whistle and a draught of ale to season it. "Why
who did you see?"

"The lady of the house herself—the mistress of poor little
Molly."

"The mistress?—and what's the name of her mistress?"

"Miss Elizabeth Brownrigge, to be sure! Didn't I tell you
so?"

"Miss Elizabeth Brownrigge!" exclaimed the young and
enthusiastic admirer of moral and physical beauty, with a start
of astonishment. "My good woman, you must be under a
mental delusion: why, she's a perfect paragon of goodness and
kindness!"

"She won't let me see little Mary, though," sighed Mrs. Jukes.

"This can't be! there's some mistake here," said Timothy,
taking up his hat, which was lying on the bench, and depositing
the tankard in its place: "Come along with me, and I'll see if
we can't set it all to rights. Giles, my good friend—confound the
fellow, he's drunk, and is as fast asleep as a top! What a state
for a landlord and a moralist! It's too bad—it's too bad! If a
man can't carry his liquor, he ought, as a sober man, to be
ashamed of taking his liquor. Here! House! Ho! Within!
Landlady, I'm going, do you see? So look after your husband."
And off he walked towards Elizabeth's cottage, at the rate of five
miles an hour, with Dame Jukes keeping up a shuffling run behind him, as near his heels as the fatigue of her previous exertions,
and the incumbrance of her many, ample, and thickly-quilted
petticoats, would allow of.

They had nearly reached the point of their destination, when
they fell in with Mr. and Mrs. Deacon, who were returning
home from Mr. Belvidere's at rather an earlier hour than usual.
Mrs. Deacon had felt herself somewhat indisposed, and had laid
her commands upon her husband to decline waiting for the
ducks and green peas which were preparing for supper, and

which appealed, with arguments of most savoury persuasion, to the olfactory nerves of Mr. Deacon, as he conducted his fair spouse, with an air of implicit but sullen obedience, through the hall and past the kitchen-windows of the manor-house. Our friend Timothy no sooner came within hearing of Mr. Deacon, than, with his mind full of the subject, he immediately entered upon the case of Dame Jukes and little Mary Clifford, her daughter-in-law. The apothecary and his wife both agreed with him that it was very extraordinary—the very most extraordinary thing they ever heard! The apothecary thought that " it should at once be inquired into ;" but his wife thought that " any inquiry at the present moment was impossible, as she had very good reasons for knowing that Miss Brownrigge was out, late as it was, taking an evening walk with a young gentleman." Again the apothecary surmised, " that the matter could all be very readily explained, and that the good woman before them, whose consideration for the girl was so highly to her credit, would find everything set right the moment she could obtain another interview with the young lady." But again the apothecary's wife, on the contrary, surmised no such thing ; for, " the young lady was a great tyrant, and had always treated the poor child most execrably ; and, for her part, she'd venture to swear that either the poor little dear was barbarously murdered, and actually dead and buried, and could not be produced at all, or, at least, was so black and blue with the blows she had received, that her mistress would be ashamed of producing her in the presence of so near and affectionate a relation as Mrs. Jukes !"

Timothy Hitch was quite at a loss—he did not know what to make of the matter ; and he vented his astonishment in short asides and ejaculatory sentences, without taking any part in the dialogue. Poor Dame Jukes herself could hardly utter a syllable, except the most common-place expressions of lamentation over the condition of herself and the little apprentice. She was never in a position of such publicity before, and was not only deeply interested for the sake of Mary Clifford, but was become agitated, terrified, and hysterical, at finding herself in close communication with such gentlefolks as Mr. and Mrs. Deacon, and the

L

object of interest to a group of stragglers which had gradually
gathered together, and was every moment becoming more
numerous during the discussion of the case.

But at this point we must for a few moments leave the party
at Islington, and follow the steps of Elizabeth and Alphonso
through the happy serenity of their evening walk. The lovers,
on quitting the cottage, bent their way, over fields and along
green shady lanes, towards the romantic and elevated village of
Hampstead. The spring of that year had been backward in no
ordinary degree ; and now, on the 25th of June, the summer
having at once succeeded to several weeks of heavy and continued rain, the hay-making had but just commenced. The air,
impregnated with the perfume which ascended from the meadows,
and from the wild flowers that covered the banks and strewed
their loose beauties about the hedges, scattered fragrance with
every gale that blew. The cheering voices of the labourers in
the distance, merrily dissipating the social toil of harvest-time
with many a jest, and laugh, and snatches of old songs—the
myriads of insects murmuring their busy tale to the still ear of
evening—the deep blue of the cloudless sky gradually melting
away towards the west, in the yellow glow of sunset ;—all the
accessories of the scene harmonised with the serenity of the
hour, and conduced to the diffusion of a corresponding feeling
over the young and tender hearts of Alphonso and Elizabeth.
Full of such sweet thoughts as love is pregnant in, and wearing
out the way in the responsive communication of them, Alphonso
had completely lost all recollection of the subject which engaged
him at dinner, and, indeed, of the existence of the Deacons and
their accusations. Our hero and heroine had already strolled
along the rich and beautiful meadows that skirt the foot of
Muswell Hill, and had reached a retired and shadowy spot
somewhat to the north of Mother Red Cap's, when, suddenly
emerging from a gap in the hedge, a little in advance of them,
started forth the female stranger who, at an earlier stage of our
narrative, presented herself in so extraordinary a manner at the
porch of the Red Cabbage. Her air was more wild, and her
dress still more disordered, than when she first was introduced
to the reader as interrupting the philosophic conference of

Timothy Hitch and his host Giles Fillup. Elizabeth, agitated at the unexpected appearance of the figure, exclaimed, " Good heavens ! there's that poor mad creature again !" and, for the first time in her life, placed her arm within that of Alphonso, as if claiming the support of his affection ; but her lover, flung off his guard by so new and so unhoped-for a condescension, involuntarily pressed it to his side, and the arm was immediately removed.

" Let me protect you," said Alphonso.

" Thank you," rejoined Elizabeth—" I'm not alarmed. It was mighty idle of me to be thus startled at a mere trifle ;" and, folding her arms composedly before her, she withdrew to the other side of the pathway.

As they approached the stranger, the stranger also advanced nearer towards them ; till, coming immediately opposite Eliza- beth, she at first fixed her eyes directly upon hers, with as strong an expression of stern defiance as her fair and youthful features were capable of exhibiting, and then, her countenance gradually relaxing from the severity of its character into a look of the deepest tenderness, prostrated herself upon the earth before her, and, her eyes streaming with tears, exclaimed, " Mistress, forgive me—oh, forgive me !"

" Forgive you, young woman !" replied Elizabeth ; " surely you have mistaken me for another ; I never was any mistress of thine ! Till this day I am not conscious of ever having seen you before."

" Am I so altered, then ? O, I see ! It is this dress of shame —these badges of disgrace—this detested finery !" And she began to tear the straggling feathers and flowers from her head- dress. " It is this disguise of sin that——"

" Hold, hold !" interrupted Elizabeth ; " young woman, I command you to restrain this violence !"

The poor girl, either impressed by the natural dignity of Miss Brownrigge's manner, or influenced by long habit of obedience to the voice by which she was addressed, let her hands fall down passively by her side, and, with a look in which affection, fear, and submission were strangely mingled, cried, " Oh ! Miss Brownrigge !"

"My name too!" exclaimed Elizabeth: "what is the meaning of all this? Who are you?—where do you come from?"

"What, miss! have you then indeed forgot me? Don't you remember Mary Jones?"

"My runaway apprentice! Are you, then, that wicked girl, who broke her indentures?"

"Don't say *wicked*, miss," exclaimed Mary Jones, rising quickly from the ground; "only think, miss, what I had to undergo."

"Undergo, ingrate that you are! Do you presume to insinuate that I was a harsh or unreasonable mistress to you?"

"O no! O no, indeed!" cried the girl, shrinking back, and looking up with a suppliant eye that seemed to deprecate the effects of the fair Elizabeth's anger.

"If," resumed the lady, "you did your duty well, did I not always deal kindly by you? if ill, did I not universally deal justly?"

"Yes—yes," rejoined the girl, "if I behaved well, I had pudding and no flogging; and if ill, I had a flogging and no pudding."

"Alas, alas!" exclaimed Elizabeth, "how are the most well-considered and most ably-digested systems of discipline rendered ineffectual by the grossness of the natures to which they are applied! And is it possible that thy intellect, Mary Jones, could have been so obtuse as to apprehend no deeper aims in the duly graduated scale of rewards and punishments under which the domestic economy of my house has always been conducted, than the pudding which was the recompense of your diligence, or the flogging that was the penalty of your offences! Did the sanctions of those laws and ordinances, which I had so carefully established as secondary means of appealing to the affections of your inmost soul—as exciting motives to your emulation—as prevailing arguments to your sense of shame, reach no farther, as inducements to virtue and discouragements from vice, than the mere palate which they gratified or the back they grieved? Are there, then, really any beings in the world to whom the moral is nothing, and the physical is all in all?"

During the progress of this very eloquent apostrophe, while

Alphonso was wrapped in silent admiration of the wisdom of his love, Mary Jones, no longer awed by that feeling of habitual submission which had returned upon her at first encountering her deserted mistress, had been rapidly relapsing into her former state of mental bewilderment and delirium; and the moment the last tone of Elizabeth's voice passed away from the life of music into the death of silence, she shrieked aloud,

"Whack, whack!—whack, whack!" Alphonso shuddered at the sounds: he seemed to hear in the exclamation the echo of the lashes from which the shrieks that so startled him before dinner had received their origin. "But no double thonging," continued the girl—"no double thonging for Mary Jones now! No, no! that time's gone for ever! If you're a miss, my lady, let me tell you that I'm a miss too! The best of silks and satins to wear—hooped petticoats, fly-caps, laced ruffles, and a chariot to ride in! No floggings for me! Me!—where's such another equipage as mine? who so fine and so grand as I, either at the park or the play? 'That's Miss Jones!—that's the beautiful Miss Jones!—that's the old Viscount of Darling's Miss Jones!' cry the gentlemen. 'Which, which?—where, where?' cry the ladies. 'There! that young, beautiful creature in the front box, with the high head and the diamonds, and the elderly gentleman sitting beside her!' reply the gentlemen. And then the people whisper to one another, and stare and talk, and talk and stare, and turn all their attention to me, and never think of the players."

"Mary Jones! Mary Jones!" cried Elizabeth, "are you not ashamed, after the lessons which I inculcated upon you in your childhood, to attach yourself to such passing vanities as these?"

"Passing!—yes, yes!—passing enough, Heaven knows; but then my poor mother was to blame. That was never any fault of mine, you know. I'm sure I tried to persuade my old lord to give her the money; and if he wouldn't, that was no reason why she should write his name upon a paper, and pretend that he had given it her, and send poor brother Tom to get it cashed at the banker's. They called it forgery—ah, ah, ah!—forgery! What fools these lawyers are! They did not mean any forgery, poor souls! They only wanted to get the money as quickly as they could, without troubling the gouty old lord any further. But he had them hanged, nevertheless, though he did profess such love for me all the time."

" Your mother and your brother hanged !" exclaimed Elizabeth ; and she turned pale with horror at the thought. " Unhappy Mary ! and you live to tell the tale ! "

" Ay, ay ! More's the pity ! more's the pity !—death were better, far better," muttered the girl, in low, deep, hurried accents ; and then, turning briskly round to Alphonso, demanded, with a sudden change of voice, " Pray, sir, did you ever see an execution ? "

" Oh, no !—never !" replied he impatiently, for his attention was drawn towards Elizabeth, whose self-possession, imperturbable as it generally was, appeared to fail her at the continued mention of such appalling subjects—" Never—and I trust I never shall !"

" I have ! I have !" shouted Mary Jones, with a cry of wild exultation—" I was in my chariot, too. When mother and brother were carried to Tyburn, I followed close beside them all the way. Little did the mob suppose that the fine lady, who sat there all alone, dizened out in her carriage, was daughter and sister to the condemned wretches that were dragged so slowly along in the cart, with Timothy Hitch and the chaplain ! Ah ! ah ! ah ! Only think : wouldn't they have prettily hissed and pelted me if they'd found that secret out ? But I sat back, crying all the while, with my handkerchief up to my eyes, so they saw nothing of me. And when the ropes were round their necks, and the caps drawn over their eyes, and the white handkerchief raised for the signal, I gave a scream, and before it fell to the ground, burst open the door of the carriage, and I've run, and run, and run, to get away from the sight in my eyes and the sound in my ears, and the aching of my heart, and the burning in my brain ;—but then they follow—follow—follow, and will follow me wherever I go."

" Be silent !—for mercy's sake, be silent !" cried Alphonso, observing the nerves of Elizabeth were seriously affected by the girl's story—" Let me entreat you to pursue this theme no further."

" Mary Jones," interposed Elizabeth, with a strong effort of self-command, "here you perceive the lamentable effects of a single error. Had you but remained under the safeguard of my protection, till your principles were sufficiently confirmed to be intrusted with the conduct of that most attractive and pernicious beauty, all might have still been well. I only hope and trust that these events may for ever act as warnings to you, and serve as future beacons to guide you over the tempestuous surges of the world. Adieu! Be wiser and better; and bear with you the good wishes of a friend."

"Oh! but let me kiss that hand once more," said the girl.

"The request is granted," replied Elizabeth, drawing off the glove from her right hand, which she kindly extended towards her. Mary Jones bent her knee to the ground, kissed it eagerly, and in an instant disappeared through the broken hedge-row by which she had made her approach.

The lovers turned away, and directed their steps towards Elizabeth's cottage. The sun had now sunk beneath the horizon; the evening was closing in fast around their path; the stars were beginning to shew themselves in the deep, unfathomable expanse of the heavens; the noise of the harvest-men had ceased; and no sounds any longer interrupted the stillness of the hour, but the heavier drone of the beetle, the lowing of the distant kine, and, from time to time, the melodious complaining of the nightingale. This interview with Mary Jones had recalled to the mind of young Belvidere the recollection of the cries which he had lately heard issuing from the dwelling of Elizabeth, and of the interpretation put upon them by the malice of Mrs. Deacon. He desired, yet feared, to demand an explanation of them. He desired to hear Elizabeth's vindication pronounced by her own lips; and yet he feared to touch upon the theme, lest he should seem to imply a doubt of her gentleness and tenderness of heart. But, anxious that no reservation of thought on his part should ever interfere with the perfect confidence that subsisted between them, he resolved, boldly and openly, to address his companion on the subject, and without any preliminary circumlocution, at once demanded the origin and the reason of those fearful shrieks which had so startled him in the afternoon.

"The cries were uttered by Mary Mitchel, my eldest apprentice," replied Elizabeth, with undisturbed serenity of voice and manner; "and were occasioned by the correction which I found it incumbent on me to administer."

"Had she done anything to excite your anger so violently against her?"

"I never," answered Elizabeth, with the dignity of conscious and suspected virtue, "am tempted to be angry at all; or, if I am, it could not but have subsided very long before the hour of castigation. The fault for which the chastisement was dealt took place the day before yesterday. I never punish, or allow any one to punish, a child intrusted to my protection at the moment of the offence, lest the correction, received as the result of thoughtless passion rather than of deliberate justice, should produce but a slight and transient impression upon the offender, and inflict pain upon the body, without producing any concomitant improvement of the heart and mind."

"Wise and right, as all your counsels are! Yet surely the chastisement which little Mary received must have been very severe, to elicit such loud and piercing shrieks of suffering."

"Alas!" rejoined Elizabeth, and she looked down, as she closed her eyes a moment to disperse the tears that were gathering over them—"Alas! the stripes were severe."

"Was, then, the offence so very great?"

"I am not aware of any scale by which we may measure the relative magnitude, and decide upon the proportionate dimensions of offences. The essence of crime consists in a vicious will, and not in the vicious act. All voluntary and predetermined sins bear, in my estimation, an equal degree of guilt. If a person would steal a pin, or utter a prevarication, or do a fellow-creature an injury, it is only cowardice, and not principle, that deters him from housebreaking, or perjury, or murder. Only let the world awaken from its present miserable state of moral and metaphysical blindness, and punish what are so ignorantly accounted as the slighter offences with the severity which their natural malignity deserves, and it would very soon discover that none of the larger offences remained to be punished."

" Oh, Elizabeth !" exclaimed Alphonso, " how has thy soul become enriched with such wisdom ? "

" By self-examination," she replied, gravely. The knowledge of my own frailty, and the consideration of the measures that were best adapted to the eradication of it, have been my only masters ; but they are masters who, I trust, have afforded me no slight stock of good, and sound, and valuable instruction."

In the course of this conversation, the lovers had reached the turning which brought them in view of the houses of Mr. Deacon and Elizabeth, and they were surprised at observing a large assembly of people upon the spot. " What can this disturbance mean ? " said Alphonso ; " I suppose some drunkard has ——"

" It is in vain," interrupted Elizabeth, " to amuse ourselves with suppositions upon the subject. They who would draw their conclusions from such mere external circumstances, without an accurate knowledge of the particulars, resemble those idle folk who pretend to discover figures in the clouds, each as his own imagination shapes them, and one sees a calf or a weasel in the self-same collection of vapour, which another converts into a whale or a camel."

" Most justly argued ! To be with you, and to listen to the accents of that voice, is to imbibe wisdom in music ! But, at least, let us not part at this spot, as usual. My own Elizabeth must permit me to conduct her through the throng of that turbulent and assembled mass of people, and see her safely established in the peaceful paradise of her home."

" By no means ; I thank you for the offer, Alphonso, but cannot assent to it. Your attending me would carry you just so far out of the way on your road to the manor-house, and could not render me any effectual service. Adieu, Alphonso ! I shall not volunteer the inconvenience of threading the mazes of yonder boisterous multitude, but shall effect my entrance to the cottage by the back door, and through the kitchen-garden. And so, again, farewell ! "

With these words Elizabeth withdrew. Alphonso watched her, the power of his vision gaining strength from the intensity of his affection, till, penetrating the dim twilight, he distinctly saw her pass unobserved into the garden, and heard the gate closed after her. And then, supposing it impossible he could have any interest in the affair which had collected and agitated the distant crowd, he bent his way, slowly and contemplatively, towards his father's house.

During the time of the lovers' walk, the assembly of people in front of Miss Brownrigge's cottage, of which Mr. and Mrs. Deacon, Dame Jukes, and Timothy Hitch had formed the nucleus, had been increased to a very considerable amount, by the addition of all the stragglers from the ale-house—the idlers of the village —the artisans let loose from the stall or the shop-board—the haymakers returning from the surrounding fields—the greater part of the female inhabitants of the neighbourhood—and every child above two years old who was allowed to be at that time out of bed. Among this mass of persons, the tale of Dame Jukes and Mary Clifford had, in the course of frequent repetition, became strangely and variously altered from the original; and while all were clamorously employed in recounting to any audience they could obtain the most exaggerated versions of the story, there were no two individuals to be met with whose version was the same.

"Oh, it's a shame ! a shame and a sin !" cried a hundred voices together. " It's a shame to a Christian country ! "

" Hey day ! what's the matter here ? " demanded a newly-arrived limb of the mob.

" All along of that poor old woman there."

" Oh, dear ! oh, dear ! " cried Dame Jukes. " My child ! my child ! What shall I do ? where shall I go ? what will become of me ? "

" Never mind, my good woman, we'll see you righted."

" That we will—that we will ! If we don't, we're no English-men," shouted a hundred consolatory voices at once.

" Righted ! who's injured her ? I say what's the matter ? "

" The lady of this house has kidnapped her baby."

" Nonsense : kidnapped ! no such thing. She bought her only daughter of her, ever so many years ago, for a new gown and a guinea, and has sold her for a slave to the Algerines."

" That an't so, Gilbert."

" I say it is."

"No; I tell you it an't. The poor old countrywoman came up here to see the child, who is but a baby of ten months old, and when she saw it she did not know it for her own—there was not a whole place in its body. You could not tell that it was a human creature, the poor baby was so barbarously beat about."

"That an't it a bit!"

"What is it, then?"

"Why, I'll tell you the whole long and short of it. She wasn't allowed to have a sight of the child. How should she? Why, everybody knows that the poor thing was murdered a week ago, when Mr. Deacon, the apothecary, heard the voice of a female infant crying murder, three times, in the dead of the night!"

"Oh, it's a shame! it's a sin!"

Here the mob became highly excited, and set up a horrid yell, with their faces directed towards Elizabeth's cottage, and shaking their fists up at the windows. In the midst of this riotous vociferation, a boy more zealous than the rest took up a small pebble, and flung it with some violence against the wall of the house.

This was hailed as the signal for a general attack, and all hands became immediately armed with stones, and all arms were raised to hurl them; when Timothy Hitch, ashamed at the lawless proceedings of the people, and terrified for the safety of the beautiful Elizabeth, rushing forward into the van of the mob, and raising his deep sonorous voice to the loudest pitch, so as to be audible above the clamour by which he was surrounded, succeeded for one moment in arresting their attention, while he maintained the following interrupted dialogue:

Tim. H. "My friends! my good friends! hear me for one moment."

Mob. "Hear him! hear him!"

Tim. H. "Let me implore you, as men of judgment, sobriety, and discretion—which I am sure the present assembly is composed of ——."

Mob. "Hear, hear! that's right!—that's sense, now!"

Tim. H. "Let me implore you not to prosecute this outrage

any further. Even to the greatest offender, I'm sure no man amongst you, as an Englishman ——"

Mob. "Hear him ! hear him !"

Tim. H. "As an Englishman—I repeat it—would deny the privilege which the free institutions of this country afford, and refuse the liberty ——"

Mob. "Hurra ! Liberty for ever ! Liberty and reform ! Hurra !"

Tim. H. "If Miss Brownrigge be really criminal ——"

Mob yells. "She is—she is ! we know it ! Down with her ! Down with her !"

Tim. H. "I cannot believe it."

Mob yells. "Yah ! yah ! yah !"

Tim. H. "Has not her whole life been a course of kindness and humanity ? Has she not been the friend of thousands ? and has she ever done an injury to a single human being among you ?"

Mob. "Down with him !" (*Loud yells : as they die away, a single voice bawls out*—"If she did do us any good, she had her own ends to serve !" *which cry is violently repeated by the mob.*)

Tim. H. "If she has committed any wrong, I don't wish to stand between a culprit and her punishment. Heaven forbid that I should ! But is she not amenable to the courts of justice ? and will not the government take care that the laws are not defrauded of their dues ?"

Mob. "Down with her ! No laws—no justice—no government —no nothing !"

In the midst of this most reasonable cry for the annihilation of the moral and material world, volleys of stones and other missiles were hurled violently against the windows of the house ; and one man, half-drunk with spirits, and half-mad with the excitement of mob enthusiasm, having possessed himself of a torch, was hastening forward, with the intention of setting fire to the building.

Timothy Hitch, whose influence with the multitude had been rapidly departing, from the moment that he had ceased to flatter and presumed to address a word of salutary counsel to them, here exerted the last effort of his lungs, and made a final trial of the extent of his popularity, by laying hold of the ruffian, and exclaiming,

" For Heaven's sake, my friends, beware what you're about! As to Miss Brownrigge, I do not interpose for her ; but will you burn the poor innocent apprentices ? "

This appeal, bursting upon them in that dull interval of silence which, even in the most turbulent and numerous multitudes, always precedes a moment of action, produced an instantaneous effect. The mass of people rushed forward, with a single impulse, to seize upon Elizabeth, and to rescue the children. The poor girls, who were discovered in the coal-shed, clinging to each other, terrified by the clamours, and grievously bruised by many stones which had been cast from the hands of their friends, were immediately removed, under the care of Mr. Deacon, to the parish work-house. Elizabeth, the object of the hostility of the mob, was nowhere to be found.

END OF BOOK THE FIRST.

BOOK II.

CHAPTER I.

*A Departure—Female Pedestrianism—Masquerading—Eliza-
beth Canning.*

" Behold them wandering on their hopeless way,
Unknowing where they stray ;
Yet sure where'er they stop to find no rest."—SOUTHEY.

Την δ ἀπομειβομενη προσεφη πολυμητις.—HOMER.

" So we grew together,
Like to a double cherry, seeming parted ;
But yet a union in partition—
Two lovely berries moulded on one stem."—SHAKESPEARE.

ON quitting Alphonso, and entering the garden, Elizabeth found
herself accosted by Mary Jones, who, deeply interested in the
safety, and anticipating the movements, of her young mistress,
had stationed herself in the garden with the intention of warning
her of the impending danger, and preventing her return to the
cottage. The poor girl wildly but accurately informed our
heroine of the origin of the riot, which was every minute
gathering strength, of the strange rumours that circulated among
the populace, of their exasperation against her, and of the
violence to which she would inevitably be exposed should she
venture to encounter them in their present infuriated state.
Elizabeth, undismayed by the intelligence, answered her attached
and humble friend with a simple expression of compassion for
the state of the poor deluded people, and began, with her usual
equability of mind and composure of manner, to retrace her
steps towards the road.

" The philosopher has said," she muttered in soliloquy, but
still loud enough to be overheard by Mary Jones, who, at a
respectful distance, followed her into a path that led over the

fields towards Gray's Inn Lane and Holborn Bars — "the philosopher has said, that if he were accused of any even the most impossible crime—if he were charged with having purloined the church steeple and carried it away in his waistcoat-pocket, his first measure would be flight."

"And by far the best measure too!" cried Mary Jones; "who that had their wits about them would stay to be baited by bum-bailiffs and shoved about by sheriffs' officers, if——"

"Inconsiderate creature that I am!" interrupted Elizabeth, suddenly recollecting the absence of her dog; "I protest, in my hurry, I have forgotten Muggletonian. He'll fall a victim to the fury of the mob. Not finding the object of their indignation, they'll vent their blind and ignorant malice upon my unoffending favourite. It were unjust and cruel to abandon him to such a fate! Instantly will I return and seek him."

"No, no, Miss Elizabeth!" exclaimed her companion; "stay you there in safety, behind the trunk and beneath the spreading shade of yonder oak, where the branches are so closely interwoven that not a single ray of moonlight can make its way, and discover your concealment, while I go back to the house. The people won't know me, or, if they should, they'll allow me to pass without annoyance. Do you wait here, and in a trice I'll return with little Muggy."

"Call him Muggletonian," said Elizabeth: "I have a great dislike to all senseless abbreviations."

It may be questioned whether Mary Jones heard this rejoinder of our heroine; for the faithful creature had no sooner expressed her determination of going in search of the absent animal, than she disappeared with the speed of lightning from the spot; and, before Elizabeth supposed it possible that she could have reached the cottage, her voice was again heard behind her, exclaiming, in a hurried whisper of exultation, "Come along—come along, my mistress! the mob have entered and are ransacking the cottage. I saw them in the parlour; but I passed them unobserved, and have rescued the object of your anxiety."

"Rescued him!—where is he?" demanded Elizabeth; "no Muggletonian do I see!"

"See him!—how should you?" replied Mary; "why, bless

your heart, my mistress, the little fellow's fast asleep in my pocket!"

I need not remind my antiquarian readers, that while in the benighted days of the eighteenth century no mantua-maker had yet advanced so far on the march of intellect as to approach the discovery of a reticule, the lap-dogs of those times were small, and the pockets were capacious.

The party being thus completed, they, for a short space, wound their way in silence beneath the bright eye of the silver moon, across the dewy fields and along the green winding paths that conducted to the metropolis. They had reached the top of Gray's Inn Lane before Elizabeth, who, during the progress of their walk, had been taking counsel with herself alone upon the course which it would be most advisable for her to adopt, had fully matured her plans of operation, and began, in the following words, to open her intentions to her companion :—

" You left me of your own accord, Mary, and in violation of the terms of your indentures : I apprehend you repent yourself of that unhappy measure ? "

" Repent me of it !—O, how bitterly ! "

" I attempt not to put any constraint upon your inclinations ; you are now at liberty to remain with or to leave me. Make your choice freely ; but, Mary Jones, make it firmly, and once for all."

" With you—O, with you ! " cried the affectionate girl, eagerly seizing and kissing the hand of Elizabeth ;—" with you, wherever you go, and whatever may be your destiny ! "

" That is well ! " rejoined our heroine, giving a slight pressure of acknowledgment to the hand by which her own was respectfully but affectionately grasped ; " and from this moment, Mary, no longer regarded as an apprentice, but as a friend, I receive you, as the depositary of my most secret thoughts, to the confidence which your fidelity deserves."

" Me !—your confidence ! O, Miss Brownrigge ! "

" It would be wiser, Mary, to designate me by that name no longer. Nothing can be more foreign from my principles or my inclinations than ' to do evil that good may come.' Never would I attempt to seek an ignominious safety from the persecutions of my enemies beneath the shelter of falsehood or prevarication. I do not, therefore, propose, as perhaps might be the case with many persons of a lower tone of morals, when placed in such an emergency as ours, to assume an *alias*. It is not my intention to change my name altogether, but I shall no longer make use of more than half of it : instead of denominating me Miss Elizabeth Brownrigge, you will henceforth remember, Mary, that my appellation is Mistress Eliza Brown."

" Mistress ? "

" Ay—*Mistress*, Mary Jones ! The unwedded wife, the virgin widow, of Alphonso Belvidere ? "

" Widow, ma'am ? "

" From this hour, true to the memory of him to whose love I am for ever dead, and from whose presence I am for ever severed, the lonely sense of widowhood will perpetually rest upon my heart, and the dark weeds of widowhood shall be the constant habiliments of my person."

" O, you cannot surely be so cruel ! What ! give up poor, dear Mr. Alphonso—such a clever, sweet, virtuous young gentleman—who stands six feet two without his shoes, and who loves you with such devotion ? "

" It is because he loves me—because I love him, my friend, that this resolution has been formed. Alphonso is no ordinary man ; and his wife, like that of Cæsar, ought not only to be immaculate in herself, but unsuspected by others. The reproach which attaches to me, and from which I fly, is to *my* conscience, and ought to be to *his*, as an irreversible sentence of divorcement. It is *his* duty to forget a name that has been linked in the public voice with dishonourable epithets ; and it is *my* duty to prevent its being ever recalled to his recollection."

" O dear, Miss——"

" Mistress, Mary—remember, Mistress ! "

" Mistress Elizabeth——"

" Eliza ! "

" Well, well !—O dear, Mrs. Eliza Brownri——"

" Brown ! that's enough."

" O, Mrs. Eliza Brown ! Can you have the heart to jilt that beautiful gentleman ? "

" I do not *jilt* him, Mary.—As an act of self-devotion, I offer up my own happiness as a voluntary sacrifice on the altar of his future respectability in life."

" And what, for mercy's sake, do you mean to do, ma'am ? "

" That thought is opportunely suggested," replied Elizabeth. " It is, indeed time that we should provide for the present need. A strict search after us will immediately be set on foot. This we must endeavour to elude. It is first necessary that we should make an alteration in our attire. Attend me here. I'll proceed to yonder warehouse, over the door of which the three golden balls are pendant and the large lamp is blazing, and purchase whatever may be requisite to complete the change of our appearance; and in effecting that change, the deserted stable to our right will afford the decent shelter of its roof."

Elizabeth had no sooner determined upon this plan, than, with that promptitude of execution by which her character was distinguished, she took measures for its instant accomplishment. She calmly entered the pawnbroker's, and deliberately made her bargain for the articles required: and after completing her purchases, many minutes did not elapse before she and her companion issued from the deserted building to which they had retired, entirely metamorphosed in their apparel and appearance. The stained and tattered finery of Mary Jones had given place to the decent linen gown, the close cap, the black bonnet, and the red cloak of a country maid-servant; while our heroine, according to the intention she had previously expressed, assumed the dark garments of widowhood. The watchmen—in those days they still existed—were now vociferating, each upon his peculiar beat, " Past ten o'clock ! " Hitherto our fair and interesting friends had proceeded on their way almost unobserved and altogether without interruption ; but, on reaching the Holborn end of Gray's Inn Lane, their progress was impeded by the intervention of a dense crowd, which reached from one side of the street to the other, and threatened to oppose a formidable obstruction to their passage. This mass of people were collected together near the gate of Gray's Inn, and their heads turned back, their mouths open, and their eyes at the fullest stretch, were listening, with intense and silent interest, to a little chimney-sweeper, who, perched on the top of a lamp-post, was bawling forth to the surrounding audience the contents of a large printed bill. As the fair friends approached this peculiar and novel kind of rostrum, they could not help catching a sufficient number of the words which the shrill-tongued urchin was vociferating to enable them to comprehend the import of his communication : and as the phrases, " eloped from her chariot," " foot of the gallows," " Tyburn," " young lady," " sixteen years of age," " fashionably attired," struck upon the ear of Mary Jones, she drew closer and closer to Elizabeth : and when she heard that £200 were offered as the reward of her restoration, she was seized with fear and trembling, and whispered her mistress in a voice scarce audible, and broken by apprehension, " O, ma'am, 'tis I—'tis I ! They'll find me out and take me from you ! O, what shall I do ? "

" Be calm ! " rejoined our heroine, grasping her wrist with an air of dignified authority ; " subdue this idle agitation, and follow me in silence ;—detection is impossible ! Remember you are again yourself, and no longer disguised as a woman of quality !"

The expression " *disguised* " somewhat jarred upon the ear and vanity of Mary Jones : but she felt consoled by the reflection that her identity with the person described in the placard was not likely to be discovered ; and, obedient to the directions of the superior mind in subjection to which she acted, she quietly followed in the path that was opened for them as the crowd retired on either side, with an involuntary feeling of respect, before the commanding brow and elevated deportment of Elizabeth. On regaining the open street, our heroine recommenced the detail of those plans for the future, in arranging which her mind had been actively engaged, even while acknowledging, with a graceful inclination of her head from side to side, the kind attention of the mob, and sustaining the fainting spirits of her more dependent and less self-possessed companion.

" We shall soon leave this country for ever, and no more return to it again ! Will it grieve you, Mary ! "

" Nothing can grieve me as long as I am with you."

" You'll not object, then, to residing in America, whither I purpose retiring to seek an asylum from the tyranny of my persecutors, in the arms of friendship and in a land of liberal opinions."

"Friends in America! I never heard, ma'am, before," cried Mary Jones, "that you had any friends in foreign parts."

"Yes, Mary," replied Elizabeth, with a sigh of tender recollection, "the dearest and the earliest friend I·have has long been an unwilling emigrant from her native land, the martyr of inflexible virtue and the victim of an indiscriminating jury. You have, perhaps, heard of Elizabeth Canning?"

"To be sure I have; you mean the girl that was transported for perjury, and who wanted to swear away the life of old Mother Squires, of Enfield Wash!"

"O, Elizabeth, Elizabeth! my school-girl friend! my childhood's monitress! And is it thus that truth and purity like yours are perverted by the misapprehensions, and profaned by the calumnies, of the multitude!"

"Why, la! ma'am," cried the astonished Mary, "is it possible that that wicked woman was really an acquaintance of yours?"

"Hear me, my young friend," replied her mistress, with a calm and gentle tone of admonition, "and ever after learn to mistrust the erring representations of common fame, and to reverence those as the most virtuous of their race whom the voice of public rumour most clamorously condemns. The parents of Elizabeth Canning and myself were not only connected by the ties of blood, but by the far closer ties of affectionate and long-continued intimacy. Their children—playmates from their birth, and sisters by adoption—became the natural inheritors of the friendship by which their fathers and mothers were so inseparably united. The daughter of Mr. and Mrs. Canning was a few months my elder; but I cannot call to mind the time in which we did not share every study and every amusement together—in which I did not find the hours hang heavy on my hands that were not irradiated by the presence of Elizabeth—the pleasure joyless that was not participated by her—and the lesson uninstructive that was not recommended to my attention by the desire of her approval and the consciousness of her companionship. She was just so much my senior as to be capable of assisting, without leading,

me—of facilitating my progress, without directing my studies—
of preceding and clearing away the difficulties in the paths of
erudition, without outstripping me in the attainment of the
goal to which they led. Her principles, formed from childhood by the counsels and the examples of the best and wisest
of the human race—I mean her parents and my own—were
exalted to a pitch of heroic elevation ; and, in whatever guise
temptation might assail her, its assaults fell powerless, and
rebounded from her invincible purity of character like the
spears of the Trojans from the invulnerable body of Achilles.
She bore a charmed spirit ; and her high-enduring constancy of
soul was capable of sustaining every species of allurement, and
defying every form of intimidation. O, Mary Jones !" cried
Elizabeth, " imagine, if I loved such virtue ! Did I love her ?
O, she was my life, my joy, my happiness, my supplemental
conscience, my second self, my counsellor, my friend !"

" And this," said Mary, indignantly, " was the person whom
the world had the barbarity to send to gaol and try as a
criminal ! "

"The *world* was unworthy of her !" exclaimed our heroine.
" When her tale of oppression was related—When it was told
that my fair and admirable friend—kidnapped, stunned, and
stripped by a band of ruffians ; threatened with loss of life ;
confined for eight-and-twenty days in a cockloft, and deprived of
all sustenance, during the time of her imprisonment, but about
a quart of water, a few slices of stale bread, and a penny mince-
pie that she happened to have in her pocket*—when it was told
that such unparalleled inflictions were endured, amid the hardest
severities of winter, by a young girl like Elizabeth, at the hands
of the most barbarous of men and the most fiend-like of women,
because she would not mingle in the pollutions of their orgies,
the tale appeared incredible to the multitude. Incapable of
comprehending the height of her virtue, they gave belief to the
slanders of her oppressors. A judge, a jury, and an English
mob, insensible to every feeling of magnanimity themselves,
could readily enough imagine that a meek and inexperienced

---

* See the trial of Elizabeth Canning for perjury.

maiden might invent a falsehood and sustain it by perjury; but they were unable to raise their petty souls to the conception of a fortitude like that of Elizabeth Canning, who suffered the bitterest oppressions in the cause of virtue, and whose virtue was thus tried and confirmed, but was not at all shaken, by the bitterness of the oppressions which she suffered."

"Admirable girl! O, how I repent the injurious opinions I have been taught to entertain of her! How I long to fling myself at her feet, and implore her pardon for my error!"

"That meeting may not be long delayed," resumed Elizabeth: "a vessel will, I know, shortly sail for New England; in it we will take our passage from an ungrateful and benighted land. Till the time of its departure a retired but respectable asylum must be found for us in the neighbourhood of London. O, my ever dear, my oppressed, and most injured friend, my impatience of absence is increased by the probability of our speedy reunion! It is painful to remember that I am separated from the society of so exalted a creature; but that state of separation will have an almost immediate conclusion; and in the meantime it is my duty to be resigned to the inevitable privation."

After this eulogistic apostrophe to Elizabeth Canning, Miss Brownrigge took the arm of her attendant, and bent her way towards Wandsworth, with a view of seeking some quiet lodging, in which she might reside unknown till she bade an everlasting farewell to the country of her birth.

CHAPTER II.

The Cottage—the Apprentices—Mrs. Deacon—a Lover—a Billet-Doux—Despair—a Discovery.

" Dead for a ducat, dead ! "—SHAKESPEARE.

" The lunatic, the lover, and the poet,
Are of imagination all compact."—*Midsummer Night's Dream.*

" Heaven, sure, form'd letters for some lover's aid."—POPE.

" Qualis populeâ mœrens philomela sub umbrâ
Amissos queritur fœtus; quos durus arator
Observans nido implumes detraxit ; at illa
Flet noctem, ramoque sedens miserabile carmen
Integrat, et mœstis latè loca questibus implet."—VIRGIL.*

DISAPPOINTED by our heroine's escape of a living object on which to vent their indignation, the mob were with difficulty prevented, by the humanity of Timothy Hitch, who was penetrated with the kindest interest for the property of Elizabeth, and by the prudence of Mr. Deacon, who dreaded the probable effects of a conflagration on premises so nearly connected with his own, from proceeding to set fire to the cottage. The principle of destructiveness—which may be always regarded as the idiosyncratic and predominating principle of all large masses of the human race—when once excited, is never allowed to pass away without producing its natural effects. It is not more certainly true, that " nothing can come of nothing," than that " something always comes of something "; and the present mob, faithful to the prevailing instinct of all mobs, did not think of dispersing till they had left in mischief the traces of their having met. They were not, indeed, afforded an opportunity of gratifying their savage propensities, by the murder of a young, lovely, and unoffending woman, or by burning her cottage to the ground, with the chance of involving half the village of

---

[* *Georgicon,* lib. iv., 511-515.—ED.]

Islington in the blaze; but they consoled themselves for the forcible check to which their inclinations were thus subjected, by shattering the carved ivory cabinets, the curious clocks, and the various articles of ornamental furniture—by smashing the glass and china into a thousand pieces—by dashing the pokers through the pictures and mirrors—by tearing up the flowers, trampling upon the borders, levelling the fences, breaking the windows—and by finally effecting a predatory and exterminating inroad on the abundant contents of the cellars, larders, and store-closets.

On the morning of the 25th of June, 1765, the sun shone brightly on the fair abode, the smiling garden, and the well-ordered dwelling of Elizabeth, as on a kingdom happily thriving under the kindly auspices of a Tory administration; on the morning of the 26th the same sun shone full as brightly, but it looked down upon a scene of ruin and devastation, like the same kingdom passed into other hands, and suffering, after a distracting clamour for liberty and reform, under the all-withering government of the Whigs and the Economists.

But the ravages which laid waste the cottage and the surrounding garden of our heroine were not all attributable to the hands of this lawless assembly: devastations were committed for which they were not responsible. They, indeed, had made the premises a wilderness; but it was rapidly converted into a desert by the crowd of inquisitive and curiosity-seeking *virtuosi*, who, on the following Sunday, came flocking to the village of Islington for the sake of gratifying their eyes with the sight of the spot in which such atrocities had been perpetrated; and each of whom carried away some portable relic as a memorial of his visit, till nothing portable remained to be carried away.

Most eager were the inquiries after the two little girls, Mary Mitchell and Mary Clifford. They had been conveyed, as we have already stated, to the poor-house; where, under the care of the respectable Mrs. Deacon, and under the eye of an incessant succession of visitors, every relief which medical skill and universal sympathy could afford was most liberally administered. The whole country was interested in their fate. The parish authorities found it so impossible to answer individually the numerous inquiries after their health, that a bulletin, signed by three eminent disciples of Esculapius, was posted at the church-door, and changed from hour to hour, as any alteration was discovered in their symptoms.

The public, by the by, had been unfairly dealt with on the occasion; for the first account which they received of this transaction, through the medium of those most veracious of all organs, the newspapers, had declared that both the children were found covered with bruises, beaten to death, and tied up with the same rope to a large beam in the roof of the coal-cellar. Now this was a very striking and impressive story indeed, and was altogether very highly gratifying to his majesty's loyal subjects of England, Wales, Ireland, Scotland, and the town of Berwick-upon-Tweed. It afforded them an ample opportunity for indulging in what Jeremy Bentham has so aptly designated "the pleasures of malevolence," by rancorous denunciations on the head of the fair Elizabeth; for placing their own tenderness of heart in advantageous contrast with her barbarity, by exaggerated expressions of astonishment at her conduct; and for a cheap exercise of the virtue of charity, by pathetic lamentations over the sufferings of her apprentices. The succeeding post-day, on the other hand, brought intelligence altogether as disappointing; by correcting the falsehood, it very materially diminished the interest of the narrative. Two *sick* children in a poor-house, desperate as their case was reported to be in a letter signed by Galen Deacon himself, was a sad falling-off from two *dead* girls in a coal-cellar. But there was still much to keep public curiosity on the stretch, and idle tongues in motion. Their mistress—struck, as it was said, with remorse and alarm—had suddenly disappeared; and the uncertainty of her apprehension was a very interesting circumstance. Then, again, it was doubted whether either, or which of the children, could recover; and the suspense of their fate was an extremely interesting circumstance indeed. To be sure, both might get well—a result which a very humane lecturer against West Indian slavery deprecated with the most earnest fervour of his piety; lest, as he said, "that horrid woman their mistress—if the police were fortunate enough to discover her—

should escape the hanging she deserved." Indeed, this last
supposition involved such a shameful fraud upon the dues of
public justice, that no one could endure to contemplate it for a
moment. The restoration of both children was not to be
thought of; in fact, Mr. Deacon was pledged to the public for
the death of one of them. In his printed letter on the subject,
he had expressed very slight hopes of the recovery of Mary
Mitchell, and none at all of Mary Clifford. So one murder
still appeared to be certain, if not two; and the multitude lived
in eager expectation of the realisation of at least half of the
original report, which they hoped to find followed by the highly-
important supplement of the detection, trial, confession, last
dying-speech, and execution of the murderess.

During this period of excitement, nothing could be more important than Mrs. Deacon's position in the world of Islington
and its vicinity. She was at the poor-house the first thing in
the morning and the last thing at night; and had always the
most correct information to give, either from personal inspection
or from the immediate intelligence of her spouse. She had
suddenly swoln into a person of distinction. Like Lord Byron,
the morning after the publication of *Childe Harold*, this lady,
the morning after the flight of Elizabeth, "awoke and found
herself famous." She heard of nothing but her penetration,
her perseverance, and her humanity—she had always seen
through the hypocrisy of Miss Brownrigge—she had always
known that there was something mysterious about her conduct
—she had always suspected how the case really stood—she had
always predicted that something would be discovered at last—
she had afforded poor, old, excellent Mrs. Jukes the first intimation of the deplorable condition in which her daughter-in-law
was placed—she it was who insisted on having the house
searched, who had directed that the dear children should be
carried to the poor-house, and who had undressed them and
anointed their bruises with her own hands—she was, besides,
the wife of the apothecary that attended them; and "from night
till morn, from morn till dewy eve," she bustled about from
house to house, and from neighbour to neighbour, pouring all
that she knew, guessed, or could invent, upon the leading topic

of the day, into the thirsty ears of her credulous and curious
auditors. This lady was one of those who, from the first, had
augured the death of both the apprentices. Her opinion was,
that " though Deacon was very clever, and could save a patient's
life as long as there was any life in him to save, mortification
must inevitably ensue, as the consequence of such bruises as
both the children had received ; and, as a doctor's wife, she
thought her opinion of some value." This opinion she pro-
mulgated, indeed, to all the innumerable friends with whom she
was so kind as to communicate on the subject ; and when Mary
Mitchell was reported better, though the same bulletin declared
Mary Clifford dead, it may be doubted whether she was not
more *grieved* by the falsification of her prediction than *gratified*
by the success of her husband's skill. The case of the apprentices,
however, was now, and finally, set at rest. Mary Clifford was a
corpse in St. Andrew's churchyard, and Mary Mitchell was disposed of to another mistress, a Jew slopseller in the neighbourhood of Rag-Fair. Such being the case, the full and active
interest of Mrs. Deacon's mind was directed into another
channel, and became wholly occupied with wondering, and sur-
mising, and inquiring about the retreat of Elizabeth ; against
whom the coroner's inquest had delivered a verdict of *wilful
murder*, and for whose apprehension a reward of £500 had been
offered in the Gazette.

Far different from the feelings of Mrs. Deacon and her friends
were those of Alphonso Belvidere. Removed as his father's
residence was from the scene of tumult, the riot, and the
attendant devastation of Miss Brownrigge's cottage, on the night
of the 25th of June, passed away without its inhabitants
receiving any intimation of the event ; and when, on the succeeding morning, the baker arrived at the kitchen-door with
the hot rolls for breakfast, and the freshest news of the neighbourhood, the domestics, each dreading to be the repeater of any
tidings that were injurious to the fame of Miss Brownrigge,
after a long discussion on the expediency or inexpediency of
relating what they had heard, unanimously resolved to keep
silence upon the subject, and leave the knowledge of events so
important to their young master's happiness to extend itself as

chance might direct. In total ignorance, therefore, of all the miserable circumstances that had taken place, his fancy bright as the morning, his spirits light as the summer gales that were playing about his cheeks, his mind full of delightful recollections, and his heart bounding high with animating hopes, Alphonso, after a rapid repast, started from the breakfast-table, that he might snatch a moment of brief converse with his Elizabeth, before the hour in which the Islington stage started for the Bank. Happy in himself, he dreamt not of aught but happiness around him—at peace with his own breast, he could not entertain a thought of enmity against another; and when he met Mr. and Mrs. Deacon advancing, with a hurried step and an air of bustling importance, towards the poor-house, he quickened his already rapid pace, and, forgetting the disagreeable skirmishes of the preceding afternoon, approached them with a smile of welcome, and extended to either neighbour the hand of frank and cordial salutation. To his surprise, the offered courtesy, which was but coolly answered by Mr. Deacon, was disdainfully rejected by the lady. Till that moment, Alphonso had never given a second thought to the extraordinary dialogue in which he had so recently exposed himself to her indignation. But as the recollection of it shot across his mind, a sense of the ridiculous nature of his position was simultaneously engendered, which exhibited itself in the involuntary sparkling of his eye and the playful curling of his upper lip. The expression, slight and fleeting as it was, did not escape the jealous and irritable glance of Mrs. Deacon. Her whole soul was stirred within her; she felt insulted in thought; and perceiving that Alphonso was still unconscious of the events at the cottage, she found herself in possession of the means of extorting an ample vengeance for the contumely he had offered to her charms, and resolved to make the fullest use of the advantage which was thus afforded her by a chance so favourable to her malignity.

"A wretched business, this!" said Mrs. Deacon, her eye glancing a look of insolent triumph, her cheeks and lips chilled and white with the icy touch of malice, her voice half choked with passion, and its accents rendered peculiarly offensive by an abortive attempt to assume a tone of compassion—"a wretched business this ! But I always foretold how it would turn out."

" No better—no better this morning," said Mr. Deacon; " I've already been twice to look at the bruises, and examine the effect of my lotions ; but I don't entertain a hope."

" Scarified from top to toe," said his wife ; "great wales all over the back and loins, as big as my fist, and striped all manner of colours, like a rainbow."

" There's not a chance of life," said Mr. Deacon.

" No, not a chance ! mortification must inevitably take place," added his wife.

" Whom are you speaking of ? " demanded Alphonso ; " whose life is in danger ? who has been thus barbarously treated ? "

" Oh !" replied Mrs. Deacon, " it's just as I related—just as I said ; though Mr. Belvidere and Mr. Alphonso Belvidere did so peremptorily *put* me down. It's all as I predicted ; and your Miss Elizabeth——"

" Good Heavens !" exclaimed the agonised Alphonso ; " what of Elizabeth ? Has she got great wales on her back ? has she been beaten black and blue ? is her life in danger ? "

" Yes, that indeed is it," replied Mrs. Deacon, bridling up, and kindling as she spoke with the anticipated triumph of an embryo repartee. " Mightily, indeed, is her life in danger, if the constables can but get hold of her ; and, though her neck is so delicate, she may yet chance to find it too large for the halter."

" Woman ! woman ? " cried Alphonso, " if you are not lost to every feeling of compassion as of shame, at once disclose the meaning of these horrible enigmas."

" Woman !—Shame !—Compassion !—Enigmas !"—ejaculated Mrs. Deacon, with a little titter of complacent malice, and still swelling more and more with the rapid and abundant secretion of that black venom which, engendered of jealousy and revenge, she was preparing to vent forth in one annihilating gush upon her victim. " Why the meaning's plain enough, Mr. Alphonso Belvidere, since you are so anxious for the discovery of ' my *enigma*,' as you call it ; the meaning is, that your sweet, beautiful, amiable Miss Brownrigge, has whipped her two dear little apprentice girls till they've been carried all but dead to the poor-house; and my young lady has had the prudence to take herself off, and nobody knows where to look after her!"

The words were no sooner uttered than, as if a pistol had been fired through his brain, our hero fell as one dead at the feet of his informant.

Now this was more than Mrs. Deacon designed: it was not her wish to kill him altogether. She would not have been displeased if her words had given him a brain fever, or a serious fit of illness. Had the result been a strait waistcoat or a consumption, it would have gratified her extremely; but his sudden death was neither expected nor desired. Mrs. Deacon was a philanthropist, according to the modern school of philanthropy. She patronised slow and lingering inflictions. With regard to our criminal law, she had universally professed herself to be a zealous reformer, on the score of humanity. Her mild and tender heart had always sickened at the very thought of a capital punishment. She was a steady advocate for the substitution of labour for life, and solitary imprisonment in its place; and when she saw Alphonso lying pale and senseless on the ground before her, reflecting on the world of excruciating anguish which he would necessarily be spared, while the fate of the children was in doubt, and during the pursuit, the prosecution, and perhaps the final condemnation of Elizabeth—like a cat, which will not destroy, but loves to keep her prey in the agony of a suspended destruction—she became intensely anxious that the animation of which her intelligence had deprived him should be quickly and effectually restored. Actuated by these feelings in his favour, Mrs. Deacon earnestly implored her husband to administer his professional assistance. That gentleman's ready lancet was immediately in his hand; and, after the loss of a good deal of blood, and swallowing a small quantity of water, the connubial and medical pair had the gratification of seeing the young man conveyed to his father's house on a litter, greatly exhausted in body, and in a high state of mental delirium.

By the by, though I forgot to mention it before, the full and particular account that Mrs. Deacon was enabled to give of this event, which, according to the lady's report, occurred while she was endeavouring to break the matter to poor Mr. Alphonso as tenderly as possibly, conduced in no trifling degree to enhance the temporary consideration which she enjoyed during the state of public excitement on Miss Brownrigge's cause.

Alphonso was confined to his room, and perfectly unconscious of the momentous occurrences that were happening around him for several days. During this state of insensibility little Mary Clifford died; his love was publicly gazetted as a murderess; and the most diligent exertions were made to discover her retreat. The sole and indefatigable attendant on his illness and his affliction was his father. By night, Mr. Belvidere kept silent watch beside his couch; by day, he was ever near to administer the appointed medicines, and catch, in the direction of his eye or the slightest motion of his hand, the intimation of his wishes or his wants. When, at length, his delirium left him, and the powers of his mind were restored, a far higher and more important office devolved on the excellent parent of Alphonso. It was then his task to counsel his son with the lessons of his wisdom and experience, and to fortify his failing spirits under the accumulated burden of the distresses which were pressing on him, by the energy of his own moral and religious principles. Seldom has a case occurred in which such succours were more urgently required. Our hero was not only afflicted by the absence of his Elizabeth; he did not only grieve over the uncertainty of her fate, and the perils by which she was surrounded; but he was suffering from her voluntary and most unexpected rejection of him. On the morning of his recovered consciousness, the following letter reached the manor-house, by means of the penny post:—

"*July* 1, A.D. 1765, N.S.

" Dear Sir,

"Having every reason for confiding in your late assurances of esteem and regard, I am not without apprehension that this communication may occasion you some degree of inconvenience. Circumstances over which I had no control, and which you must at this writing be fully acquainted with, have rendered it expedient that I should travel abroad. It is my intention never to return to England. We shall, consequently, meet no more. Want of time prevents me having the pleasure of detailing the reasons which have induced this determination ; but that good opinion of my judgment and discretion which you have so frequently described yourself as entertaining, will be sufficient to satisfy you that it has not been adopted without strong and substantial grounds. You will be so good as to present my compliments to any neighbours that may be interested in my welfare ; and with my best respects to *your* honoured father and *my* very kind friend, Mr. Belvidere, senior, I beg leave to subscribe myself,

Dear Sir,

Your humble and obedient servant,

ELIZABETH BROWNRIGGE.

" *For Mr. Alphonso Belvidere,*
    Manor House, Islington."

This letter, with the post-mark " Cheapside " upon it, and destitute of any other clue that might serve to guide him to her retreat, was the only intimation that our hero received of the existence of his mistress. That her resolution was formed on principles of the most perfect wisdom, he had not the temerity to doubt ; but, alas ! our consent to the justice of the sentence which may be passed upon us affords very little alleviation for the misery which we may suffer from its infliction. Alphonso's wretchedness was extreme : the sun of his existence had set. He only lived on the hope of calling Elizabeth his own. All the prospects of his ambition, all the exertions of his genius, had her happiness for their object ; and the sole enjoyment which he anticipated from the success and affluence that awaited him was to result from witnessing the blessings which they would enable him to lavish upon her who was so inestimably dearer to him than himself ;—and that she should give him up ! That he should be abandoned by one for whom he would have been content to die in torture, and without whom existence was a burden too intolerable to be endured,—the very thought was madness to him ! Why, at the slightest hint from her, he would willingly have relinquished his home, family, country, fortune, fame—all his possessions in the present, all his expectations for

the future—and have deemed it delight and privilege enough
to be allowed to labour for her support, and procure for her the
necessaries and the conveniences of life by the sweat of his
brow, an unregarded stranger in the midst of strangers, and an
alien in the stranger's land! And then, to be put away so
calmly, and for ever, and without a single expression of regret !
The consideration of these things drove him to desperation ; and,
in the changeful paroxysms of his agony, he would now clench
his fists, and stamp violently upon the ground, and beat his
breast, and tear his hair, and utter the most piercing shrieks and
exclamations of suffering ; and then—as if the more acute sense
of pain was blunted by continued endurance, and nature, exhausted by the excess of torture, had relapsed into insensibility,—
he would sit silent, motionless, and abstracted, with the tears
fast-flowing, like rivulets from ever-springing fountains, down
his cheeks, and without exhibiting the slightest consciousness of
the presence of the persons or circumstances around him. Still,
reduced as Alphonso was by the loss of his Elizabeth, his own
sufferings had not abated, or in the least degree diminished his
interest for her safety ; and the dread of her apprehension was
another poisoned shaft from the bow of destiny that rankled in
his so severely-wounded breast. Aware, however, of her intention to depart from England, and finding that several weeks of
vain pursuit had already elapsed during which the police authorities had been baffled in all their attempts to discover her abode,
both he and his father had begun to lose much of their first apprehension on her account, and to trust, with considerable confidence,
to the probability of her having succeeded in effecting her escape.

Such was the posture of affairs when, on the evening of Saturday the 15th of August, Mr. Belvidere persuaded his son to
leave his room, and essay the tranquillising effects of a brilliant
sunset, and of the fair and fertile scenery of Islington, in giving
a happier direction to his thoughts. At the earnest request of
Alphonso, they had quitted the precincts of the manor-house,
and bent their steps towards the spot on which Elizabeth's
cottage had once smiled. *" Campos ubi Troja fuit."* Mr. Belvidere had suggested to his son, that the review of scenes once
so dear, and now so pregnant of painful recollections—once so

fair, and now so devastated—would be too severe a trial of his fortitude; but Alphonso overruled every objection; and the kindhearted father assented to his wishes, extending the aid of his age-enfeebled arm to sustain the tottering steps of his emaciated and grief-enfeebled son.

"When this sad visit is over, my boy," said Mr. Belvidere, "I trust that the extreme bitterness of your grief will be past; that we shall have attained the climax of our sorrow, and that we may look for brighter and happier days to come."

"Oh, my father," said Alphonso, "you can never have known what *real* grief is, or you would not speak thus."

"At your early years, Alphonso, I certainly was not acquainted with affliction: there are few, indeed, that are. Yours is a peculiar and a mournful exception from the common lot; but who ever reached my time of life without being well informed of the flavour of the cup of sorrow? In early life, with good spirits and good looks, which are as strong magnets that draw love and friendship towards us, almost every thing around us conduces to elate our souls; but, in after-life, as our spirits and our looks decline, friendship becomes languid, and love falls from us, and there is scarcely anything that does not tend to depress them."

"Oh! you talk of the ordinary casualties of life, and the regrets and disappointments which are incident to ordinary men; but you have never grieved as I have grieved,—you have never wept such scalding tears as those which, like streams of burning lava, are now flowing from my eyes."

"And, yet, I have shed tears of much bitterness, Alphonso."

"Father, you cannot have fathomed those extreme depths of sorrow which I have been marked out by the inveteracy of fate to penetrate and explore; you have not been doomed to undergo that concentration of all agonies in one—the loss of the object of your love."

"Do you forget, Alphonso, whose tomb it is that stands on the right of the chancel-door?"

"Oh! but did that loss excruciate the inmost recesses of your soul? Did the contemplation of it scarify your brain, and send molten lead and liquid fire circulating instead of blood throughout your veins ? Did it turn your meat to poison, your drink to gall, your sleep to unimaginable horror ? Did it make the light of day a torture to the eye, and the darkness of night an appalling oppression to the soul ? Did that loss, my father, work for you what the loss of my Elizabeth has wrought for me ? Did it convert the universe into one vast gloomy dungeon ; and the solid globe on which we stand into an instrument of torture ; and every pulse that reports the assurance of our existence to the mind into another stretch of agony upon the wheel, or another blow from the iron bar of the executioner ? "

" No, my poor child, my grief certainly did not afflict me in the way you speak of ; but when your dear mother died, after twenty years of happiness together, if you had not looked up from your cradle and smiled upon me, I think it would have broken my heart."

As they were thus conversing, Mr. Belvidere and his son arrived at the ruins of Miss Brownrigge's cottage, and were joined by Mrs. Deacon. That lady had observed their approach from the gate of her garden, and advanced to meet them, with many kind inquiries after the health of Mr. Alphonso, and many voluble congratulations on seeing him again abroad.

To our hero, every word she uttered was as a poisoned arrow to his soul. Mrs. Deacon knew it was so ; and the pleasure which she experienced in contemplating his emaciation, and goading by sly touches the raw and wounded places of his breast, would not allow her to retire from the society into which she had impertinently obtruded herself, though Mr. Belvidere scarcely deigned her a reply, and Alphonso remained wrapped in moody and impenetrable silence. As the lady was thus bestowing the full fruits of her vocabulary and her humanity on the gentlemen, in the front of the ruined flower-beds and depopulated parterres of Elizabeth's dwelling, her eloquence was interrupted by an exclamation from Alphonso, who, after having for some time fixed his eyes attentively on a particular spot of the garden, where a broken rose-tree was lying along the path, suddenly cried out—" It is he ! I thought so from the first ; it is poor dear Muggletonian himself !" and then, breaking with a strong effort from his father's side, he rushed towards the place where the little animal was crouching, covered with dust, panting with fatigue, and wasted from want of food. Though conveyed away from the premises in Mary Jones's pocket, Muggletonian had contrived to find its way back again to Islington. Directed by that sure instinct with which some animals are so wonderfully endowed, the little creature had left his mistress in her new abode, and hastened, with a love of place that particularly distinguished him, to regain the well-known haunts of his early and accustomed home. Alphonso, intoxicated with delight at obtaining anything which had been possessed and was valued by his Elizabeth, caught Muggletonian eagerly in his arms, and pressed him to his breast, and smothered him with a multitude of kisses. In this operation, his eye fell upon the collar; it was inscribed," *E. B., Wandsworth, Surrey.*"

"Father, my father, she's found! she's found! I have discovered the abode of my Elizabeth!" cried Alphonso, losing all presence of mind in the ecstasy of his joy,—"Let us not delay a moment! Let us instantly away. Father, see here; she's at Wandsworth!"

The exertion that he had made, and the violent excitement of his strongest and most inward affections, were more than his debilitated frame could support, and he fainted in his father's arms.

"Wandsworth!" muttered Mrs. Deacon to herself; and she gave a hint of the direction in which Elizabeth was to be sought before she sent the assistance, that she had pretended to go in search of, to the relief of Alphonso.

CHAPTER III.

The Apprehension—Elizabeth's Defence—Death—Conclusion.

"Since laws were made for every degree,
To curb vice in others as well as in me,
I wonder we han't better company
Upon Tyburn tree.
But gold from law can take out the sting;
And if rich men like us were to swing,
'Twould thin the land, such numbers to string
Upon Tyburn tree."— GAY, *Beggar's Opera.*

'Αι, αι, αι, αι, δαιμων, δαιμων,
'Απολωλ', ω ταλας.—SOPHOCLES.

ELIZABETH, attended by Mary Jones, the temporary disturbance of whose intellect had entirely disappeared on a return to her accustomed habits of submission, and seemed to have been cast off with the trappings of her sin and vanity,—Elizabeth, with this her humble friend and companion, had established herself in an elegant and commodious apartment in the romantic village of Wandsworth. The house she had selected for her abode belonged to a Mr. Dunbar, who with his wife and children occupied the upper and lower stories, leaving the drawing-rooms at the disposal of their lodger. Our heroine, always anxious to discover and to improve an opportunity of benefiting her fellow-creatures, did not allow her residence in this family to pass away without their deriving some advantage from her sojourn amongst them. By adopting the Socratic mode of questioning the children, she led them to comprehend the meaning of the lessons which they had previously only known by rote. She instructed her host in an easier and less complex mode of bookkeeping, an admirable refinement, of her own invention, on the system of double-entry; she also imparted some highly valuable hints on the subject of domestic economy to her hostess, by which she was enabled to reduce her monthly bills from 7 to 7½ per cent. on their former amount, and dispense with the hire of a weekly charwoman. Thus, "dropping the manna" of her wisdom in the way of an ignorance-starved people, Elizabeth by the means of her intellectual superiority—heightened as its influence was by the splendour of her beauty and the dignity of her manners—won "golden opinions from all sorts of people." The affections of every heart, and the praises of every tongue, were prodigally bestowed on her; and when, on the evening of Saturday the 15th of August, she informed Mr. and Mrs. Dunbar that it was her intention on the following Monday to quit their lodgings, and embark on board the vessel that was to convey her to America, they were afflicted at the intelligence as at the thought of parting with some well-beloved relative, and volunteered a very considerable abatement of the rent and much additional accommodation, with the hope of inducing her to remain an inmate of their dwelling. The kind solicitude of the elder, and the tears of the younger Dunbars, were necessarily unavailing. With danger and bitter enemies in England, with security and Elizabeth Canning in America, our heroine could have no hesitation with regard to the course she ought to follow. She remained fixed in her original determination; but yet the kindness and the interest which these honest people exhibited for her could not fail of adding another to the many causes of regret which already existed in carrying that determination into execution.

No suspicion had ever entered the minds of Mr. and Mrs. Dunbar that, in the person of the fair and gentle widow, Mrs. Eliza Brown, whom they and their family cherished with so sincere an affection, they were affording concealment to the notorious culprit for whose apprehension a large reward was offered; whom, under the designation of Mother Brownrigge, every tongue was talking of with execration; with the account of whose barbarity the newspapers were teeming; and whose features and manners, portrayed by the hand of prejudice, were represented as indicating, in distinct and not-to-be mistaken characters, the peculiar ferociousness of her disposition. In conversing with our heroine, her host and hostess had often enlarged upon the recent events at Islington, and expressed their abhorrence of the treatment which the little apprentices had received at the hands of their mistress ; but not a word or look had ever evinced that their lodger entertained the slightest knowledge or interest in the fate of the person they condemned. She had sometimes, indeed attempted to mitigate the rancour of their feelings and expressions, by suggesting general arguments of charity, and reminding her friends that, according to the laws of England, every individual, of whatever crime accused, was considered as innocent till he or she was proved to be guilty ; but this mild and temperate view of the subject occasioned no surprise, as being in harmony with her constant practice ; and, besides, she at the same time acknowledged that, if the facts were true, their indignation was completely justified. What, then, must have been the astonishment of these worthy people when, on the morning of Sunday the 16th of August, about half past ten, as the bells were ringing for church, and the whole family were preparing to obey the summons, a post-chaise drove up to the door, and they saw the fair object of their attachment suddenly seized by a couple of tipstaves, under the name of Elizabeth Brownrigge, and ordered to mount the carriage and to accompany them to town. The scene existed but for a moment—a brief and agitated moment. Mr. Dunbar was in tears—Mrs. Dunbar in hysterics—Mary Jones fainted away ; the elder children clung to Elizabeth and screamed— the younger children ran to their mother and squalled ;— Elizabeth, the incomparable Elizabeth! was the only one whose constancy was not disturbed. Releasing herself from the friendly embraces that delayed her movements, and casting on the assembled group a smile of inexpressible tenderness and pity, she said, " Allow me, Mr. Dunbar, to offer you my thanks for the many civilities which I have received during the time of my residence under your roof. Have the kindness, also, to express my obligations to the worthy lady your wife, when those distressing paroxysms of which I have been the unintentional cause, are over. Pray, add to the many favours for which I am already your debtor, by informing my servant, when she comes to herself, that I shall expect her attendance in London. My young friends, I hope to hear of your continuing to be good children, and proving the source of happiness and credit to your parents. Adieu! Gentlemen, I am ready to attend you." And, with these words, one of the sheriffs' officers having entered before her, she placed her foot upon the steps of the post-chaise, and ascended the vehicle with her accustomed air of calm and dignified composure.—The magnanimity of her soul, like Mr. Smeaton's *pharos* on the Eddystone, was firmly fixed upon the rock of the soundest principles, and diffused a light around it, for the guidance of those who were beating the waves upon the dark and troubled ocean of adversity, but was itself unshaken by the storm.—The other bailiff jumped in after her, the door of the carriage was closed, and they started on the road to London as fast as four horses could carry them.

Elizabeth was immediately conveyed to Newgate, where Mary Jones joined her in the course of the day. She would admit no other person to her presence. Alphonso and his father repeatedly solicited an interview ; but, though our heroine tempered her refusal by the most considerate expressions of her esteem and regard, she could not be prevailed upon to accede to their requests. The grounds of her objections were two-fold. In the *first* place, from the prejudices excited against her in the public mind, she felt convinced that an impartial judge and jury could never be assembled for the trial of her cause ; and therefore, as her condemnation was certain, the meeting her friends again could prove neither more nor less than a vain renewal of the misery of parting from them. And, in the *second* place, limited as she was, during her residence in Newgate, to the use of a single apartment, she had no chamber but the one in which she slept for the reception of her guests ; and the feeling of female delicacy pleaded, in confirmation of the conclusions of her judgment, against the admission of their visits. Till the day of her trial at the Old Bailey, attended only by Mary Jones, and excluding herself from all society except the stated and official calls of the chaplain, the fair and excellent Elizabeth adopted, as nearly as circumstances would allow, the same admirable disposition of her time to which she had been accustomed when inhabiting her own romantic bower in the village of Islington. She completed a large stock of baby-linen

for the poor ; she perused and commented upon the principal
new publications of the day ; and she composed an elaborate
parallel between the characters of Socrates and Lady Jane Grey,
after the manner of Plutarch. These are the two distinguished
personages, in the whole range of authentic history, who in
their strength of mind, purity of life, and extensive accomplish-
ments, bore the strongest resemblance to herself; and to them,
perchance, the attention of our heroine was more particularly
directed in the quiet and retirement of her cell by the many
points of similarity which subsisted between their destiny and
her own.

On Saturday the 12th of September, Miss Brownrigge was
conducted, at nine o'clock in the morning, from her cell at
Newgate, to undergo her trial at the Old Bailey. The yells
and hootings of the mob that greeted her were deafening and
terrific ; but, prepared, as the fair Elizabeth was, for their dis-
play of misdirected indignation, and sustained under it by the
consciousness of innocence, the clamour of their insults past
by her unregarded ; and even when, on entering the dock, the
dense crowd collected in the court began to exhibit the rancour
of their enmity towards her by hissings and reproaches, she did
not deign to yield them any other notice of their contumely
than a smile of the gentlest and most elevated compassion.

Elizabeth had requested her friends, as a last and especial
favour, to abstain from attending this most momentous scene.
Their presence, she was well aware, could not afford her any
additional encouragement or support; while the consciousness
of the pain which they were undergoing on her account, might
have the effect of shaking her resolution and impairing her
self-possession. Her commands had been attended to. Mr.
Belvidere and Alphonso had taken their station at a neighbouring hotel, hoping against hope, that virtue might triumph
over prejudice—that an acquittal might be the result of the
proceedings—and that the sun of happiness might yet again
shine full upon their fortunes ; but they did not presume to
appear in the hall of the Old Bailey, in opposition to the desire
which the fair object of their interest and attachment had so
touchingly expressed. Around her and before her, in the judge

upon the bench, in the jury, in the witnesses, and in the whole
congregated multitude, Elizabeth did not perceive a single eye
that was not turned upon her with an expression of sternness
and of loathing; nor could she believe that a single individual
was to be found in the assembly who did not deem all further
inquiry a mere form of supererogation, or who was not prepared, at once and unheard, to condemn her to the scaffold.
Still, her fortitude never for a moment failed her. As soon as
the disturbance consequent on the entrance of our heroine into
court had ceased, the trial commenced. Elizabeth pleaded "Not
Guilty;" but the plea was followed by shouts of exasperated
derision; and the judge, in commanding silence, seemed to par-
ticipate in the sentiments of the multitude, while he checked
the expression of them as disorderly. The depositions of the
witnesses were quickly given, and allowed to pass unsifted by
the salutary process of cross-examination. After Mr. and Mrs.
Deacon, Mrs. Jukes, the master of the poor-house, &c., &c., had
delivered their evidence, Miss Brownrigge was asked whether
she had any witnesses to call, or anything to urge in her defence.
She had been allowed a chair in the dock during the progress of
the case against her. On being addressed by the bench, she
rose slowly, but firmly, from her seat; and while all was hushed
around her, replied in the following words :—

"My lord, if it were my intention or my desire to influence
the judgment of those on whom the determination of this cause
depends, by any other arguments than such as may immediately
apply to the facts of the case, and address themselves exclusively
to the reason, I should, on the present occasion, attempt to deprecate the severity of my hearers, and conciliate their benevolence, by directing their attention to the age, the sex, the fortune,
the well-known character, and the previous conduct of the individual who now appears in the degraded situation of a prisoner
at your lordship's bar. But I have no such wish. I stand here
to vindicate my much-calumniated name ; to rebut the imputa-
tion of a crime most abhorrent from my nature ; to justify my
plea of 'Not Guilty;' and, as far as in me lies, to nullify that
unjust sentence of condemnation which has already been passed
upon my conduct, and which, deeply engraven by the iron pen

of malice on the adamantine rock of popular prejudice, no testimony can ever effectually eradicate, and not even an acquittal at this august tribunal could have the power of totally reversing. But, hopeless as my case may be—judged, as I already am, by the voice of public opinion, I disdain to have recourse to the vain arts of the rhetorician in my defence; and, whether I stand or fall, my exculpation shall rest upon the simple foundations of truth and reason, and of truth and reason alone.

"I am accused, my lord, of having whipped my little apprentice girl Mary Clifford to death. Supposing that my heart was as insensible to the cries of infant suffering, and my moral principles as perverted as my enemies would represent, what motive could have induced the perpetration of so abominable an act of inhumanity? What benefit could I derive from her decease? They who impute the crime should find out in what manner I could be benefited by the commission of it. Has the whole course of your lordship's experience ever brought you in contact with a culprit who was guilty of a gratuitous homicide, and who volunteered incurring the severest penalties of the law, without the prospect of gratifying some prevailing passion of our common nature, or securing to himself some anticipated advantage? No such being ever lived. Your lordship's acquaintance with the ordinary springs and general motives of human conduct must convince you, that such an offender would prove a monstrous and unheard-of anomaly in the history of the human race. Yet, my lord, such is the unfruitful folly of guilt, such is the objectless delirium of iniquity, which the witnesses for the prosecution have had the unblushing effrontery to lay this day to my charge.

"My lord, I had no reason for desiring or seeking the death of the child; on the contrary, it was for my advantage that she should retain her activity unimpaired, and her strength unbroken. Every accident that befell Mary Clifford was to my own especial injury; for to what end was she bound my servant, but that I might profit by her services?

"The child is dead. Granted. But does it therefore follow that she must have died in consequence of a blow? The deceased and Mary Mitchell, her fellow-apprentice, were, we learn, both conveyed to the poor-house, terrified at the riotous attack which had been made by a band of misguided ruffians upon the humble dwelling of their mistress. May not the fright have been too powerful for nerves so weak as hers, and have produced the dissolution of the younger child, though the elder was strong enough to survive its operation? Is death an unfrequent consequence of terror? But again, my lord, supposing that she did not fall the victim of her apprehensions, but that her end was really hastened by a *blow*, why should the chastisement which was dealt by the friendly hand of a mistress, with a rod, upon her back, be fixed upon as the cause, when it is notorious that the child had received many and very severe contusions on more vital parts of her body, inflicted by the stones and missiles of the multitude?

" My lord, this is not all: the deceased was for several days exposed to the peril of the draughts, and pills, and lotions of Mr. Deacon. What reason have we for presuming that instruments, which have so often proved mortal in other cases, were wholly innocent in the case of my late unhappy apprentice?

" My lord, I have but one word more to add: it relates to the extreme supposition, that the child really suffered from the correction which I thought it my duty to inflict. Admitting such to be the case, is it possible that the voice of justice can attach the *guilt* of murder to my act, or the laws consider me as obnoxious to the *penalty* of murder? The chastisement which I dealt the child was dealt as lovingly as to a child of my own; it was given after much deliberation, with feelings of deep regret, and with a view to her temporal and eternal welfare. Was I to blame, my lord, in administering such correction? No; my conscience acquits me; and I am satisfied that your lordship's better judgment sends back a responsive echo to that silent but most satisfactory acquittal. All errors of conduct are symptoms of moral diseases; punishment is moral medicine. I may, perchance, actuated by too eager a desire for the rapid cure of my little and much-cherished patient, have dispensed my alteratives too liberally, and produced an untoward, an unexpected, and a most deeply-lamented consequence; but am I, therefore, to be condemned as guilty? In the analagous case of the physician, whose too-abundant anodynes may have lulled the sufferer to endless slumbers, or whose too copious phlebotomy may have let out the fever and the life at one and the same moment from the veins, would this most harsh and unmerciful measure be applied? My lord, you know that it would not; and, admitting the fact, which I most decidedly disbelieve—but admitting the fact of my having caused the death of Mary Clifford, as no malice on my part can be imputed—no object but her ultimate good presumed —no motive but correction ascribed to me, I demand from the justice of your lordship and a jury of my countrymen—as a matter not of mercy, but of right—the same impunity in *my* case which would be accorded, freely and unasked, under parallel circumstances, to the medical practitioner."

With these words our heroine resumed her seat. The elo- quence of her style and the forcible arguments of her defence produced a most extraordinary effect upon the audience. Not a single look or even murmur of disapprobation was again levelled at her during the period of her remaining in the court.

The summing-up of the judge inclined most favourably towards her. The jury hesitated in their decision; and it was supposed by several who were present, and saw how far the sentiments of the jury had been conciliated by the powerful influence of her speech, that Elizabeth would certainly have been acquitted altogether, but for a stratagem of Mrs. Deacon. That lady, who was still in court, perceiving that the jury were in doubt, and anxious for the condemnation of her rival, sud- denly screamed out that she saw the ghost of Mary Clifford, standing in a menacing attitude at the side of the prisoner in the dock; and then caused herself to be carried out of the court in a state of violent hysterics. This event decided the cause. The jury were awe-stricken; they came, at once, to a unanimous decision; and the foreman delivered in the verdict, "GUILTY OF WILFUL MURDER."

Elizabeth, as soon as the sentence of death had been passed, made her curtsey with grace and dignity to the bench and the jury-box, and was conducted to the condemned cell, to await till the following Monday her execution at Tyburn. With less than forty hours to linger in this world, she requested that no one should be allowed to intrude upon her privacy, and applied herself to the final arrangement of her affairs with that equanimity of mind which had distinguished her in every other period of her life. The cell in which she passed her time between the trial and her death has been consecrated by the muse of George Canning, in some most expressive lines, which may be found in the early pages of the *Poetry of the Anti-Jacobin.**

The morning of Monday the 14th of September at length arrived. I will not recapitulate all the formal ceremonies that preceded the departure of the procession from Newgate—the breakfast of the sheriffs and their friends—the throng of curious visitors who assembled in the press-yard—the leave-taking with Mary Jones—the solemn address which Elizabeth delivered to her fellow-prisoners—the mounting the fatal cart—and the funeral procession to Tyburn. The fair and innocent victim of popular prejudice was followed by a repetition of those incessant yells and vulgar execrations to the place of execution, which had accompanied her, on the preceding Saturday, to the place of judgment. The train at length reached the spot which had been mortal to the lives of thousands. Elizabeth was still firm in the energy of her high resolves and her conscious integrity. Timothy Hitch alone was agitated and in tears. His hands trembled to such a degree, from the excitement of his nerves, that they could scarcely fasten the fatal cord about her neck.

The awful moment had now arrived. Our heroine's last communication with the ordinary was over; she had expressed the forgiveness of all her enemies—she had bestowed a last memorial of her regard on the gentle Timothy—and she was preparing to utter a few sentences of parting exhortation to the assembled multitude—when, rising several inches above the crowd that pressed upon him, and immediately in front of the scaffold, pale with sickness and with grief, she suddenly caught a glimpse of Alphonso Belvidere. As their eyes met, he raised a phial to his mouth, and cried, " Elizabeth, my own Elizabeth, our love has been on earth!—our spousals shall be in the grave ! We may not live, but we will die together !"

---

* *Vide* note *suprà*, p. 117.

" No, Alphonso ! for the sake of your father and of my fame," she exclaimed, " dismiss so wild, so inexcusable an intention.— You will not obey !—What !— How is this ?—Good people, tear away, I entreat you, yon vile and deadly potion from that madman's hand ! "

The people obeyed her mandate—the laudanum was dashed upon the ground; but Alphonso's hand was immediately turned to the butt-end of another weapon of death, which lay concealed in the side-pocket of his coat.—There was a pause.—The gaze of the mob was again directed towards Elizabeth.—The cap was drawn over her eyes—the final signal was given—the drop fell, and, as it fell, the explosion of a pistol was heard on the spot where Alphonso stood.—The attention of the multitude was diverted from the struggles of Elizabeth to the agonies of her lover.—The ball had taken effect.—He tottered, and sank into the arms of the by-standers, crying, as the last breath of life departed from him, " I come—I come, love ! I could not live without thee in the world, and I hasten to join thee for ever in the tomb ! "

The reader may perhaps be anxious to know the fate of the rest of the personages of my historic tale. Old Mr. Belvidere died of a broken heart soon after the transactions which we have recorded, and left the amount of his large fortune in charities, with an annuity to an elderly resident of Islington, on the condition of her seeing Elizabeth's lap-dog, Muggletonian, supplied with a kennel in the neighbourhood of the cottage that he was so attached to, and the daily allowance of sixpenny-worth of cat's meat.

Mary Jones, to whom Elizabeth had bequeathed the whole of her property, married Timothy Hitch, who withdrew from public life to pass the residue of his days, with his young and beautiful wife, in a romantic retirement near the Lake of Windermere.

The rapid increase of Mr. Deacon's practice enabled him to purchase a Scotch doctor's degree, and to set up a snuff-coloured chariot, in which he was accustomed to drive about collecting the guineas of his patients for the greater part of the twenty-four hours; till, at the age of seventy-two, he was found dead in the inside of it, with the last guinea he had received grasped tightly in his hand.

Mrs. Deacon, who survived her much-respected husband nearly twenty years, succeeded to the immense accumulations which he had secured by the exercise of his profession. She had the chariot painted a bright yellow, and drove about in it nearly as many hours every day as its original occupant. Having attained extreme old age, possessing all her faculties to the last, with a large house, a good table, and a hospitable disposition, she eventually attained the designation of " the *venerable* Mrs. Deacon " ; and, having lived the universal favourite of the neighbourhood, she died as universally lamented.

Advertisement.—The Author of the foregoing Tale begs leave to state, that he is prepared to treat with any liberal and enterprising publisher, who may be inclined to embark in the speculation, for a series of novels, each in 3 vols. 8vo., under the title of " Tales of the Old Bailey, or Romances of Tyburn Tree ; " in which the whole *Newgate Calendar* shall be travestied, after the manner of *Eugene Aram.*

Letters (post-paid) addressed to X. Y. Z., 215 Regent Street,* will receive immediate attention.

---

* Then (1832) the publishing office of *Fraser's Magazine*, in which the tale of *Elizabeth Brownrigge* originally appeared.—ED.

CONTRIBUTIONS TO "THE SNOB."

[CAMBRIDGE : 1829.]

OUR "SNOB'S" BIRTH, PARENTAGE AND EDUCATION.*

"EVER shall I forget," said an old crone to me the other day, who, as far as we know, is cotemporary with the alley in which we live—"Never shall I forget the night, in which you, Mr. Tudge, made your first appearance among us. Your father had, in his usual jocular manner, turned every one from the fire-side, and putting a foot on each hob, with a pot in one hand, and a pipe in the other, sat blowing a cloud." "Ay, Mrs. Siggins," said I, "νεφεληγερέτα Ζεὺς,† I suppose, as the blind bard has it." "Keep your Latin for the collegers," said she; "I know nothing on 't. Well, lo and behold, as I was saying, we were all sitting quiet as mice, when just as I had turned over the last page of the "Skeleton Chief, or Bloody Bandit," a sound, like I don't know what, came from overhead. Now, no one was up stairs, so, as you may well suppose, the noise brought my heart into my mouth,—nay more, it brought your dad to his legs, and you into the world. For your mother was taken ill directly, and we helped her off to bed." "*Parturiunt montes, nas* ——"‡ said I, stopping short in confusion,—thank Heaven, the old woman knew not the end of the proverb, but went on with her story. "Go, Bill," says your father, "see what noise was that."

* *The Snob.* No. 3. Thursday, April 23, 1829, pp. 11-12.

† [νεφεληγερέτα Ζεὺς. (HOM. *Iliad., α.* 511, 517, *et sæpius*), i.e. "cloud-compelling Jove."—ED.]

‡ [*Parturiunt montes, nascetur ridiculus mus.*—HOR. *De Art. Poet.*—139. —ED.]

O

Off went Bill, pale as a sheet, while I attended to your mother. Bill soon came laughing down. "The boot-jack fell off the peg," says he. "It's a boy," screams I. "How odd !" says your dad. "What's odd?" says I. "The child and the jack —it's ominous," says he. "As how?" says I. "Call the child Jack," says he. And so they did, and that's the way, do you see, my name was Jack Clypei Septemplicis Ajax.

Early in life I was sent to a small school in the next street, where I soon learnt to play at marbles, blow my nose in my pinafore, and bow to the mistress. Having thus exhausted her whole stock of knowledge, I migrated to Miss G——'s, in Trumpington-street, and under the tuition of the sisters, became intimately acquainted, before I was nine years of age, with the proper distribution of letters in most three-syllable words of the British tongue, *i.e.* I became an expert speller.

(*To be continued.*)

MRS. RAMSBOTTOM IN CAMBRIDGE.*

Radish Ground Buildings.

DEAR SIR,—I was surprised to see my name in Mr. Bull's paper, for I give you my word I have not written a syllabub to him since I came to reside here, that I might enjoy the satiety of the literary and learned world.

I have the honour of knowing many extinguished persons. I am on terms of the greatest contumacy with the Court of Aldermen, who first recommended your weekly dromedary to my notice, knowing that I myself was a great literati. When I am at home, and in the family way, I make Lavy read it to me, as I consider you the censure of the anniversary, and a great upholder of moral destruction.

When 1 came here, I began reading Mechanics (written by that gentleman whose name you whistle). I thought it would be something like the Mechanics Magazine, which my poor dear Ram used to make me read to him, but I found them very foolish. What do I want to know about weights and measures and bull's-eyes, when I have left off trading ? I have therefore

---

* *The Snob.* No. 7. Thursday, May 21, 1829, pp. 39-40.

begun a course of ugly-physics, which are very odd, and written by the Marquis of Spinningtoes.

I think the Library of Trinity College is one of the most admiral objects here. I saw the busks of several gentlemen whose statutes I had seen at Room, and who all received there edification at that College. There was Aristocracy who wrote farces for the Olympic Theatre, and Democracy who was a laughing philosophy.

I forgot to mention that my son George Frederick is entered at St. John's, because I heard that they take most care of their morals at that College. I called on the tutor, who received myself and son very politely, and said he had no doubt my son would be a tripod, and he hoped perspired higher than polly, which I did not like. I am going to give a tea at my house, when I shall be delighted to see yourself and children.

Believe me, dear Sir,

Your most obedient and affectionate

DOROTHEA JULIA RAMSBOTTOM.

A STATEMENT OF FAX RELATIVE TO THE LATE MURDER.

BY D. J. RAMSBOTTOM.*

"Come I to speak in Cæsar's funeral."
MILTON, JULIUS CÆSAR, *Act III.*

ON Wednesday the 3rd of June as I was sitting in my back parlour taking tea, young Frederick Tudge entered the room; I reserved from his dislevelled hair and vegetated appearance, that something was praying on his vittles. When I heard from him the cause of his vegetation, I was putrified! I stood transfigured! His father, the Editor of "The Snob," had been macerated in the most sanguine manner. The drops of compassion refused my eyes, for I thought of him, whom I had lately seen high in health and happiness; that ingenuous

---

indivisable, who often and often when seated alone with me has "made the table roar," as the poet has it, and whose constant aim in his weakly dromedary was to delight as well as to reprove. His son Frederick, too young to be acquainted with the art of literal imposition, has commissioned me to excommunicate the circumstances of his death, and call down the anger of the Proctors and Court of Aldermen on the phlogitious perforators of the deed.

It appears that as he was taking his customary rendez-vous by the side of Trumpington Ditch, he was stopped by some men in under-gravy dresses, who put a pitch-plaister on him, which completely developed his nose and eyes, or, as Shakespeare says, "his visible ray." He was then dragged into a field, and the horrid deed was replete! Such are the circumstances of his death; but Mr. Tudge died like Wriggle-us, game to the last; or like Cæsar in that beautiful faction of the poet, with which I have headed my remarks, I mean him who wanted to be Poop of Room, but was killed by two Brutes, and the fascinating hands of a perspiring Senate.

With the most sanguinary hopes that the Anniversary and Town will persecute an enquiry into this dreadful action, I will conclude my repeal to the pathetic reader; and if by such a misrepresentation of fax, I have been enabled to awaken an apathy for the children of the late Mr. Tudge, who are left in the most desultory state, I shall feel the satisfaction of having exorcised my pen in the cause of Malevolence, and soothed the inflictions of indignant Misery.

D. J. RAMSBOTTOM.

P.S.—The publisher requests me to state that the present No. is published from the MS. found in Mr. Tudge's pocket, and one more number will be soon forthcoming containing his inhuman papers.

"THE NATIONAL STANDARD."

[1833.]

FOREIGN CORRESPONDENCE.

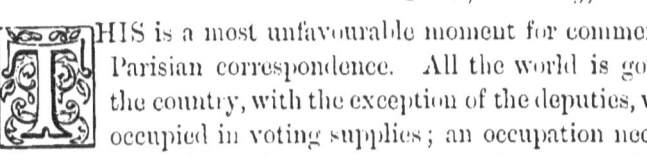

Paris, Saturday, June 22.

THIS is a most unfavourable moment for commencing a Parisian correspondence. All the world is gone into the country, with the exception of the deputies, who are occupied in voting supplies; an occupation necessary, but not romantic, and uninteresting to the half million of Englishmen who peruse the "National Standard." However, in all this dearth of political and literary news, the people of France are always rich enough in absurdities to occupy and amuse an English looker-on. I had intended, after crossing the Channel to Boulogne, to have staid there for a while, and to have made some profound remarks on the natives of that town, but of these, I believe, few exist; they have been driven out by the English settlers, one of whom I had the good fortune to see. He did not speak much, but swore loudly; he was dressed in a jacket and a pair of maritime inexpressibles, which showed off his lower man to much advantage. This animal, on being questioned, informed me that the town was d—— pretty, the society d—— pleasant, balls delightful, and cookery excellent. On this hint, having become famished during a long and stormy voyage, I requested the waiter of the hotel to procure some of the delicacies mentioned by the settler. In an hour he returned with breakfast: the coffee was thin, the butter bad, the bread sour, the delicacies, mutton-chops. This was too much for human patience. I bade adieu to the settler, and set off for Paris forthwith.

I was surprised and delighted with the great progress made by the Parisians since last year. Talk of the "march of mind" in England, La jeune France completely distances us: all creeds, political, literary, and religious, have undergone equal revolutions, and met with equal contempt. Churches, theatres, painters, booksellers, kings, and poets, have all bowed before this awful spirit of improvement, this tremendous "Zeitgeist." In poetry and works of fiction, this change is most remarkable. I have collected one or two specimens, which I assure you are taken from works universally read and admired. I have, however, been obliged to confine ourselves to the terrific; the tender parts are much too tender for English readers. In England it was scarcely permitted in former days to speak of such a book, as the Memoirs of the celebrated M. de Faublas; in France it was only "a book of the boudoir," taken in private by ladies, like their cherry-brandy; now the book is public property. It is read by the children, and acted at the theatres; and for Faublas himself, he is an absolute Joseph, compared to the Satanico-Byronico heroes of the present school of romance. As for murders, &c., mere Newgate-Calendar crimes, they are absolute drugs in the literary market. Young France requires something infinitely more piquant than an ordinary hanging matter, or a common-place *crim. con.* To succeed, to gain a reputation, and to satisfy La jeune France, you must accurately represent all the anatomical peculiarities attending the murder, or crime in question: you must dilate on the clotted blood, rejoice over the scattered brains, particularize the sores and bruises, the quivering muscles, and the gaping wounds; the more faithful, the more natural; the more natural, the more creditable to the author, and the more agreeable to La jeune France.

I have before me a pleasing work with the following delectable title: "Champavert: Immoral Tales. By Petrus Borel the Lycanthrope!"* After having perused this pretty little book, I

---

* [*Champavert. Contes Immoraux.* Par Petrus Borel le Lycanthrope. The edition before us is a Brussels reprint, bearing date 1872.—ED.]

give the following summary of it, for the benefit of English readers.

Tale 1. "M. de L'Argentière," contains a rape, a murder, an execution.

Tale 2. "Jaquez Barraou," concludes thus :

"Immediately he seized him by the throat—the blood gushed out, and Juan screamed aloud, falling on one knee and seizing Barraou by the thigh ; who in turn, fastened on his hair, and struck him on the loins, while, with a back-stroke, *il lui étripe le ventre*. (The manœuvre is extraordinary, and the language utterly untranslateable.) They rolled on the ground : now Juan is uppermost, now Jaquez—they roar and writhe !

"Juan lifted his arm, and broke his dagger against the wall. Jaquez nailed his in Juan's throat ! Covered with wounds and blood, uttering horrid screams, they seemed a mere mass of blood flowing and curdling ! Thousands of obscene flies and beetles might be seen hovering round their mouths and nostrils, and buzzing round the sores of their wounds.

"Towards night a man stumbled over the corpses. 'They are only negroes,' said he ; and went his way."

It is, as the reader will see, quite impossible to translate properly this elegant passage ; it displays a force, originality, and good taste, which can never be transferred to our language.

Tale 3. "Andréa Vésalius." Three adulteries, four murders. The victims are a wife and her three lovers, murdered first, and dissected afterwards, by Andréa Vésalius.

Tale 4. "Three fingered Jack." Contains only one suicide, and the death of Jack in fair fight.

Tale 5. "Dina." One rape, one murder, one suicide.

Tale 6. "Passereau." Two murders, and some intrigues— very prettily described.

Tale 7. "Champavert." This is the history of Lycanthrope himself. He was an extraordinary and melancholy young man, remarkable for a strong poetical genius and a long beard, both of which he had manifested from the age of seventeen. This history contains a couple of seductions, a child murder, and two suicides. Whether Champavert were a fictitious or real personage, I know not ; there is, however, a long circumstantial account of his suicide here given; and I trust, for the honour of France, that the Lycanthrope actually lived and died in the manner described in the book.

My dear young ladies, who are partial to Lord Byron, and read Don Juan slily in the evening; who admire French fashions, and dishes, and romances,—it is for your profit and amusement that this summary has been made. You will see by it how far this great nation excels us in genius and imagination, even though Bulwer and D'Israeli still live and write.

The costume of Jeune France is as extraordinary as its literature. I have sent a specimen, which I discovered the other day in the Tuileries. It had just been reading the *Tribune*, and was leaning poetically against a tree; it had on a red neckcloth and a black flowing mane; a stick or club, intended for ornament as well as use; and a pair of large though innocent spurs, which had never injured anything except the pantaloons of the individual who wore them. Near it was sitting an old gentleman, who is generally to be seen of a sunny day in the Tuileries, reading his Crebillon or his prayer-book: a living illustration of times past,—a strange contrast with times present !*

Paris, Saturday, June 29.

There is no doubt that the "National Standard," though the best conducted Journal in the world, has a most senseless, impotent, and unmeaning title: National Standard; what does it signify? It may be a newspaper, or a measure for brandy; a banner for King William, or a flag for King Cobbett: you should take advice by the papers of this country, and fix on a name more striking. These observations have been inspired by the title of a journal which is about to appear here, " Le Necrologe: Journal des Morts; " a pretty romantic and melancholy title, printed on a sentimental paper, handsomely edged with black, and bearing an urn for a frontispiece. O death ! O life ! O *jeune France*, what a triumph of art and taste is here ! Fancy " *The Mourning Advertiser; the Sexton's Mis-*

---

* Here, in *The National Standard*, appears an admirable sketch, which, indifferently drawn as it is, has much of the spirit and humour of Thackeray's maturer illustrations of his own text.—ED.

cellany; *The Raw Head and Bloody Bones; the Undertaker's Manual; the Pickaxe, or Grave-digger's Vade Meeum,"* published every morning for breakfast, and treating of all the most fashionable deaths, murders, suicides, and executions in Europe. What a pleasing study for melancholy young men and tender young ladies! Then one has the advantage of swallowing sentiment and history at the same time, and (as *Figaro* says,) while living, one is a subscriber to it; when dead, an article. The November suicides in England used to be a staple article of French satire; they used to think that London-bridge was built for the mere convenience of throwing one's self from it into the Thames, and that our lamp-posts were only cast-iron substitutes for gibbets : in regard to lamp-posts, however, we borrowed our learning from them ; and, as to suicides, the advantage is now decidedly on the French side. Half-a-dozen fellows "asphixient" themselves every morning, and servant-maids with low spirits and wages, generally adopt this means of retirement, as one easy, expeditious, and certain. I heard just now of a young gentleman who had arrived at the mature age of sixteen, and of another more venerable by a couple of years, who some time ago brought their lives to a conclusion in charcoal. They had, together, written a drama, which was represented at the Porte St. Martin, and succeeded ; it procured for them, no doubt, a few dozen francs, and an eternity of half-a-dozen nights, which seemed entirely to answer their hopes and satisfy their ambition. Their enjoyment was complete, their cup of fame was full; and they determined, like young sages as they were, to retire from the world before their happiness should fade, or their glory tarnish, thinking no doubt that their death, their last and noblest action, would establish beyond all question their spiritual immortality.

So they purchased the means of their death, (it is very cheap, twopenny-worth will kill half a thousand young poets ;) they retired to their *sixième*, they shut out the world, and closed up the windows ; and when, some hours after, the door of their apartment was forced open, their spirits and the charcoal-smoke flew out together, leaving only the two corpses to be admired by the public, and buried by the same. In

France they dropped tears on their bodies; they would have employed stakes, instead of tears, in our less romantic country. However, peace be to their ashes! they are now, no doubt, comfortably situated in that heaven where they will find Cato and Addison, and Eustace Budgell, and all the suicidal philosophers; and some day or other, Liston, Talma, and all the great tragedians.

I asked my informer the names of these young unfortunates, and the title of their tragedy. He had forgotten both! So much for their reputation.

The theatres are in a flourishing condition: they have all at this moment some piece of peculiar attraction. At the *Ambigu Comique* is an edifying representation of "Belshazzar's Feast." The second act discovers a number of melancholy Israelites sitting round the waters of Babylon, with their harps on the willows! A Babylonian says to the leader of the chorus, "Sing us one of the songs of Zion;" the chorus answers, "How can we sing in a strange land?" and so on: the whole piece is a scandalous parody of the Scripture, made up with French sentiment and French decency. A large family of children were behind me, looking, with much interest and edification, at the Queen rising from her bath! This piece concludes with a superb imitation of Martin's picture of Belshazzar. Another piece at the *Porte St. Martin*, called "Bergami," vivifies Hayter's picture of the House of Lords, at Queen Caroline's trial. There was a report this morning that a courier had arrived from England, for the express purpose of forbidding this piece; and supposing, from that circumstance, that it must contain something very terrible, I sallied to the *Porte St. Martin* to see it; but I was sadly disappointed: for there was nothing in it but a little Platonic dialogue between Bergami, who is an angel, and the queen, who is an injured woman. Bergami appears first in the character of a post-boy, and makes such delightful remarks on the weather, the scenery, and Italian politics, that the warm-hearted queen is subdued at once, and makes him forthwith her equerry. The first act ends, and the queen gets into a carriage. In the second she gets into a packet, (that unlucky packet!) in the third she gets into

a balcony; in the fourth she gets into a passion, as well she
may, since Bergami is assassinated by Lord Ashley, (on which
fact we beg to congratulate his lordship ;) and accordingly, she
goes to the House of Lords to make her complaint against him
for this act of impoliteness; here the scene is very animated
(it is taken from the picture). *Sir* Brougham makes a speech
about injured women, patriotism, and so forth; Lord Eldon
replies, the Ministerial bench cheers, the Opposition jeers, and
the queen comes in majestically, bowing right and left, and
uttering the noblest sentiments. Presently a row is heard in
the streets: the mob is in arms for the queen! Lord Eldon
motions the Minister of War; he rushes out to quell the disturbance, the queen follows him, but the attempts of both are
ineffectual; windows are broken, stones are flung, Lord Eldon
disappears, Sir Brougham bolts, and Lord Liverpool, (a stout
man in a white waistcoat, with a large tin star,) falls to the
earth, struck violently in the stomach with a leather brick-bat,
and the curtain, of course, drops with the Prime Minister. The
French nation was exalted by this exhibition to a pitch of
immoderate enthusiasm, and called stoutly for the *Marseillaise.*
I did not see the fifth act, in which the queen is poisoned,
(Lord Ashley again !) but returned home to give an account of
this strange tragedy. There is a third play, of much more
importance than the two former, of which I had wished to give
some account, " Les Enfans d'Edouard," by M. Casimir Delavigne,
one of the best acted tragedies I had ever the good fortune to
see ; but I have made this letter so long, that I must reserve this
for some future day. I could not, however refrain from sending
a little sketch of Ligier,* who performs the part of *Richard,* in
this play, in a manner, I think, which Kean never equalled.

Beside Ligier is the admirable Mademoiselle Mars, and that
most charming, gay, graceful, *naïve* actress, Madame Anais
Aubert. It would be worth an English actor's while to come
to Paris, and study the excellent manner of the French
comedians ; even Cooper might profit by it, and Diddear go
away from the study a wiser and better man. Here is too

* The sketch appears with the letter in *The National Standard:* we
regret to be unable to reproduce it here.—ED.

much about theatres, you will say; but after all, is not this subject as serious as any other?

THE CHARRUAS.

Paris, July 5.

The wondering reader may fancy that the scene here given was designed in the wilds of America, rather than·in this gay city of Paris; but he will see, if he takes the trouble of reading the following article (from the pen of M. Jules Janin), how the figures above* represent three unfortunate Charruas Indians, who have quitted South America to shiver under the cold Parisian sun.

" Allons! let us go and see the savages; they are lodged in the Champs Elysées, in one of those half-built houses, those ruins of yesterday, the view of which is sad without being solemn. Here are the heroes of our drama, not taller than the brave Agamemnons and Alexanders of the Theatre Français, but well-built and active, bold cavaliers, and gallant horse-tamers. They are perfidious, idle, revengeful, cruel cannibals, some of them; perfect dramatic characters, in fact. In truth, they possess all the qualities requisite for the modern drama; they can ride, fight, betray, revenge, assassinate, and eat raw flesh; it is true that they don't know a word of French; but what of that? it is all the better for the theatre now-a-days.

" When I saw them huddled together in their court, I declare I thought that I was looking at some modern tragedy: these brave savages wore costumes hideous and fanciful; they were all three seated in different solemn attitudes. First, the cacique, with hair uncombed, and fierce and heavy looks; he would have made a capital tyrant for a melo-drama : the next, a lean, livid animal, with a sidelong look, and an indefinable smile, reminded me of Cooper's *Magua*; the third was gay, careless, and merry enough: and then came the timid and gentle Guynuya. She sate alone in a corner of the court, with her head on her bosom, bending under the weight of her captivity, like a princess of Ilium of old. This woman is truly sublime: it is true she is fickle and faithless, that she loves pleasure and change, that she has not our ideas of conjugal fidelity; but she has more passion and love than all the

* A sketch of the Charruas headed this letter in *The National Standard.*—ED.

heroines of our tragedy ; and above all, she has the passion of grief. I was much touched by this woman and her sorrows ; her arms are all scarred over with wounds, and each of these wounds is the history of a sorrow. They were inflicted by herself : there is a scar for each friend she has lost; for every child of which she has been deprived there is a finger gone ; she has lost two fingers, and there are near eighty scars on her arm : and this woman is not yet eighteen years old !

"Have you, in all the range of your drama, such an heroine as this ? Have you, in all your poetry, so profound a grief as hers ? And, for heroes, here is one whose shoulder has been laid open by a hatchet ; and who, for the last miserable white Frenchwoman, who blunders through your ballets and your choruses, would go gladly to the Bois de Boulogne, and defy a dozen gentlemen at once ! You call your heroes cruel, and your heroines tender : Here is a hero who poisons his own arrows, and a woman who gashes her arms with a wicked knife with as much ease as you would flourish a fan. Poor dramatists ! See how utterly you are beaten off your ground by the first arrival from the plains of Paraguay. Thus, in fact, it is: as soon as one quits the poetical drama for that of the heart, and literary truth for common truth, one must expect to be vanquished by the first matter-of-fact competitor, whether savage or not ; by all which I mean to say, as Lord Byron has said before, that truth is stranger than fiction.

"Now, these heroes of the Champs Elysées are as poetic as the heroes of Homer. Vaimaca Peru is a great chief, a veritable cacique, a specimen, in fact, of vagabond royalty, no more called on to uncover his head than are other vagabond royalties. Senaqué is the devoted friend of his chief, a subject faithful and sorrowful, more sorrowful indeed than his destitute master ; and this is a common case about ruined thrones. The next, the young man, is careless and brave ; and, although conquered, happy still, because he is young, and looks to the future. The woman Guynuya is truly the epic heroine, resigned to her fate ; her very smile is full of tears, her sufferings are consoled by her weaknesses. Do you know that these savages have come from the extremity of Southern America ?

that they were made prisoners after long and bloody battles; that they have come hither to Paris, as a last asylum; and that this is the St. Helena of the vanquished cacique? For a long time they fought under Ribera; a year ago their tribe was destroyed, and they fled into the desert, bearing with them, not their harps, like the Hebrews, but the skulls of their enemies, the ornaments of their cabins. And now, vanquished prisoners, fugitives, they have come so far to find an asylum, and to receive the visit of that amateur of monsters, M. Geoffroy St. Hilaire.

" How times are changed ! Formerly, when the grand king-dom of France was a Christian kingdom, the arrival of these savages would have caused a sensation amidst all the catholi-cism of Paris. There would have been a tender solicitude evinced for the welfare of their immortal souls. They would have found, most likely, the king's mistress for a godmother, and the king's brother for a godfather ; they would have been the objects of infinite dissertations, philosophical and religious : Jansenists and Jesuits would have disputed over these four souls with a ferocity altogether ecclesiastical. Our savages meanwhile would have been baptised, fêted, and amused, and sent back to their country loaded with presents and honours. At present, what is their fate, poor monarchs of the deserts ? They have been received by the Academy of Sciences; and next, they will go to St. Cloud, and see the king, that is, if the master of the ceremonies permits it. The director of the opera will give them a box some night when all the boxes are empty; then they will go to the Porte St. Martin, then to Franconi's, and then to some cabaret of the lower order, where the grisette, come out for her Sunday, will scarcely deign to look at them, seeing that she prefers her quadrille to all the savages in the world. Poor fellows ! they will be lucky enough if they do not, like their brethren of the North,* die in the hospital, with a sister of charity on each side of them.

" I did not forget to caress the ostrich which gallops about in the court ; he is a careless and gentle ostrich, who much pleased me: having nothing to give him, I offered him a piece of

---

* The Osages, who were exhibited at Paris some years ago, and died there.

money, which he did me the honour of accepting, and which he swallowed and pocketed with the grace of a civilized individual.

"JULES JANIN."

I have curtailed this article of M. Janin's, which is, I think, a tolerable specimen of the French style of periodical writing. It concludes with a long paragraph, expressing the writer's joy at escaping from the savages into the Champs Elysées; and some remarks on the civilized world in general. The paragraph proves that M. Janin was in a fright, and no wonder; three cannibals with knives and poisoned arrows are not pleasant companions even for a brave Frenchman. In the sketch given above, the stout man is the chief; the lady Guynuya has her back turned, a piece of unpoliteness in which she persisted during the whole of my visit. They play cards all day, laugh, eat raw beef, and drink all they can get.

Paris, July 13.

The figure above* is a copy of the statue which shortly is to decorate the column in the Place Vendôme. It is, as everybody knows, to be elevated about the 29th of the month; but his majesty the king of the French, being averse to *émeutes dépenses* of all kinds, has determined that it shall be erected privily in the night season, and shall have no needless extravagance or unnecessary publicity to accompany its elevation.

The statue has been cast of bronze, or brass made of Austrian cannon (the victories of Napoleon are, luckily, not all used up), and represents, as the reader beholds, the little corporal in his habit of war. The column, up to 1814, was surmounted with a representation of the Emperor Napoleon, with robes and sceptre imperial; it bore on its base the following sonorous inscription :

Neapolio Imp. Aug.

Monumentum Belli Germanici

anno MDCCCV.

Trimestre spatio profligati

ex ære capto

Gloriæ exercitus maximi dicavit.

---

* A sketch of Napoleon on the Vendôme Column headed this letter in *The National Standard.*—ED.

In 1814 the inscription was removed, the statue torn down, and a dirty white flag replaced it. It seemed a lame and impotent conclusion to the series of victories which are carved on the column itself, and wind from the base to the summit, as if these battles had been fought and won for the sole purpose of re-establishing the white flag aforesaid.

Next week, however, Napoleon will make his second appearance on the column. He certainly ought to make a short speech on the occasion, which, we should think, would run something in this manner.

The emperor, after having raised his bronze spy-glass to his brazen eye, and regarded the multitude who are waiting to hear his oration, begins

" Ladies and gentlemen ! (*Tremendous applause.*)

" Unaccustomed as I am to public speaking, and overpowered by feelings of the deepest and tenderest nature, you may readily fancy my inability to address you with the eloquence demanded by your presence, and by this occasion.

" Ladies and gentlemen : This is the proudest moment of my life ! (*Bravo, and cheers.*)

" I thank you for having placed me in a situation so safe, so commanding, and so salubrious : from this elevation I can look on most parts of your city. I see the churches empty, the prisons crowded, the gambling-houses overflowing ; who, with such sights before him as these, gentlemen, and *you*, would not be proud of the name of Frenchmen ? (*Great cheers.*)

" The tricolor waves over the Tuileries as it used in my time. It must be satisfactory to Frenchmen to have re-established their glorious standard, and to have banished for ever the old white flag ; and, though I confess myself that I cannot perceive any other benefit you have wrought by your resistance to a late family, you of course can. (*Applause, mingled with some unseemly groans from the police.*)

" I apprehend that the fat man* with the umbrella, whom I see walking in the gardens of the Tuileries, is the present

---

* Napoleon here makes an irreverent and personal allusion to King Louis Philippe. His stoutness and his umbrella were depicted some two months ago, in our paper [*vide infra, p.* 211].

proprietor. May I ask what he has done to deserve such a reward from you? Does he found his claim on his own merits, or on those of his father? (*A tremendous row in the crowd: the police proceed to empoigner several hundred individuals.*) "Go your ways," (said the statue, who was what is vulgarly called a dab, at an impromptu;) "go your ways, happy Frenchmen! You have fought, you have struggled, you have conquered: for whom? for the fat man with the umbrella!

"I need not explain what were my intentions and prospects, if I had had the good fortune to remain among you. You were yourselves pleased to receive them with some favour. The rest of Europe, however, did not look on them in the same light, and expressed its opinion so strongly, that we, out of mere politeness, were obliged to give up our own.

"I confess myself that I was somewhat arbitrary and tyrannical: but what is our fat friend below? Is it not better to be awed by a hero than to be subdued by a money-lender? to be conquered by a sword than to be knocked down by an umbrella? (*Here there was an immense cry of "*A bas les Parapluies!*" Some further arrests took place.*)

"Perhaps, if it be not a bore, (*go on,*) you will allow me to say a word concerning those persons who so strongly voted my own removal, and the re-establishment of the white cloth, now folded up for ever.

"The Russians are occupied in strangling, murdering, and banishing; I could not possibly have chosen for them a better occupation.

"The English, with their £800,000,000 of debt, have destroyed their old institutions, and have as yet fixed on no new ones. (*Here a further crowd were marched off by the police.*) I congratulate you. Gentlemen, *they* too have policemen.*

"The Portuguese are fighting about two brothers, both of whom they detest. Heaven preserve the right, whichever he may be.

"From Italy there are delightful accounts of revolts, and deaths thereon consequent.

---

* This struck us as rather a vulgar allusion on the part of the statue.

"The Germans are arresting students for want of a better employment. The Spaniards are amusing themselves with sham fights: what a pity they cannot be indulged with real ones!

"And the family! for whom about five hundred thousand lives were sacrificed,—where are they? The king is doting, and the dauphin is mad in a chateau in Germany; and the duchess must divide her attentions between her son and her daughter!

"And yourselves, gentlemen, you have freedom of the press, —but your papers are seized every morning, as in my time. You have a republic, but beware how you speak of the king! as in my time also. You are free; but you have seventeen forts to keep you in order. I don't recollect anything of the sort in my time.

"Altogether, there is a most satisfactory quantity of bullying, banishing, murdering, taxing, and hanging, throughout Europe. I perceive by your silence "—Here the emperor stopped: the fact was, there was not a single person left in the Place Vendôme; they had all been carried off by the police!

LOUIS PHILIPPE.*

HERE is Louis Philippe, the great Roi des Français,
(Roi de France is no longer the phrase of the day :)
His air just as noble, his mien as complete,
His face as majestic, his breeches so neat ;
His hat just so furnish'd with badge tricolor,
Sometimes worn on the side, sometime sported before,
But wherever 'tis placed, much in shape and in size,
Like an overgrown pancake " saluting men's eyes."
From hat down to boots, from his pouch to umbrella,
He here stands before you, a right royal fellow.

Like " the king in the parlour " he's fumbling his money,
Like " the queen in the kitchen," his speech is all honey,
Except when he talks it, like Emperor Nap,
Of his wonderful feats at Fleurus and Jemappe ;
But, alas ! all his zeal for the multitude's gone,
And of no numbers thinking, except number one !
No huzzas greet his coming, no patriot-club licks
The hand of " the best of created republics."
He stands in Paris as you see him before ye,
Little more than a snob—There's an end of the story.

---

* This and the four following pieces were accompanied with caricature
portraits, by the author, of the persons described, on their original appearance in *The National Standard.*—ED.

MR. BRAHAM.

SONNET.—By W. Wordsworth.

Say not that Judah's harp hath lost its tone,
Or that no bard hath found it where it hung, .
Broken and lonely, voiceless and unstrung,
Beside the sluggish streams of Babylon ;
Sloman !* repeats the strain his fathers sung,
And Judah's burning lyre is Braham's own !
Behold him here. Here view the wondrous man,
Majestical and lovely as when first
In music on a wondering world he burst,
And charm'd the ravish'd ears of sovereign Anne !†
Mark well the form, O ! reader, nor deride
The sacred symbol—Jew's harp glorified—
Which circled with a blooming wreath is seen
Of verdant bays ; and thus are typified
The pleasant music and the baize of green,
Whence issues out at eve, Braham with front serene !

———

N. M. ROTHSCHILD, Esq.

Here's the pillar of 'Change ! Nathan Rothschild himself,
   With whose fame every bourse through the universe rings ;
The first‡ Baron Juif ; by the grace of his pelf,
   Not " the king of the Jews," but " the Jew of the kings."

* It is needless to speak of this eminent vocalist and improvisatore. He nightly delights a numerous and respectable audience at the Cider-cellar ; and while on this subject, I cannot refrain from mentioning the kindness of Mr. Evans, the worthy proprietor of that establishment. N.B. A table d'hôte every Friday.—W. Wordsworth.

† Mr. Braham made his first appearance in England in the reign of Queen Anne.—W. W.

‡ Some years ago, shortly after the elevation (by the emperor of Austria' of one of the Rothschilds to the rank of Baron, he was present at a soirée in Paris, which he entered about the same time as the Duc de Montmo-

The great incarnation of cents and consols,
Of eighths, halves, and quarters, scrip, options, and shares;
Who plays with new kings as young Misses with dolls;
The monarch undoubted of bulls and of bears!

O, Plutus! your graces are queerly bestow'd!
Else sure we should think you behaved *infra dig.*
When with favours surpassing it joys you to load
A greasy-faced compound of donkey and pig.

Here, just as he stands with his head pointed thus,
At full-length, gentle reader, we lay him before ye;
And we then leave the Jew (what we wish he'd leave us,
But we fear to no purpose,) *a lone* in his glory.

A. BUNN.

I.

WHAT gallant cavalier is seen
So dainty set before the queen,
    Between a pair of candles?
Who looks as smiling and as bright,
As oily, and as full of light,
    As is the wax he handles?

II.

Dress'd out as gorgeous as a lord,
Stuck to his side a shining sword,
    A-murmuring loyal speeches,
The gentleman who's coming on
Is Mr. Manager A. Bunn,
    All in his velvet breeches.

------

renci. "Ah!" said Talleyrand, "voici le premier baron Chrétien, et le premier baron Juif." The Montmorencies boast, and we believe justly, that they are the first Christian barons. We all know that the Rothschilds may make the same claim of precedence among the Jews.

III.

He moves our gracious queen to greet,
And guide her to her proper seat,
   (A bag-wigg'd cicerone.)
O Adelaide! you will not see,
'Mong all the German com-pa-ny,
A figure half so droll as he,
   Or half so worth your money.

PETRUS LAUREUS.

Who sits in London's civic chair,
With owlish look and buzzard air,
The wise and worshipful Lord Mayor?
          Sir Peter!

Who, spectacle astride on nose,
Pours forth a flood of bright bon-mots,
As brilliant and as old as Joe's?
          Sir Peter!

Who, sworn to let thieves thrive no longer,
Shows to the rogues that law is stronger,
And proves himself a *costermonger?*
          Sir Peter!

Who, fairly *saddled* in his seat,
Affords the Queen a *bit* to eat,
And *bridles* up before the great?
          Sir Peter!

O happy be your glorious *rein*,
And may its *traces* long remain,
To *check* and *curb* the rogues in grain!
          Sir Peter

And when to *leathery* ease
Return'd, you give up London's keys,
May luck thy patent-axles grease,
          Sir Peter!

LOVE IN FETTERS.*

A TOTTENHAM-COURT-ROAD DITTY,

*Showing how dangerous it is for a Gentleman to fall in love with
an "Officer's Daughter."*

AN OWER TRUE TALE.

1.

I FELL in love, three days ago,
With a fair maid as bright as snow,
  Whose cheek would beat the rose ;
The raven tresses of her hair
In blackness could with night compare,
  Like Venus's her nose :
Her eyes, of lustre passing rare,
  Bright as the diamond glow'd,
If you would know, you may go see,
If you won't go, pray credit me ;
    'Twas at the back
    Of the Tabernac,
In Tottenham Court Road.

2.

The street in which my beauty shone
Is named, in compliment to John ;
  Her house is nigh to where
A massy hand all gilt with gold,
A thundering hammer doth uphold,
  High lifted in the air :

---

* When it originally appeared in *The National Standard* this " Ditty "
was accompanied with an illustration by the author.—ED.

What house it is you shall be told,
    Before I end my ode,
If you would know, go there and see,
If you won't go, then credit me ;
        'Twas at the back
        Of the Tabernac,
In Tottenham Court Road.

3.

Smitten with love, at once I wrote
A neat triangular tender note,
    All full of darts and flame ;
Said I, " Sweet star,"—but you may guess
How lovingly I did express
    My passion for the dame ;
I sign'd my name and true address,
    But she served me like a toad.
If you would know, pray come and see,
If you won't come, then credit me ;
        'Twas at the back
        Of the Tabernac,
In Tottenham Court Road.

4.

Next morn, 'tis true, an answer came,
I started when I heard my name,
    As I in bed did lie ;
Says a soft voice, " Are you the cove
Wot wrote a letter full of love ?"
    " Yes, yes," I cried, "'tis I :"
" An answer's sent," said he—O Jove !
    What a sad note he show'd.
If you would know, pray come and see,
If you will not, then credit me ;
        'Twas at the back
        Of the Tabernac,
In Tottenham Court Road.

5.

By a parchment slip I could discern
That by me stood a bailiff stern,
   My Rosamunda's sire!
I served the daughter with verse and wit,
And the father served me with a writ,
   An exchange I don't admire:
So here in iron bars I sit,
   In quod securely stow'd,
Being captivated by a she,
Whose papa captivated me;
     All at the back
     Of the Tabernac,
In Tottenham Court Road.

DADDY, I'M HUNGRY.

A Scene in an Irish Coachmaker's Family,

Designed by Lord Lowther, July, 1843.

A sweet little picture, that's fully desarving
    Your lordship's approval, we here riprisint—
A poor Irish coachmaker's family starving
    (More thanks to your lordship) is dhrawn in the print.

See the big lazy blackguard! although it is Monday,
    He sits at his ease with his hand to his check,
And doin' no more work nor a Quaker on Sunday,
    Nor your lordship's own self on most days of the week.

And thim's the two little ones, Rory and Mysie,
    Whom he'd dandle and jump every night on his knee—
Faith he gives the poor darlin's a welcome as icy
    As I'd give a bum-bailiff that came after me!

He turns from their prattle as angry as may be,
    "O, daddy, I'm hungry," says each little brat;
And yonder sits mammy, and nurses the baby,
    Thinking how long there'll be dinner for that.

For daddy and children, for babby and mammy,
    No work and no hope, O! the prospect is fine;
But I fancy I'm hearing your lordship cry—"Dammee,
    Suppose they *do* starve, it's no business of mine."

Well, it's "justice," no doubt, that your lordship's observing,
    And that must our feelings of hunger console;
We're five hundred families, wretched and starving
    But what matter's that, so there's *Justice for Croal?*

THE

Bibliography of Thackeray

A BIBLIOGRAPHICAL LIST

ARRANGED IN CHRONOLOGICAL ORDER

OF THE

PUBLISHED WRITINGS IN PROSE AND VERSE
AND THE SKETCHES AND DRAWINGS

OF

WILLIAM MAKEPEACE THACKERAY

(FROM 1829 TO 1886)

[This Bibliography was first published, in a separate form, in the winter of 1880 : in the present issue it has been thoroughly revised and considerably enlarged.]

THE BIBLIOGRAPHY OF THACKERAY.

1829.

THE SNOB: *A Literary and Scientific Journal, not "conducted by Members of the University."* Cambridge: Published by W. H. Smith, Rose-crescent. 1829, 12mo, pp. 64.

Consisting of eleven weekly numbers, printed on paper of several different colours, commencing Thursday, April 9, and ending Thursday, June 18, 1829.

1832.

ELIZABETH BROWNRIGGE: *A Tale, in Two Books. Fraser's Magazine,* August—September, 1832, vol. vi. (pp. 67-88, 131-148).

1833.

Contributions in verse and prose to *The National Standard and Journal of Literature, Science, Music, Theatricals and the Fine Arts.* London: Thomas Hurst, 65, St. Paul's Churchyard. 1833, 4to.

The contributions distinctly traceable as Thackeray's are as follows (though probably others might be identified) :—

Vol. i. (1833.)

May 4, p. 273. Louis Philippe (Verses and Sketch).

May 11, p. 289. Mr. Braham, "Sonnet by W. Wordsworth," and Sketch.

May 18, p. 305. N. M. Rothschild, Esq. (Verses and Sketch).

June 1, p. 345. A. Bunn (Verses and Sketch).

June 8, p. 362. Love in Fetters ; a Tottenham-court-road Ditty (with Sketch).

June 15, pp. 380-381. Covent Garden (with Sketch).

June 22, p. 395. Petrus Laurens (Verses and Sketch).

June 29, pp. 412-413. Paris Correspondence (with Sketch).

Vol. ii. (1833).

July 6, pp. 10-11.⎫
July 13, pp. 28-29. ⎬Paris Correspondence (with three Sketches).
July 20, pp. 42-43.⎭

August 10, pp. 85-86. ⎱The Devil's Wager (with an Illus-
August 24,* pp. 121-122.⎰ tration).

The Devil's Wager, with the same illustration reproduced, is reprinted in *The Paris Sketch Book* (1840), vol. ii., pp. 83-101. There are some verbal alterations throughout, and the words of the incantation of Father Ignatius are omitted in the later version.

1836.

FLORE ET ZEPHYR. BALLET MYTHOLOGIQUE PAR THÉOPHILE WAGSTAFF.—London : Published March 1st, 1836, by J. Mitchell, Library, 33, Old Bond-street. A Paris, chez Rittner & Goupil, Boulevard Montmartre. Folio.

Eight plates, lithographed by Edward Morton, of which the following is the letterpress description :

1. La Danse fait ses offrandes sur l'autel de l'Harmonie.
2. Jeux Innocens de Zephyr et Flore.
3. Flore déplore l'absence de Zephyr.
4. Dans un pas-seul il exprime son extrême desespoir.
5. Triste et abattu, les séductions des Nymphes le tentent en vain.
6. Réconciliation de Flore et Zephyr.
7. La Retraite de Flore.
8. Les Délassements de Zephyr ; and vignette on wrapper-title.

" In 1836 his first attempt at independent authorship appeared simultaneously at London and Paris. This publication, at a time when he still hoped to make his bread by art, is, like indeed everything he either said or did, so characteristic, and has been so utterly forgotten, that an account of it may not be out of place,' perhaps more minute than its absolute merits deserve.

' It is a small folio, slightly tinted, entitled *Flore et Zephyr, Ballet Mythologique dédié à—par Théophile Wagstaff.* Between "*à*" and "*par*" on the cover is the exquisite *Flore* herself, all alone in some rosy and bedizened bower. She has the old jaded smirk, and, with eyebrows up and eyelids dropped, she is looking down oppressed with modesty and glory. Her nose,

---

* With this number Thackeray's contributions appear to have ceased ; though the Journal itself continued to exist until February 1, 1834, completing a second volume and running on to a fragment (eighty pages) of a third.

which is long, and has a ripe droop, gives to the semicircular smirk of the
large mouth, down upon the centre of which it comes in the funniest way,
an indescribably sentimental absurdity.   Her thin, sinewy arms and large
hands are crossed on her breast, and her petticoat stands out like an inverted
white tulip—of muslin—out of which come her professional legs, in the
only position which human nature never puts its legs into; it is her special
pose.   Of course, also, you are aware, by that smirk, that look of being
looked at, that though alone in maiden meditation in this her bower, and
sighing for her Zephyr, she is in front of some thousand pairs of eyes, and
under the fire of many double-barrelled lorgnettes, of which she is the focus.

"In the first plate, *La Danse fait ses offrandes sur l'autel de l'harmonie,* in the
shapes of Flore and Zephyr coming trippingly to the footlights, and paying
no manner of regard to the altar of harmony, represented by a fiddle with
an old and dreary face, and a laurel wreath on its head, and very great
regard to the unseen but perfectly understood " house."   Next is *Triste et
abattu, les séductions des Nymphes le tentent en vain,* Zephyr looking
theatrically sad.   Then *Flore* (with one lower extremity at more than a
right angle to the other) *déplore l'absence de Zephyr.* The man in the orchestra
endeavouring to combine business with pleasure, so as to play the flageolet
and read his score, and at the same time miss nothing of the deploring, is
intensely comic.   Next Zephyr has his turn, and *dans un pas seul exprime
sa suprême désespoir*—the extremity of despair being expressed by doubling
one leg so as to touch the knee of the other, and then whirling round so as
to suggest the regulator of a steam-engine run off. Next is the rapturous reconciliation, when the faithful creature bounds into his arms, and is held up
to the house by the waist in the wonted fashion.   Then there is *La Retraite
de Flore,* where we find her with her mother and two admirers—Zephyr, of
course, not one.   This is in Thackeray's strong unflinching line.   One lover
is a young dandy without forehead or chin, sitting idiotically astride his
chair.   To him the old lady, who has her slight rouge, too, and is in a
homely shawl and muff, having walked, is making faded love.   In the
centre is the fair darling herself still on tiptoe, and wrapped up, but not too
much, for her *jucre.*   With his back to the comfortable fire, and staring
wickedly at her, is the other lover, a big, burly, elderly man, probably well
to do on the Bourse, and with a wife and family at home in their beds.   The
last exhibits *Les délassements de Zephyr.*   That hard-working and homely
personage is resting his arm on the chimney-piece, taking a huge pinch of
snuff from the box of a friend, with a refreshing expression of satisfaction,
the only bit of nature as yet.   A dear little innocent pot-boy, such as only
Thackeray knew how to draw, is gazing and waiting upon the two, holding
up a tray from the nearest tavern, on which is a great pewter-pot of foam-
ing porter for Zephyr, and a rummer of steaming brandy and water for his
friend, who has come in from the cold air.   These drawings are lithographed
by Edward Morton, son of "Speed the Plough," and are done with that
delicate strength and truth for which this excellent but little known artist

is always to be praised. In each corner is the monogram, W. T., which appears so often afterwards with the M added, and is itself superseded by the well-known pair of spectacles. Thackeray must have been barely five-and-twenty when this was published by Mitchell in Bond Street. It can hardly be said to have sold."—DR. JOHN BROWN (*North British Review*, February 1864).

1837.

CARLYLE'S FRENCH REVOLUTION.—*Times*, Thursday, August 3, 1837, fol. 6, col. 4-6.

" I understand there have been many reviews of a very mixed character. I got one in the 'Times' last week. The writer is one Thackeray, a half-monstrous Cornish giant, kind of painter, Cambridge man and Paris news-paper correspondent, who is now writing for his life in London. . . . His article is rather like him, and I suppose calculated to do the book good."— *Carlyle to his brother:* 'Scotsbrig, August 12, 1837.' (*Carlyle's Life in London*, i. 113).

THE PROFESSOR. A TALE. By Goliah Gahagan.—*Bentley's Mis-cellany*, September, 1837 (vol. ii., pp. 277-288).

Reprinted in *Comic Tales and Sketches* (1841), vol. ii., and in the Col-lected Works of Thackeray, vol. xxv. (1885), but not in any intermediate edition.

THE YELLOWPLUSH CORRESPONDENCE. Fashionable Fax and Polite Annygoats. By Charles Yellowplush, Esq.—*Fraser's Magazine*, November, 1837 (vol. xvi., pp. 644-649).

A review of a volume entitled "My Book, or the Anatomy of Conduct," by a Mr. John Henry Skelton.

Reprinted in Thackeray's Collected Works, vol. xxv. (1885).

1838.

THE YELLOWPLUSH CORRESPONDENCE :—

No. II.   Miss Shum's Husband.
No. III.   Dimond cut Dimond.
No. IV.   Skimmings from the Dairy of George IV.
No. V.   Foring Parts.
No. VI.   Mr. Deuceace at Paris.
        The End of Mr. Deuceace's History.
        Mr. Yellowplush's Ajew.

Fraser's Magazine, January to August, 1838, vol. xvii., pp. 39-49, 243-250, 353-359 ; 404-408, 616-627, 734-741 ; vol. xviii., pp. 59-71, 195-200.

Reprinted in *Comic Tales and Sketches* (1841).

Strictures on Pictures. A Letter from Michael Angelo Tit-marsh, Esq.—*Fraser's Magazine*, June, 1838 (vol. xvii., pp. 758-764).

With sketch by the author of "Titmarsh placing the laurel-wreath on the brows of Mulready."

Reprinted in Thackeray's Collected Works, vol. xxv. (1885).

Twelve Plates illustrative of "Men of Character. By Douglas Jerrold. In three volumes.—London : Henry Colburn. 1838."

List of Plates : Vol. I. Practical Philosophy of Adam Buff ; The Fall of Pippins ; Job Pippins a Murderer ; Jack Runnymede's Dream. Vol. II. John Applejohn's Humane Intentions ; Maximilian Tape before the "Lords ;" Final Reward of John Applejohn. Vol. III. Barnaby Palms "feeling his way ; " Cheek's Introduction to a new subject ; The Ghost of Kemp ; Matthew Clear not "seeing his way ;" Introduction of Titus Trumps to "Miss Wolfe."

"The illustrations were by Mr. W. M. Thackeray, now the renowned novelist."—*Life and Remains of Douglas Jerrold, by his son Blanchard Jerrold.* London : 1859, p. 144.

The Story of Mary Ancel.—*New Monthly Magazine.* (London : Colburn), October, 1838 (vol. liv., pp. 185-197).

Reprinted in *The Paris Sketch-Book* (vol. i., pp. 254-290).

1838-1839.

SOME PASSAGES IN THE LIFE OF MAJOR GAHAGAN.—*New Monthly Magazine.* London : Colburn. February, March, November, December, 1838, and February, 1839 (vol. lii., pp. 174-182, 374-378 ; vol. liv., pp. 319-328, 543-552 ; vol. lv., pp. 266-281).

Reprinted in *Comic Tales and Sketches* (1841), vol. ii.

1839.

STUBBS'S CALENDAR ; OR, THE FATAL BOOTS. With twelve illustrations by George Cruikshank.—*Comic Almanack* for 1839. London : Charles Tilt.

Reprinted in *Comic Tales and Sketches* (1841), vol. ii.

Contributions to *The Corsair*, 1839 :—

Letters from London, Paris, Pekin, Petersburg, &c. By the Author of "The Yellowplush Correspondence," the "Memoirs of Major Gahagan, &c. (signed T. T.)

No. 1, dated " Hotel Mirabeau, July 25, 1839."

No. 2, dated " Paris, 16th August, 1839 " (*Madame Sand and Spiridion*).
No. 3, ...
No. 4, dated " 31 August."

*The Corsair: A Gazette of Literature, Art, Dramatic Criticism,
Fashion and Novelty* (Office in Astor House, No. 8, Barclay-
street. Edited by N. P. Willis and T. O. Porter. New York:
August 24, September 14, 21, October 5, 26, 1839, vol. i.
pp. 380-382, 429-430, 445-447, 473-475, 521-523.

The first three contributions were reprinted substantially, under the titles
of "An Invasion of France," "Madame Sand and the New Apocalypse," and
" The Fêtes of July," in *The Paris Sketch-Book* (1840), vol. i. pp. 1-22, 59-75 ;
vol. ii. pp. 102-151, although several paragraphs appearing in *The Corsair*
are omitted or altered. The fourth contribution was not reprinted, and is
now only accessible in the late Mr. Hotten's volume, entitled " The Students'
Quarter." (*Vide infra*, p. 252-253).

1839-1840.

CATHERINE: A STORY.   By Ikey Solomons, Esq., junior.—
Fraser's Magazine, May, June, July, August, November, 1839 ;
January, February, 1840.

With four full-page illustrations by the author : Mrs. Catharine's
Temptation ; The Interrupted Marriage ; Captain Brock appears at Court
with my Lord Peterborough ; Catharine's Present to Mr. Hayes.
Reprinted in the Collected Editions of Thackeray's Works.

1839.

A Second Lecture on the Fine Arts, by Michael Angelo Titmarsh, Esq.—*Fraser's Magazine*, June, 1839 (vol. xix., pp.
743-750).

Reprinted in Thackeray's Collected Works, vol. xxv (1885).

The French Plutarch, No. 1.   1. Cartouche.   2. Poinsinet.—
Fraser's Magazine, October, 1839 (vol. xx., pp. 447-459).

Reprinted in *The Paris Sketch-Book*, 1840.

On the French School of Painting—in a Letter from Mr.
Michael Angelo Titmarsh to Mr. MacGilp of London.—
Fraser's Magazine, December, 1839 (vol. xx., pp. 679-688).

Reprinted in *The Paris Sketch-Book*, 1840, vol. i.

1840.

BARBER COX, AND THE CUTTING OF HIS COMB.   With twelve

illustrations by George Cruikshank.—*Comic Almanack* for 1840. London : Charles Tilt.

Afterwards, when first reprinted in Thackeray's *Miscellanies* (1856), entitled " Cox's Diary."

Epistles to the Literati. Ch-s Y-ll-wpl-sh, Esq., to Sir Edward Lytton Bulwer, Bart. John Thomas Smith, Esq., to C—s Y—h, Esq.—*Fraser's Magazine*, January, 1840 (vol. xxi., pp. 71-80).

Reprinted in *Comic Tales and Sketches*, 1841, vol. i.

THE BEDFORD-ROW CONSPIRACY. In two Parts.—*New Monthly Magazine*, January, March and April, 1840 (vol. lviii., pp. 99-111, 416-425, 547-557).

Reprinted in *Comic Tales and Sketches* (1841), vol. ii.

THE PARIS SKETCH-BOOK. BY MR. TITMARSH. With numerous designs by the author, on copper and wood. In two volumes, pp. 304, 298.—London : John Macrone, 1840.

CONTENTS OF VOL. I.

An Invasion of France.	On some French Fashionable
A Caution to Travellers.	Novels.
The Fêtes of July.	A Gambler's Death.
On the French School of Painting.	Napoleon and his System.
The Painter's Bargain.	The Story of Mary Ancel.
Cartouche.	Beatrice Merger.

CONTENTS OF VOL. II.

Caricatures and Lithography in Paris.	The Case of Peytel.
	Imitations of Béranger.
Little Poinsinet.	French Dramas and Melo-
The Devil's Wager.	dramas.
Madame Sand and the New Apocalypse.	Meditations at Versailles.

The Preface is dated " London, July 1, 1840."

An Essay on the Genius of George Cruikshank, with numerous illustrations of his works (from the *Westminster Review*, No. lxvi.), with additional Etchings. Henry Hooper, 13, Pall Mall East, 1840, pp. ii., 59.

Reprinted separately from the *Westminster Review*, June, 1840 (vol. xxxiv. pp. 1-60), where it originally appeared.

A Pictorial Rhapsody, by Michael Angelo Titmarsh. With an Introductory Letter to Mr. Yorke.—*Fraser's Magazine*, June, 1840 (vol. xxi., pp. 720-732).

A Pictorial Rhapsody, concluded, and followed by a remarkable statement of facts by Mrs. Barbara.—*Fraser's Magazine*, July, 1840 (vol. xxii., pp. 112-126).

Reprinted in Thackeray's Collected Works, vol. xxv. (1885).

Going to see a Man Hanged.   Signed W. M. T.—*Fraser's Magazine*, August, 1840 (vol. xxii., pp. 150-158).

Reprinted in several of the Collected Editions of Thackeray's Works, among "Sketches and Travels in London."

A SHABBY GENTEEL STORY.   In Nine Chapters.—*Fraser's Magazine*, June, July, August, October, 1840.

Reprinted in Thackeray's *Miscellanies*, 1857, vol. iv, pp. 221-324), with a brief note of fourteen lines added at the end, signed "W. M. T." and dated "London : April 10, 1857."

SKETCHES BY SPEC.   No. 1.—Britannia protecting the Drama. Published by H. Cunningham, 3, St. James' Square [1840]. Print and letterpress Explanation.

This work, if ever actually issued, does not appear to have been continued. The only known copy of the only number known to exist, is in the possession of Mr. Charles Plumptre Johnson, under whose auspices, and with a prefatory note written by him, it was reproduced in facsimile by the Autotype Company in 1885, in a wrapper, privately printed.

Captain Rook and Mr. Pigeon.   By William Thackeray.   With two illustrations by Kenny Meadows.—*Heads of the People : or, Portraits of the English. Drawn by Kenny Meadows. With Original Essays by distinguished writers.* London : Robert Tyas, 1840, pp. 305-320.

1841.

The Fashionable Authoress.   By William Thackeray.   With an illustration by Kenny Meadows.—*Heads of the People. Drawn by Kenny Meadows.* London : Robert Tyas, 1841, pp. 73-84.

The Artist.   By Michael Angelo Titmarsh.   With an illustration by Kenny Meadows.—*Heads of the People.* London : 1841, pp. 161-176.

These three contributions to Kenny Meadows's *Heads of the People* were reprinted in Thackeray's collected *Miscellanies* (London, 1856), vol. ii, pp. 443-494.

COMIC TALES AND SKETCHES.   EDITED AND ILLUSTRATED BY MR. MICHAEL ANGELO TITMARSH.   In two volumes.   London :

Hugh Cunningham, 1841, 12mo (vol. i., pp. vii., 299 ; vol. ii., pp. 370).

The Preface is dated " Paris, April 1, 1841."

Contents of Vol. I. :—THE YELLOWPLUSH PAPERS.—1. Miss Shum's Husband ; 2. The Amours of Mr. Deuceace — Dimond cut Dimond ; 3. Skimmings from the Dairy of George IV. ; 4. Foring Parts ; 5. Mr. Deuceace at Paris, in ten chapters ; 6. Mr. Yellowplush's Ajew ; 7. Epistles to the Literati.

Contents of Vol. II. :—Some Passages in the Life of Major Gahagan ; The Professor ; The Bedford-Row Conspiracy ; Stubbs's Calendar, or the Fatal Boots.

THE SECOND FUNERAL OF NAPOLEON ; in Three Letters to Miss Smith, of London, and The Chronicle of the Drum. By Mr. M. A. Titmarsh. London : Hugh Cunningham. 1841, pp. 122.

With frontispiece of "Tomb in the Chapel of the Invalides," and vignette drawn by the author on the coloured wrapper.

" The Second Funeral of Napoleon " was reprinted (with prefatory note), from the original manuscript, in the *Cornhill Magazine*, January 1866 (vol. xiii., pp. 48-80). A small portion of the manuscript is facsimiled in *The Autographic Mirror* of February 20, 1864 (vol. i., p. 6).

The Chronicle of the Drum was reprinted in Thackeray's collected *Ballads* (1855). The original manuscript, twenty pages quarto, is in Mr. Frederick Locker-Lampson's Collection of Autographs (see Catalogue, p. 217).

Memorials of Gormandising. In a letter to Oliver Yorke, Esq., by M. A. Titmarsh.—*Fraser's Magazine,* June, 1841 (vol. xxiii., pp. 710-725).

On Men and Pictures. Apropos of a Walk in the Louvre.— *Fraser's Magazine,* July, 1841 (vol. xxiv., pp. 98-111).

Men and Coats.—*Fraser's Magazine,* August, 1841 (vol. xxiv., pp. 208-217).

The above three papers are reprinted in Thackeray's Collected Works, vol. xxv. (1885).

THE HISTORY OF SAMUEL TITMARSH AND THE GREAT HOGGARTY DIAMOND. Edited and illustrated by Sam's Cousin, Michael Angelo.—*Fraser's Magazine,* September to December, 1841 (vol. xxiv.).

THE HISTORY OF SAMUEL TITMARSH AND THE GREAT HOGGARTY

DIAMOND. BY W. M. THACKERAY.—London : Bradbury and Evans, 1849, pp. xii., 189.

With engraved title and nine full-page illustrations by the author. The Preface is dated " Kensington, January 25, 1849."

Little Spitz. A Lenten Anecdote, from the German of Professor Spass. By Michael Angelo Titmarsh. With woodcut illustration by George Cruikshank.—Printed in *George Cruikshank's Omnibus*, No. vi., October 1841. London : Tilt and Bogue, pp. 167-172.

The King of Brentford's Testament. By Michael Angelo Titmarsh.—Printed in *George Cruikshank's Omnibus*, No. viii., December, 1841, pp. 244-246.

Reprinted in Thackeray's collected *Ballads* (1855).

1842.

Dickens in France (with two illustrations by the author).— *Fraser's Magazine*, March 1842 (vol. xxv., pp. 342-352).

Sultan Stork : being the One Thousand and Second Night. By Major G. O'G. Gahagan, H.E.I.C.S. Part the First.—The Magic Powder. Part the Second.—The Enchanted Princess. With two illustrations on wood by George Cruikshank.— *Ainsworth's Magazine*, February and May, 1842 (vol. i. pp. 33-38 ; 233-237).

An Exhibition Gossip. By Michael Angelo Titmarsh.— *Ainsworth's Magazine*, June, 1842 (vol. i., pp. 319-322).

Contributions to *Punch* :—

Vol. iii. (1842.)

MISS TICKLETOBY'S LECTURES ON ENGLISH HISTORY. With twenty-three illustrations by the author.

	PAGE
A Character (to introduce another Character) . .	8— 9
Miss Tickletoby's Lecture	12—13
Miss Tickletoby's Second Lecture . . .	28—30
Lecture III. The Sea-kings in England . .	58—59

With a ballad of eight stanzas (24 lines), '.Ethlfred Koning Murning Post redinge,' and 'The Song of King Canute,' twenty-four stanzas (72 lines), afterwards reprinted in *Rebecca and Rowena*, pp. 32-35.

Lecture IV. Edward the Confessor—Harold—William the	
Conqueror	70—72
Lecture V. William Rufus	84—85

Reprinted in Thackeray's Collected Works, vol. xxv. (1885).

Vol. iv. (1843.)

Mr. Spec's Remonstrance (signed "Alonzo Spec, Historical Painter.") With two illustrations by the author, pp. 69-70.
A Turkish Letter concerning the Divertissement " Les Houris." With two illustrations, one signed with the spectacles, p. 199.
Second Turkish Letter, &c. With one illustration, p. 209.

1842-1843.

FITZ-BOODLE'S CONFESSIONS.—*Fraser's Magazine*, June, 1842 (vol. xxv., pp. 707-721).

PROFESSIONS BY GEORGE FITZ-BOODLE. Being appeals to the unemployed younger sons of the nobility.—*Fraser's Magazine*, July, 1842 (vol. xxvi., pp. 43-60).

FITZ-BOODLE'S CONFESSIONS. Miss Löwe.—*Fraser's Magazine*, October, 1842 (vol. xxvi., pp. 395-405).

CONFESSIONS OF GEORGE FITZ-BOODLE. Dorothea.—*Fraser's Magazine*, January, 1843 (vol. xxvii., pp. 76-84).

CONFESSIONS OF GEORGE FITZ-BOODLE. Ottilia.—*Fraser's Magazine*, February, 1843 (vol. xxvii., pp. 214-224).

CONFESSIONS OF GEORGE FITZ-BOODLE. Men's Wives. Mr. and Mrs. Frank Berry.—*Fraser's Magazine*, March, 1843 (vol. xxvii., pp. 349-361).
With an illustration by the author.

CONFESSIONS OF GEORGE FITZ-BOODLE. Men's Wives, No. II. The Ravenswing. In eight chapters.—*Fraser's Magazine*, April to June, August and September, 1843.

MEN'S WIVES. BY GEORGE FITZ-BOODLE. No. III. Dennis Haggarty's Wife.—*Fraser's Magazine*, October, 1843 (vol. xxviii., pp. 494-504).

MEN'S WIVES. BY GEORGE FITZ-BOODLE. No. IV. The ——'s

Wife.—*Fraser's Magazine*, November, 1843 (vol. xxviii., pp. 581-592).

The "Fitzboodle Papers" were collected in Thackeray's *Miscellanies* (1857), with the exception of *Dorothea* and *Ottilia*, substantially reprinted for the first time in the posthumous editions of his Works, *Miss Löwe*, first reprinted in the supplementary twenty-fifth volume, and *Men's Wives*, No. IV. *The ——'s Wife*, which, together with the third of Fitzboodle's "Professions," have never been reprinted.

THE IRISH SKETCH-BOOK. BY MR. M. A. TITMARSH. With numerous engravings on wood, drawn by the author. In two volumes, 12mo. London: Chapman and Hall, 186, Strand, 1843. (Vol. i., pp. vi. 311 ; vol. ii., pp. vi. 327).

The Dedication, to Dr. Charles Lever, is dated "London, April 27, 1843."

A literary treasure of singular appositeness has lately turned up in the form of a preface, written by Thackeray for the second edition of his 'Irish Sketch Book,' but suppressed by the publishers as being too out-spoken. This preface forms a long essay on the political situation in Ireland. In it Thackeray strongly supports not merely the disestablish-ment of the alien English Church, which, he says, "will no more grow in Ireland than a palm-tree in St. Paul's Churchyard," but even the Repeal of the Union. He goes so far as to venture on a prophecy that the latter concession will be eventually wrung from Sir Robert Peel. The paper is said to be written in Thackeray's most vivacious and characteristic style, and to form a curious contrast to the acid comments by Carlyle on Irish affairs lately given to the world. This preface was some time ago announced as about to appear in the *Century Magazine*, but was for some reason again suppressed, and has not yet seen the light.

1843.

Daddy, I'm hungry.—A Scene in an Irish Coachmaker's Family, designed by Lord Lowther, July, 1843. (Six stanzas of four lines each, with woodcut illustration, from a drawing by the author.—Printed in *The Nation* (Dublin), Saturday, May 13, 1843 (vol. i. no. 31, fol. 492, col. 1).

Reprinted, with the illustration, in Sir Charles Gavan Duffy's *Young Ireland*, Lond. 1880, p. 243.

1 LETTERS ON THE FINE ARTS. No. 1.—The Art Unions. From M. A. Titmarsh, Esq., to Sanders M'Gilp, Esq.—*Pictorial Times*, No. 1, Saturday, March 18, 1843, fol. 13-14 (signed Michael Angelo Titmarsh).

2 ――――― No. 2. The Objections against Art Unions.— *Pictorial Times*, April 1, 1843, fol. 43.

3 ――――― No. 2. (concluded).—*Pictorial Times*, April 8, 1843, fol. 61-62.

4 The Water-Colour Exhibitions.—*Pictorial Times*, May 6, 1843, fol. 125.

5 Letters on the Fine Arts. No. 3. The Royal Academy.— *Pictorial Times*, May 13, 1843, fol. 136-137.

6 Letters on the Fine Arts. No. 4. The Royal Academy. Second Notice.—*Pictorial Times*, May 27, 1843, fol. 169-170.

[*The Pictorial Times: A Weekly Journal of News, Literature, Fine Arts, and the Drama: illustrated with engravings on Wood by Henry Vizetelly and others.* London: Office, 135, Fleet Street, 1843.]

Jerome Paturot. With Considerations on Novels in General. In a letter from M. A. Titmarsh.—*Fraser's Magazine*, September, 1843 (vol. xxviii., pp. 349-362).

Bluebeard's Ghost. By M. A. Titmarsh.—*Fraser's Magazine*, October, 1843 (vol. xxviii., pp. 413-425). ·

Grant in Paris. By Fitz-Boodle.—*Fraser's Magazine*, December, 1843 (vol. xxviii., pp. 702-712).

A satirical notice of a book by Mr. James Grant, entitled " Paris and its People."

The above three pieces are reprinted in Thackeray's Collected Works, vol. xxv. (1885).

1844.

THE LUCK OF BARRY LYNDON. A Romance of the Last Century. By Fitz-Boodle.—*Fraser's Magazine*, January to September, November and December, 1844 (vols. xxix. and xxx.).

First re-issued in a separate form, under the title of " Memoirs of Barry Lyndon," in Thackeray's *Miscellanies*, 1856.

A Box of Novels.—*Fraser's Magazine*, February, 1844 (vol. xxix., pp. 153-169).

Reprinted in Thackeray's Collected Works, vol. xxv. (1885).

THE HISTORY OF THE NEXT FRENCH REVOLUTION. (From a

forthcoming History of Europe.)—*Punch*, February 24; March 2 to 30; April 6 to 20, 1844 (vol. vi.). With fourteen illustrations.

Reprinted in Thackeray's Collected Works, London : 1879, Vol. xv., pp. 163-201.

TITMARSH'S CARMEN LILLIENSE.—*Fraser's Magazine*, March, 1844 (vol. xxix., pp. 361-363).

Reprinted in Thackeray's *Ballads* (1855).

Review of " A New Spirit of the Age, by R. H. Horne."— *Morning Chronicle*, Tuesday, April 2, 1844, *fol.* 6.

This notice is referred to and quoted as the work of Michael Angelo Titmarsh in the late Mr. Horne's Introductory Comments to the second edition of his " New Spirit of the Age."

Reprinted in Thackeray's Collected Works, vol. xxv. (1885).

LITTLE TRAVELS AND ROAD-SIDE SKETCHES. By TITMARSH. (From Richmond in Surrey to Brussels in Belgium.)—*Fraser's Magazine*, May, 1844 (vol. xxix., pp. 517-528).

LITTLE TRAVELS AND ROAD-SIDE SKETCHES. By Titmarsh. No. II. Ghent—Bruges.—*Fraser's Magazine*, October, 1844 (vol. xxx., pp. 465-471). No. III. Waterloo—*Fraser's Magazine*, January, 1845 (vol. xxxi., pp. 94-96).

May Gambols ; or, Titmarsh in the Picture Galleries.—*Fraser's Magazine*, June, 1844 (vol. xxix., pp. 700-716).

Reprinted in Thackeray's Collected Works, vol. xxv. (1885).

The Partie Fine, by Lancelot Wagstaff, Esq.—Arabella ; or, the Moral of " The Partie Fine " (signed TITMARSH).—*Colburn's New Monthly Magazine*, May and June, 1844, (vol. lxxi., pp. 22-28, 169-172).

Greenwich—Whitebait. By Mr. Wagstaff.—*Colburn's New Monthly Magazine*, July, 1844, pp. 416-421.

The last-named paper is reprinted in Thackeray's Collected Works, vol. xxv. (1885).

Wanderings of our Fat Contributor.—*Punch*, August 3, 1844 (vol. vii., pp. 61-62).

With three illustrations by the author.

TRAVELLING NOTES BY OUR FAT CONTRIBUTOR.—*Punch*, August 10, 1844 (vol. vii., pp. 66-67).

With an illustration by the author.

August 17, 1844 (vol. vii., pp. 83-84).
With three illustrations by the author.

November 30, 1844 (vol. vii., p. 237).
With two illustrations by the author.

December 7, 1844 (vol. vii., pp. 256-257).
With three illustrations by the author.

December 14, 1844 (vol. vii., pp. 265-266).
With four illustrations by the author.

1845.

PUNCH IN THE EAST. FROM OUR FAT CONTRIBUTOR.—*Punch*, January 11, 1845 (vol. viii., pp. 31-32).
With an illustration by the author.

January 18, 1845 (vol. viii., pp. 35-36).
With two illustrations by the author.

January 25, 1845 (vol. viii., p. 45).
With three illustrations by the author.

February 1, 1845 (vol. viii., p. 61).
With two illustrations by the author.

February 8, 1845 (vol. viii., p. 75).
With an illustration by the author.

Picture Gossip: in a Letter from Michael Angelo Titmarsh.— *Fraser's Magazine*, June, 1845 (vol. xxxi., pp. 713-724).
Reprinted in Thackeray's Collected Works, vol. xxv. (1885).

The Chest of Cigars. By Lancelot Wagstaff, Esq. *Colburn's New Monthly Magazine*, July, 1845 (vol. lxxiv., pp. 381-385).

Bob Robinson's First Love. By Lancelot Wagstaff, Esq. *Colburn's New Monthly Magazine*, August, 1845 (vol. lxxiv., pp. 519-525).

The Pimlico Pavilion. By the Mulligan (of Kilballymulligan). *Punch*, August 9, 1845 (vol. ix., p. 66).

Meditations on Solitude. By our Stout Commissioner.—*Punch*, September 13, 1845 (vol. ix., p. 123).
With an illustration by the author.

Beulah Spa. By " Punch's" Commissioner.—*Punch*, September 27, 1845 (vol. ix., pp. 137-138).
With two illustrations by the author.

The Georges.—*Punch*, October 11, 1845 (vol. ix., p. 159).

A LEGEND OF THE RHINE. BY MICHAEL ANGELO TITMARSH. With fourteen woodcut illustrations by George Cruikshank.— Printed in *George Cruikshank's Table Book*. London: Published at the *Punch* Office, 1845.

Divided into thirteen chapters, published in instalments, commencing in the sixth and ending in the twelfth and last number.

Notice of N. P. Willis's *Dashes at Life.*—*Edinburgh Review*, October, 1845 (vol. lxxxii., pp. 470-480).

Two letters to Mr. Macvey Napier, Editor of the *Edinburgh Review*, dated, "St. James's-street, July 16, 1845," and "October 16, 1845," and signed "W. M. Thackeray."—*Correspondence of the late Macvey Napier*, edited by his son. London: Macmillan and Co., 1879, pp. 498-499.

Barmecide Banquets with Joseph Bregion and Anne Miller. George Savage Fitz-Boodle, Esquire, to the Rev. Lionel Gaster. —*Fraser's Magazine*, November, 1845 (vol. xxxii., pp. 584-593).

Reprinted in Thackeray's Collected Works, vol. xxv (1885).

Brighton. By "Punch's Commissioner."—*Punch*, October 11, 1845 (vol. ix., p. 158).

With three illustrations by the author.

A Brighton Night Entertainment. By "Punch's Commissioner." —*Punch*, October 18, 1845 (vol. ix., p. 168).

With four illustrations by the author.

Meditations over Brighton. By "Punch's Commissioner." (From the Devil's Dyke.)—*Punch*, October 25, 1845 (vol. ix., p. 187).

With an illustration by the author.

A Doe in the City. By Frederick Haltamont de Montmorency. —*Punch*, November 1, 1845 (vol. ix., p. 191).

With an illustration by the author.

About a Christmas Book. In a Letter from Michael Angelo Titmarsh to Oliver Yorke, Esq.—*Fraser's Magazine*, December, 1845 (vol. xxxii., pp. 744-748).

A notice of "Poems and Pictures: A Collection of Ballads, Songs and other Poems. With designs on wood by the principal artists; 4to. London: James Burns, 1845."

A Lucky Speculator. (With "Jeames of Buckley-square, A
Heligy.")—*Punch*, August 2, 1845 (vol. ix., p. 59).
With an illustration by John Leech.

A Letter from "Jeames of Buckley-square."—*Punch*, August 16,
1845 (vol. ix., p. 76).

Jeames on Time Bargings.—*Punch*, November 1, 1845 (vol. ix.,
p. 195).
With an illustration.

1845-1846.

JEAMES'S DIARY.—*Punch*, November 8 to 29 ; December 6, 13,
1845 (vol. ix.) ; December 27, 1845 ; January 3, 10, 17, 31 ;
February 7, 1846 (vol. x.)
With twenty illustrations by the author.
First reprinted in collected form in Thackeray's *Miscellanies*, 1856.

1846.

NOTES OF A JOURNEY FROM CORNHILL TO GRAND CAIRO, by way
of Lisbon, Athens, Constantinople and Jerusalem. Performed
in the Steamers of the Peninsular and Oriental Company.
By Mr. M. A. Titmarsh. London : Chapman and Hall, 1846.
With coloured frontispiece and numerous woodcut illustrations by the
author. The Dedication, to Captain Samuel Lewis, is dated "London :
December 24, 1845."

Ronsard to his Mistress. Signed "Michael Angelo Titmarsh."—
Fraser's Magazine, January, 1846 (vol. xxxiii., p. 120).
Reprinted in Thackeray's collected *Ballads* (1855).

A Brother of the Press on the History of a Literary Man,
Laman Blanchard, and the chances of the Literary Profession.
In a Letter to the Reverend Francis Sylvester at Rome, from
Michael Angelo Titmarsh, Esq.—*Fraser's Magazine*, March,
1846 (vol. xxxiii., pp. 332-342).
Reprinted in Thackeray's Collected Works, vol. xxv (1885).

Titmarsh v. Tait. Letter to Mr. Punch. Signed "Michael
Angelo Titmarsh," and dated "Blue Posts, March 10, 1846."
—*Punch*, March 14, 1846 (vol. x., p. 124).

On some Illustrated Children's Books. By Michael Angelo
Titmarsh.—*Fraser's Magazine*, April, 1846 (vol. xxxiii. pp.
495-502).

Jeames on the Gauge Question.—*Punch*, May 16, 1846 (vol. x., p. 223). With an illustration.

Mr. Jeames again.—*Punch*, June 13, 1846 (vol. x., p. 267).
With an illustration by the author.

Proposals for a Continuation of Ivanhoe. In a letter to Monsieur Alexandre Dumas, by Monsieur Michael Angelo Titmarsh.—*Fraser's Magazine*, August and September, 1846 (vol. xxxiv., pp. 237-245, 359-367).

This was the germ of the Christmas book afterwards published under the title of *Rebecca and Rowena*.

1847.

MRS. PERKINS'S BALL. BY MR. M. A. TITMARSH.—London : Chapman and Hall, 186, Strand. 1847, pp. 46.

With illustrations by the author, coloured in some of the copies.

1846-1848.

THE SNOBS OF ENGLAND. BY ONE OF THEMSELVES.

With numerous illustrations by the author, commencing in *Punch* of February 28, 1846 (vol. x., p. 101), and ending February 27, 1847 (vol. xii., p. 86). (Prefatory Remarks and fifty-two Chapters.)

THE BOOK OF SNOBS : BY W. M. THACKERAY. London : *Punch* Office, 1848, pp. viii, 180, in green wrapper (with the original illustrations and a vignette on title, not appearing in the *Punch* issue).

The following Chapters are omitted in this Collected Edition : Chapter XVII.—On Literary Snobs, in a letter from "One of themselves" to Mr. Smith, the celebrated penny-a-liner (*Punch*, June 27, 1846, vol. x., p. 261); Chapter XVIII. On some Political Snobs (*Punch*, July 4, 1846, vol. xi., p. 4) : Chapter XIX. On Whig Snobs (July 11, 1846, vol. xi, p. 19); Chapter XX. On Conservative or Country-Party Snobs (July 18, 1846, vol. xi., p. 23) ; Chapter XXI. Are there any Whig Snobs ? (July 25, 1846, vol. xi., p. 39) ; Chapter XXII. On the Snob Civilian (August 1, 1846, vol. xi., p. 43) ; Chapter XXIII. On Radical Snobs (August 8, 1846, vol. xi., p. 59).

"On reperusing these papers," writes the author, p. 66, *note*, "I have found them so stupid, so personal, so snobbish—in a word—that I have withdrawn them from this collection."

The "stupid" papers, thus repudiated by the author, are with questionable judgment, reprinted separately in the second supplementary volume of Thackeray's Collected Works (vol. xxvi.), published by Messrs. Smith Elder and Co. in the winter of 1885.

1847.

A Grumble about the Christmas Books. By Michael Angelo Titmarsh.—*Fraser's Magazine*, January, 1847 (vol. xxxv., pp. 111-126).

1847-1848.

VANITY FAIR. A NOVEL WITHOUT A HERO. BY WILLIAM MAKEPEACE THACKERAY. With Illustrations on Steel and Wood by the Author.—London : Bradbury and Evans. 1848, pp. xvi., 624.

Issued in monthly instalments in yellow wrappers, originally bearing the title, " Vanity Fair : Pen and Pencil Sketches of English Society. By W. M. Thackeray." On the wrapper is an illustration by the author not reproduced in the body of the work. No. 1 is dated January, 1847, and Nos. 19 and 20 (double number), July, 1848.

The Preface ("Before the Curtain") is dated " London : June 28, 1848."

1847.

An Eastern Adventure of the Fat Contributor.—*Punch's Pocket-Book*, for 1847, pp. 148-156.

With full-page illustration by the author.

The Mahogany Tree.—*Punch*, January 9, 1847 (vol. xii., p. 13).

The second stanza is omitted in Thackeray's Collected Ballads (*Miscellanies*, vol. i. 1855, pp. 47-48).

Two Letters to William Edmondstoune Aytoun, dated " 13, Young-street, Kensington, January 2," and " January 13, 1847," and signed " W. M. Thackeray."—Printed in *Memoir of William Edmondstoune Aytoun*, by Theodore Martin. Blackwood and Sons, Edinburgh and London, 1867, pp. 131-135.

Mr. Jeames's Sentiments on the Cambridge Election.—*Punch*, March 6, 1847 (vol. xii., p. 102).

LOVE-SONGS MADE EASY.— " What makes my heart to thrill and glow ? " Song by Fitzroy Clarence.—*Punch*, March 6, 1847 (vol. xii., p. 101).

With an illustration by the author.

LOVE-SONGS BY THE FAT CONTRIBUTOR.—The Domestic Love-

Song. " The Cane-Bottomed Chair."—*Punch*, March 27, 1847
(vol. xii., p. 125).
With two illustrations by the author.

LOVE-SONGS OF THE FAT CONTRIBUTOR.—The Ghazul, or Oriental
Love-Song. The Rocks. The Merry Bard. The Caïque.—
Punch, June 5, 1847 (vol. xii., p. 227).
With two illustrations by the author.

PUNCH'S PRIZE NOVELISTS :—

1. George de Barnwell.—*Punch*, April 3-17, 1847.
   With three illustrations by the author.

2. Codlingsby. By B. de Shrewsbury, Esq.—*Punch*, April 24,
   May 15 to 29, 1847.
   With four illustrations by the author.

3. Lords and Liveries.—*Punch*, June 12 to 26, 1847.
   With three illustrations by the author.

4. Barbazure. By G. P. R. Jeames, Esq.—*Punch*, July 10
   to 24, 1847.
   With five illustrations by the author.

5. Phil. Fogarty. A Tale of the Fighting Onety-Oneth. By
   Harry Rollicker.—*Punch*, August 7 to 21, 1847.
   With five illustrations by the author.

6. Crinoline. By Je-mes Pl-sh, Esq.--*Punch*, August 28,
   September 4, 11, 1847.
   With six illustrations by the author.

7. The Stars and Stripes.—*Punch*, September 25, October 9,
   1847.
   With two illustrations by the author.

Brighton in 1847.   By the F. C.—*Punch*, October 23, 30,
1847 (vol. xiii., pp. 153, 157-158).
With three illustrations by the author.

TRAVELS IN LONDON, by SPEC.—*Punch*, November 20, 1847 (vol.
xiii., p. 193).
With an illustration.

TRAVELS IN LONDON. The Curate's Walk, November 27, 1847.

TRAVELS IN LONDON. A Walk with the Curate. December 4,
1847. A Dinner in the City. December 11, 25, and 31,
1847.
With nine illustrations by the author.

1848.

TRAVELS IN LONDON. A Night's Pleasure.—*Punch*, January 8-29 and February 12, 19, 1848. With ten illustrations by the author. A Club in an Uproar.—*Punch*, March 11, 1848 (vol. xiv., pp. 95-96). With two illustrations by the author. A Roundabout Ride.—*Punch*, March 25, 1848 (vol. xiv., p. 119). With an illustration by the author.

"OUR STREET." BY MR. M. A. TITMARSH. London : Chapman and Hall. 1848, pp. 54.
With illustrations by the author, coloured in some of the copies.

The Persecution of British Footmen. By Mr. Jeames.—*Punch*, April 1 and 8, 1848 (vol. xiv., pp. 131, 143-144).
With three illustrations.

The Battle of Limerick.—*Punch*, May 13, 1848 (vol. xiv., p. 195).

On the New Forward Movement. A Letter from our old friend, Mr. Snob, to Mr. Joseph Hume.—*Punch*, May 20, 1848 (vol. xiv., p. 207).
With an illustration.

Mr. Snob's Remonstrance with Mr. Smith.—*Punch*, May 27, 1848 (vol. xiv., p. 217).
With an illustration.

A LITTLE DINNER AT TIMMINS'S.—*Punch*, May 27 ; June 17 and 24, and July 1, 8, 22 and 29, 1848 (vol. xiv., pp. 219-223, 247, 258 ; vol. xv., pp. 5, 13, 33-34, 43).
With eight illustrations by the author.
Reprinted in Thackeray's *Miscellanies*, 1856.

Letters to a Nobleman visiting Ireland.—*Punch*, September 2-9 1848 (vol. xv., pp. 95-96, 107).
With two illustrations by the author.

Science at Cambridge.—*Punch*, November 11, 1848 (vol. xv., p. 201).
With an illustration.

A Bow Street Ballad. By a Gentleman of the Force (Signed " Policeman X. 54 ").—*Punch*, November 25, 1848 (vol. xv., p. 229).
With an illustration.

R

Death of the Earl of Robinson. (In the manner of a popular Necrographer.)—*Punch*, December 2, 1848 (vol. xv., p. 231).
With an illustration.

Bow Street Ballads. No. II. Jacob Omnium's Hoss. *Punch*, December 9, 1848 (vol. xv,, p. 251).
With an illustration.

The Great Squattleborough Soirée.—*Punch*, December 16, 1848 (vol. xv., pp. 253-254).
With an illustration by the author, representing Dr. Johnson and Boswell walking together.

The Three Christmas Waits.—*Punch*, December 23, 1848 (vol. xv., p. 265).

1848-1850.

THE HISTORY OF PENDENNIS ; HIS FORTUNES AND MISFORTUNES, HIS FRIENDS AND HIS GREATEST ENEMY. BY WILLIAM MAKEPEACE THACKERAY. With illustrations on steel and wood by the Author. In two volumes (pp. viii. 384, xii. 372). London : Bradbury and Evans, 1849-50.
Originally issued in monthly numbers in yellow wrappers, No. 1 being dated November, 1848, and Nos. 23 and 24 (double number) December, 1850. After the appearance of the eleventh number (dated September, 1849), the publication was suspended during four months, on account of the author's illness. The twelfth number bears date January, 1850. The Preface is dated " Kensington, November 26, 1850."

1849.

An Interesting Event. By Mr. Titmarsh.—Printed in *The Keepsake*, 1849, *edited by the Countess of Blessington.* London : David Bogue. 1849, pp. 207-215.

DOCTOR BIRCH AND HIS YOUNG FRIENDS. BY MR. M. A. TITMARSH. London : Chapman and Hall. 1849, pp. 49.
With vignette title and fifteen full-page illustrations by the author, coloured in some copies. The " Epilogue " is in verse.

Contributions to *Punch* :—

Child's Parties: and a Remonstrance concerning them,— *Punch*, January 13 and 27, 1849 (vol. xvi., pp. 13-14, 35-36).
With two illustrations by the author.

Paris Revisited. By an Old Paris Man.—*Punch*, February 10, 1849 (vol. xvi., pp. 55-56).
With an illustration.

THE BALLAD OF BOUILLABAISSE.   From the Contributor at Paris.—*Punch*, February 17, 1849 (vol. xvi., p. 67).

Two or Thrêe Theatres at Paris.—*Punch*, February 24, 1849 (vol. xvi., p. 75).

> With an illustration by Richard Doyle.

On Some Dinners at Paris.—*Punch*, March 3, 1849 (vol. xvi., p. 92).

> With an illustration by Richard Doyle.

MR. BROWN'S LETTERS TO A YOUNG MAN ABOUT TOWN :—

Introductory.—*Punch*, March 24, 1849 (vol. xvi., p. 115).

On Tailoring and Toilettes in General.—March 31, 1849, p. 125.

The Influence of Lovely Woman upon Society.—April 7, 1849, pp. 135-6.

Some More Words about the Ladies.—April 14, 1849, pp. 145-6.

On Friendship.—April 28, May 5, 1849, pp. 165-6, 184-5.

Mr. Brown the Elder takes Mr. Brown the Younger to a Club. —May 12 to 26, 1849, pp. 187-8, 197-8, 207-8.

A Word about Balls in Season.—June 9, 1849, pp. 229-230.

A Word about Dinners.—June 16, 1849, pp. 239-240.

On some Old Customs of the Dinner-table.—June 23, 1849, pp. 249-250.

Great and Little Dinners.—July 7, 1849 (vol. xvii., pp. 1-2).

On Love, Marriage, Men, and Women.—July 14, 1849, pp. 13-14 ; July 21, 1849, p. 23 ; August 4, 1849, p. 43.

Out of Town, August 11 and 18, 1849, pp. 53, 66-69.

> With sixteen illustrations.

THE THREE SAILORS.   (With Reminiscences of Michael Angelo Titmarsh at Rome).—Printed in *Sand and Canvas ; A Narrative of Adventures in Egypt, with a Sojourn among the Artists in Rome*, by Samuel Bevan.   London : Charles Gilpin, 5, Bishopsgate street-without, 1849, pp. 336-342.

THE THREE SAILORS.   Autograph copy sent to Mr. Bevan (with note commencing " Dear Bevan," and signed " W. M. Thackeray ") for insertion in *Sand and Canvas.*—Facsimiled in *The Autographic Mirror*, November 1, 1864 (vol. ii., p. 156).

In the *North British Review*, February, 1864 (vol. xl., p. 254), appears a printed version of " The Three Sailors," under the title of " Little Billee," differing considerably from the above.

1850.

Rebecca and Rowena : A Romance upon Romance. By Mr.
M. A. Titmarsh. With Illustrations by Richard Doyle.
London : Chapman and Hall, 186, Strand.   1850, pp. viii., 102.
The Preface is dated " Kensington, December 20th, 1849."
In some copies the full-page illustrations are coloured.
The substance of this *jeu d'esprit* had already appeared in *Fraser's Magazine*
for August and September, 1846.   *Vide supra.*

The Dignity of Literature.   To the Editor of the *Morning
Chronicle.*   Letter dated " Reform Club, Jan. 8," and signed
"W. M. Thackeray."—*Morning Chronicle*, Saturday, January 12,
1850.
In answer to some remarks in a leading article which had appeared in
the *Morning Chronicle* of Thursday, January 3.
Reprinted in Thackeray's collected Works, vol. xxv. (1885).

Sketches after English Landscape Painters.   By Louis Marvy.
With short notices by W. M. Thackeray.   London : David
Bogue, 86, Fleet-street.   4to. [1850].
The letter-press consists of a Preface and twenty short notices of
Callcott, Turner, Holland, Danby, Creswick, Collins, Redgrave, Lee,
Cattermole, Müller, Harding, Nasmyth, Richard Wilson, Cooke, Con-
stable, De Wint, Cox, Gainsborough, Roberts, and Stanfield.   There is no
pagination to the volume.

Capers and Anchovies.   To the Editor of the *Morning Chronicle.*
Letter of nearly a column, dated " Garrick Club, April 11,
1850," and signed " Wm. Thackeray."—*Morning Chronicle*,
Friday, April 12, 1850.

Contributions to *Punch :*—

The Proser : Essays and Discourses, by Dr. Solomon Pacifico.

Vol. xviii. (1850.) pp. 151-152.	1. On a Lady in an Opera-Box. (With an illustration.)
„ „ 173.	2. On the Pleasures of being a Fogy. (With an illustration.)
„ „ 197-198.	3. On the Benefits of being a Fogy.
„ „ 223-224.	4. On a good-looking young Lady. (With an illustration.)
„ „ 234-235.	5. On an Interesting French Exile.
Vol. xix. (1850.) pp. 7- 8.	6. On an American Traveller.
„ „ 59.	7. On the Press and the Public. (With an illustration.)

BALLADS OF POLICEMAN X.
  Vol. xviii. (1850.)
The Ballad of Eliza Davis. With an illustration, p. 53.
The Lamentable Ballad of the Foundling of Shoreditch. With an illustration, p. 73.
Lines on a Late Hospicious Ewent, p. 189.
The Wofle New Ballad of Jane Roney and Mary Brown, p. 209.
Damages Two Hundred Pounds, vol. xix. (1850), p. 88.

1851.

THE KICKLEBURYS ON THE RHINE. By Mr. M. A. TITMARSH.
Second Edition. With Preface, being an Essay on Thunder
and Small Beer. London : Smith, Elder, and Co. 1851, pp.
xv. 87.
  With fifteen illustrations by the author, coloured in some of the copies.

Voltigeur. By W. M. Thackeray, Esq.—Printed in *The Keepsake for* 1851, *edited by Miss Power.* London : David Bogue,
1851, pp. 238-250.

MAY DAY ODE, containing nineteen stanzas of eight lines
each, dated "April 29," and signed "W. M. Thackeray."—
Times, Wednesday, April 30, 1851.

1852.

THE HISTORY OF HENRY ESMOND, ESQ., a Colonel in the service
of Her Majesty Q. Anne. Written by himself. In Three
Volumes. London : printed for Smith, Elder, and Company,
over against St. Peter's Church in Cornhill. 1852, pp. 344,
vi. 319, vi. 324.
  The half-title runs as follows :—"ESMOND : A STORY OF QUEEN ANNE'S
REIGN. By W. M. THACKERAY."

1853.

THE ENGLISH HUMOURISTS OF THE EIGHTEENTH CENTURY. A
Series of Lectures delivered in England, Scotland, and the
United States of America. By W. M. Thackeray. London :
Smith, Elder, and Co. 1853, pp. 322.

Mr. Thackeray in the United States. To the Editor of *Fraser's
Magazine.—F. M.,* January, 1853 (vol. xlvii., pp. 100-103).
Signed " John Small."
  Reprinted in Thackeray's collected Works, vol. xxv. (1885).

The Pen and The Album. (Stanzas.)   By W. M. Thackeray.—
The Keepsake for 1853, edited by Miss Power.   London :
David Bogue, pp. 48-50.

Preface to a Selection from his Contributions to *Punch*, pub-
lished in America.   1. Mr. Brown's Letters to a Young Man
about Town ; with The Proser and other Papers.   2. Punch's
Prize Novelists, The Fat Contributor, and Travels in London.
By W. M. Thackeray.   Two volumes.   New York : D.
Appleton and Co.   1853, pp. 256, 306.

This selection was made by the author himself during his first visit to
America.   The Preface, of five pages, is signed "W. M. Thackeray," and
dated " New York : December, 1852."

The Proser contains the following papers : 1. On a Lady in an Opera
Box ; 2. On the pleasures of being a Fogy ; 3. On the benefits of being a
Fogy." The Miscellanies that follow comprise : 1. Child's Parties, and a
Remonstrance concerning them ; 2. The Story of Koompanee Jehan ; 3.
Science at Cambridge ; 4. A Dream of Whitefriars ; 5. Mr. Punch's
Address to the Great City of Castlebar ; 6. Irish Gems ; 7. The Charles
the Second Ball ; 8. The Georges ; 9. Death of the Earl of Robinson.

1853-1855.

THE NEWCOMES.   MEMOIRS OF A MOST RESPECTABLE FAMILY.
EDITED BY ARTHUR PENDENNIS, ESQ.   With illustrations on
steel and wood, by Richard Doyle (vol. i., pp. viii. 380 ; vol.
ii., pp. viii. 375).   London : Bradbury and Evans, 11,
Bouverie-street.   1854-1855.

Issued in monthly numbers in yellow wrappers ; the first dated
October, 1853, and the last (Nos. 23-24—a double number), August,
1855. The last chapter is dated at the end, " Paris, 28th June, 1855."

1853.

" Mr. Washington."   To the Editor of the *Times*.   Letter dated
" Athenæum, Nov. 22," and signed " W. M. Thackeray."—
Times, Wednesday, November 23, 1853.

In answer to some strictures of the New York Correspondent of the
Times (dated " New York, Nov. 8," printed in the *Times* of Nov. 22, 1853),
respecting a passage in the first number of *The Newcomes*, which had given
offence in the United States.

1854.

Lucy's Birthday,
        " Seventeen rosebuds in a ring."
Three stanzas of eight lines each, dated " New York, April 15."

Printed in *The Keepsake*, 1854, *edited by Miss Power*. London : David Bogue. 1854, p. 18.

LETTERS FROM THE EAST BY OUR OWN BASHI-BAZOUK.—*Punch*, June 24, July 1, 1854 (vol. xxvi., pp. 257-258, 267-268) ; July 8 to 29, August 5, 1854 (vol. xxvii., pp. 1-2, 11-12, 21-22, 31-32, 41).

With seven illustrations by the author.

Pictures of Life and Character. By John Leech.—*Quarterly Review*, December, 1854 (vol. xcvi., pp. 75-86).

1855.

THE ROSE AND THE RING ; or, the History of Prince Giglio and Prince Bulbo. A Fire-side Pantomime for Great and Small Children. By Mr. M. A. Titmarsh. London : Smith, Elder, and Co. 1855, pp. iv. 128.

With illustrations by the author, plain in all the copies. The Preface, or " Prelude," is dated " December, 1854."

Reminiscences of Weimar and Goethe, in a letter addressed to Mr. G. H. Lewes, dated "London, 28th April, 1855," and signed " W. M. Thackeray."—Printed in *Lewes's Life and Works of Goethe*. London : David Nutt. 1855, vol. ii., pp. 442-446.

Letter to Mr. Edmund Yates, dated " Michaelmas Day, 1855," and signed " W. M. Thackeray."—*Edmund Yates, his Recollections and Experiences*. London : Bentley. 1884, vol. i., p. 280.

1856.

The Idler. By W. M. Thackeray. Eleven stanzas of eight lines each, signed " Essel."—Published in *The Idler, Magazine of Fiction, Essay, Belles Lettres and Comedy. Edited by Edward Wilberforce*. (London : Robert Hardwicke, Piccadilly), No. 3, March, 1856, pp. 172-173.

Reprinted in Thackeray's collected Works, vol. xxv. (1885).

1857.

Address to the Electors of Oxford, dated " Mitre, July 9, 1857," and signed " W. M. Thackeray."

A Letter of Thackeray (to Captain George Francklin Atkinson, in acknowledgment of his illustrated work entitled " Curry and Rice," dated "Hotel Bristol, Place Vendôme, December 27, 1858," and signed "W. M. Thackeray.")—Facsimiled in *The Leisure Hour*, September, 1883. (London), pp. 560-561.

1857-59.

THE VIRGINIANS : A TALE OF THE LAST CENTURY. BY W. M. THACKERAY. With illustrations on steel and wood by the Author. In Two Volumes (pp. viii. 382, viii. 376). London : Bradbury and Evans. 1858-1859.

Issued in twenty-four monthly numbers (in yellow illustrated wrappers), commencing November, 1857, and ending October, 1859.

Letter to Mr. Anthony Trollope, dated " 36, Onslow-square, October 28 " [1859], and signed "W. M. Thackeray."—*An Autobiography by Anthony Trollope.* Blackwood, 1883, vol. i., pp. 183-184.

Letter to Henry Wadsworth Longfellow, dated " 36, Onslow-square, November 16, 1859," and signed " W. M. Thackeray." —Printed in the *Life of Henry Wadsworth Longfellow, edited by Samuel Longfellow.* London : Kegan Paul. 1886, vol. ii., p. 346.

1860.

Nil Nisi Bonum.—*Cornhill Magazine*, February, 1860 (vol. i., pp. 129-134).

The Last Sketch. (A short paper signed W. M. T., prefixed to " Emma, a Fragment of a Story by the late Charlotte Brontë.") —*Cornhill Magazine*, April, 1860 (vol. i., pp. 485-487).

Vanitas Vanitatum. (Sixteen stanzas of four lines each).— *Cornhill Magazine*, July, 1860 (vol. ii., pp. 59-60).

1861.

A Leaf out of a Sketch-Book. By W. M. Thackeray.—Printed in *The Victoria Regia, a Volume of Original Contributions in Poetry and Prose, edited by Adelaide A. Procter.* London : Emily Faithfull and Co. 1861, pp. 118-125.

With two sketches by the author.

1860-1861.

LOVEL THE WIDOWER. BY W. M. THACKERAY. With illustrations. London : Smith, Elder, and Co. 1861, pp. 258.

Originally published in monthly instalments in the first six numbers of the *Cornhill Magazine* (January to June, 1860).

"The Wolves and the Lamb," the original of the story of *Lovel the Widower* (printed for the first time in Thackeray's collected Works, London : Smith, Elder and Co., 1879, vol. xxiv., pp. 125-175), was written for the stage, and refused by the management of the Olympic about 1854.

THE FOUR GEORGES.   BY W. M. THACKERAY.   With illustrations. London : Smith, Elder, and Co.   1861, pp. 226.

Originally published in the *Cornhill Magazine*, July to October, 1860 (vol. ii, pp. 1-20, 175-191, 257-277, 385-406).

1861-1862.

THE ADVENTURES OF PHILIP ON HIS WAY THROUGH THE WORLD ; SHEWING WHO ROBBED HIM, WHO HELPED HIM, AND WHO PASSED HIM BY.   BY W. M. THACKERAY.   In Three Volumes, pp. 329, 304, 301.   London : Smith, Elder, and Co., 65, Cornhill.   1862.

Originally published in instalments, with illustrations, in the *Cornhill Magazine*, commencing January, 1861 (vol. iii. p. 1), and ending August, 1862 (vol. vi., p. 240).   The illustrations do not re-appear in the three-volume edition of the book.

1860-1863.

ROUNDABOUT PAPERS.   *Reprinted* FROM THE CORNHILL MAGAZINE, WITH ILLUSTRATIONS.   BY W. M. THACKERAY.   London : Smith, Elder, and Co.   1863.

These papers originally appeared in the *Cornhill Magazine*, as follows :—

No. 1. On a Lazy, Idle Boy.—January, 1860 (vol. i., pp. 124-128).

No. 2. On Two Children in Black.—March, 1860 (vol. i. pp. 380-384).

No. 3. On Ribbons.—May, 1860 (vol. i., pp. 631-640).

No. 4. On some late Great Victories.—June, 1860 (vol. i., pp. 755-760).

No. 5. Thorns in the Cushion.—July, 1860 (vol. ii., pp. 122-128).

No. 6. On Screens in Dining-rooms.—August, 1860 (vol. ii., pp. 252-256).

No. 7. Tunbridge Toys.—September, 1860 (vol. ii., pp. 380-384).

No. 8. De Juventute.—October, 1860 (vol. ii., pp. 501-512).

 A Roundabout Journey ; Notes of a Week's Holiday.—November, 1860 (vol. ii., pp. 623-640).

No. 9. On a Joke I once heard from the late Thomas Hood.)—December, 1860 (vol. ii., pp. 752-760).

No. 10. Round about the Christmas Tree.—February, 1861 (vol. iii., pp. 250-256).

No. 11. On a Chalk-mark on the Door.—April, 1861 (vol. iii., pp. 504-512).

No. 12. On Being Found Out.—May, 1861 (vol. iii., pp. 636-640).

No. 13. On a Hundred Years Hence.—June, 1861 (vol. iii., pp. 755-760).

No. 14. Small-Beer Chronicle.—July, 1861 (vol. iv., pp. 122-128).

No. 15. Ogres.—August, 1861 (vol. iv., pp. 251-256).

No. 16. On Two Roundabout Papers which I intended to write.—September, 1861 (vol. iv., pp. 377-384).

No. 17. A Mississippi Bubble.—December, 1861 (vol. iv., pp. 755-760).

No. 18. On Letts's Diary.—January, 1862 (vol. v., pp. 122-128).

No. 19. On Half-a-Loaf.—A Letter to Messrs. Broadway, Battery and Co., of New York, Bankers.—February, 1862 (vol. v., pp. 250-256).

Nos. 20 to 22. The Notch on the Axe. A Story *à la Mode*. In Three Parts.—April,* May and June, 1862 (vol. v., pp. 508-512, 634-640, 754-760).

No. 23. De Finibus.—August, 1862 (vol. vi., pp. 282-288).

No. 24. On a Peal of Bells.—September, 1862 (vol. vi., pp. 425-432).

No. 25. On a Pear-Tree.—November, 1862 (vol. vi., pp. 715-720).

No. 26. Dessein's.—December, 1862 (vol. vi., pp. 771-779).

No. 27. On Some Carp at Sans Souci.—January, 1863 (vol. vii., pp. 126-131).

No. 28. Autour de mon Chapeau.—February, 1863 (vol. vii., pp. 260-267).

On Alexandrines. A Letter to some Country Cousins. April, 1863 (vol. vii., pp. 546-552).

On a Medal of George the Fourth.—August, 1863 (vol. viii., pp. 250-256)-

"Strange to say, on Club paper."—November, 1863 (vol. viii., pp. 636-640).

1863.

Cruikshank's Gallery. (Notice of a column and a quarter.) Printed in *The Times*, Friday, May 15, 1863.

" Kind Thackeray came, with his grave face, and looked through the little gallery, and went off to write one of his charming essays, which appeared in *The Times*."—*Life of George Cruikshank*, by Blanchard Jerrold.

---

* On the reverse of the title of the *Cornhill Magazine* for April, 1862, is a valedictory address of the Editor " To Contributors and Correspondents," on resigning his post, dated " March 18, 1862," and signed " W. M. T."

POSTHUMOUS.

1864-1885.

DENIS DUVAL. By W. M. Thackeray.—London: Smith, Elder, and Co. 1867, pp. 275.—*Cornhill Magazine*, March to June, 1864, with illustrations (vol. ix., pp. 257-291, 385-409, 513-536, 641-665).

Mrs. Katherine's Lantern. (Written by W. M. Thackeray in a Lady's Album).— *Cornhill Magazine*, January, 1867 (vol. xv., pp. 117-118).

The Anglers. By the late W. M. Thackeray. Seven stanzas of eight lines each.—*The Princess Alexandra Gift Book, edited by John Sherer*. London: Hamilton, Adams, and Co. 1868, pp. 22-23.

THE ORPHAN OF PIMLICO, AND OTHER SKETCHES, FRAGMENTS AND DRAWINGS. BY WILLIAM MAKEPEACE THACKERAY. With some Notes by Anne Isabella Thackeray. London: Smith, Elder, and Co. 1876; 4to, pages unnumbered.

Prefixed is a portrait of the author, " copied by Mr. Thackeray from a drawing by D. Maclise about 1840." The Preface (signed "A. I. T.") is dated " London, November 20, 1875."

Etchings by the late William Makepeace Thackeray while at Cambridge, illustrative of University Life, etc. Now first published from the Original Plates. London: H. Sotheran and Co., Piccadilly. 1878.

List of Subjects : 1. Departure for Cambridge ; 2. Arrival from Cambridge ; 3. Worldly Study ; 4. Imposition ; 5. First Term ; 6. Second Term ; 7. Work Within ; 8. Pleasure Without ; 9. Collera Morbus ; 10. Scene from the Deluge ; 11. Ah, Mr. Goldfinch !

Miscellaneous Essays, Sketches and Reviews.—Contributions to " Punch " (not previously reprinted). By William Makepeace Thackeray. With Illustrations by the Author (forming Volumes xxv. and xxvi. of the Works of William Makepeace Thackeray). London: Smith, Elder, and Co. 1885-1886, pp. x. 468 ; xii. 404.

In Vol. xxv. (pp. 355-372) appears a Lecture on " Charity and Humour," previously unpublished.

SKETCHES AND CARICATURES.

1

CHARLES IX. firing at the Huguenots out of the windows of the Louvre. Sketched on the blank portion of the yellow paper cover of a French drama.—Facsimiled in *The Recollections and Reflections of J. R. Planché.* London: Tinsley Brothers, 1872, vol. i. to face p. 171.

2

Signor Balfi. Sketch made in Mr. Planché's box during the performance of Balfe's opera, " The Siege of Rochelle," 16th November, 1835.—Facsimiled in Planché's *Recollections and Reflections,* vol. i., p. 241.

3

THE " WHITEY-BROWN PAPER MAGAZINE."—Suggested to be issued in 1838-9, as a weekly publication.

A series of humorous sketches, with brief descriptive letterpress, in prose and verse, representing the fortunes and misfortunes of Dionysius Diddler, facsimiled in the first eight numbers of *The Autographic Mirror,* February 20 to June 1, 1864 (vol. i., pp. 6, 15, 28, 39, 40, 60, 68, 76).

4

THE STUDENT'S QUARTER, or Paris Five-and-Thirty Years Since, by the late William Makepeace Thackeray. Not included in his Collected Writings. With original coloured illustrations. London: John Camden Hotten, Piccadilly (*n.d.*), pp. 202.

This volume consists (1) of four original contributions to *The Corsair,* a New York weekly journal, Aug.-Oct. 1839 (*vide suprà,* pp. 225-226), of which three were reprinted, with slight alterations, omissions and additions, in the *Paris Sketch-Book* (1840), vol. i. pp. 22-24, 59-75; vol. ii. pp. 445-447, under the titles of " An Invasion of France ;" " The Fêtes of July ;" "Madame Sand and the New Apocalypse." It also contains (2) two articles by Thackeray,—" Cartouche," and " A Ramble in the Picture Galleries,"— which had, before their appearance in *The Corsair,* already appeared in *Fraser's Magazine,* where the latter paper bore the title, " On the French School of Painting," which it afterwards retained in *The Paris Sketch-Book,* where both these articles likewise reappear.

The chief if not sole literary interest which Mr. Hotten's volume possesses consists in the preservation of the suppressed paper, there christened "More Aspects of Paris," though bearing no title in *The Corsair,* published in that journal in the number for October 26, 1839 (vol. i. pp. 521-523)—the only letter which justifies the legend of the title-page, "not included in Thackeray's Collected Writings." Those desirous of more minute information on the subject may refer to two letters entitled "Thackeray's 'Paris Sketch-Book,'" in *The Athenæum* of August 7, 14, 1886.

It should be added that the coloured illustrations which figure in this volume were not executed to accompany the letter-press, even if, as seems probable, they are rightly attributed to Thackeray's pencil.

5

Note addressed to Mr. Planché, and signed " W. M. Thackeray," dated "13, Great Coram-street, Brunswick-square, with pen-and-ink sketch of the State visit of the Queen and Prince Albert to Covent Garden Theatre, 1840.—Facsimiled in Planché's *Recollections and Reflections*, vol. ii. p. 40.

6

The Gamblers. A Sketch.—Facsimiled in *The Autographic Mirror*, March 15, 1864 (vol. i., p. 27).

7

Note dated " 36, Onslow-square, 26th March, 1855," and signed " W. M. Thackeray."—Facsimiled in *The Autographic Mirror*, *ubi suprà.*

8

Caricature Sketch of himself seated, writing on the banks of the Nile, sketched on the first page of a copy of " Cornhill to Cairo," presented to his friend, William Bevan, and two letters, dated "36, Onslow-square, Brompton, February 21, 1855 " one commencing, " My dear W. B." [William Bevan], and the other, " My dear S." ; both signed " W. M. Thackeray." —The sketch and the two letters facsimiled in *The Autographic Mirror* (October 1, 1864), vol. ii., p. 139.

9

THE THREE SAILORS, by the late W. M. Thackeray (Sketch and Anecdote).— *The Editor's Box, A Midsummer Annual.* London: Cecil Brooks and Co., Strand, 1880, p. 80.

A reproduction in facsimile of a page from the autograph album of the late Mr. Shirley Brooks.

1

THACKERAY'S Writings.—*Edinburgh Review*, January, 1848 (vol. lxxxvii., pp. 46-67).

2

" Esmond."—*Essays by the late George Brimley, M.A.* Cambridge : Macmillan and Co., 1858, pp. 258-269.
Reprinted from the *Spectator* of November 6, 1852.

3

Essay on the Newcomes.—*Oxford and Cambridge Magazine.* London : Bell and Daldy, 1856, pp. 50-61.
Thackeray and Currer Bell.—*Ibid.*, pp. 323-335.

4

The Modern Novel.—Dickens, Bulwer, Thackeray. *Essays in Biography and Criticism by Peter Bayne, M.A. First Series.* Boston : Gould and Lincoln, 1857, pp. 363-392.

5

Thackeray, Humourist and Satirist, his Works, Original Characters, and Comic Writings. A Lecture, principally treating on *Vanity Fair.* By Thomas Edward Crispe. London : printed by William Davy and Son, 8, Gilbert-street, 1857, pp. 34, coloured wrapper.

6

William Makepeace Thackeray.—*Novels and Novelists from Elizabeth to Victoria.* By J. Cordy Jeaffreson. London : Hurst and Blackett, 1858, vol. ii., pp. 262-281.

7

British Novelists and their Styles : a Critical Sketch of the History of British Prose Fiction. By David Masson, M.A. Cambridge : Macmillan and Co., 1859.
Pages 233-253 are devoted to a consideration of Dickens and Thackeray.

8

Thackeray.—*Calcutta Review*, December, 1861 (vol. xxxvii., pp. 245-280).

9

William Makepeace Thackeray. With portrait from a photograph by Herbert Watkins.—*Illlustrated London News*, January 9, 1864.

A memorial notice (signed "S. B.") written by the late Mr. Shirley Brooks.

10

IN MEMORIAM. BY CHARLES DICKENS.

Historical Contrast, May, 1701; December, 1863 (Dryden and Thackeray), by Lord Houghton, signed " Hᵒ."

W. M. Thackeray. By Anthony Trollope.

Cornhill Magazine, February, 1864 (vol. ix., pp. 129-137).

11

Thackeray.—*North British Review*, February, 1864 (vol. xl., pp. 210-265).

By the late Dr. John Brown, of Edinburgh, author of *Horæ Subsecivæ*. The paper is accompanied by a fac-simile of a drawing by Thackeray, representing Johnson and Goldsmith passing the shop of Filby, the tailor, with a street-boy and his little sister stepping out in mimicry of the two.

12

The National Shakespeare Committee and the late Mr. Thackeray. London : Joseph Clayton, 265, Strand [1864], pp. 23.

13

THACKERAY, THE HUMOURIST AND THE MAN OF LETTERS. THE STORY OF HIS LIFE, including a Selection from his Characteristic Speeches, now for the first time gathered together. By Theodore Taylor, Esq. With photograph from life by Ernest Edwards, B.A., and original illustrations. London : John Camden Hotten, Piccadilly, 1864, pp. vii. 223.

"Theodore Taylor" was merely a *nom-de-guerre*. The book (mainly a scissors-and-paste production) was compiled by the publisher himself, whom no one would at this distance of time wish to deprive of any credit or discredit that might attach to it.

14

Thackeray.— *Westminster Review*, July, 1864. Reprinted in *A Scratch Team of Essays, never before put together.* By Sept. Berdmore. London: W. H. Allen and Co., 1883, pp. 97-122.

15

Mr. Thackeray, Mr. Yates, and the Garrick Club. The Correspondence and Facts. Stated by Edmund Yates.—Printed for Private Circulation. 1859, pp. 15.

Contains a letter to Mr. Edmund Yates, dated "36, Onslow-square, June 14," and signed " W. M. Thackeray ;" a letter to the Committee of the Garrick Club, dated "36, Onslow-square, June 19, 1858," signed "W. M. Thackeray ;" a letter to Charles Dickens, dated "36, Onslow-square, 26th November, 1858 ;" and a letter to the Committee of the Garrick Club, dated "Onslow-square, November 28, 1858," both signed "W. M. Thackeray."

The substance of this narrative, and the correspondence appertaining to it, re-appeared in an article entitled "An Old Club Scandal," in *Time, a Monthly Miscellany*, &c., edited by Edmund Yates, London : January, 1880 (vol. ii., pp. 385-382), with an Illustration, and again in *Edmund Yates: his Recollections and Experiences :* London : Bentley, 1884, vol. ii., pp. 9-37.

16

Footprints on the Road. By Charles Kent. London : Chapman and Hall, 1864.

The chapter on " W. M. Thackeray, the Satirist-humourist," occupies pp. 370-407.

17

Haud Immemor: A Few Personal Recollections of Mr. Thackeray in Philadelphia. (Privately printed.) William P. Kildare, 422, Walnut-street, 1864, 8vo., pp. 31.

Contains six letters from W. M. Thackeray to W. B. Reed, dated—

1. Mr. Anderson's Music Store, Penn's Avenue, Friday.
2. Neufchatel, Switzerland, July 21, 1853.
3. 36, Onslow-square, Brompton, November, 8, 1854.
4. Baltimore, January 16, 1856.
5. April 24, 1856.
6. Maurigy's Hotel, 1 Regent-street, Waterloo-place, April 2, 1859.

And a letter to Clement C. Biddle, dated Girard House (Philadelphia), January 23, 1853, and signed "W. M. Thackeray."

[The substance of this pamphlet reappeared, under the same title, as an article in *Blackwood's Magazine*, June 1872, pp. 678-690.]

18

William Makepeace Thackeray. By one who knew him (Bayard Taylor).—*Atlantic Monthly*, March, 1864 (vol. xiii., pp. 371-379).

19

A Brief Memoir of the late Mr. Thackeray. By James Hannay. (Reprinted from the *Edinburgh Courant*.) Edinburgh : Oliver and Boyd ; London : Simpkin, Marshall and Co., 1864, pp. 31.

20

Studies on Thackeray. By James Hannay. London: Routledge and Sons [*n. d.*], pp. 107.

With vignette portrait on title. Divided into four chapters : "Thackeray as a Novelist," "as a Humourist and Satirist," "as a Critic and Essayist," "as a Poet."

21

A Memorial of Thackeray's School-days. (Signed J. F. B.)— *Cornhill Magazine*, January, 1865 (vol. xi., pp. 118-128).

With five sketches by Thackeray.

22

Thackerayiana. Account of an Album containing five inedited designs by W. M. T., in a Letter to the Editor of the *Times*, dated " Paris, Oct. 7," and signed " J. Augustus O'Shea."— *Times*, Wednesday, October 9, 1867.

23

Personal Recollections of Thackeray. (With Letters to Mr. Bedingfield).—*Cassell's Magazine*, April, 1870, new series, vol. i., pp. 296-299.

Recollections of Thackeray. With some of his letters, anecdotes and criticisms. By his cousin, Richard Bedingfield.— *Cassell's Magazine*, vol. ii. (1870), pp. 12-14 ; 28-30 ; 72-75 ; 108-110 ; 134-136 ; 230-232.

24

Yesterdays with Authors. By James T. Fields. London : Sampson Low, 1872.

The chapter on Thackeray occupies pp. 11-37.

25

The Best of all Good Company. By Blanchard Jerrold.—A Day with W. M. Thackeray. With facsimile page of extract from MS. letter.—London : Houlston and Sons, 1872; 8vo. (numbered pp. 315-392).

26

Anecdote Biographies of Thackeray and Dickens. Edited by Richard Henry Stoddard. New York : Scribner, Armstrong and Co., 1874.

The biography of Thackeray occupies the first 196 pages. A facsimile is given of one of his letters, with sketch.

27

THACKERAYANA : Notes and Anecdotes, illustrated by nearly six hundred sketches by William Makepeace Thackeray, depicting humorous incidents in his school-life, and favourite scenes and characters in the books of his every-day reading. London : Chatto and Windus, Piccadilly, 1875, pp. xx. 492.

Compiled by Mr. Joseph Grego.

28

Thackeray and Leech.—*Forty Years' Recollections of Life, Literature and Public Affairs, from 1830 to 1870.* By Charles Mackay, LL.D. London : Chapman and Hall, 1877, vol. ii. pp. 294-304.

29

An Essay on the Writings of W. M. Thackeray. By Leslie Stephen. Printed in the twenty-fourth volume of the Works of W. M. Thackeray. London : Smith, Elder and Co., 1879, pp. 313-378.

With two facsimile leaves of autograph letter to Mr. Smith, dated " Sat. 29 Oct.," and Postscript to Roundabout Paper, dated " Dec. 16 " (1861).

30

Thackeray. By Anthony Trollope. London : Macmillan and Co., 1879, pp. vi., 210.

One of the series of " English Men of Letters, edited by John Morley."

31

Studies of English Authors. By Peter Bayne.—W. M. Thackeray.—*Literary World*, September 12, 1879 to March 19, 1880.

32

Great Novelists : Scott, Thackeray, Dickens, Lytton. By James Crabb Watt. Edinburgh : Macniven and Wallace, 1880.

The chapter on Thackeray occupies pp. 97-159.

33

Stray Moments with Thackeray : his humour, satire, and characters. Being Selections from his Writings, prefaced with a few Biographical Notes. By William H. Rideing. New York : D. Appleton and Co., 1880, pp. 192.

34

Thackeray as a Draughtsman. By Russell Sturgis. (With numerous illustrations.) — *Scribner's Monthly*, New York : June, 1880, vol. xx., pp. 256-274.

35

THE BIBLIOGRAPHY OF THACKERAY. A Bibliographical List, arranged in chronological order, of the published Writings in Prose and Verse, and the Sketches and Drawings, of William Makepeace Thackeray, from 1829 to 1880. London : Elliot Stock [1880], pp. viii., 62.

Compiled by Richard Herne Shepherd.

36

Thackeray's Relations to English Society. By E. S. Nadal. With a pen-sketch by Robert Blum of Boehm's statuette of Thackeray.—*Scribner's Monthly*, February, 1881, vol. xxi., pp. 535-543.

37

Extracts from the Writings of W. M. Thackeray, chiefly philosophical and reflective. (With portrait, engraved by J. C. Armytage, from a photograph.) London : Smith, Elder, and Co., 1881, pp. xiv., 395.

38

An Essay on the Genius of George Cruikshank. Reprinted, with illustrations, from the *Westminster Review*. With Prefatory Essay on Thackeray as an art-critic, by W. E. Church. London : George Redway, 1883.

39

W. M. Thackeray.—*Essays in History and Biography.* By John Skelton ("Shirley"). Edinburgh : Blackwood, 1883, pp. 293-295.

40

In the Footsteps of Thackeray. By William H. Rideing. (With Illustrations by Hubert Herkomer and others, and a Portrait engraved by W. B. Closson, from a daguerreotype taken by Brady during Thackeray's visit to America.)—*The Century, Illustrated Monthly Magazine*, October, 1883, pp. 830-844.

41

Thackeray's London. A description of his haunts and the scenes of his novels. By William H. Rideing. London : J. W. Jarvis and Son ; Boston, U. S.: Cupples, Upham and Co., 1885, pp. 103.

With a reduced engraving of Mr. G. Barnett Smith's large etching of Thackeray.

42

Unpublished Drawings by Thackeray.—*The Century*, July, 1884.

43

Hints to Collectors of Original Editions of the Works of William Makepeace Thackeray. By Charles Plumptre Johnson. London : George Redway, 1885, pp. 48.

44

The Works of W. M. Thackeray contemplated or commenced, but not completed. By Charles P. Johnson.—*Walford's Antiquarian*, August, 1885 (vol. viii., pp. 81-87).

An account of *The Whitey-Brown Paper Magazine, Sketches by Spec* (*vide supra*, p. 228), *Dinner Reminiscences*, and other works announced or projected, but not carried out.

INDEX.

T

262   *INDEX.*

Brownrigge, Elizabeth. See *Elizabeth Brownrigge*
Bruges, 234
Brussels, 234
Brussels point-lace, 125
Budgaroo, transmutations or metamorphoses of, 6
Bulwer, E. L., his book on Athens, 111; his *Eugene Aram*, 114-118, 200; letter to, from Yellowplush, 227
Bunn, Alfred, lines on, 213-214
Byron, Lord, 41; his *Don Juan*, 43, 200; effect of the publication of his *Childe Harold*, 170; on truth and fiction, 205

Cadger's Cavern, 34, 35
Cadger's Hall, 35
Cæsar, death of, 196
Cæsar's wife, must be unsuspected, 161
Calcott, Sir Augustus, golden landscapes of, 52
Canning, Elizabeth, 164, 165, 166, 182
Canning, George, his lines on Elizabeth Brownrigge, quoted, 117, 141, 190
Cant, the worst of sins, 108, 111
"Capers and Anchovies," 244
Carlyle, Thomas, his *French Revolution*, reviewed, 99-113, 224; his description of Thackeray, *ib.*; his comments on Irish affairs, 232
Caroline, Queen, trial of, 202
Carrick, Mr., his miniatures, 78
Cartouche, 227
Catnach's ballads, 64
Chalon, Mr, his ogling beauties, 56, 78
Champavert, *Contes Immoraux*, 198-200
Chapone, Mrs., 96
Charcoal, asphyxiation by, 201
Charruas, The, 204-208
Childe Harold, publication of, 170
Chilly, as Ralph Nickleby, 38

Chinese war, the, 60
Chronicle of the Drum, The, 229
Church, W. E., on Thackeray as an art-critic, 259
Cider-cellar, the, 212
"Claret" (blood), 46
Claude, 80
Clifford, Mary, apprentice of Elizabeth Brownrigge, 127, 142, 145, 154, 168, 170; death of, 171, 175, 187, 189; ghost of, *ib.*
Closson, W. B., engraving of Thackeray from a daguerreotype, 260
Comic Tales and Sketches, 224, 225, 227, 228-229
Cooper, Fenimore, his *Magua,* 204
Cooper, Mr., 203
Cope, C. W., his pictures feeble in hand, but beautifully tender and graceful, 54
Cornhill Magazine, 229; Thackeray's contributions to, 248, 249, 250, 251
Cornhill to Cairo, 237, 253
Corsair, The, Thackeray's contributions to, 225-226, 252
Coutts, Miss, 69
Crebillon fils, 200
Creswick, Mr., his "Welsh Girl" and "Evening," 79
Crispe, Thomas Edward, on Thackeray, 254
Croal, Mr., his contract, 218
Cruikshank, George, illustrates Thackeray's *Fatal Boots,* 225; *Barber Cox,* 226-227; Thackeray's essay on his genius, 227, 259; illustrates Thackeray's *Little Spitz* and *Sultan Stork,* 230; his illustrations to Thackeray's *Legend of the Rhine,* 236; Thackeray's notice of his Gallery, 250

"Daddy, I'm hungry," 218, 232
Danton, awful image of, 105; warrant made out, *ib.*; his prison-thoughts, 106; before the Revolutionary Tribunal, 107; in the death-cart, 108
David, French painter, 53
Decamps, M., drawings of, 49

DRYDEN PRESS : J. DAVY & SONS, 137, LONG ACRE, LONDON, W.C.

www.ingramcontent.com/pod-product-compliance
Lightning Source LLC
Chambersburg PA
CBHW030623030726

47497CB00006B/1618